Legal Vengeance

Allen Tanner

Austin, Texas

Legal Vengeance

By Allen Tanner

© 2007 Allen Tanner

Groundbreaking Press
8305 Arboles Circle
Austin, TX 78737
512-657-8780
www.groundbreaking.com

Library of Congress Control Number: 2006940804
ISBN: 0-9777795-3-X

First Edition

Senior Editor
Barbara Foley

Editor
Brad Fregger

Book Design & Production
M. Kevin Ford

Cover Design & Production
M. Kevin Ford

This book is printed on acid-free paper.

All rights reserved. No part of this book may be reproduced or utilized in any form by any means, electronic or mechanical, including photocopying or recording, or by any information storage and retrieval system, without permission in writing from the author. This is a fictional work, which takes place among imaginary people. Any resemblance to persons living or dead is purely coincidental.

For my father, who instilled in me a love for creative thinking,
And, for my mother, who had the wisdom to let her four boys just be boys.

Acknowledgments

This book was created late at night with the professional help and support of Betty, Diana, Esther, Nancy, and Susan—thank you all very much!

I also want to thank Sherri, Ilana, Jeremy, Jed, Bobby, Casey, Cathy, Jim, and Andrea for their help, advice, and support.

Finally, I want to thank Brad, Barbara, and all the others at Groundbreaking Press for turning my messy manuscript into a real story.

ONE

It was a typically hot and humid Houston afternoon when Lucas Lustick finally arrived at the Beth Israel cemetery. He was late, but it didn't seem to concern him. Having never been to a funeral before, he wasn't too excited about going to this one. After parking his car, he clumsily stepped out of it. Reaching into the back seat, he grabbed a dark-gray sports coat which he put on over his wrinkled white shirt. Nervously he looked around before deciding in which direction to walk. Nearly a quarter-mile away, a group of mourners gathered at a gravesite. Assuming that they were there for Amy, he headed in that direction.

Walking slowly, he thought about Amy and her life. A clear vision of her as a little girl flashed in his mind. She was barefoot, wearing a short, blue dress, running as fast as she could, with her long, dirty-blonde hair dangling to her waist. But it was the terrified look on her face that he would never forget. Though it had been a long time ago, it seemed as if it was just yesterday.

Lucas disliked most women, thinking of them as being nothing but trouble. He often referred to them as "the root of all evil." To him, it seemed their dual purpose on earth was to give men pleasure and to make their lives miserable. Anyone who knew him was aware of these feelings since he never tried to hide them. But Amy was different. To Lucas, she wasn't like any other woman. He never completely understood why he felt so differently about her, but he did. Maybe it was their childhood together.

While growing up, girls had teased him, making fun of his looks and clumsiness. As he went through college and law school, they ignored him as if he didn't even exist. But not Amy. She never teased him, never ignored him, but rather admired him, looking up to him for his intelligence and wit. She had time to spend with him when he wanted company, though those times were scarce because he was such a loner. Whatever the reason, Lucas knew deep down in his heart that he loved her. Amy was like a sister to him. She was the only woman who had ever really understood his strange personality. Now she was gone forever.

As Lucas approached the gravesite, a tall, bearded rabbi was conducting the service. The rabbi stood next to Amy's casket, which was held above the grave. There were seats right in front in which Amy's husband Rickie and her little boy Mikey were seated. Behind them were eighty or so people whom Lucas quietly joined. He felt totally out of place in this crowd. Assuming that most of the people were civil attorneys from Rickie's law firm, he didn't like being anywhere near any of them. In his mind, all civil attorneys were rude and pompous. He refused to make the slightest eye contact with anyone.

True, many of the mourners were from Johnson, Cates, and Bennington, one of Houston's most prestigious civil firms, but there were others present who weren't. There were molecular biologists and geneticists from the Baylor College of Medicine who had worked with Amy prior to her illness. There were neighbors and friends who had come to pay their respects to the family. If he had bothered to look, there was even one of his running buddies from the criminal courthouse, John O'Reilly.

All that mattered to Lucas was the little boy sitting in front of the casket. He focused on the boy, curious about what was going on inside his head. He wondered how the death of Amy would affect him. When Mikey had been born, problems during the delivery resulted in his having some sort of brain damage. Amy never talked about it, so Lucas never asked any questions. But he now wondered why a young child with mental problems was even here to watch his mother be placed into the ground in a wooden box and then covered with dirt.

"Dust you are, and to dust you shall return," voiced the rabbi, "so says the *Torah*. Amy must return to dust. To the many of you here who are dear friends to the Kassell family, but are not of the Jewish faith and are wondering why the family is having such a hurried funeral the day after Amy passed with merely a plain, unfinished coffin, let me take a moment to explain. It is our duty as Jews to see to it that Amy returns to dust as soon as possible; the *Torah* so commands us. Many a Jew has been buried wrapped merely in a blanket or sheet, placed in direct contact with the earth. This is to expedite the decomposition of the body so that it can return to dust as soon as possible."

Put her into the ground. I'm not here to learn Jewish customs, Lucas wished he could tell the rabbi.

The rabbi then talked about Amy and the life she had lived. "Putting aside her contributions to society in the field of science, let us look at what she truly cherished the most during her life. What meant most to her was being a mother to Mikey."

Walking over to Mikey, the rabbi got down on his knees. Looking into his teary eyes, he placed his hands on top of Mikey's shoulders. He was a beautiful child, blessed with the face of an angel. His sad eyes were big and brown. His dark-brown hair fell to his shoulders, its texture thin, his bangs nearly reached his eyes. Baby teeth were still intact inside his perfectly shaped mouth. Rickie had dressed him in a blue suit with a white shirt and red bow tie. As skinny as he was, he needed red suspenders to hold up his pants. A black ribbon was attached to his suit above his heart to symbolize his grief. He appeared to be scared and confused, not understanding what had happened to his mother, yet knowing it was bad.

"Where is my mommy?" he asked the rabbi. "Where did she go?"

"She is now with God. You must always remember how much she loved you. You made her the happiest woman in the world. Remember her each day of your life, for she was a beautiful and smart woman, and a great mother to you."

Tears were flowing freely from Mikey's eyes. Most of the mourners were also crying as the rabbi went back to stand by the coffin.

Lucas felt anger towards the rabbi for bringing out these emotions in Mikey. He was making the situation too dramatic for the boy to handle. Lucas turned his back to the congregation and started walking away, mumbling under his breath, "Fuck this idiot. Bury her and let's get on with things!" But after a few steps he turned back, realizing he needed to stick it out to the end of the ordeal.

The rabbi continued, "In this casket lies Amy and a picture of Mikey which she was holding when she took her last breath. In our faith, anything attached to the body at the time of passing shall be buried with it. The Lord has given and now has taken away; blessed be the name of the Lord."

Four men dressed in dark suits then lifted the coffin and held it above the gravesite as the rabbi continued, "Amy, you will be cherished and loved wherever you go."

The rabbi then motioned the bearers to lower the coffin into the grave as he signaled to Rickie and the others to join him, "*Barukh attah ... Dayan Ha-Emet*, blessed are You ... the true Judge."

The end had come. Amy was now in her final resting place. All that was left was the final honor of pouring earth onto her coffin. Rickie picked up a shovel and held it with both hands as he stuck it into the pile of dirt lying next to the grave. He then asked Mikey, "Son, will you please help me do this?"

Mikey held the wooden part of the shovel beneath the big hands of his father, and the two of them threw the dirt upon Amy's coffin. To those watching, it was a beautiful scene between a father and son, a final gesture of love for the most important woman in both their lives. It was the final goodbye to the man's wife and to the little boy's mother. As Mikey let go of the shovel, he reached down into the grave trying to open the coffin. Hysterically he screamed, "Mommy, come back! I need you! I need you! Come back, Mommy!"

Tears poured down his face, his forehead was soaked with sweat. Rickie, looking confused and upset, picked him up from behind and briskly walked towards the limousine parked on the street. Mikey was screaming and kicking as hard as he could, trying to get out of his father's grasp, but Rickie just kept squeezing him tighter.

Amy's friends were in tears as they watched Rickie carrying Mikey toward the limousine. A few chased behind them, but most just stood still, figuring that this is what happens when small children attend a parent's burial. Thoroughly disgusted with the rabbi, Lucas never moved an inch.

When Rickie finally got to the limousine, he jumped into the back seat, closed the door, and told the driver, "Please, get us out of here!" As they drove off, Mikey continued kicking and screaming for his mother. However, Rickie would not let go, holding him with both arms wrapped around his waist.

Finally, after several minutes he settled down and fell asleep in his father's arms. Rickie looked down at his son and thought about the final promise he had made to Amy right before she had died. He had promised to always take care of Mikey and to see to it that he was the happiest little boy in the world. He felt that he had already broken his promise and prayed that things would get better.

TWO

Most of the visitors remained at the gravesite. Some were visibly shaken and in no condition to drive home yet. It had been an emotional funeral. Everyone was talking about how sad and unfair life was. Friends moaned about how Amy was the one person who didn't deserve to die at such a young age. She was so smart, so sweet, and ever so lovely. How would Mikey cope without her? How would he adapt to kindergarten the following month? Everybody questioned whether Rickie would be able to take adequate care of him.

Lucas Lustick was not one of the folks who stayed around after the funeral. Just twenty feet from his car, he heard a familiar voice yelling from behind, "Wait up, Lustick! What's your fucking hurry?"

It was John O'Reilly, all five-eight, one-hundred-and-fifty pounds of him, dressed in a dark-blue suit and wearing, as always, black, pointed cowboy boots.

"O'Reilly, what are you doing here? Why aren't you at your office fucking up people's lives?"

John, shrugging his shoulders, answered, "I used to fuck her back in California so I figured I should at least come to her funeral. Besides, I knew there would be a lot of civil lawyers here—it won't hurt me when I run for judge someday."

Lucas didn't respond. Other people from the funeral were now starting to gather in the parking lot. John then moved closer to him and asked, "When are you headed to Austin and out West?"

"Fuck you for talking about Amy like that!" hissed Lucas as he started his car, gunning the motor and glaring at O'Reilly.

As he drove away, John yelled, "Have a nice drive and don't get too drunk on that flight! I'll call you tomorrow."

Looking back at the cemetery in his rearview mirror, Lucas thought about Mikey. He couldn't erase from his mind the sight of him being carried away from his mother's gravesite. Hopefully, he'd be okay.

John jumped into his Ford pickup and carefully put on his Stetson, which hid any hint of his slicked-back, blond hair. He decided to visit his parents before heading home to his wife and daughter.

Otis and Maggie O'Reilly still lived in the same house on Kirby Drive where John was raised. When they had bought the house thirty years earlier, they paid three-hundred thousand for it. Nowadays, it was worth close to three million.

When John pulled into their driveway, he could see that both cars were gone, so he quickly pulled back onto Kirby Drive and headed to his house in the Memorial Drive area. John was very close to his parents, especially his father. Otis O'Reilly was a native Houstonian who had made his money in the oil and gas business before ever marrying Maggie, a Houston socialite who was fifteen years his junior.

The two of them believed that the State of Texas was the best at everything except educating its young, so they sent John to Stanford for both undergraduate and law school. Maggie had been plenty nervous about sending her fair-haired son to California, fearing that he might be exposed to liberal ways of thinking. He'd been raised very conservatively under Texas Baptist influence. But, Otis knew there was no risk of his boy turning into a liberal, and he was absolutely right.

When John returned to Texas at age twenty-five after seven years in Northern California, he was, in his own words, "ready to prosecute every nigger, Mexican, and queer that I can get my hands on." In his five years with the Harris County District Attorney's Office in Houston, he quickly gained a reputation as a fire-breathing prosecutor who had no mercy for anyone charged with any sort of a crime. Defense lawyers hated to go up against him in trial. The redneck, racist, good-old-boy Texas juries loved him and routinely returned verdicts in his favor. He had only lost one jury trial in five years, that being a murder case he had tried nearly two weeks before Amy's funeral.

Lucas Lustick had represented the accused killer, and it tore John up inside to have lost the case to him. He'd known Lucas since his days in law school, Lucas having attended Boalt Hall at the University of California at Berkeley. That murder trial really angered John because he was planning to run for judge someday, but now he wouldn't be able to claim that he had an unblemished record as a prosecutor. In his mind, he was a far superior trial lawyer to Lucas—but everybody else around the courthouse knew that was not true.

Lucas pulled into his townhouse garage and rushed inside. Entering his bedroom, he ripped off his clothes and hurried into the shower. There he poured shampoo on his long, stringy, black hair, allowing it to run down his elephant-sized ears onto his scraggly beard. He then scrubbed his scalp and lathered up the rest of his two-hundred-and-eighty-pound frame. As he rinsed himself off, he looked down at his sunken chest and protruding stomach. He was an awful-looking specimen, but it didn't concern him enough to do anything about it. He hated all types of exercise and never went anywhere near a gym.

After getting out of the shower he dried himself off, and looking in the mirror, ran his fingers through his hair. Then he put on a pair of jeans and a white T-shirt with "WOLF-PACK" in bold red letters written across the chest.

He loved North Carolina State's basketball team. That past March they had won the NCAA basketball tournament, whipping Duke in the finals. He had won ten-thousand dollars on the game, and had bought himself this shirt in their honor.

Putting on some white socks and a pair of black sneakers, he was now nearly ready to hit the road. But first, he reached into his top-dresser drawer and pulled out two large bundles of one-hundred-dollar bills which he stuffed into his front pockets. He then opened another drawer and grabbed another huge wad of bills which he stuffed into his back pockets. Finally, he opened up a pint-size bottle of Jack Daniel's and poured himself a glassful. Adding some ice, he was finally ready to head out of town. Carrying the glass of bourbon in one hand and a suitcase in the other, he walked out to his car and soon was on the interstate heading for Austin.

There was plenty of daylight left as he sped along the highway. He put on his New York Yankees baseball cap to help shield his eyes from the sun. Since he was drinking Jack Daniel's, he stayed at the speed limit to avoid being pulled over by the police. He didn't need a DWI in some country-hick town between Houston and Austin. There wouldn't be any justice in any of these places.

He knew that to be a fact from his five years of practicing law throughout the state. In these small towns, everybody took a lawman's word as gospel and believed anything he said in a court of law. Lucas had tried cases in small Texas towns like Columbus and Seguin, and even proven to juries that the police were flat-out lying, but the redneck jurors would usually convict anyway, and then slap the officers on their backs as they left the courthouse. This type of encouragement led the police to lie even more because they knew that they could do it with impunity. It drove Lucas crazy. He simply hated all Texas cops, the ones from the small towns as well as those from Houston.

His hatred of the police made him one of the top defense lawyers in the city of Houston. He was successful in nearly ninety percent of his jury trials, which in and of itself was unheard of. The typical defense attorney was successful in less than ten percent of his trials. The difference was in Lucas' ability to cross-examine police officers. His grueling style set him apart from his colleagues, many of whom feared insulting the police during cross-examination.

In Houston, officers were used to good-old-boy, court-appointed lawyers going easy on them during trials. This was not the case with Lucas, who always tore into them and won many cases because of it. Judges and prosecutors alike hadn't ever seen a lawyer like him. One judge described him as a "Mack Truck in the courtroom" because of the recklessness he displayed when in trial. Nothing ever stopped him in fighting for the rights of one of his clients.

As Lucas cruised west along Interstate 10, he eventually reached Columbus and turned north onto Highway 71 which would take him to Austin, his favorite Texas town. Parts of it reminded him of Berkeley, where he had spent his college and law school days. There were plenty of places where he could buy whiskey or score some marijuana if he so desired.

It was a town where he could find a hundred-dollar whore, which, of course, was important to him since he never dated women. He desired them solely for sexual gratification. His idols were the cavemen who inhabited the earth thousands of years earlier. He saw modern-day men who needed wives and girlfriends as being weak. Women ran the world, in his eyes, only because men allowed them to.

As he drove into Austin, he realized that he had four hours to kill before catching the late-night flight to Vegas. He'd meet with Art on Sixth Street and then maybe have time to visit Mama before catching his flight.

Sixth Street in Austin was Texas' answer to Bourbon Street in New Orleans and Telegraph Avenue in Berkeley. After parking his car, Lucas quietly blended into the large crowd. People were walking in both directions on the crowded sidewalks. Just as he liked it, nobody knew him and he knew nobody.

Anxiously he walked into a bar called Forks. It was a dingy-looking place with marked-up walls and a hardwood floor which appeared to have never been refinished. There must have been two-hundred people crowded into the small space allotted this popular Sixth Street joint. Music blasted from loud speakers hanging from the ceilings. People poured down beers and margaritas as they tried to converse over the blaring music. Lucas ordered a drink from the bar and then started focusing on the people inside.

Most of the men were wearing blue jeans and colored T-shirts with various logos on them. Some of the women wore short skirts, while others wore jeans. Nobody looked real clean. The cigarette smoke engulfing the room clearly added to the decadent environment for which Forks was known. It was the type of place where people came to drink alcohol, smoke cigarettes, and listen to loud music, thereby escaping the problems of everyday life. People from all walks of life patronized the establishment. There were students, legislators, electricians, lawyers, plumbers, nurses, laborers, and accountants, all trying to relax and forget their everyday problems.

Lucas felt comfortable here. It was his type of place. As he downed his drink, he checked out the women. However, he knew they were not for him. These were women who had jobs during the day and liked to party at night. His type of woman slept all day and worked at night.

He ordered another drink, and as he paid the bartender, he noticed people staring at a young man standing at the front door. The doorman carded him to assure that he was old enough to enter. Several patrons approached him and asked for autographs. Standing five-nine and weighing barely a-hundred-and-sixty pounds, wearing blue jeans and an orange T-shirt, he looked ordinary, a typical blond-haired college kid. But a typical college kid he was not. Art Kiser was the University of Texas' pre-season, All-American quarterback candidate, getting ready to start his senior year. He had run the Texas offense that led the NCAA in total yardage the previous year.

That Longhorn team had been undefeated before being blown out 51-0 in the Cotton Bowl by a powerful Penn State team. This year it would be different. Texas' skill-position players were all seniors and hopefully wouldn't be overwhelmed come bowl season. Head Coach Bucky Seymour promised the UT faithful that their Longhorns were not going to come up short of a National Championship this time around.

Kiser was a great all-around athlete. He could throw deep, and he had pinpoint accuracy and touch on his short routes. Nobody in the land had an arm like him, and he could run, too. He ran a 4.4 forty, and when he needed to use that speed, he did, often scrambling for big yardage. What Lucas liked the most about Art was his height. The fact that he stood only five-nine meant that no matter how great a talent he was, he wasn't ever going to play in the National Football League on Sundays. NFL teams had little interest in drafting quarterbacks under six feet.

Art knew it, too. Once his days of playing college ball were over, he'd be selling cars in his hometown of Midland, Texas. This was his last year to be a star, his last year to get the girls, his last year to make some money playing football.

As Art walked towards the bar to order a drink, he didn't see Lucas but knew he was there. Lucas always showed. Art talked to several people and then headed towards the bathroom. Pushing open the door, he walked inside. It was dark except for the dim light from a bare forty-watt lightbulb hanging from the ceiling. There was one dirty toilet and a sink which looked like it hadn't been cleaned in six months. There wasn't a towel, soap, or toilet paper in sight.

Thirty seconds after he entered the bathroom, there was a knock at the door. It slowly opened and Lucas stepped inside. Locking the door behind him, he turned and greeted Art.

"Lucas, I'm in a hurry! I shouldn't be in this fucking place!"

Lucas handed him a thick wad of bills from his pocket and told him, "It will be easy to win by less than twenty-four points. You don't need to blow them out. Also, try to stay under forty-six total points. The parlay is very important to us."

Art, shaking his head, said, "I can keep it under forty-six as long as our defense don't score, but I can't stop them from scoring! If our defensive guys recover fumbles or pick off passes, they'll score. You know man, our defense, they're all fast as shit and they all love to score. Then they do that fucking dancing in the end zone!"

Lowering his voice, Lucas whispered, "Just do the best you can with the offense. Try to control the ball so their offense doesn't get a chance to turn it over. Try to make it 20-3 or 24-10, something like that. That way you guys win the game and we'll hit all our plays!" The two then shook hands and both headed back out to the bar.

It was getting late and Lucas had an eleven p.m. flight to catch. Immediately he left the bar and headed towards his car parked off Sixth Street. Before reaching it, he decided to walk into an Asian modeling studio where he was greeted by an aging Korean woman who went by "Mama."

She recognized him from past visits and in broken English asked, "What you need tonight? We got four girl working, two Korean, two Thai, all very young, twenty-one year at most. They all very pretty."

Lucas, handing her a one-hundred-dollar bill, said, "Mama, just give me your best one, but hurry. I'm heading out of town tonight and need to get to the airport."

Mama, taking quick, short steps, walked to an adjoining room where she pushed open the door and then disappeared from sight. A minute passed, then two, then three, and finally she reappeared with a beautiful young Korean girl whom she introduced as "Youme."

Lucas nodded to Mama that he was quite satisfied. Youme then grabbed his hand and led him down the hallway. As he walked with her, he was trying to figure out her age. She stood nearly five-foot-five and weighed less than a hundred pounds. She had long, straight, black hair, falling freely to the middle of her back. She looked sixteen, but giving her the five-year allowance he reserved for Asian women, he figured her to be twenty-one. She led him into a small, dimly lit room furnished only with a queen-sized bed with a white sheet on it. He watched her as she closed the door. It would be only moments before he ravished her.

"What your name?" she asked.

"Lucas."

"You very hansum," she said as she looked down at the floor.

Even though he knew she was lying, he loved the sweetness in her voice. In fact, he loved everything about her. Beautiful, feminine, and quietly sexy, she was the product of many generations of Asian culture. A culture which throughout the centuries prided itself in turning out submissive females. Before she even undressed, he knew that she'd be an uninhibited partner in bed, much like the other Asian women he'd been with before.

She did not prove him wrong; he had an amazing time with her. Quickly he hugged her goodbye and handed her a one-hundred-dollar tip for the pleasure she had just given him. This was as close as he ever wanted to come to having a girlfriend. Glancing down at his watch, he knew he needed to hurry to catch his flight.

"Goodbye," Youme said. "Please come see me other time."

"I'll visit you the next time I'm in Austin." He knew damn well he'd never see her again.

As he approached the gate for his Las Vegas flight, he glanced around at the roughly seventy-five people who were waiting to board. They looked different from folks who were traveling to other destinations. They appeared more decadent. Most of the men wore baseball caps. Some wore jackets which advertised the names of their favorite casinos, such as

Binion's, The Desert Inn, or The Flamingo. Some of the women dressed like old maids, others looked downright trashy. Everyone had a look of confidence that they were going to win big this time.

    Once Lucas boarded the plane, he walked to the very back, sat down, and waited for takeoff. Exhausted, he was ready to fall into a deep sleep. It had been a long day. The captain dimmed the cabin lights and Lucas shut his eyes as the plane gently left the runway and ascended into the night sky.

THREE

Sitting on the brown-leather sofa in the den, Rickie propped his feet up on the glass coffee table in front of him. It was quiet and peaceful, much different than the day's events which were now behind him. It had been a long day, seeming like forty-eight hours instead of twenty-four. So many people had come to show their final respects to Amy. Everyone expressed how sad they felt, and some wanted to help in anyway they could.

Amy's best friends offered to drive Mikey to-and-from school each day and to take care of him until Rickie came home from the law firm. They wanted to take him to his activities and to help with his schoolwork. Some offered to cook dinner on weeknights.

Everyone was so kind; however, Rickie had already hired a nanny who would soon be arriving from England. Her services were expensive, but cost didn't matter since she'd be taking care of Mikey the many hours he would be working at the firm. He needed somebody who in her own way would serve as a mother figure.

Rickie glanced around the room. He had never felt lonelier. The big, two-story house seemed empty without Amy.

The downstairs was so quiet, calm—too quiet. Lifelessly he sat there, wearing only a light-blue bathrobe. Only his eyes moved. The rest of him remained motionless.

He glanced at the pictures hanging on the walls; each one had been framed and hung by Amy. So many of them were of her with Mikey. These were pictures of events which she had always wanted to remember, times she had cherished.

Rickie reminisced about how deeply he had loved her as he stared at a picture of her during her college days, standing with her girlfriends in front of a North Beach Italian restaurant in San Francisco. If only he could turn back time and make the picture come alive, then he could spend one more night with her in beautiful San Francisco. He would step right into the picture, squeeze her hand, and just keep walking down Stockton Street. She would be young, happy, and carefree as they enjoyed the night together. He would hear her laugh, listen to her talk about her classes—they would hug and kiss.

Feeling tears starting to fall, he quickly looked away and focused on another picture on a different wall. Amy was young in this picture, too. It showed her with him, Lucas Lustick, and John O'Reilly in front of Scoma's Restaurant at Fisherman's Wharf. Behind them were people standing in a long line, since nobody could ever make reservations at Scoma's. In the picture, John was holding up a twenty-dollar bill with a big grin on his face. Rickie now smiled as he remembered the actual night. John was preparing to bribe the maitre'd so that they wouldn't have to wait in line. He said something like, "That's how we do things in Texas!"

Rickie remembered that the twenty-dollar bill got them right into the restaurant. Then he remembered that someone else was at dinner that night, the guy who had actually snapped this picture. This mysterious person had known Lucas and Amy back when they were kids but had disappeared for a while. Lucas had run into him somewhere in the Bay Area and had invited him to this dinner. Something was very strange about him, but Rickie could never put his finger on what it was. He remembered that Lucas called him by some number as a nickname, like "Forty-two" or "Twenty-five." Never did he call him by his real name, whatever it might have been.

Next, he looked at a picture of Amy holding Mikey in her hospital bed the day he was born. She held him with both hands, looking right into his eyes. The expression on her face as she stared at her newborn was asking, "Well, what do we have here?" She looked so happy and so proud of her little boy. Rickie remembered bringing the two of them home from the hospital. He had pulled his black BMW to the front of the hospital on Fannin Street where he saw Amy sitting in a wheelchair holding Mikey. She looked so tired, but so relieved to be going home. She was wearing a long, white cotton dress, and Mikey was all wrapped up in a tiny blue-and-white blanket. She held him so tightly to her chest.

Amy was always with Mikey, unless she was at work. Even then, she would often come home during her lunch break to be with him. At work she'd constantly call the babysitter checking on him. Each minute of every weekend was spent with him. She'd play games, read books, and watch television with him. They were inseparable. She had little time to spend with Rickie, but he always had so much work to do that he didn't mind. He enjoyed watching the two of them together. Mikey was so happy, and Amy had a certain special glow. Rickie knew she wanted so much to give Mikey the childhood she had never experienced. It was so important to her.

Rickie finally got up from the couch and slowly walked towards the kitchen. He looked down at his bare feet as he crossed the carpeted den and entered into the kitchen, where the floor was white tile. The carpet had felt so much better. Slowly, he opened the refrigerator and grabbed a half-gallon carton of cold milk. Taking a glass from the cabinet, he poured some milk into it. As he was getting ready to take a drink, he noticed some sort of movement to his right.

It was a very quick, darting motion which his peripheral vision picked up. Quickly, he turned his head as he held the glass in his hand. Then he jumped back, spilling a little milk. Sitting on the kitchen counter was a two-inch-long, black tree roach with two long antennas sticking out of its head. It seemed as if this ugly creature was staring right at him. Rickie remained still; he knew not to take his eyes off this insect. If he did so, even for a second, it would be gone. He pondered what to do. Rickie could never get used to Texas tree roaches.

He could walk to the closet, get a broom, and then swat the roach to death. But before he would be able to get the broom, it might quickly run off and hide somewhere else in the kitchen. That would be horrible, because then, each time he walked into the kitchen for the next few days, he'd worry about where the roach was hiding. It could be on the ceiling ready to jump on him or in a cabinet ready to jump out at him. It could get into the food. *Hell*, he cringed, *it could even go upstairs and climb onto me or Mikey while we're asleep*. Rickie didn't want this roach to escape under any circumstances.

After exhausting other options for the roach's demise, he decided to grab a copy of *Newsweek* which was lying on the counter about four feet from the roach. Never taking his eyes off the insect, he tightly rolled up the magazine so that it was now a deadly weapon as far as the roach was concerned. Lifting his arm high above his head, in one fluid motion he slammed the coiled magazine down on the roach.

Rickie was surprised at the satisfaction he got from killing this pest. As he cleaned up the mess, he thought, *I got you, you bastard! You'll never bother us again!*

As he walked up the stairs, he knew that he'd have to keep himself occupied day and night to avoid thinking about Amy. His job would help serve that purpose. He loved the practice of law and was one of the hardest-working partners at his law firm, often putting in sixty-hour weeks. Now, he would work even more hours during the week. And on weekends he'd spend a lot more time with Mikey, which would be good for both of them.

At the top of the stairs he quietly entered Mikey's room. Mikey was sleeping on his stomach, wearing only a white T-shirt and a pair of underwear. He was clutching a yellow blanket that Amy had knitted for him right before he was born. It had been in his crib the day he arrived home from the hospital. He slept with it each night of his life, and tonight his little hands clutched onto it even though he was in a very deep sleep.

His head rested upon a white pillow. Next to the pillow was a picture of Amy. Earlier, when Rickie had put him to bed, he had insisted that he be able to hold this picture which had been in Rickie's and Amy's room. It was a picture from the surprise party which was held for Amy on her twenty-fifth birthday. She had a big smile on her face as she held her birthday cake. Mikey was able to go to sleep as long as this picture was near him. It was as if having it beside him made him feel that she was still with him.

Rickie gently ran his fingers through Mikey's hair, being sure not to awaken him. He had always liked doing this while he was asleep because it gave him a special feeling of intimacy with his son. Leaning over, he kissed him on his forehead, praying silently, *Dear God, please take care of my boy here. Allow him a good life.*

Leaving Mikey's room, Rickie walked down the dimly lit hallway. Knowing that he wouldn't be able to sleep, he thought that he ought to at least try. Many things were on his mind.

Where is Amy? She's dead, but where did she go? Does she not exist anymore, her soul and all, or is she somewhere safe and happy? Is she at a place where she can watch whatever she feels like watching? Maybe she's peering over me right now!

He wondered what really happened to people after they passed away. The great religions of the world all adhered to different theories on the subject. Each one believed its teachings were right, but nobody knew for sure. He closed his eyes.

Several moments later he heard a loud cry. Jumping up, he ran down the hallway. Mikey was sitting up in his bed holding his blanket and screaming, "Where did Mommy go? Where did Mommy go?!"

He kept repeating it over and over. Rickie picked him up and held him for several minutes, but the screaming didn't stop. Mikey was sweating profusely, his head and hair both soaking wet. Rickie sat in the wooden rocking chair, trying to calm him by rocking back and forth. But it did no good. The screaming and sweating only got worse. He then carried him down the stairs, opened the front door, and stepped outside. Mikey immediately looked up to the sky and then suddenly stopped crying. He kept staring at the full moon which looked so bright in the dark sky. It was as if he was in a hypnotic trance. He just kept looking up, saying, "moon, moon, moon."

Rickie placed his hand across Mikey's chest and could feel that his heart was no longer racing. The moon seemed to have mesmerized him. Rickie wondered if Amy was possibly up there in some form or fashion. Did she somehow connect with her son? After twenty minutes of being outside, Mikey finally fell asleep. Rickie carried him back upstairs and tucked him into bed. The hard day was finally coming to an end.

FOUR

"Desert Inn, Las Vegas. May I help you?"

"Yes ma'am, I'm calling for Lustick, Lucas Lustick, he's from Houston, Texas."

"One moment please, and I'll connect you."

The phone rang six times before Lucas finally answered, "Yeah."

"Hey, motherfucker, what took you so long to answer?" sneered John O'Reilly.

Lucas, looking down at his watch replied, "It's six a.m. here; why are you fucking calling this early? Hold on motherfucker."

Tossing the receiver onto the nightstand, Lucas headed into the bathroom. He could still hear John screaming into the phone for him to pick up, but he just ignored him. John didn't like being put on hold; Lucas didn't care. Flipping on the light switch in the bathroom, he ran the cold water and started brushing his teeth.

That's what he did first thing every morning, brush his teeth. He couldn't stand the dryness and bad taste caused by bacteria to which he would awaken. Brushing with a mint-flavored toothpaste made his mouth feel so fresh and clean. No matter what, it was the first part of his daily routine. There were absolutely no exceptions, least of all a phone call from John O'Reilly.

When he finished brushing, he picked up the phone and calmly asked, "O'Reilly, what's going on?"

"What the fuck did you put me on hold for?" John snapped. "You asshole!"

"Yeah, I'm real sorry," Lucas said sarcastically. "What do you want this early?"

"Did you get our plays in last night?"

"No, I didn't even get here 'til well past midnight, and all the Sports Books were closed. I saw the numbers here and at Caesars, and also over at the Hilton, but I couldn't put any money down. It was Texas minus twenty-four at all three places, and the total was forty-six at one place and forty-five-and-a-half at the other two. Kickoff is at one-thirty your time, right?"

"Yeah," John answered. "I'm headed to Austin, but I need to know the exact numbers before the game starts. Hell, the line may move down to twenty-three or up to twenty-five. The total could move two or three points either way before kickoff. I want to know my exact numbers right after you place our fucking bets. And you save the tickets so that if we lose, I know you actually placed the damn bets!"

"I'll bet SMU and the under," Lucas told him, "no matter what the fucking numbers are. Don't worry, I won't cheat you, motherfucker! If Texas moves up to twenty-five or twenty-six, you'll get it at twenty-five or twenty-six; if the total moves to forty-eight, you'll get it at forty-eight. So don't worry. I'm going back to sleep. I'm fucking tired."

Lucas didn't wait for a response before hanging up the phone. He thought, *He doesn't trust me. We've been involved together in so many crooked games yet even after all of these years the little redneck still doesn't trust me. ... Unbelievable.*

Lying there, he remembered back to law school when he and John were involved in fixing Cal games in both football and basketball. It was all so easy back then. Cal was terrible in both sports and were always huge underdogs. Lucas was in cahoots with three athletes, one being the quarterback, and the other two being hoops players. There were so many games in both sports where Cal was being blown out by halftime, and then "the boys" would take care of business in the second half, seeing to it that Cal wouldn't come back and cover the spread. Lucas or John would meet with the players the next day, give them five-hundred dollars apiece and wait a few weeks to do it all over again.

He and John were also involved in crooked horse races at Golden Gate Fields in Berkeley. Lucas had met two Mexican jockeys in the lounge of a San Francisco brothel and, after finding out what they did for a living, hooked them up with some escorts he knew out of Oakland who would go straight to their apartments. The jocks loved the idea of girls coming to them and showed their appreciation by letting Lucas know when they had a long shot which was ready to win, and when they had a favorite which they were going to hold back. This was all Lucas' inside information, but he always shared it with John and the two of them made tons of money because of it.

Ever since they started practicing law in Houston, Lucas had done so many things for John. For one thing, he placed all of his bets for him. John, being an Assistant District Attorney, would be fired if he were ever caught betting with bookmakers. Lucas also took care of setting up the crooked games involving the University of Texas, and he would tell John when to load up against the Longhorns. When a game was fixed like this one against SMU, Lucas would have to fly all the way to Vegas to bet it because the locals in Houston wouldn't handle the amounts of money which he and John wished to wager.

He remembered all the times he had allowed John to use his place to screw whores so that his wife Tammy wouldn't find out. The idea that John didn't trust him was downright upsetting. He kept tossing and turning in bed. His chances of falling back to sleep now ruined, he got up and took a quick shower. He put on a pair of jeans, a black T-shirt, and the pair of worn-out, black high-top sneakers. Now, he was ready to head into the early morning streets of Las Vegas.

The doorman asked, "Do you need a cab?"

"I sure do."

Within seconds, a Yellow Cab appeared and the doorman opened the back door so Lucas could step in.

As he did so, the driver asked, "Where to?"

"Binion's."

Slamming the door, the doorman said, "Thank you very much, asshole!" as the cabbie drove off.

"That bastard wanted a tip for opening the door to this fucking cab, but fuck him," Lucas angrily mumbled to the driver. "I could have opened the fucking door myself! I don't need some punk opening my door and then slamming it shut because I didn't give him a tip. Fuck him!"

The cabbie laughed and drove from The Strip onto the freeway heading downtown. There is little doubt that downtown Las Vegas is one of the seediest places on the face of the earth. It is home to thousands of vagrants, drunkards, and downtrodden gamblers who have lost everything. Even so, it has its own certain elegance which can't be matched in any other city.

The driver stopped at Fremont Street in front of Binion's Horseshoe Casino, and looking over his shoulder, said, "Eleven-twenty."

Lucas handed him twenty dollars and got out of the car without saying a word. The cabbie said, "Thank you," as Lucas shut the door.

After the cab sped away from the curb, Lucas looked across the street at the old Fremont Hotel and Casino. He thought of crossing the street, but quickly changed his mind. Turning back towards Binion's, he walked inside.

Binion's Horseshoe Casino was where the old-time, hard-core gamblers went to shoot dice and try their luck at cards. Built in the 1930s, it looked as if it hadn't been renovated since. It was dark and rustic-looking, lacking the glamour and elegance of the major hotel casinos on The Strip.

Lucas always thought of it as a real man's casino. Not too many of the men who frequented Binion's had a woman tagging along. In fact, women were seldom seen on the premises. Binion's players were serious gamblers from the old school, men who won or lost fortunes on one roll of the dice or a flip of a card. These were men who came to Vegas to gamble hard and that was it.

Lucas headed to the back where all the craps tables were. There were four dice games in play, the rest were closed down. It was still early morning. Later in the day, all the tables would be running at full speed. Casually, he glanced at the players standing at each table.

The shrewd pit boss watching him knew that he was in search of someone. It was the way Lucas focused on each person before shifting his eyes to the next. The pit boss was trained in watching people. He'd been doing it at Binion's for twenty years and was very good at it. He watched everybody who came near the dice pits. That was his job, watching people, those who worked for the casino and those who came to visit.

He didn't think Lucas was a crook or dice cheat who might try to slip a pair of crooked bones into the game. He simply prided himself in his ability to read faces. He surmised that Lucas was looking for a friend, but he wanted to know if he was right. It was a game to him, sort of like trying to work out a crossword puzzle. After all, he was bored with his job just like anyone else who did the same thing, day in and day out.

Lucas started watching one particular player who was hunched over at the twenty-five-dollar-minimum table. The gentleman was wearing a black Oakland Raider's cap which was pulled down over his forehead with the brim blocking his eyes and nose. He didn't look up from the table. It appeared he was bald; there wasn't any hair sticking out from under his cap. He was extremely thin. Lucas moved closer, hoping to see more of his face. As he did so, he heard him tell the dealer, "Buy the ten, two-hundred dollars."

Lucas thought he recognized the voice but wasn't sure. Creeping closer, he stood right next to the man and quietly said to him, "Two-eight."

The gambler slowly lifted his head, and when he saw Lucas, a big grin came across his face. "Lustick, my boy, how's it going?"

Lucas smiled back and the two firmly shook hands. As this was happening, the shooter rolled a seven and the house-boys raked up all the chips on the table.

"Pick up your chips and let's go eat," Lucas said. "There's something I need to tell you."

As the two left the table and headed towards the hotel restaurant, the clever pit boss couldn't help but smile, knowing that he had been right again.

"You must have something good to tell me if you came all the way out here! How'd you know that you would find me here in the middle of the morning?"

"Well, Agnew, let's just say that I know that you're a decadent, addicted, dice-shooting bastard who has always loved shooting dice all night long in this fucking run-down whorehouse of a casino. This is the only place I've ever seen you play, and I've never seen you start playing before two a.m.! Is that good enough?"

"Yeah, I forgot how smart you are. I always wished I had your brains, you smart-ass bastard."

"Fuck you!" replied Lucas.

Inside the restaurant, a washed-out-looking, dark-haired hostess wearing a white blouse and tight black skirt seated them towards the back. They sat down opposite each other at a small linoleum-topped table.

She dropped two menus in front of them, asking if they wanted coffee.

"Yes," they both said, nodding.

Lucas watched her walk away, and then looked at Agnew. With little emotion he told him, "Amy died a few days ago. They buried her in Houston yesterday."

Agnew just looked at him with his mouth half open.

"She got cancer in her uterus somehow, about four months ago. Died quickly. She was in lots of pain. They had to put her on fucking morphine the last couple weeks. There was nothing the doctors could do, and she had the best ones around."

Agnew was visibly shaken. "She was like a sister to us. I haven't seen her in years, haven't even talked to her, but goddammit, she was the closest thing to a sister I ever had."

Pausing for a moment he then asked, "Why didn't you come out here and tell me she was so sick?"

"I really don't know. I just didn't think about it. I'm sorry, man."

"Was she still married to that straight-arrow guy who went to lawyer school with you?"

"Yeah, Rickie, you met him back when we were in California. When she got her job in Houston, he followed her there. They have a five-year-old kid. He's got some mental problems. It's not that he's retarded, but he's pretty slow. Something's not right with him, but I don't know what it is. It's gonna be real hard on him. He was really attached to her."

Agnew just sat there, looking down at the table.

At that moment, a young, attractive waitress brought two cups of steaming coffee and placed them down in front of the two grieving friends.

They were both reaching for their cups when she held up her order pad and asked if they knew what they wanted.

Lucas ordered four eggs, over easy, with a double order of hash browns.

Agnew, after looking her up and down, told her, "I just want you for breakfast!"

She teased him, "You can't afford me," and Lucas started laughing, grateful for the break in the painful conversation.

"Okay," Agnew said. "If I can't have you, then get me the same thing he's having, except only two eggs and one order of hash browns. Also, throw on a piece of steak." As she walked away, he told Lucas, "I'd sure like to do her!"

"Yeah, I'm sure she's thinking the same about you."

"Fuck you, Lustick, and why are you really here? I know you didn't come all the way out here just to tell me about Amy!"

Lucas took a sip from his cup. "I'm also here to bet on a game. I have good information on a college football game going later today. Take SMU against Texas, and bet it to go under the total. Bet all you can. It's locked!"

Shaking his head, Agnew asked, "Are you still into fixing those fucking football and basketball games? You aren't ever going to outgrow that bad habit, are you?"

"No, but I'm not into it as much as I was out in California. My law practice cuts into a lot of my free time. I don't have the time to hang out with and get to know the athletes like I used to. But, I know some good ones here and there. You know, guys I can trust, who are reliable and can take care of business in certain games. That's all I need, two or three crooked games each season. It makes life interesting."

"That asshole you used to gamble with in California, I don't remember his name; you ever see him?"

Lucas, nodding his head, answered "John O'Reilly, yeah, he's down in Houston. He's in on this football game with me."

"I saw him several months ago in Reno shooting dice, but I didn't say nothing to him because I always hated the prick."

Shaking his head, Lucas assured him, "No, that wasn't fucking O'Reilly. He'd of told me if he was in Reno. I see him everyday in Houston."

Agnew said, "Well, maybe I was mistaken, but it sure looked like the motherfucker."

The waitress arrived with their breakfast and placed their plates in front of them. They started eating.

"Take your time, big boy," Agnew said. "You act like you haven't eaten in five years! The food isn't going anywhere."

After finishing off his own plate, Lucas started watching Agnew meticulously use his knife and fork to cut into his food. Agnew carefully examined what was on his fork each time before placing it into his mouth. Sometimes it was steak, other times eggs or hash browns. But, he had very little on his fork each time. Lucas watched, wondering why he ate so slowly.

Agnew was skinny, with long arms and legs. His arms looked like wire cables. They were very thin, yet firm, with good muscle definition. His fingers were long and tapered, his nails freshly manicured. Lucas thought that he must have been bred to be a burglar. With his wiry arms he could easily pull himself in through windows to climb into houses or buildings. He was thin enough to hide in a closet or under a bed. He had the foot speed necessary to run away from the police or an unexpected homeowner if he had to, and finally, he could kill without remorse if the situation merited it.

"You mentioned my bad habit from the past. What about yours, have you ever outgrown it?" Lucas asked.

Agnew smiled. "No, I'm still the same as when we were kids. Nothing's changed. It's part of me now. I can't help myself."

"How often do you indulge yourself?"

"Whenever I feel the rage deep down inside of me, then I just go do it. It just depends. Usually two, maybe three times a year. It just," he hesitated briefly, "depends."

"Two or three times a year?" Lucas asked. "That's outrageous! You're going to get caught one of these days."

"If it ever happens, then I'll call you."

"You're sick," Lucas told him as he motioned for the waitress to bring the check.

Leaving a twenty on the table he stood up and said, "Get back out on the dice tables. I'm heading back to The Strip to find the best spot to bet the football game."

The two walked out from the restaurant into the lobby and then stopped and faced each other.

"What are you doing after you bet the game?" asked Agnew.

"Oh, I'll probably go back to my hotel to get some fucking sleep," answered Lucas. "Later today or tomorrow, I'll catch a flight back to Houston. Don't forget to place a bet on the game. Load up on it. I wouldn't give you a bad play. It's good. It goes at eleven-thirty this morning."

"You've always been pretty good at picking football," Agnew told him, "but I'm going to stick with dice."

Lucas turned around and walked out of the hotel onto Fremont Street where he motioned to a Red-and-White Cab coming down the street. The driver pulled up and he jumped into the front seat.

"Where to?" asked the cabbie.

"The Barbary Coast."

* * * *

As he walked into the Barbary Coast, Lucas headed straight towards the Sports Book. The casino was noisy at this time of morning; it was alive and full of energy. Everyone had received their paychecks the day before and now were trying to win some money. The early morning sun was reflecting off the white-paved sidewalk through the open doors of the casino. The slot machines rattled loudly when quarters jingled into the metal trays. Their lights flashed red and their sirens wailed each time someone hit a winner. People were everywhere. It was Saturday morning in Las Vegas.

At the Sports Book, the college football point-spread propositions were displayed in white chalk on the wall behind two betting clerks. The early East Coast games were getting ready to start. As Lucas crept closer he could see that Texas was favored by twenty-five points and that the over-under was at forty-seven points. Figuring that these were fair numbers, he shouldered his way into one of the lines. When reaching a betting clerk, he asked, "What's the most I can play on any one game?"

"Two thousand is the max on any straight play, one thousand on parlays."

"Then get me two thousand on SMU and the same on under forty-seven. Parlay them together for a thousand."

The clerk punched out the tickets and Lucas handed him a wad of cash. Grabbing the tickets he walked off.

Exiting the casino through the front entrance, he briskly walked towards Caesars Palace which was across the street.

As he crossed Las Vegas Boulevard, he was glad he still had plenty of time left before the Texas game started. He knew that Caesars' Sports Book was the most popular one in town and expected it to be jam-packed. He also knew their betting limits were higher than the other joints, and he still had nearly ten-thousand dollars to wager on SMU.

As Lucas entered into the complex, he walked through the casino in the direction of the Sports Book. Getting in one of the lines, he waited his turn until he reached the betting clerk. He laid ninety-nine-hundred dollars to win on SMU. The clerk punched out the ticket which read "SMU (+26) $9,900 to pay $18,900." Lucas paid him and was now down on the game.

Back in his room he noticed the message light on his phone was blinking. Assuming it was a message from John, he pushed the button for the message operator.

She answered and told him, "Sir, you have one message from a John O'Reilly from Houston, to call and leave a message with his father at 713-645-9986, telling him what the numbers on the game are."

Lucas thought, *That bastard! Fuck him!*

Quickly, he undressed and got into bed. Within minutes he was sound asleep.

FIVE

"Will you please slow this damn truck down before you get us killed? You are going to make Megan an orphan. There's no need to drive this fast!"

John could tell by the tone of her voice that Tammy was dead serious. Keeping both hands on the steering wheel, he looked over at her. "I'm only going ninety-five. I'd be going a hundred-and-ten if you weren't in the car!"

He did not let up on the gas pedal at all, continuing to cruise at ninety-five miles an hour. "I need to get to Austin to watch the Longhorns destroy them SMU prima donnas!"

"Watch what you're saying; that's my alma mater!"

"I know it is; that's where all you rich girls go. It's like a country club up there; your daddies pay for you to live in sorority houses in Highland Park. It's not even like going to college. What an existence, go to class all week and then play with sorority sisters all weekend."

"First of all, we didn't just play with our sorority sisters on weekends."

Staring over at her, he asked "Well, who'd you play with?"

"That's none of your damn business who I played with while you were working your way through school in *Palo Alto, California.* I just admire the way you put yourself through college and law school without any help from your daddy. Otis just never helped you at all. The odds you overcame to get to where you are today! It's just plain amazing!"

Pushing harder on the gas pedal, John said, "My father told me never to marry a sorority bitch. Said y'all make terrible wives. But I didn't listen to him. I blame nobody but myself for marrying you. I just fell for your looks. Never really looked beyond that!"

Exchanging insults was commonplace in John and Tammy's relationship; they both enjoyed trying to outwit one another. Though he would never admit it, John appreciated the way Tammy challenged him. She wasn't all that beautiful, but she was attractive enough to keep his interest most of the time. A petite, fair-skinned blonde with blue eyes, she most definitely knew how to take care of herself. She liked wearing boots, tight blue jeans, and designer shirts.

She met John at a Memorial Park picnic the summer after graduating college. He had just graduated from law school and was studying for the Texas bar exam. The two hit it off from the very start. Before they knew it, Tammy was pregnant. The couple felt that they were in love and were quietly married by a local Justice of the Peace.

Then, the young newlyweds broke the news to their families. Tammy's parents, both psychologists, readily accepted their new son-in-law. They saw him as a well-educated young man who was ready to accept the responsibilities that go along with marriage and fatherhood. On the other hand, Otis and Maggie weren't thrilled with their son being forced into a marriage, but figured he could have done a lot worse than a Texas-bred girl with an SMU diploma to her credit. They thought she was uptown enough to serve her purpose.

As they headed past Columbus and onto Highway 71, John looked into his rearview mirror and saw in the distance, but closing fast, a black Texas state trooper's vehicle with its overhead lights flashing.

"Goddamn it! This fucking cop is after me. This could make us late to the game. Goddamn it! Goddamn it! Goddamn it! I'm barely speeding!"

"No, of course not," Tammy told him. "You're only going ninety-five! Good thing I'm in the car, otherwise, you'd be going a hundred-and-five!"

"Fuck you!" he hissed as he angrily pulled off to the side of the road. "Open the glove box and take out the papers in the white envelope. He's gonna want to see them. Also, the DA badge right under the envelope."

She handed him the badge and then the papers. The badge had a photo of him on it and printed underneath the words, "Assistant District Attorney, Harris County, Texas."

John, looking in his rearview mirror, saw the trooper getting out of his patrol car. Standing nearly six-five, the lawman must have weighed close to two-hundred-and-fifty pounds. John had always said that six-five and two-fifty seemed to be the minimum height-and-weight requirements for members of this elite Texas law enforcement group. The trooper's head was big, and his face was square. He wore a tan uniform and a tan cowboy hat, standard garb for state troopers. As he approached the car, John whispered, "These guys all look alike—they look like fucking cows! This boy isn't wearing any stripes. That means he's a nothing, just a traffic cop."

"Just be nice to him, John! Don't be so obnoxious!"

As the trooper reached the window, he looked down into the vehicle and asked, "Sir, can I see your driver's license and proof of insurance?"

"Yes, sir," John said as he handed them to him.

"Sir, do you know why I stopped you?"

"I believe I do."

"I clocked you at ninety-five miles an hour, which is way over the speed limit. Is there any reason you were driving so fast?"

"Yes, sir, there sure is. I'm going to the football game in Austin. I'm an alumnus there, and I'm meeting two old classmates outside the stadium who have our tickets. If we're late, they're just going to go in without us. I'm really sorry. I'm asking that you give me a break this time and not write me a ticket."

The trooper told him to remain in the car as he walked back to his patrol vehicle.

Tammy looked at John, and mimicking him, said, "Oh, sir trooper, please, please don't give me a ticket. I'm such an ass-kisser. I'm a UT alumnus—and by the way, it was the Palo Alto, California branch of UT that I went to! I'm just a good-old boy from Texas, just like you."

John, looking at her, said, "You just don't know how to deal with cops. I deal with them everyday."

Suddenly he got a look on his face as if he'd just remembered something. "Oh, damn it, I forgot to show him my badge!"

Beeping on his horn, he motioned to the trooper to come back to his car. Begrudgingly, the officer got out of his vehicle and started walking back to see what he wanted. John started to step out of his car and the trooper yelled, "Get back inside your car! What the hell are you doing?"

"I'm sorry," John said, as he pulled his door shut, "but I wanted to show you that I'm an assistant DA in Houston. Here's my badge to prove it."

He handed the badge to the trooper through the rolled-down window. While he carefully looked at it, John continued, "In Houston, we get professional courtesy on tickets. HPD gives it to us, and so does the Sheriff's Department. I've never been pulled over by a trooper, so I don't know if you'll extend it to us or not. But, remember, that when you police arrest people, we prosecutors are your lawyers in court."

"What court do you prosecute out of?" the trooper asked.

"The 358th, Judge Tex Adams," John lied. He had been transferred out of that court months earlier.

The trooper, looking impressed, told him, "I've heard of him. He's the hanging judge, isn't he? You boys got your work cut out for you in Houston with all that crime there, don't you?"

John, now knowing that he had the trooper on his side, responded, "The biggest problem we have is all the damn blacks running wild, killing, robbing, and selling dope. We can hardly control them anymore. It used to be that they just did crimes against their own, which is okay. We'd hardly even prosecute them for that. But nowadays, they're going out to the suburbs and hurting white folks. We've been prosecuting them real hard. Hell, our office sent three of them to death row in the past month. I sent one of them myself, two weeks ago."

The trooper grinned. "Sounds like Harris County has a lot of problems. That's why I live out here in the country."

The trooper handed John his license, insurance papers, and badge back. "It's been nice meeting you. Just slow down."

The two shook hands, and then John rolled up the window, placed his truck into drive, and headed towards Austin.

Turning to Tammy, he said, "That was one hell of a nice cop. Has a good head on his shoulders."

Nodding her head in amazement, Tammy just stared out the window. She couldn't believe that John had won over that trooper. She was, in a way, hoping that he would have gotten a ticket. Then she could ride him about it. But, no such luck; her husband had a way with rednecks. He had talked his way out of it.

About thirty miles from Austin, Tammy asked whether SMU had a chance of winning against Texas.

"No, they don't have a chance of actually winning the game," John said. "Texas wants to win the national championship and they aren't going to lose to SMU. However, I believe SMU will stay in the game. They'll lose, but I don't think they'll be blown out as bad as a lot of people think. I actually bet them plus twenty-five or so points."

"What does plus twenty-five points mean?"

"That means if I bet SMU plus twenty-five points and Texas wins 28-0, I lose the bet. If Texas wins 28-7, I win the bet. As long as SMU doesn't lose by twenty-five points or more, I'll win my bet. I'm hoping Texas wins the game, but by less than twenty-five points. If they win by ten, I'm happy that they won the game, and I'm also happy because I bet SMU plus twenty-five points. That's how you bet football."

"How much did you bet on today's game?"

"I bet a hundred on SMU, and a hundred on under forty-six points, and I parlayed them together for a hundred."

"What does under mean, and what is a parlay?"

"The under bet is a bet where I'm saying that if you add up UT's points and SMU's points after the game, together they will be less than forty-six points. If Texas wins 35-17, then the total would be fifty-two points and I would lose my bet. If Texas wins 17-0, then, of course, I would win the wager."

Tammy nodded her head, pretending she understood what he was saying.

He then explained what a parlay is. "If you bet a parlay on SMU plus twenty-five points, and the total score going under forty-six points, then, if you win both parts, say Texas wins 24-3, well, then you collect two-and-a-half times whatever the wager is. But you have to win both parts or you lose your bet. Say if Texas wins the game 42-21, you win the SMU part, but lose the under part, then the parlay bet is a loser. Parlays are tough to hit, but when you do so, they pay real well!"

"Tell me again what you bet, honey."

"I put one hundred on SMU plus twenty-five points, and one hundred on under forty-six points being scored in the game, and I put them together in a one-hundred dollar parlay. So pull for SMU to stay within twenty-five points, and pull for it to be a fairly low-scoring game."

She said, "Now that I know that you bet so much on this game, it makes me nervous."

If only she knew how much I had really bet on this fucking game.

John didn't think gambling was something that wives needed to know about. Otis had taught him at a young age that wives didn't need to know the truth about gambling, business, or girlfriends.

It was thirty minutes before kickoff as they approached Austin on Highway 71. They soon merged into heavy traffic on Interstate 35. Horns were blasting and traffic was bumper-to-bumper as John waited to get off at the 15th Street exit, which would lead them to Memorial Stadium.

Tammy had opened her purse and was grabbing lipstick and makeup to put on before reaching the stadium. She knew that there would be lots of pretty college girls at the game, and she wanted to look her best. She didn't know much about football, didn't care to. The game was a social outing, a people-watching adventure to her. She liked seeing all the different outfits which the college girls wore on a Saturday afternoon at the stadium. She loved watching the cheerleaders and the school bands.

Once John parked their car inside the north gate she was ready to go. As they walked towards the stadium, a group of college girls were chanting, "UT! UT! UT!" Tammy looked at them and screamed, "Go Mustangs! Beat UT!"

As they entered the stadium, John was wondering what betting line Lucas had gotten on the game. He stopped at a pay phone to find out if Lucas had called his dad's house and left any information on the betting numbers. Nobody answered.

Lucas had been pretty rude that morning on the telephone, but he knew that Lucas was basically a straight-up guy and wouldn't cheat him on the numbers. If the line was SMU plus twenty-seven, he knew that's what he'd get it at.

He would never admit it to Lucas, but he trusted him one-hundred percent. They'd been through too much together not to.

As they sat down on their forty-yard-line seats, the teams were about ready to begin playing. SMU had lost the coin toss and was preparing to kick off to Texas. There was a certain energy in the stadium as the fans all stood in anticipation of the opening kickoff of the season. The special team players on both sides were all pumped up, waiting for the first live hitting of the season.

To Texas fans this was a season filled with promise, a season where they could win it all. Coach Seymour had promised that they would bring home a National Championship. In Austin, being head football coach was like being God; you could make those promises.

John looked through a pair of binoculars all the way across the field at the Texas players standing on their sideline in their burnt-orange-and-white uniforms. He perused the sidelines looking for Art and spotted him with his helmet off, talking to one of the offensive coaches. He appeared loose as he stood there. John knew that Head Coach Seymour had given

Art total control over the play-calling in this, his senior year. He figured that they were talking about what to run on the first few plays of the game.

The fans all stood as the SMU place kicker approached the teed-up football and kicked it through the Texas end zone. Texas would have first possession on their own twenty-yard line. Art Kiser led the offensive unit onto the field to a long-standing ovation from the fans. They huddled, then broke as the linemen rushed up to the line of scrimmage. Art then walked behind the center. He had two backs set behind him and wideouts flanked to each side of the field. He took the snap from the center, dropped back into the pocket, and hit one of his receivers running a twenty-five-yard post pattern across the middle of the field. The fans cheered loudly after this first completion.

John thought that Kiser could burn this SMU secondary all day if he chose to do so. He whispered to Tammy, "Hell, both of the SMU safeties are white boys! They don't have the speed to keep up with the coons Texas has!"

On the second play from scrimmage, the Longhorns set up a slot-back to the right, who ran a crossing pattern with the wideout. The SMU defender covering the slot-back forgot to switch in his coverage, and the wide receiver found himself wide open across the middle of the field at the SMU twenty-five-yard line. Art tossed a perfect spiral which he caught as he strutted untouched into the end zone. The Texas fans went crazy as the cannons fired and the players jumped all over each other. They were celebrating their first score of the season, knowing well that there would be many more occasions to celebrate as the season progressed.

John clapped his hands after the score but wished that Art had taken a little bit more time off the clock before scoring. Hell, he had the "under." The game was only forty seconds into the first quarter, and it was already 7-0. However, after this initial score, the game slowed down considerably. SMU tried to keep the ball away from Kiser by trying to control it themselves. They had a couple of bruiser-type running backs who kept running the ball off-tackle. They were averaging about four yards per carry, which allowed them to control the ball by picking up first downs. Two of their drives ended on missed field goals deep in Texas territory.

Had someone gotten to the SMU kicker? John wondered. He'd been all-conference the past season, but today had already shanked two field goals.

Texas scored a second touchdown early in the second quarter on a Kiser twenty-yard-touchdown pass. But after that, Art looked bland the rest of the first half. His timing was off with his receivers, and the television announcers at halftime noted that he had been sacked five times in the first half. This was not normal for Kiser, who was known as a great scrambler. Texas led 14-0 at intermission.

The third quarter was scoreless until late in the period when a Texas defensive back intercepted a pass and returned it for a touchdown. The Texas fans went berserk and started chanting, "Number one! Number one! Number one!"

John thought, *Oh, fuck, it's 21-0. One more Texas touchdown and the game ends 28-0.* He and Lucas would then lose a lot of money. He just hoped that Art would keep Texas from scoring again and that the game would end 21-0. *Hell, that's what he was paid to do.* But Art had no control over keeping the defense from scoring.

The score remained 21-0 well into the fourth quarter. Art was keeping his part of the bargain. He'd hand the ball to his backs who would then dive into the SMU line, usually picking up two or three yards per carry. He was doing great at running down the clock. When he needed to pass, he'd intentionally throw the ball five feet beyond his receivers' outstretched hands. With two minutes left to go in the game, the SMU quarterback was intercepted at mid-field by a Texas safety who then broke through four tackles by SMU players en route to a fifty-yard-interception return for a touchdown. The score was now 28-0!

The stadium was in an uproar. The fans knew that the line was twenty-five or so points, and lots of them had bet the game, laying the points. Texas was finally covering the spread!

Coach Seymour, glowing from ear-to-ear, was down on the field congratulating his defensive unit for the late touchdown. He knew how important it was for him to be able to win games not only straight-up, but against the spread. It was called, "keeping your alumni happy." He knew that alumni bet heavily each week on Texas, and what mattered to them aside from the National Championship was the Longhorn's covering the line. During the history of college football, many coaches had lost their jobs by not being able to cover the spread.

John was fuming. Silently he was cussing out the SMU players for missing tackles. Tammy, looking at him, could tell that he was very angry. She told him, "Be happy! Your Longhorns are winning the game!"

"Yeah, but by too many points. Did you see those SMU pussies miss all those tackles! They quit! They have no heart, no guts! I'm going to lose a lot of dough!"

Tammy patted him on his back and said, "It's only three-hundred dollars. Please don't get so upset."

Three-hundred dollars my ass! John cringed at Tammy's attempts to make him feel better.

SMU received the kickoff and returned it to their own forty-yard line. However, the return man fumbled the ball, giving possession to Texas with one minute and forty-five seconds left in the game. Kiser handed the ball to his fullback on first down, and he picked up five yards.

In the huddle before the next play, Art called a, "Blue, 15 down and out," which was a pass play whereby one of his receivers runs fifteen yards downfield and then cuts to the sideline where he expects the ball to be thrown. One of the lineman asked, "Why are we running a pass play with just a minute left and we're leading 28-0?"

Art told him, "We need to win bigger. Just line up and run the fucking play!"

The offensive team lined up, and Art took the snap and dropped back to pass. He threw the ball towards the wideout, only it slipped out of his hand when he released it. It was intercepted by an SMU cornerback who returned it for a touchdown. The play had nothing to do with who would win the game. Texas still led by a score of 28-7 with only a minute left to play. However, Art's bad pass certainly upset a lot of people.

An angry Coach Seymour met him when he came back to the sidelines. "What the fuck was that? I've got alumni and fucking boosters who bet us to win this game by over twenty-five points! What the fuck are you doing out there!"

"I'm sorry, coach. I didn't know what the spread was. Had no idea. I was just trying to get another completion."

Texas then recovered SMU's onside kick with sixty seconds left in the game. Art took two snaps from center and on each play just put his knee down. It sure sounded as if you could hear more boos than applause coming from the Texas fans during this last minute of the game. Time ran out with Texas winning 28-7.

John was all smiles as he and Tammy left their seats and headed to the truck. It had been more of a "sweat" than he wanted, but Art had come through for him at the end. Tammy, however, was upset that SMU had lost. Her throat hurt from screaming so much during the game. Sitting in traffic in the parking lot, John patted her knee. "Honey, SMU did just fine. They covered the spread."

"But I really wanted them to win!"

John was thinking how much money he and Lucas had just won.

In Las Vegas, Lucas had slept throughout the entire game. When he awakened, he didn't know who had won or what the final score was.

It was the middle of the afternoon and he had a terrible headache. He headed downstairs to the casino Sports Book where he could see the scores posted. There he saw that SMU had covered the spread and that the game had gone under forty-seven points. But he had no idea just how close it had been.

He went to the front desk at the hotel and rented a safe-deposit box where he stashed his winning tickets from both Caesars and the Barbary Coast. He was planning to fly to Reno that evening and didn't want to carry a large amount of cash. He would cash in his winning tickets when he returned to Vegas the following day.

SIX

As the judge entered the courtroom, Richard, the court bailiff, stood, and in a loud, deep voice announced, "The 268th District Court of the great State of Texas is now in session. Everybody please rise."

Judge Frank Grant, dressed in a black robe, walked up two steps and sat down in a large, black, leather chair which was positioned behind the judicial bench facing the courtroom. Across the front of the bench read, "Judge Grant, 268TH District Court." As Frank sat down, Richard announced, "Everybody please be seated."

Frank Grant looked around the old courtroom and saw numerous lawyers whom he knew, chatting amongst themselves. The courtroom was divided into two parts: the attorney part, which consisted of the counsel tables and the jury box, and the spectator part, which consisted of the numerous wooden benches where court spectators could sit. The spectators consisted mainly of defendants who were out on bond, witnesses in various cases, and family members of defendants who were in custody. The two sections were clearly divided by a wooden railing. The lawyers were free to be on either side of the railing, while the others weren't allowed on the attorney side unless accompanied by their lawyer or one of the prosecuting attorneys. At times, the judge would ask certain defendants on bond to approach the bench, but that was rare.

Frank Grant looked out at the forty-or-so people sitting on the spectator benches and whispered to his chief prosecutor, "Is it my imagination or do those people out there look as scummy as I think they look? I mean, don't they even get dressed decently when they come to court?"

John O'Reilly whispered back, "Your Honor, of course they look scummy. Most decent people don't get charged with felonies. What do you expect them to look like? Have you or any of your kids been charged with felonies lately?"

"I guess you're right," Frank replied, "but it's just depressing."

John then asked, "Judge, do you want to go to trial today, or do you want me to try to work the cases out?"

"I'm trying to tee-off at one o'clock at Brandywine, so try to move what you can." Looking at his watch, he continued, "My ride is coming at noon."

John, nodding his head, said, "Yes, sir, I'll see to it that we move things today so that nothing keeps you from your plans."

John had a lot of respect for the old judge. Frank Grant had been a career prosecutor with Harris County for many years before taking the bench. Never the most talented trial lawyer in the office, he was better known for his administrative abilities. His final fifteen years there, he was head of the trial bureau. His duties were to supervise all the trial lawyers in the office. He would assign them to various courts, attempting to place them in spots where they were compatible with the judge of the court. He also had the authority to promote prosecutors to higher positions when he thought they were ready. Often, he would transfer them from one court to another for whatever reason he deemed necessary.

In addition, he had to deal with the everyday problems of the two-hundred-and-fifty trial lawyers within the office. His easygoing, gentlemanly style made him very popular amongst his troops, most of whom were half his age. Eighty percent of them had been out of law school for less than five years. They had come to the District Attorney's Office for the main purpose of getting trial experience, and while many of them had huge egos, some had very fragile ones.

Frank was comforting to young prosecutors after they had lost cases or had been whipped up on in court. He would try to rebuild their self-confidence in a fatherly fashion. Many a depressed, young lawyer would find himself or herself in Frank's office at times of need. At the other extreme, guys like John O'Reilly always had a place where they could go and brag about their great accomplishments in the courtroom to somebody who seemed to care. Frank was a great listener and knew that trial lawyers had a psychological need to be heard.

His great patience and popularity made him the perfect candidate to be appointed by the governor as judge of the 268th District Court when the former judge, Billy Harmon, resigned to accept a position as a racing steward at a Louisiana horse track. The governor appointed Frank to the bench based on the many high recommendations which were forwarded on his behalf.

With his appointment as judge, Frank bid the District Attorney's office farewell and accepted his position among the Harris County Judiciary. Wearing a black robe didn't change him. After a year on the bench he was still the same patient, easygoing, loveable Frank. That's why John wanted to see to it that there would be nothing in the courtroom preventing him from teeing off at one o'clock. He remembered that when Frank was with the office, he saw to it that John was assigned to the most prosecution-oriented courts where he was able to hammer away at criminals day-in and day-out with the support of the judge. It enabled him to obtain his reputation as the top trial lawyer in the office. Now it was time to pay Frank back for the opportunities he had given him.

John motioned to both of his assistants to meet with him in the back hallway behind the courtroom. They each momentarily excused themselves from the defense lawyers with whom they were dealing and followed him into the narrow, brightly lit hallway. In sharp contrast to the dark courtroom they had just been in, it was like being in a dermatologist's office where the intense lighting seemed to magnify everyone's facial flaws. As John spoke, both assistant prosecutors watched him and listened to what he was telling them about settling their cases on the docket that morning.

Mary Meggs, a tall blonde who didn't particularly like working under John, focused on the long, uncut hairs sticking out from his nose as he talked. She thought he looked disgusting. She didn't like the idea of settling all of her cases at reduced punishments just to move the docket so that the judge could go play golf that afternoon instead of presiding over a trial. But she knew not to buck John because doing so would mean that she would get a bad evaluation when the day came.

Mary knew that a bad evaluation from John O'Reilly would pretty much signify the end of her career as a trial lawyer in the District Attorney's Office. She would never be promoted to the position of chief prosecutor in a court. She would most likely end up being assigned to an undesirable position in the hot-check or family-violence divisions, where she would rot away like an old tomato left in the bottom drawer of a refrigerator. So she hustled back towards the courtroom, now knowing that she had to settle all of her trial cases.

Following behind her was Dennis Medley, a young, redheaded prosecutor who was quite pleased with John's instructions. Dennis had been drinking and gambling all weekend and was in no mood to pick a jury and try a case. Besides, he had to meet his bookmaker across town in Pasadena at two o'clock to pay off his football losses from the weekend. He went 1-6 on the college games that Saturday and 0-5 on the Sunday NFL card. He was depressed after getting beaten so badly but had to keep it to himself that he was betting the games because it could lead to his firing if it were known. Earlier that morning, on the elevator, he had heard John telling some people that he had attended the Texas game that weekend and how well he thought they played. Dennis thought, *If only O'Reilly knew how much I lost because they didn't cover the spread. I think they played like shit, them non-covering bastards!*

As Mary and Dennis re-entered the courtroom, eight or so defense lawyers were crowded around the counsel tables, each wondering what the status of their case was. Were they going to trial or were they going to be offered reduced plea-bargains which their clients might accept?

Mary picked up her five trial folders and started talking to her opposing lawyers, one-by-one, trying to work out her cases. She didn't want any of them to know that she had been ordered to resolve the cases regardless of how low she would have to go on her plea-bargain offers. In one particular drug case, she had only two weeks earlier offered the defendant fifteen years in prison as a plea bargain. Now she reduced the offer to twelve years. The defense lawyer ran it by his dope-dealing client who rejected it. Mary was frustrated, knowing that if the case was tried, she'd probably get forty years from a jury. She could get this punk off the streets for a long time. Now, since she was forced to move the case, she lowered her offer to ten years, but the defendant still rejected it. His lawyer told her that he would take, "a nickel, nothing more," and she agreed to give it to him. She felt powerless as she filled out the plea papers for the five-year sentence. The defendant quickly signed the papers, realizing that he was getting a great deal for waiving his right to a jury trial.

She settled all her cases in this manner except for a rape case which she reduced from a fifty-year offer all the way down to fifteen years. Refusing to waive his right to a jury trial, the defendant still rejected it. His lawyer told her that he'd take six years; otherwise, he wanted a trial. Mary was furious, knowing that if she were allowed to try the case, she'd get life on this pervert easily. He was an ex-con who had broken into a woman's apartment at three o'clock in the morning, held a butcher knife to her throat, and sexually assaulted her. She went to John and told him that she couldn't in good conscience offer below fifteen years.

"It is a horrible case!" she cried out.

John was standing against the wall in the back of the courtroom facing Lucas Lustick, who had arrived just moments earlier. He didn't have any cases that morning, but had stopped by to talk about his weekend trip to Vegas which John, of course, had great interest in.

John turned and asked Mary, "What's the name of the rape victim?"

Wondering why he asked such a question, she replied, "Her name is Ann Hall."

John, who couldn't tell her race by her name, then asked, "Is Ann Hall white or black?"

"What's the difference?"

"Just answer my question."

"She's black."

John ordered her, "Go fill out the papers for six years."

Mary stared at him in total disbelief and then stomped off.

Lucas asked, "What's her problem?"

John answered, "These women are so emotional. They try to make so much more out of their cases. Some nigger was raped. Who gives a fuck!"

Lucas just shook his head back and forth, amazed that John had these strange thoughts about justice.

As they continued to converse about the Vegas trip, across the courtroom, Dennis Medley was working out all of his trials. He bluntly told the defense lawyers that plea bargains on all his cases were "on sale." He would allow the defendants to take nearly whatever they desired if they agreed to waive jury trials and plead guilty. It was simply "giving away the courthouse" in order to move cases. Defendants who were looking at five-to-twenty years on cases were now walking off with probation or just fines.

At eleven-thirty, Judge Grant proceeded to take the pleas of each defendant. Each of them smiled as he pronounced their sentences in accordance with the plea bargains. They were getting the deals of their lives, and they all knew it.

Mary Meggs stood to the side, thinking, *What a day for the criminals in the Fighting 268th. This is disgraceful!*

She wondered why she even got into criminal law. She could have gone to work for some fancy civil firm. What a big mistake she made going to work for the District Attorney's office; she felt like quitting!

Frank finished taking all the pleas and then asked if anyone had any more court business. Looking across the courtroom he saw John wink at him. Nodding his head he got up from the bench and left the courtroom. John knew that the old judge was proud of him for moving the docket so that he could make his tee-time.

Lucas and John then left the courtroom, each heading to Lucas' law office on Smith Street where they could split up the loot from the crooked football game. It was a ten-minute drive from the courthouse. Lucas parked in front of the two-story building at 2009 Smith Street and stood outside his car and waited for John to pull up. Moments later, he arrived and the two walked into the old office building.

There were four law offices on the ground floor and one private investigator's office. Upstairs, there were five law offices, one of which was leased by Lucas on a month-to-month basis. The lawyers in the building were criminal lawyers, all of them solo practitioners. Each one was basically broke, barely making it month-to-month, with the exception of Lucas. He had plenty of clients, and they paid him well for his services. Clients who visited his office were always surprised that he didn't office in one of the big, fancy buildings on Travis or Louisiana Street. This was Lucas' first office when he started practicing law, and he had no intention of leaving it. It was good enough for him then, and it was good enough for him now.

He and John stood on the first floor, awaiting the elevator. After a minute or so, John kicked the elevator door and asked, "What's wrong with your fucking elevator?"

Lucas replied, "It runs slow."

John angrily said, "Let's just walk up the fucking stairs!"

As they climbed the stairs, John asked, "Why don't you move to a decent fucking building? You're making a lot of money. Get out of this fucking dive!"

"It's fine for me," Lucas said, as he reached into his pocket for his keys.

They briskly walked down the dimly lit hallway to Lucas' office. He unlocked the wooden door and the two walked in. It was dark and very quiet.

"Where's your fucking secretary?" asked John. "What kind of business are you running here?"

Lucas, turning on the lights, replied, "Oh, she just works part time. She dances at night, and a lot of days she's too tired to come in."

"You've got to be kidding!" John seemed amazed. "You're one of the best criminal lawyers in the state, and you don't have someone answering your phones around the clock or at least from eight to five? What the fuck is wrong with you? And this office, look how dirty it is—fuck! Doesn't anyone ever clean it?"

Lucas didn't pay any attention to John's comments. This was where he was comfortable. It was where he could study his law books and read court opinions, hoping to maybe find some technicality or seldom-used law that might help his clients win their freedom. He kept a messy office, but it was none of John's damn business.

Kneeling down, he unlocked a file cabinet next to his desk and removed two white envelopes which he handed to John, saying, "It's all in here."

After opening both envelopes, John counted the money to make sure that Lucas didn't short him. Lucas had actually included an extra one-hundred-dollar bill, just to see if John would be honest and tell him. When John finished counting the money, he told Lucas, "Perfect," and then he placed the envelopes into his suit jacket inside pocket. "Good work, boy," he said.

Lucas assured him, "I'll get back with Art in about three or four weeks. Let them crush some teams the next few games, and then they'll be giant favorites against Baylor or Kansas State, and we'll do it all over again."

John, nodding his head, said, "Yeah, we can't do this every week."

Lucas then sat down at his desk and started reading a case file. John asked him what he was looking at, to which he answered, "It's a federal case which I'm going to try next week."

John inquired, "Haven't you been kicking ass over there in federal court lately?"

"Yeah, I've won three straight dope cases; now they're gunning for me. I fucked hard with the DEA agents each time. I turned them inside out, those lying bastards. A couple of them would put a bullet in the back of my head if they thought they could get away with it. And those federal prosecutors—I hate to brag, but I've kicked the shit out of them in each trial. They don't know how to handle it when I start fucking with them!"

John, laughing, told him, "Okay, tough guy. Keep working. I've got to go."

Turning around, he walked out of the office and headed down the stairs. He knew that he, too, had a full afternoon of work ahead. He needed to prepare for a murder case which was scheduled to start the following week. As he climbed into his truck, he reached inside his jacket to give the two envelopes of money a pat of satisfaction. *And ... an extra hundred to boot.*

SEVEN

"Find out everything that you can on this lawyer. Where is he from? Where did he go to school? What does he do in his spare time? How much tax does he pay? Anything you can find on him—who he sleeps with, what type of family he comes from, anything, just get it for me!"

"Yes sir, Mr. Calhoun. I'll be flying to Virginia on Thursday night to train some new recruits at the academy. I'll get it all together for you before I leave. It will be typed and delivered to your office on Friday morning, if that's okay. If you need to talk to me about anything in the report, you can call me in Quantico. I'll be available for you."

Preston Calhoun expressed his gratitude to the young FBI agent and bid him farewell. He then walked to the antique hat rack in the back of his office. It stood proudly, almost eight-feet tall and three-feet wide, solid mahogany, with yellow-brass hooks to hang hats or even sport coats upon. It had a rectangular mirror attached to it at face level where Preston always checked himself out before leaving his office.

He was a proud Irishman, always wanting to look his very best. If his reddish-gray hair wasn't neatly in place, he'd brush it. If he had anything in his nose, he'd be sure to wipe it away. He'd rub away any crud near his eyes, and brush off any dandruff from his suit jacket. Close to fifty, Preston had the vanity of a man much younger. An impeccable dresser, his suits were made by a private tailor, his shoes and ties imported from Europe.

Everyone who worked for him knew that he was a perfectionist. Everything had to be done just right. He expected his people to maintain a professional attitude in the way they carried themselves when at work and away. The FBI did complete background checks on all his staff lawyers, and even the secretaries who worked in the office. Everyone needed to be squeaky clean to be hired by him. There wouldn't be any gamblers, drinkers, wife-beaters, or adulterers working for Preston Calhoun. He thought it a great honor to be able to work for the United States government. Ever since the President had appointed him to the post of United States Attorney for the Southern District of Texas, he had taken great pride in his work and that of his staff.

Preston was responsible for prosecuting criminals charged with federal crimes committed within the jurisdiction. Whereas the local District Attorney's Office prosecuted street crimes such as murder, rape, and robbery; the U.S. Attorney's Office took the more complex cases involving crimes such as drug trafficking and white-collar offenses committed against the United States government. Very seldom would the U.S. Attorney's Office prosecute crimes of violence. They usually left that to the state prosecutors to pursue. But on occasion, in the case of a bombing of a federal building, or the murder or attempted murder of a federal agent, then they might intervene and take control in the prosecution of the case.

Once his office accepted responsibility in prosecuting a case, it was up to Preston to assign the case to a federal prosecutor working under him. He had great confidence in all of them; after all, he had handpicked them. They were all career types. None of them were there to learn the ropes, to then quit and become defense lawyers. Preston let them know when he hired them that he wasn't going to train them and have them become what he called a "Benedict Arnold," who would someday leave the office to help criminals get off—with trial skills he had taught them. The few who had left his office over the years either went to work for civil firms or left town. No one ever dared to become a practicing criminal defense lawyer in Houston if they had worked under him.

Preston walked out of his office down the hallway towards his secretary's desk. He asked her to bring him the Ralph Pond file from Mike Miller's office since he had decided to take the case away from Mike.

Judy had been his secretary for fifteen years and had never before seen him take a case back which he had already assigned to another prosecutor. She wondered why he was doing so in this case, but knew not to ask. He wasn't the type of boss who liked to be asked questions. She simply went to Mike Miller's office, took the Pond file off his desk, and brought it back to Preston. He took it, thanked her, and then headed back into his office, shutting the door. Judy then left a note on Mike Miller's desk informing him that Mr. Calhoun had requested the Pond file and that he was now going to be handling the case.

She knew that Mike would be raising hell as soon as he returned from court and saw her note. Things would get real interesting that afternoon. She was, in a way, waiting for his return from court so that the excitement would begin.

It did, right before the noon hour.

Mike stormed out of his office and went straight to her desk, asking, "What the hell is going on?"

Judy meekly answered, "I don't know." And then after pausing, "He's in his office now. Go talk to him."

Mike headed to Preston's office. Judy had never seen him this angry. Mike was the golden boy of the office; tall, blond, blue-eyed, Ivy League all the way. Though raised in Houston, he attended college in New Jersey, at Princeton. Then, he returned for law school at UT and had been with Preston's office ever since. Known for his extraordinary efforts in preparing his cases, Mike had put many, many hours into the preparation of the Ralph Pond case and couldn't believe that Preston had the nerve to take it off his desk without even talking to him about it. This was a case he really had his heart set on trying to a jury. It involved the attempted murder of an FBI agent in the course of his work. It was more exciting than most of the white-collar crimes that were usually assigned to him. This wasn't a Medicare fraud case against a doctor, or a complicated tax-evasion case against some politician. No, this was a case against some street punk who had tried to kill a federal agent. This case had some meat to it, and Mike was highly upset that the big boss was taking it away.

He knocked on the door and Preston shouted, "Hold on!"

Preston expected Mike's reaction. Rising up from his chair, he walked to his hat rack to check on himself in the mirror before opening the door. Satisfied that he saw no flaws, he opened the door. Politely, he greeted Mike, asking him to come in. Mike sat down in a leather chair directly across from Preston's desk. Preston sat down in the wooden chair behind his desk, and asked, "So what brings you down to my office today, young man?"

"I think you know why I'm here! Why did you take the Pond case from me?"

Preston just looked at him and reached into his shirt pocket for a toothpick, which he then placed between his teeth. As he bit down, Mike continued, "I had that case all worked up for trial. It's set for Monday!"

Preston still didn't respond, as he continued chomping on the toothpick. Now, he wasn't even looking at Mike; but instead, he stared out the window to his right.

Finally, still looking out the window, Preston said in his calm, assuring voice, "Mike, don't worry. It has nothing to do with you. I've just decided to handle this case. I'd let you sit second with me, but you know my policy on that."

Preston never assigned two lawyers to the same case unless it involved prosecuting multiple defendants in a single trial. He thought it to be a waste of resources. "But I need your help in preparing for Monday. Please call all of our main witnesses and have them here at two o'clock Friday so that I can go over their testimony with them."

Mike slumped down in his chair. Though disappointed, he felt relieved knowing that he hadn't done anything wrong to cause Preston to take the case away from him. There was some reason Preston wanted this case, but it didn't appear that he intended to share the reason with him. Mike assured Preston that he'd get all the witnesses to his office on Friday, and then stood up and started walking out the door.

Preston then offered, "Michael, come back in here and sit down! I'll tell you what's going on."

Mike walked back to the chair and sat down, curiously looking at his boss, wondering what he had to say.

"Michael, I got a call last night from a county prosecutor I know by the name of John O'Reilly. He keeps me informed of what's going on at the county courthouse from time to time. Wants to be a judge someday, and he's going to want my support, so I guess that's why he even talks with me. Well, anyhow, he told me that there is some defense lawyer he knows who is bragging about how he's whipped up on our office in court. Says our prosecutors are pansies and have no fight in us. Says the most fun he's ever had was kicking our federal butts in trial!"

"Who is it?" Mike asked.

"His name is Lucas Lustick. Do you know of him?"

"I know of him, but I've never met him," Mike answered. "He has never even shown up for any of our preliminary hearings in this case. But I've heard about him. Had an acquittal against Mel three-or-so weeks ago in some dope case. Mel said he was a strange-looking guy with long hair, huge ears, and the widest nose he'd ever seen on a human being. Supposedly, he usually practices in state court. Mel told me that he ripped into the DEA agents beyond belief. Tore them apart. Said he'd never seen anyone do it like he did!"

Preston continued, "Well, I checked all the trial records in our office for the past three years and this Lustick character has gotten three acquittals in all three cases which he's tried against us. Besides Mel's case, he walked a major trafficker from Columbia against Lopez, and then some local dealer against Dave Davis. It's the only cases either Davis or Lopez have lost in over fifteen years here.

"Anyhow, Mr. O'Reilly told me that Lustick was going to try a case here next week, so I went through our trial logs to see where he was set. I was going to take it no matter whose case it was. It just turned out to be yours. You see, it's my office which he is mouthing off about. I take personally what he's been saying and I'm going to take care of it myself."

Mike responded, "I totally understand. I'd be doing the same if I was in your shoes. You need to just kick him around the court like a rag doll!"

Preston, now nodding his head and smiling, told him, "Don't worry, I will."

Mike stood up to leave and said, "Good luck. If you need anything, just call me."

Preston now felt much better about having pulled rank over Mike. He had explained things and Mike handled the situation well. Mike understood why he had to take over the case. It was simply a matter of pride, and who better than Mike Miller would understand that?

Preston started reading through the government's file which contained the usual paperwork. There was an offense report which was prepared by the lead detective assigned to the case. It consisted of a detailed crime-scene investigation and written statements given by the police officers and federal agents involved in the case. After reading through everything, he realized that there weren't any pre-trial motions filed by Lucas Lustick included within the file.

This was very unusual. In most cases, defense lawyers file pre-trial motions related to the discovery of all the government's evidence in a case. These so called "discovery motions" require that the government show to the defense all the evidence which they intend to use during a trial in attempting to obtain a conviction.

Preston's office policy had always been that once a defense lawyer filed such a motion, his office would hand over the entire case file to the lawyer to read and take any notes from. He basically had an open-file policy which allowed defense lawyers to know exactly what they would be facing in court. But here, it appeared there were no discovery motions ever filed by Lustick on behalf of Mr. Pond. Preston then got on the phone to Judy and asked her to connect him to Mike Miller.

"Has this Lustick character ever filed any discovery on this case?"

Mike answered, "No, none that I received notice of."

Preston asked, "Has he ever come by to read our file?"

"No, I've never heard from or seen the guy. Like I told you, he's never even shown up for court! The judge finally got really upset and just set the case for trial because he never shows up."

"So, he just never comes to court?"

"No," replied Mike, "not on this case."

"Thanks," said Preston, and he hung up the phone. Next, he asked Judy to find Lucas Lustick's phone number.

Moments later, she came to his office and handed him a piece of paper with the phone number on it.

He didn't take the paper from her. Instead he asked her if she would please call Mr. Lustick and ask him if he wanted to read the government's file prior to trial. She started walking to her desk, but he stopped her, "Come back here; use my phone." He wanted to hear the conversation.

Judy dialed the number and a male voice answered on the other end, "Law office."

She asked, "Is Attorney Lustick in?"

"This is Lustick."

There was a pause for several seconds, and then she said, "I'm calling from Preston Calhoun's office. You are set to go to trial in the Pond case on Monday, and Mr. Calhoun wanted me to call you and let you know that he is leaving his file open for you to read if you want to come by our office."

Lucas paused, and then told her, "Well, tell Mr. Calhoun that I appreciate it, but I'm going to have to turn down the offer. I just get too nervous every time I step into your building. I feel like I'm being secretly taped or I'm being watched by hidden cameras. I'm real uncomfortable in there. The federal building just isn't my type of place."

Judy, listening to his sarcastic response, looked at Preston and rolled her eyes. She then told Lucas that if he overcame his paranoia, he was welcome to come over and look at the file.

After saying, "Goodbye," she hung up the phone and told Preston, "What a jerk! Thinks that when he comes over here we're secretly taping everything he does with some hidden camera. He really sounds like a low-life. Doesn't even have a secretary answering his phone. I wonder what he looks like? I bet he's fat and ugly."

Preston laughed, "Well, thanks, Judith, for at least trying. We did all we could to help him out. By the way, get a hold of Mel, Dave, and Lopez, so that I can ask them about, well, never mind—forget that—just get back to your own work."

Preston wanted to talk to them about their trial experiences with Lucas Lustick, but decided not to do so. He didn't want it to appear that he was too concerned about his courtroom opponent. Staring down at his pocket watch he saw that it was nearly one-thirty. He left his office and started walking to the YMCA where he could run two or three miles on the indoor track, as he usually did during his lunch break.

As Preston was running, Lucas was meeting with a process server who had come by to pick up some subpoenas to serve for the Pond case. Lucas handed him one-hundred dollars along with two subpoenas to serve. That was it for his preparation. In his mind, he was ready for trial.

Preston, on the other hand, worked the rest of the week preparing for the trial. He visited the crime scene, interviewed people, and took pictures. He read and then re-read all the statements in the offense report. He worked on his opening statement and his final argument.

On Friday, Preston met with all of his witnesses in his office where he woodshedded them so that their statements would be consistent and sound credible in court. He was not going to leave any stone unturned in this case. A very competitive man, he was planning to lower the hammer on Lucas Lustick, and in doing so, convict Ralph Pond.

It wasn't until nearly four o'clock on Friday, when the FBI memo was delivered to Preston's office. He quickly removed it from the envelope. It read:

> *We can't find a birth certificate anywhere in the U.S.A. or any other place in the world to which we have access. We can find no early school records. We found that at age eleven or twelve, he moved into Briaridge Orphanage, north of San Francisco, California. It is thought, but cannot be confirmed, that his birth mother was a waitress-prostitute and his biological father possibly a professor at a northern California university. The source as to this information about his natural parents spoke on condition of anonymity and my promise not to ever disclose her name to anyone. However, I have that information if you need it.*
>
> *At the orphanage, young Lustick's records reveal that he had very deep psychological problems from the time he was admitted until the day he left at age seventeen. However, the medical record-keeping is very sketchy and incomplete. Numerous papers are missing from his file. It appears that a doctor who at one time*

treated him, described him as brilliant, though extremely paranoid, with major anti-social tendencies.

There are notes entered by an unknown source which also indicate that he might be psychotic. However, this diagnosis is not signed or dated and there are no test results in his charts to support such opinion. Other notes indicate he had excessive anger, aloofness, anxiety, and antisocial thoughts. Counseling records speak of his hatred of all authority figures, his hatred of females, and his distrust of everyone with the exception of two other orphan children, one named Amy and the other Agnew, who both entered the orphanage at the same time as he. Records show that they are of no blood relationship to him. Of note, two counselors who treated Lustick emphasized that "loyalty" was of utmost importance to him.

His IQ test score was 160. He received his secondary education at a school near the orphanage, but the school has since burned down. I would need more time to find his high school records. He scored an 800 on his math SAT and a 740 on his verbal SAT. He attended Cal Berkeley on a full academic scholarship for undergraduate and law school. He was known as being very antisocial throughout his years at Berkeley. We have internal, university police reports which target him as being involved in point-shaving scandals by Cal Berkeley football and basketball players. However, the investigations were never completed, and he was never made aware of them. During his years at Berkeley, he frequented two area racetracks, one in Berkeley, the other south of San Francisco. He was never known to date anyone during his seven years at Berkeley. There is no indication that he is homosexual.

> *Following law school, Lustick left California and moved to Houston to practice criminal defense law. He has lived in Houston for five-and-a-half years. He has become a very successful lawyer, primarily in state court. He is known as a ruthless, talented trial lawyer. He is hated by almost all prosecutors in the Harris County District Attorney's Office. He has reported income in each of the last three years at well above two-hundred-thousand dollars. He lives by himself in a modest townhouse with few furnishings, enjoying a spartan existence. He likes to drink, and often dates topless dancers. He has no close friends that we are aware of.*

Preston couldn't believe what he'd just read, so he read it again. Then he called Judy into his office so she could read it. She just shook her head and said, "He sounds like a real winner."

Preston responded, "He looks to be a sick man. Very sick." As he said this, he was thinking to himself about what he had just read. He knew that Lucas Lustick would be different than any lawyer he had ever faced.

Judy left for the weekend, and Preston stayed in his office well past midnight. He was the only person left in the building with the exception of Don, the night watchman, who wandered from floor to floor. When Don walked the eighth floor, he heard a loud voice coming from Preston's office. The voice was that of Preston delivering his final argument to the walls. Don, a retired cop, chuckling to himself, thought, *These fucking lawyers are so insecure about themselves that they need to practice what they're going to say in court by talking to the walls beforehand! Geesh.*

While Preston prepared for trial, Lucas left Houston for the evening and drove on I-10 East to Louisiana for a night of gambling. He visited Vinton, a Cajun town, long known for its fast women who occupied the interstate truck stops, and its slow horses which raced for cheap claiming prices at Delta Downs Racetrack. He arrived at the track in time to bet the daily double. After purchasing the *Racing Form,* he started handicapping the races. The first race was a three-thousand-dollar claiming race for fillies and mares, the second, a five-thousand-dollar claiming race for horses who had never won.

Standing near the betting windows, Lucas studied the *Racing Form*, making comparisons of all the horses. Mumbling out loud, he said, "What a bunch of pigs running at this fucking track!"

The guy next to him, an overweight, unshaved, transplanted New Yorker, responded, "This is the best these hicks have down here. I sure miss Belmont and Aqueduct! The only good racing in the country is in New York!"

Another track regular chirped in, "That's not true. I'm from Baltimore. Baltimore's got Pimlico, Laurel, and Bowie! They're all great tracks, especially Pimlico. There you just bet speed; it's true at that track!"

When Lucas heard the man talking of "betting speed," it caught his attention. He had always favored betting horses which had early speed out of the gate. He looked up at the man; a skinny, gray-haired, washed-up derelict. Lucas sized him up as a man who had been to a track or two in his day. He asked him, "That's where the Preakness is run every year, isn't it?"

"Sure is, two weeks after the Derby, each-and-every year. I've been to almost every one of them since I was a kid. My father took me there for my first in 1945 when Polynesian won." Pausing, he then asked Lucas, "Have you ever been to Baltimore?"

Lucas shook his head and answered, "No."

"Oh, it's a fine city all around. It's a segregated city, if you know what I mean? All the Wops live in one part of town, the Polacks all live in another part, the Jews stay where they stay, and the niggers are all together. It's on the water. The city is well known for its crabs, they are the best in the world; and the crab cakes, you can eat them all day long! But the best thing about the city is Pimlico. Like I said, you can make money there betting speed all day. It holds, the turns are narrow, and horses that go wide coming home end up swaying all the way out to the grandstand."

Lucas enjoyed listening to the man, but now needed to move away from the regulars so that he could concentrate on reading the *Racing Form*. He did so, but then finally decided after reviewing all the entrants in the first two races that it was a waste of effort trying to handicap these horses. These were all such cheap ponies; there wouldn't be any consistency to any of them. The prize purses were so low that the only way the horse owners could make any money here was to fix races. Lucas knew that he wasn't in on any of the fixes at this track, so he decided just to sit near the finish line and bet long shots all night—and, of course, drink some Jack Daniel's.

The best any of his horses did all night was to finish fourth. His wallet was empty when he drove off from Delta Downs. He didn't even save enough money to get himself a girl at one of the truck stops. But he was relaxed; it had been a fun evening.

EIGHT

Mikey was sitting in the den on his father's lap when the two of them heard a soft knock at the front door. Rickie had been showing him a picture book about a mother bear who had been killed, and the father bear had raised the cubs by himself.

"Let's get up and see who's come to visit," Rickie gently suggested.

It was around four-thirty Saturday afternoon, and Rickie thought he knew who it was. Holding Mikey's left hand, the two of them walked towards the door.

Mikey asked, "Who is it, Daddy? Maybe it's Mommy!"

"It won't be Mommy," Rickie told him, "but I bet it's somebody nice. Maybe it's a new friend who will love you very, very much."

As they approached the door, there was another soft knock. "We're coming," Rickie said, starting to unlock the door.

As he fiddled with the lock, he looked through the peep hole and saw two women in plaid dresses. He recognized one of them whom he had met at the agency several weeks earlier. The other one he figured must be the nanny from England.

She wasn't supposed to arrive in America until Monday, but had arrived two days early. The agency had called him that morning and asked if he would like her to start working that day or wait until Monday. He thought it would be best for her to start right away so that she could get to know Mikey over the weekend.

As Rickie opened the door to greet the women, Mikey grabbed onto his trousers and wouldn't look up.

"Good to see you, ladies," said Rickie. "Please come in."

Tapping Mikey's head, he said, "These are nice ladies. Say hello to them."

But Mikey still wouldn't look up.

Rickie led the way into the den and pointed to a leather couch for both women to sit on. He sat in a leather chair with Mikey on his lap, burying his head in his daddy's chest. He tried to explain Mikey's shyness, but it was unnecessary. Both women thought he was adorable.

The woman from the agency introduced herself as Linda Thompson, and Rickie, nodding his head, acknowledged that he knew who she was. He had forgotten her name but acted as if he hadn't. She then introduced the younger woman as Sarah Leach, the nanny from overseas.

Rickie finally got Mikey to look up at the women, but he still refused to talk. "This is Miss Sarah. She's going to live with us and help us around the house. She will help you with your schoolwork and with getting dressed in the morning.

She's from far away, and she came here just to help you and me. Is that okay with you?"

Mikey slowly nodded his head. It appeared as if he even smiled slightly.

Sarah Leach was a lovely young woman, appearing to be at the most, seventeen or eighteen years old. Her dark hair was pulled back into a bun, fully exposing her high cheekbones and chiseled jaw. She had a tiny nose and thin lips; her pale skin was soft and exceptionally clear. Standing five-foot-seven, she weighed somewhere near one-hundred-and-ten pounds. It was hard to see her figure because of the frumpy dress she wore with white socks and saddle shoes.

Rickie, smiling, asked, "Where are you from in England?"

"Basingstoke," she said in her crisp British accent. "It's a town south of London."

As Sarah explained what Basingstoke was like, Linda felt quite pleased about having recruited her. Rickie appeared happy with her, and Linda hoped he might refer other lawyers to her agency.

"Sarah speaks the Queen's English," she said. "It will be very good for Mikey. He will learn to be proper from her."

Rickie acknowledged what she was saying but knew better. He'd been to Basingstoke for two weeks one summer while he was in law school. It was a lower-middle-class town, where people spoke not the Queen's English, but English with a cockney accent. The locals would work all day and then head to the pubs at night. They liked loud music, throwing darts, and wearing designer clothes. He remembered referring to the people of Basingstoke as "Euro Trash."

But, he congratulated Linda on finding Sarah. She was going to be "it" for the time being. There was no sense in making fun of her. Big deal if she was going to try to act proper even though she wasn't necessarily raised that way. Besides, Mikey seemed to be taking to her. He had gotten off Rickie's lap and was slowly edging towards Sarah. He would make eye contact with her and then coyly shift his eyes away.

"Mikey," Sarah said, "you are such a funny boy. You are a good boy, too, I've been told."

He then looked over at Rickie and said, "Daddy, she talks funny."

"Son, she's from England, which is very far away. People there talk differently than we do. She probably thinks that we talk funny."

Mikey giggled and asked her, "Do you think we talk funny?"

Rickie asked Linda, "Where are Sarah's suitcases?"

"They're in the trunk of my car."

"You stay right here with Sarah, okay?" Rickie told his son. "I'm going outside with Miss Thompson to get Sarah's luggage."

"Okay, Daddy," he replied.

"Would you like to sit on my lap, Mikey?" Sarah asked.

Without hesitation, he did so.

"That's a very pretty shirt you're wearing. What color is it?"

"Red," he answered.

"No, Mikey, it's yellow, sweetheart," she smiled indulgently at him. "What color is my hair band?"

"Green," he said.

Sarah hid her surprise. Her hair band was red. "Sweetie, do you know your colors?"

"Yes, I do," he proudly said.

Realizing that he thought he did, she assured him, "Mikey, I'll teach you all your colors. We will work on them everyday until you learn them all. Okay, sweetheart?"

He answered, "But I know my colors. I'm not stupid!"

Sarah studied him; he looked so sad. It was like he realized that he didn't really know his colors but couldn't admit it to himself. Sensing his feelings of inner anguish, she quickly changed the subject. "Mikey, what does a dog say?"

"Ruff, ruff!" he answered with a big grin on his face.

"What does a cow say?"

"Moo, moo, moo!" He then started laughing.

She went on with different animals and he was having the time of his life responding with the appropriate sounds; he was so proud of himself. Grinning from ear to ear, he knew that he had this game mastered.

"You got them all right! You are such a smart little boy. Give me a big hug."

He wrapped his arms around her neck and squeezed so tightly that Sarah felt a chill go down her spine. She had never felt this wanted, this needed by anybody in her entire life. She had been abandoned by her mother when she was only two, left to be raised by one of her aunts, who already had six kids of her own. Her older boy cousins started molesting her before she learned her ABCs, and continued doing so until she was old enough to fight back. But, by then, it had already taken its toll on her life; she trusted nobody. Her aunt had allowed her sons to abuse her without any repercussions.

Throughout middle school and high school, Sarah turned to her schoolbooks as an escape from the real world. Carving herself out a tiny area in the living room of her aunt's house, she would study late at night while her cousins all slept. By candlelight she would lie on the floor and read. When she was ready to go to sleep, she'd blow out the candles and lay her head down on the worn carpet. She indulged in her lessons much more than was required, studying on weekends as her classmates attended dances and other functions. She was an honor student in English, Latin, and history, but she had problems in math and science.

In class, people noticed her, but she was not very social. She was distant from everyone, preferring to keep to herself. She felt safest when she was alone. She never dated, fearing the boys would try to touch her. She knew that she would never marry, that she would rather live her life alone somewhere, in a dark flat, with her candles burning, very peaceful, very safe.

* * * * *

Carrying several suitcases, Rickie and Linda passed Sarah and Mikey on their way upstairs to Sarah's bedroom. Rickie carried the larger one which he placed on her bed. Her room was right next to Mikey's and down the hall from the master suite. She and Mikey would share a bathroom nearby. Her room consisted of a queen-size bed with a dark-green quilt, a white dresser, and a matching nightstand. There was one small window that would allow her to look into the backyard. The lighting was dim; there were only two lamps in the room, one on the dresser, and the other on the nightstand.

Sarah and Mikey shortly thereafter followed them up the stairs. The two seemed to have a certain sort of chemistry, as if they both needed each other at this point in their lives. Sarah wouldn't be here except for the nanny advertisement she had responded to in the *London Times*, and Mikey would never have had a reason to meet her if not for the premature death of his mother.

When Sarah and Mikey walked into what was now Sarah's new room, Linda got up from the bed, saying, "Sarah, you have a beautiful room here. Why don't you start to unpack. I'm going to leave now and let y'all be alone."

Hugging Sarah and Mikey goodbye, she then walked down the stairs. Rickie walked her to her car and thanked her for finding Sarah. He told her, "She and Mikey sure seem to be hitting it off."

Linda nodded. "I think you'll be very satisfied with her, both you and Mikey."

As she drove away, Rickie headed back inside his house. He didn't bother to go upstairs to check on Sarah and Mikey, but rather went straight to his soundproof study located on the first floor. Now alone with his law books, he locked the door and began working. This was what he was put on Earth to do, simply practice law. Having found somebody to take care of Mikey, he could start billing hours again.

Sarah and Mikey spent the rest of the afternoon and evening together, mostly playing games and reading stories. She was giving him the attention he was used to getting, the attention he needed.

Several of Amy's friends visited the house and offered Sarah any help she might need in taking care of Mikey. They all knew that Rickie was a workaholic, and even though he wanted to help with the raising of Mikey, he would most likely continue to work long hours. They offered to help her with carpools, shopping, cooking, whatever she might need. They all had been true friends to Amy, and now that she was gone they offered to help in any manner they could.

Amy's best friend, Laura Dorsey, was especially relieved to see Mikey in such good spirits. She was worried that he might not be able to cope without his mother. She spent almost an hour with Sarah, telling her all about Amy, as the two of them watched Mikey work on some puzzles. He kept looking up at them. Laura commented, "Children are so strong, so self-centered. As long as they keep busy, they can overcome the death of a parent. It's important that routines in their life remain the same, their activities, school, their friends."

Laura liked Sarah and felt she was already becoming attached to Mikey. She believed that Sarah would treat him almost as if he was her own child. She'd raise him with nearly the same love and nurturing that Amy had. If Amy had been able to pick her own replacement, Sarah would have certainly measured up.

Later that evening Sarah got Mikey ready for bed. She helped him change into his pajamas and tucked him in. After she shut the light off, his room was dark except for light coming in from the hallway.

"I want to rock, I want to rock," he said, turning towards his rocking chair.

Getting him out of bed, she lifted him onto her lap and started rocking back and forth.

"Tell me story, tell me story."

"Mikey, it's tell me *a* story, not tell me story. Say that, sweetheart, tell me *a* story."

"Tell me story," he said.

Sarah repeated the phrase again, but he still refused to do it her way. He was getting upset. "Tell me story, now! Tell me story!"

Sarah then told him about a young English girl who kept a pet elephant in her backyard. He listened carefully and finally fell asleep in her arms. She sat holding him and just kept staring at him. It had been a long day. Running her fingertips across his forehead, she wondered if he was dreaming anything. How sweet and innocent he was.

She thought about how she, too, had no mother at his age. Did he think his mom had abandoned him, or did he understand that it was God who took her away? She realized that he wasn't too bright. It seemed like he didn't quite understand certain things. By now, he should know his colors and be able to converse using proper sentences. But it didn't matter. Her job was to help him, teach him those things.

Her assistance was needed now, and she had never felt needed before. This little boy's whole life was now in her hands. He would rely on her for love and help throughout his childhood and maybe even longer.

When he finally fell into a deep sleep, she carried him to his bed and gently placed him down. After putting his blanket over him, she slowly tiptoed out of the room, quietly closing the door behind her so that he wouldn't be disturbed by the bright hallway lights. Walking down the hallway, she turned into her room, shut the door, and stood there, not knowing what to do next.

Should she get undressed? Maybe take a warm bath or shower? Possibly unpack her suitcases and tidy up her room? Should she wander downstairs and get something to eat or drink, or just flop on the bed, close her eyes, and fall fast asleep?

Indecisive, she chose to do nothing. Gazing around the room, she looked at her suitcases and realized that inside were all the things she owned. And, of course, the simple black shoes she was wearing and the clothes on her back. She looked through her window into the dark night. It was pitch black outside, haunting. There was not a sound inside or out. It was as quiet as a graveyard in an abandoned town.

She decided to walk downstairs to the kitchen to get a drink of cold water. As she went down the staircase, she felt scared. This house was so big and empty, and so far from her aunt and cousins in Basingstoke. She was far away from the small house where everyone would fight for a bed to sleep in, fight for warm clothes to wear in the winter, fight for food to eat. The small house where the walls were dirty, the carpets worn through to the wooden floors. She remembered the mildewed bathroom with everybody's toothbrushes and toiletries always scattered around the small, square, cast-iron sink.

There were always noises in that tiny, overcrowded house. There were smells. Here, there was only silence, and no smells except the scent of pipe smoke which escaped from the study.

When she reached the kitchen, she poured herself a glass of cold water from a pitcher in the refrigerator. Standing there drinking it, she remembered an article she had once read in a psychology book. It was about an old man who lived in a high-rise apartment somewhere in New York City, and every night a noisy train went by his window at midnight, but he always slept right through it. Then one night at midnight, the train didn't come by, and the old man woke up and couldn't fall back to sleep. Even though the train was a noisy nuisance, the old man missed it when it was gone.

That was kind of what Sarah felt now. She was very homesick. She'd never been away from her cousins or that little house in Basingstoke. It hadn't been a perfect life, not close to it, but it was all she had ever known. Now her life was changing. She was in America, in some place called Texas, taking care of a little boy, living in a great big, fancy house.

NINE

"To what do I owe this pleasure?" asked the tiny, middle-aged woman sitting behind the large, glass desk.

"I'm here to try a case, Your Honor," answered Preston. "If it's alright with you."

"Of course it is, but I didn't see your name on the court docket this morning."

"It's on the Pond case," Preston answered. "I'm taking it over from one of my assistants. His name is probably still associated with the case."

"Preston, you know what my next question is."

"Yes, I know what it is. You want to know why I'm subbing in."

Nodding her head, she replied, "Yeah, I'm curious if you want to tell me."

Preston coyly responded, "Well, of course, I'll tell you. You and I go way back."

After hesitating, he continued, "This Ralph Pond character charged in this case is also the main suspect over in the state system as a serial rapist. The police are certain he's the guy, but they just can't get enough evidence on him to file charges. I need to make certain he gets convicted on this federal charge so that he never gets a chance to hit the streets again. The DA's Office won't have to worry about being able to make the rape cases if I lock him up forever on this case."

The judge said, "I see. I knew there had to be a reason you were over here."

"Yes, ma'am, there sure is. It's been nice talking with you, Your Honor. I need to check in the courtroom to see if any of my witnesses have shown up yet."

Turning around, he left her chambers. The veteran federal prosecutor had just pulled off one of the oldest tricks in the book. He had prejudiced the judge against Ralph Pond by lying about Ralph being a suspected serial rapist so that she might slant her rulings anyway she could in helping him gain a conviction on the pending federal charge. And then, after a conviction by the jury, she would most certainly sentence Ralph Pond to the maximum sentence, life in the federal penitentiary.

Preston looked around the large federal courtroom. He walked to the counsel table where he had earlier placed his trial notebook. Looking at his watch he saw it was now ten minutes before nine o'clock. The jury selection part of the trial was scheduled to begin sharply at nine. Several U.S. Marshals were in the hallway, lining up potential jurors for the case. A pool of sixty citizens, from whom a jury of twelve would be selected, had been called to court by federal summons.

Preston was the only person inside the courtroom. He wondered where Lucas Lustick was. He was curious to see what he looked like.

At two minutes before nine, a Federal Marshal brought Ralph Pond, who had been locked up in the courtroom holding tank, into the courtroom. Escorting him to the defendant's table, he told him to sit in one of the two chairs there. Ralph was wearing a dark-blue suit and a maroon tie, which his mother had left for him at the federal holding facility where he had been an inmate since his arrest. Glancing around the courtroom, he looked for his lawyer or his mother. However, neither was there.

Preston carefully watched Ralph. He thought him to be a good-looking, young black man, somewhere near twenty years of age, appearing scared to death, alone in the giant courtroom. Ralph's and Preston's eyes met, and then Ralph looked away.

At nine o'clock, two Marshals led all the jurors into the courtroom. They were told to sit in six rows. Each one of them was given a number between one and sixty. As they took their places, many of the jurors stared at Ralph and Preston, sitting across from one another at the counsel tables. Two Marshals stood behind Ralph, giving jurors the impression that the young man seated at the counsel table might be very dangerous. As Preston watched the jurors, he determined which ones looked like they'd be good for his side. He liked the looks of almost all of them. They appeared to be conservative, redneck Texans. There were four blacks whom he figured he'd get rid of by using some of his peremptory challenges. Each side was given ten peremptory challenges which allowed them to strike certain jurors for any reason they so desired. He wouldn't take a chance of letting a black get on this jury. One of them might have sympathy for Ralph Pond.

At five minutes past nine, the judge entered the courtroom. Everybody stood and then sat back down after she took her seat behind the judicial bench. Though physically tiny, Ann Hudson was very powerful. She had been appointed to this bench six years earlier by the President of the United States. It was a position she would hold for the rest of her life, unless she ever chose to retire. She never would face an opponent in any sort of election as would her counterparts in the State Court system. State Court judges had to run for re-election every four years and, therefore, were held accountable to the public for their performance.

Federal judges were not accountable to anyone. She would just do her job as she saw fit, with no one to whom she had to answer. Her background was in admiralty law; she had been a full partner at Lipman, Benge, and Baker, one of the nation's finest admiralty firms. She knew nothing about criminal law when she had accepted the appointment six years earlier. In presiding over criminal cases, she simply followed the lead of the prosecution, for she had learned that they would usually guide her down the right path. She had a reputation for always ruling against defendants on trial in her courtroom, whether they were in the right or not. The last thing she cared about was protecting the rights of those accused.

She addressed the jurors, "Ladies and gentlemen, I'm Judge Ann Hudson. You've been called to this United States courtroom to sit as a jury panel in which twelve of you will ultimately be selected as jurors to sit in judgment of an accused citizen who is before this court today.

"I want to take this moment to personally thank each and every one of you for sacrificing valuable time in your lives to be with us today. If not for people like you, our system would fail. Under our legal system, juries make the important decisions. I visited several judges in the Soviet Union last year, and there the judges decide the important cases. When I told them that here in America we let citizens decide our cases, they were shocked to hear that we trusted the masses to make our most important decisions."

The jurors listened carefully as she spoke. They all felt very powerful and important because of their jury service.

Judge Hudson announced, "I now call to trial the case of the United States of America versus Ralph Pond."

Preston stood and said, "Preston Calhoun representing the government. I announce ready for trial, Your Honor."

Her honor then asked for an announcement from the defense.

Ralph looked at her, and then out at the jurors. He was scared and didn't know what to say. The judge asked him to stand, which he did. She asked him where his lawyer was. The courtroom was dead silent. At that moment, the courtroom door opened loudly. In walked Lucas Lustick, dressed in a gray pin-striped suit, a maroon tie, and a pair of scuffed-up, black penny loafers. He walked to the counsel table and set down his legal pads. Paying no attention to anyone else in the room, he started whispering to Ralph.

Judge Hudson watched him in amazement. Finally she spoke to him in an angry voice, "Counsel, this trial was set for nine o'clock! It is now ten minutes past nine! I was here at nine, Mr. Calhoun was here at nine, the good citizens of this jury panel were here at nine. Why were you not here?"

Lucas started to respond, but she interrupted him, ordering him to stand when addressing her. He was thinking to himself that men judges wouldn't make such a big deal about being ten minutes late; this was a woman thing. Now standing, he told her, "I apologize to you and to everyone else that I am late."

She responded, "That's not good enough! I want to know why you are late."

"Because I am."

She growled, "Don't get smart with me. I demand to know why you were late." The jurors were enjoying watching her dress down Lucas. To them, it was the tough, likable judge on her home turf, against this lazy, low-life defense attorney.

Lucas turned around and looked out at the panel. They all stared right back at him, all sixty of them. He thought, *You goody, goody pieces of shit out there. You're all enjoying watching this miserable bitch chew me out. Fuck all of you!*

He then looked back at the judge and thought that he'd better come up with an answer to satisfy her. "I just overslept—my alarm didn't go off."

"Well, that will cost you a five-hundred-dollar fine payable to the Federal District Clerk's Office. Next time, you will be sentenced to serve jail time. Are you ready to begin this trial?"

Nodding, Lucas answered, "Yes, I am."

Judge Hudson then told the jurors that she was going to conduct *voir dire* examination and it was important that everyone be truthful in answering all of her questions. She told them what Ralph Pond was charged with and explained the various elements to the offense which the government needed to prove in order to make their case. She explained that the burden of proof as to Mr. Pond's guilt was "beyond a reasonable doubt," and she went on to explain what the federal definition of "beyond a reasonable doubt" actually was.

Next, she told everyone that they might hear from police officers or federal agents during the trial and that they must promise not to believe them solely because they worked in law enforcement. She also asked several personal questions of various jurors. What she was basically doing was qualifying each juror to be able to sit on this case. The whole proceeding took less than twenty minutes.

Lucas then stood and requested that he be allowed to question the panel so that he could make a determination as to which jurors could and couldn't be fair in this case. She denied his request. In disbelief of her ruling, he decided to make a more formal request for the record in the event Ralph ever had to appeal this case. He told her, "Your Honor, I need to individually question the jury panel in various areas of the law so that I can attempt to challenge certain jurors for cause, and so that I can also intelligently exercise my peremptory challenges in providing effective assistance of counsel to my client. I believe that your questioning of the panel was totally inadequate. Not allowing me to conduct additional *voir dire* denies Mr. Pond a fair trial as guaranteed by the United States Constitution."

Judge Hudson angrily denied Lucas' request and told him and Preston to each make their ten strikes so that she could then seat a jury. Lucas used his peremptory strikes against the most redneck-looking jurors, while Preston used his against the blacks and a few people who had raised their hands when the judge asked if anyone had family members with a criminal record. At ten o'clock, Judge Hudson called out the names of the twelve jurors who would serve and asked them to be seated in the jury box. She excused the remaining members of the panel and thanked them for their time.

She next asked Ralph to stand while Preston read the indictment against him. The jurors focused on Ralph as the charges were read out loud. Judge Hudson then asked him how he pled to the charges, and he looked at her and said, "Not guilty."

Judge Hudson then explained to the jury that she didn't allow opening statements in her court; the evidence ought to speak for itself. Looking at Preston, she told him, "Call your first witness."

The jurors appeared to be happy with the judge's manner. Things would move in her courtroom; there would be no wasting of their time. The tiny woman was in total control!

Preston announced, "Your Honor, the government calls Agent R.K. Lyons."

Judge Hudson then ordered the court clerk, "Swear the witness in." The clerk asked Agent Lyons to raise his right hand, and then asked him if he swore to tell the truth, the whole truth, and nothing but the truth.

He answered, "I do."

After taking the witness stand, Preston began questioning him as to what had happened back in May when he had first met Mr. Ralph Pond. Lyons testified that he was a DEA agent assigned to the Drug Task Force, and on that night, he was conducting undercover surveillance at a location in the southwest part of Houston. He was sitting in an unmarked car in a suburban neighborhood. Things were quiet and his eyes were on one particular house to observe the amount of traffic to and from it. He recorded the license plate numbers of people who visited this house.

As he sat in his car at the location, he heard over his police radio that a black male driving a white Ford pickup truck with Texas plates SFD-411 was in the area. The dispatcher stated that the vehicle was stolen and for all police to be on the lookout for it. Lyons further testified that the stolen vehicle with Texas plates SFD-411 pulled up on the curb in front of the house he had been watching. The driver was a black male who parked the vehicle and turned the motor off. "At this point, I drew my weapon and exited my car. I approached the stolen vehicle and announced in a very loud voice, 'Police! Get out of your truck!' The black male got out with his hands up, and I told him he was under arrest for auto theft."

Preston then asked him if he could identify the black man he had placed under arrest that night.

"Yes, I can. He's sitting at counsel table wearing a dark-blue suit and maroon tie." He pointed to Ralph Pond.

Preston then asked, "What happened next?"

"I had my gun drawn on him, and I was getting ready to handcuff him. Then, somehow, he grabbed my gun from me. It was a .380 automatic, fully loaded. We struggled over it, but he ended up with it. He pointed it at me and yelled, 'Hey, pig, you're gonna die tonight!'" Mesmerized by the testimony, the jurors were now all sitting forward in the jury box.

Preston asked, "What was going on in your mind as Mr. Pond was pointing this gun at you and telling you that you were going to die?"

R.K., looking down at his lap, answered, "I started thinking of my kids and my wife, and that I'd probably never see them again. I thought this was the end." Several of the jurors were crying during his very emotional testimony.

Preston asked what happened next.

"I dove on the ground toward my car and he fired at me, two or three rounds! He missed. I got to my car and hid behind it. Then he fired three or four more rounds at me, but still missed. I was ducking behind the car. After that, he ran towards an open field where it was pitch black; there were no lights."

"What happened next?"

"I got on my radio and called for assistance."

"Did help arrive?"

"Yes, four county units, one of them being a canine unit, came to my assistance. The officers were all in uniform. I showed them the field where the defendant had run, and they began pursuit. I remained at my car."

"Did you see the defendant later that night?" asked Preston.

"Well, yes I did, after they arrested him. They brought him back to my vehicle so I could identify him."

"And did you do so?"

Before he could answer, Lucas stood and objected, saying, "Before any in-court identification is made by this witness, I'm requesting a hearing outside the jury's presence as to the improper suggestibility of the identification made at the scene."

Judge Hudson asked, "Mr. Lustick, did you file a pre-trial motion as to this?"

Lucas told her, "No I didn't, but I'm still entitled to raise the issue at this time."

"No, you're not," she curtly said. "Your objection is overruled. Proceed with the testimony, Agent Lyons."

Looking up at her, R.K. said, "I forgot the question. Can you please have the prosecutor ask it again?"

"Sure," answered the judge.

Preston then asked, "Did you see the defendant later that night?"

R.K., nodding his head, answered, "Yes sir, I did, when the uniformed officers brought him back to my car, I immediately recognized that he was the person who took my weapon and tried to kill me."

Preston asked, "Did he look any different than when you saw him earlier that evening, when he was aiming the gun at you?"

"The only difference I observed was that now his clothes were torn, and it appeared that he had some dog bites on his arms."

Preston glanced over at the jury, and asked, "Did you see Mr. Pond any more that night?"

"Yes, I did. When the uniformed police transported him downtown, I rode with them so that I could give a written statement as to the events that transpired that evening. When we got to the police station, I filed my written report with their agency, and made a copy which I gave to my supervisors at the DEA."

Preston then stood and announced, "I pass the witness."

To everybody's surprise, Lucas only asked one question on cross-examination. He asked R.K. if he had ever placed a hand on Ralph Pond that evening, to which he replied, "Certainly not."

Preston was shocked that Lucas didn't at least try to impeach R.K.'s testimony. The DEA agent had just testified in dramatic fashion as to each element of attempted murder of a federal agent. The prosecutor had the jury eating out of his hands, and Lustick, this allegedly great lawyer, did nothing to soften the impact. Judge Hudson, too, was surprised by Lucas' cross-examination, or lack of one. She figured that her ripping into him for being late to court that morning had something to do with it; it must have made him timid. She then asked Preston to call his next witness.

He called Ed Wood, who was sworn by the clerk in the same manner as was R.K. Lyons. Preston then asked him how he was employed, and he responded that he was a deputy with the Harris County Sheriff's Department, assigned to the canine unit. He told the jurors his partner was a German Shepherd dog named Tar Heel. He explained that Tar Heel was trained to use his keen sense of smell to detect certain drugs and to search out human beings. He was often used to help find prison escapees or other people hiding from the law. Occasionally he was used to try to locate lost children. On this evening he had been brought to the crime scene to help find the person who had attempted to kill R.K. Lyons.

Legal Vengeance

Preston asked if Tar Heel was present in court this day.

Ed replied, "No, he wasn't subpoenaed." The whole courtroom, including Ralph, erupted into laughter. Even Lucas found some humor in the deputy's answer. Ed continued, "But I do carry his picture."

Preston asked if he could have the picture to show the jury.

Ed answered, "No problem."

Preston had the photograph of Tar Heel marked as an exhibit and offered it into evidence.

While Preston was doing this, Lucas whispered to Ralph, "You should've shot that fucking dog."

Preston asked Ed, "Did Tar Heel help in the apprehension of the man who attempted to take Agent Lyons' life, and if so, can you tell the jurors how?"

Lucas objected, but the judge overruled his objection and told him to be seated. She told the witness that he could answer the question.

"Well," said Ed, "Tar Heel and I were sitting in the parking lot of Dunkin' Donuts at 6359 Westheimer, when I received a call on my radio to respond to the 4200 block of Hudson Avenue to assist in the apprehension of a suspect who fired shots at an officer. We arrived at the scene at ten fifty-five p.m. and there were other marked units there already."

Preston then asked, "And what did you and Tar Heel do once you arrived at the scene of this attempted police killing?"

Ed, looking at the jurors, continued, "Well, I was advised of the situation by DEA Agent R.K. Lyons. He led Tar Heel, me, and the other deputies to a field where he said the culprit had run. It was an extremely dark evening. I released Tar Heel into the field with a command to search for the smell of human flesh."

Preston then asked, "Did Tar Heel find anything?"

"Yes, about three minutes later, he started barking. It was a ferocious bark. I then ran toward the direction of the barking and observed him fighting with a black male. He wasn't supposed to attack unless the human provoked him, so he was fighting to defend himself."

All the jurors were now looking at Ralph with astonished looks on their faces. They were wondering what type of person would fight with a German Shepherd.

Preston stood and said, "Ed, you don't have to raise self-defense on Tar Heel's behalf; he's not on trial."

The jurors were now laughing hysterically. This was becoming a very entertaining trial. Ed then continued, "Tar Heel was getting the best of the suspect when I gave the command to release him. I then drew down on him, as did Deputy Sears, and we placed him under arrest."

Preston then asked, "What was the condition of the suspect when you arrested him?"

"He was lying on the ground; he had several bites on his arms and legs. He had a lot of dirt and blood all over his body. He wasn't bleeding that badly that we felt he needed an ambulance."

"And so what did you do?"

"Deputy Sears and I read the suspect his rights and told him that he was under arrest. We walked him back to the shooting scene, where R.K. Lyons saw him and identified him as the person who earlier had attempted to take his life. Then Tar Heel and I left the scene in our vehicle, and I made my report the following morning."

Preston asked, "Who took control of the suspect once you left?"

"Deputy Sears was responsible for transporting the suspect downtown."

Preston then asked him whether he recognized the suspect from that evening anywhere in the courtroom.

Ed answered, "Yes. He's the black man sitting at counsel table, wearing a blue suit and maroon tie."

Preston then asked to allow the record to reflect that the witness had just identified the suspect, Ralph Pond. The judge stated, "The record shall so reflect."

Preston then passed the witness to Lucas, who first asked, "Do you know who went with Deputy Sears when he took Mr. Pond to the downtown jail house?"

"I believe another deputy was with him, and R.K. Lyons also."

Lucas then asked, "Why did R.K. Lyons ride downtown with the suspect?"

"I don't know. It must have been just out of convenience. He had to enter a report with our agency."

Lucas didn't push the issue. He then asked him if he ever recovered a weapon at the location where Mr. Pond was arrested, to which he answered, "Yes, I recovered a .380 automatic pistol about ten feet from where he was fighting with Tar Heel."

Lucas then asked, "He never tried to shoot your dog, or fire at you, or at any other officers, is that correct?"

"That is correct."

Lucas then passed the witness, telling the judge that he had no further questions.

Preston now realized that he had forgotten to cover the testimony about the gun being recovered.

He then asked Ed if the particular .380 automatic which was recovered was brought to court that day.

"I'm not sure. I haven't seen it today."

Preston then opened a large, yellow envelope and pulled out a .380 automatic pistol and had it marked by the court reporter as an exhibit. He then asked Judge Hudson for permission to approach the witness for the purpose of showing the gun to him. She granted the request and Preston walked up to the witness stand and handed the gun to Ed, asking him, "Have you ever seen this gun before?"

"Yes sir, I believe it is the same .380 automatic that I recovered from the scene of Mr. Pond's arrest that evening."

Preston then recalled R.K. Lyons to the witness stand. As R.K. was coming back into the courtroom, Lucas whispered across the counsel table to Preston, "Hey, Man, did you forget to go through all this about the gun when you were putting your case on? You should have allowed Mike Miller to stay on this case."

Preston heard Lucas trying to irritate him but refused to acknowledge him. He looked at R.K. Lyons, and showing him the same gun which Ed had just testified as to having recovered from the arrest scene, asked him, "Do you recognize this gun?"

R.K. answered, "Yes sir, that's my gun. It's the same gun which Mr. Pond took from me that night and then tried to kill me with."

Preston had no further questions of R.K. and then Lucas told the judge that he had no questions at this time. Preston then stood and looked at the jurors. He proudly announced, "The government rests its case."

The judge broke for lunch and told all involved that the case would resume promptly at one-thirty. She sternly told Lucas to be ready to put his case on at that time.

At one-thirty, Lucas was nowhere to be found, and the judge was fit to be tied. She sat angrily looking down from her bench, wondering where the surly lawyer was. The twelve jurors were seated in the box, watching her every move, her feline-like eyes glued to the large courtroom door, waiting for the tardy mouse to dare to appear, so she could pounce on him, humiliate him, and then eat him alive. It would be a great scene, and all of the jurors were anxiously waiting for it to happen. The courtroom was very tense, and the judge, at one-forty, ordered a Marshal to take the jurors to the jury room. She knew that she was going to severely sanction Lucas whenever he came back to court and feared that if she did so in front of the jury, it could prejudice Mr. Pond, and could later cause the case to be reversed on appeal. She wisely wanted to avoid that risk.

At one-fifty, Lucas sauntered into the courtroom. He walked to the counsel table and sat down next to Ralph. He looked up at the judge, who told him to stand and approach the bench. She stared right into his eyes. "I don't want to hear any excuses, Counselor, as to why you are late once again." Lucas just looked back at her without responding. She went on, "I'm holding you in contempt of this court and sentencing you to thirty days in jail immediately following this trial. You have the right to appeal my sentence to the Fifth Circuit if you so desire."

Lucas, shaking his head, said, "No, I'll do the time. It'll give me the chance to pick up some new clients."

The judge wasn't amused by his response, and told him, "You keep it up and you'll be in there for six months. Is that clear?"

Lucas looked at her, saying nothing, but she knew what he was thinking.

Judge Hudson then told the Marshals to bring back the jurors. They took their seats in the jury box. They all looked at Lucas, knowing that they had all been deprived of the pleasure of watching his sanctioning by the pesky judge. But they knew that now it was time to get back to business, for this was a serious trial. Lucas stood up and announced, "I call the defendant to the stand."

Judge Hudson told Ralph to approach the clerk where he was sworn to tell the truth. He sat down in the cushioned chair."

Lucas asked, "Will you state your name for the record?" and Ralph's testimony was now underway. After going into background testimony, Lucas asked, "How did you come about meeting R.K. Lyons?"

Ralph, looking at the jurors, began, "I was drivin' this white truck, you know, one night, which I had borrowed from a neighbor of mine. I was cuttin' through some neighborhoods, you know, lookin' for a store my mom had sent me to go get her some things."

"Who was this neighbor from whom you borrowed the truck?"

Ralph answered, "His name is George. I don't know his last name. You know, he just comes and goes. I think he just stays at his lady friend's house, you know, near my mom's house, when he's in town."

"Did you know the truck was stolen?"

Ralph, looking right at him, answered, "No sir, he didn't tell me, you know, nothin' about that. I thought it was his truck."

Lucas nodded and then asked, "What happened next?"

Ralph paused, looked at the jury, then back at Lucas, and continued, "Then the lawman, you know, Mr. Lyons, the one here before, while I'm slowly drivin' down this street, he jumps in front of my truck, you know, and points his gun at me. He was actin' crazy, you know, screamin' at me, to get my 'black fuckin' ass out from the truck.' Those were his words. So, you know, I stop the truck, and get out." He again paused.

Lucas told him, "Go on."

"Next thing I know, he's standin' behind me, crackin' me on the back of my head with the butt of his gun."

Lucas asked, "Did it hurt?"

Ralph answered, "Shit, yes," and then he looked at the judge who was peering down at him from the bench. He said, "Excuse me, Your Honor. I mean, yes, it hurt."

He looked back to Lucas who asked him to explain what happened next.

"He said to me, 'I'm tired of you fuckin' niggers stealin' cars and breakin' into homes,' and then, you know, he hit me on the back of my head with that gun again. He was still standin' behind me, sayin', 'The only good nigger is a dead one,' you know. Then I got scared."

Lucas asked, "What was going on in your mind then?"

"I thought he was goin' to kill me, you know, and then dump me into one of the bayous."

Lucas asked, "So what did you do next?"

Ralph, looking right at the jurors, continued, "I turned and wrestled his gun away from him, you know, I took it from him."

"What did you do with the gun?"

"I didn't know what to do with it. I was scared. He was a lawman and I didn't know what to do. I didn't want to shoot him, but I knew if I gave him back the gun, he'd of shot me."

"How did you know that he'd of shot you?"

Ralph raised his eyebrows and answered, "Because I'd just gotten down on him, you know, embarrassed him. No lawman is goin' to be too happy, you know, about you takin' his gun right out of his hands."

"So what did you do?"

"Well, I backed up from him, and I fired the gun high into the air and down into the ground as I backed away. I never fired at the lawman." He paused. "Then I ran away, you know, into that field where the dog caught me."

"Now Ralph, did you have any intentions of killing Agent R.K. Lyons?"

"No sir, none at all. I just wanted to get away from him."

Lucas then asked, "After being arrested by that stupid dog, what happened?"

Preston jumped up to object, but didn't say anything. He didn't like Lucas referring to Tar Heel as a stupid dog but, not knowing how to word his objection, just sat back down.

Ralph continued, "A lawman handcuffed me behind my back and put me into some patrol car."

Lucas, now looking at the jury, asked, "Did you have the bad fortune of seeing R.K. Lyons again on that night?"

"Yes sir, I did. He come into the patrol car, and he sat next to me all the way downtown to the police station."

Lucas asked, "Did anything happen in the patrol car?"

"Yes sir, it did." He hesitated and then continued. "He kept punchin' me in my eyes, all the way into, you know, downtown. He kept on callin' me names, called me a nigger, a coon, spearchucker, and, you know, he just kept hittin' me."

Lucas asked, "Did the other officers in the car try to stop him?"

"No, they just laughed. One of them up front made threats, you know, to dump me in the bayou."

Preston now looked at the jurors and shook his head sideways as if to say he didn't believe a word that was being spoken.

Lucas then passed the witness, and Preston spent the next thirty minutes cross-examining Ralph. He repeatedly called him a liar, accusing him of fabricating the whole story. When he finished, the judge then excused the jurors for a fifteen-minute recess.

Following the break, Lucas called to the witness stand the Custodian of Records at the jail and offered into evidence Ralph's booking photos taken the night of his arrest at the Sheriff's Department. He showed the photos to Preston, who looked at them and objected to them as being irrelevant to the case. To everyone's surprise, the judge overruled his objection and admitted them into evidence.

Lucas did not ask to have them displayed before the jury. He then called the Custodian of Medical Records at the jail and asked her if she brought with her any medical records belonging to Ralph Pond which showed treatment during his incarceration on this case. She stated that she had brought such records with her. Lucas then asked that they be tendered into evidence. Preston reviewed the records, and as he did so, got a sick feeling in his stomach. He objected to their admissibility but was overruled again. The judge admitted the records into evidence. Lucas then asked the witness if the records indicated whether there were any times when Ralph Pond appeared in the jail clinic to receive medical attention.

She said, "Yes sir, according to these records, upon his arrival at the jail, he was treated for severe lacerations to the back of his scalp. The wounds were deep into the scalp, and he was bleeding profusely. Twenty stitches were applied by the doctor to close the scalp. There were three follow-up visits over the next two weeks."

Lucas told the judge that he had no further questions and passed the witness to Preston, who asked, "You don't know from the records where the inmate received these lacerations, do you?"

She answered, "No sir."

He went on, "These lacerations to the scalp could have happened during a fight in the jail. Is that correct?"

"That's possible."

Preston passed the witness. Lucas then pointed out through her that Ralph was booked into the jail at twelve-thirty a.m. and was taken straight from booking to the medical floor where he was treated at one-thirty a.m.

The judge then asked Lucas if he had any more witnesses, to which he replied that he did. She said, "Go ahead, call your next witness."

He stood, and said, "I call R.K. Lyons back to the stand."

This totally surprised Preston, who looked at the judge. The two of them made eye contact, both wondering why Lucas was recalling the government's key witness. A Marshal got R.K. from the hallway and escorted him to the witness stand where he appeared to be as surprised as anybody that he had been recalled by the defense to testify. After all, earlier that day he had some of the jurors in tears following his testimony.

Lucas asked the judge, "Can I begin?"

She said, "Go ahead."

Lucas then began a blistering cross-examination of the DEA agent. He berated him for coming into court and telling so many lies. Standing up, he asked him, "How did Mr. Pond receive the wounds to his head?"

R.K. kept saying that he knew nothing about the head wounds, claiming that he never hit Ralph in any form or manner, that Ralph may have received the wounds earlier that evening, even before their encounter. "Maybe your client fought somebody. You know how dopers get into fights, or maybe he got into a fight at booking!"

Lucas asked him, "If you did lie to this jury during your testimony earlier this morning as to what actually transpired that night between yourself and Mr. Pond, would you admit to us now that you had lied earlier?"

The jurors all focused in on R.K., watching his demeanor as he thought of an answer. It was an impossible question to answer, and Lucas knew it. That's why he asked it. If R.K. answered the question, "No," then, that told the jurors that R.K. Lyons was the type of guy who could lie in court, and then even after given a period of time to reflect upon his mistake, wouldn't correct it by telling the truth. If he answered the question, "Yes," that he would admit that he had earlier lied under oath, well, that's a damn lie for sure; nobody would ever believe that a cop would do that!

R.K. answered, "If I lied earlier, yes, I would admit it to you now."

Lucas looked into the jury box. The jurors now knew that R.K. was lying to them. Lucas couldn't believe that he had pulled this question off without even an objection from Preston. He knew that Preston had no clue as to what he had just done.

Standing up, Lucas approached the court reporter. She had the booking photos of Ralph which were offered into evidence earlier.

As he reached down to pick up the photos, he heard a loud screech coming from the judge. In an angry voice, she said, "Counsel, I didn't give you permission to approach the court reporter. You go back to where you were. You know the proper courtroom etiquette!"

Lucas slowly walked back to the counsel table, thinking that Her honor wasn't doing any harm to her courthouse reputation as, "The Ice Bitch." He then asked her if he could please have her permission to approach the court reporter. She told him to go ahead. Slowly he walked towards the court reporter, picking up the booking photos from her desk. He asked the judge to allow the jury members to view the photographs. She responded, "Give them to the Marshal so that he can publish them to the members of the jury."

Lucas did so, and a Marshal then walked to the jury box and handed the photos to the closest juror so she could view them. She did so and then passed them to the other jurors. The booking photos showed that Ralph's eyes were very swollen; actually, they were barely open. It was quite obvious that someone had used his face as a punching bag. Lucas watched the jurors as they each finished viewing the photographs. Each of them would glance at R.K. who was seated on the witness stand. It was not only the way they looked at him, but the way they cocked their necks, crossed their arms, and stiffened their lips, that showed Lucas that these people were quite angry with R.K. Lyons. After the last juror looked at the pictures, she gave them back to the Marshal, who then handed them to Lucas.

Lucas then asked R.K., "Is it true that you pounded your fists into Ralph Pond's eyes as he sat handcuffed in the Sheriff Department's patrol car?"

R.K. answered very calmly, "Of course not."

Lucas looked directly into his eyes, without saying anything. And R.K. stared right back, not willing to back down to his accuser. The courtroom was silent. This went on for several moments.

Finally, the judge broke the silence. She told Lucas, "Move along." He didn't acknowledge her; he just kept staring at R.K., who now had broken off any eye contact and was staring at the floor. Finally, Lucas asked, "Well, if you didn't give Mr. Pond the black eyes which we see he has in the pictures, then who did?"

R.K. looked back up at Lucas and answered, "Tar Heel, the dog, he must have done it."

Several of the jurors gasped, and Preston dropped his forehead all the way down to the counsel table. He could not believe what he had just heard his witness say. He mumbled to himself, "Oh, fuck." His case had just blown up in front of his very own eyes. Lucas had just set up the witness, frustrating him so, that he gave an answer which would now force the jurors to interpret the rest of his testimony with great skepticism.

Lucas kept looking at R.K., who stared back at him, and asked, "Agent Lyons, you stick by your story, is that correct?"

R.K. answered, "Yes sir, that's correct."

At this point, Preston stood and asked the judge for a ten-minute recess.

Lucas stood up and angrily objected to any recess. He was going for the kill and had all the momentum. R. K. Lyons was on the ropes, and the government's case was taking a hard fall. But the judge granted Preston's request, and had a Marshal escort the jury out of the courtroom.

Lucas stormed the bench and told her, "This is bullshit, Judge! You can't let them call timeout when I'm in the middle of kicking their ass!"

"You better watch your mouth in my courtroom, Mr. Lustick! You just earned yourself another thirty days in the slammer."

She then got up and left the courtroom. Lucas was furious. He went up to Ralph and said, "They're trying to fuck us!"

His heart was racing and he was sweating heavily as he stomped off to the rear of the courtroom. Kicking open the courtroom door, he saw R.K. Lyons and Preston together, down the hallway. They were standing face-to-face, but only Preston was talking. Lucas knew that they were conspiring on how to get out of the mousetrap which they were in. He knew that the "bluecoats" would do anything to win. Justice meant nothing to Preston; winning was everything. Going back inside the courtroom, he sat down next to Ralph, and told him, "I hate the fucking government! Lying, motherfucking whores!"

Ralph then whispered, "I should'a killed him that night. What really happened after I got his gun, you know, was he got on his hands and knees and started cryin'. Started beggin' for his life, you know, said he had a wife and three kids. Said one of the kids was mentally retarded and couldn't make it without him. That's the only reason I spared him. I showed weakness, you know, for the retarded kid, because my baby sister is retarded. Now he comes into court and lies on me and tries to send me away for life, so I can't be around to help my little sister. Damn it, I should'a put the lead between his eyes. It's my fault he's here to lie against me."

Lucas looked at Ralph and asked, "Do you swear to me that's what happened out there that night?"

Ralph, holding up his hand, said, "I swear."

Lucas then got up and headed back out to the hallway. He spotted R.K. now standing by himself, puffing away on a cigarette. He walked up to him and said, "R.K., let's put all this courtroom bullshit aside and lets talk man-to-man about what's real important in life."

R.K. nodded and said, "Go ahead."

"My client says that he would of killed you that night except that you told him that you had a retarded child. Is it even true that you do have a retarded child?"

"Yes it is," R.K. answered, "but what does that have to do with anything?"

"A lot," Lucas continued, "Ralph has a retarded little sister that he needs to take care of. I've seen her; she's messed up bad.

She has been crying for Ralph every night since he's been locked up. Why don't you just tell Preston to drop the charges in this case? Tell him the truth—that Ralph spared your life that night, and then the case will be over. You know you've been lying. I know you've been lying. I won't ever say anything to anybody, I promise you that. You won't ever get into any trouble at all. Preston just drops the case, Ralph goes home, you go back to work, I go on to my next case. That's it; it's over."

R.K. didn't say anything, but Lucas knew he was thinking mighty hard. Finally, he said, "Let me go talk with Preston."

Lucas encouraged him, "Go ahead ... tell him the whole deal! Hopefully he'll understand."

R.K. then went back into the courtroom searching for Preston. Lucas knew that it was a great deal for Preston, too, because it would prevent him from getting a "not guilty" verdict from this jury. What a deal for the crooked, lying government. He was sure that Preston would go along with the idea. Waiting outside in the hallway, he expected that Preston would soon appear. However, he never did. The only person who came into the hallway was a Marshal who told Lucas to come back into the courtroom, for the judge was ready to proceed with the trial.

Lucas went back inside the courtroom and slowly walked to the counsel table, eyeing Preston the whole way. Keeping his eyes on the yellow legal pad in front of him, Preston didn't even look up. Lucas sat beside Ralph and now needed to proceed with his cross-examination of R.K. Lyons.

The judge then said, "Mr. Calhoun, you can now question the witness."

Lucas stood and yelled out, "Judge, I was still cross-examining the witness. I wasn't done yet!"

Judge Hudson, sternly looking down at him said, "Mr. Lustick, I run this courtroom! I just told Mr. Calhoun that he can begin questioning the witness. You sit back down and remain quiet!"

Feeling his blood pressure rising, Lucas angrily cried out, "I object to this!"

"You're overruled. Now sit down, or I will sanction you!"

Lucas couldn't believe what was happening. He figured that Preston must have gotten to her during the recess. Why else would she allow him to question the witness out of turn? This was unheard of behavior by any judge.

Preston then asked R.K., "Why did you tell Mr. Lustick that the dog was responsible for Mr. Pond's two black eyes?"

R.K., then looking at the jurors, answered, "Because I was frustrated, was why I said it. The lawyer over there," pointing at Lucas, "he frustrated me so much with all his questions that I told him that the dog did it to his client. I didn't mean it. It was just a sarcastic answer which I didn't mean, and never should have given."

At this point Lucas, in disbelief, stood up and shouted, "I object to this whole trial! Miss Eva Braun up there," as he pointed to the judge, "is in bed with the government!" With his finger still pointed at her, he shouted, "You're a fucking bitch! Fuck you and your fucking circus you run in here!"

Judge Hudson screamed to a Marshal, "Take him into custody! Place him under arrest!"

The Marshal grabbed Lucas from behind and then pulled his hands behind his back so that he could cuff him. Lucas offered no resistance and walked with him to the courtroom holdover cell.

The Marshal told him, "You've got balls. I couldn't have said it better myself—Eva Braun! What a great line! That's just who she is—Adolph Hitler's girlfriend. Wow, that was great!"

Lucas told him not to forget about Ralph, who was now sitting in the courtroom unattended. The Marshal said, "I'll get fired if he escapes," and he hurried back into the courtroom.

Ralph was just sitting there. The courtroom looked like it had before. The judge was on the bench, the jury in the box, R.K. on the stand, Preston at his table. The only thing that changed was that Lucas was no longer sitting next to Ralph. But, the trial could not go on without him. Only he could try to protect Ralph from the lying DEA agent, the crooked federal judge, and the federal prosecutor who cared only about winning and nothing about justice.

Judge Hudson declared a mistrial and excused the jurors. She then told Ralph that he would be given a new trial date several months away. She advised him to find a new lawyer, telling him that his lawyer was very unprofessional and would not be allowed to practice law in her courtroom ever again. She then told her clerk, "Add three months to Mr. Lustick's contempt sentence, and draft a letter to the State Bar grievance committee for me to sign, outlining Mr. Lustick's conduct during Mr. Pond's trial." Standing up, she declared that court was now in recess, and left the courtroom.

Lucas sat alone in the holding tank until nearly five p.m., when a Marshal opened the door to allow a federal public defender inside to talk to him. Lucas shook hands with Casey Baker, a spanking-new lawyer who was assigned to help him in his contempt action. Casey offered to get him out on bond by five-thirty, but Lucas declined, saying, "I'm just going to serve out my sentence. I don't want to fight anything."

Casey tried to convince him to get out and fight the case, but Lucas was adamant that he'd serve his one-hundred-and-fifty-day sentence.

He said, "I'd rather do my time than get out and see that fucking-bitch judge again."

Casey asked if there was anything he could do to help, and Lucas told him, "Yeah, call my secretary at 229-1234. Her name is Jill. She'll be there tomorrow morning. Tell her to close up my office and to sell my furniture. Tell her to keep the money. Also, tell her to call all my clients and tell them they need to get new lawyers because I'm in the hole. Tell her to be truthful with them. Also tell her I'll call her collect at the club."

Casey asked, "Are you sure you want to do this?"

"Yes, I'm positive. Please just do what I ask."

The young public defender didn't understand his reasoning, but knew to respect it. The many lines on his client's face convinced him that the incarcerated lawyer had been through much worse in his life. Shaking Lucas' hand, he quietly left the holding tank.

Ten minutes later, two Marshals came to take Lucas to the county jail on Franklin Street. They transported him in the same manner that they would any other federal prisoner. He was handcuffed and placed into the back seat of an unmarked federal police car where he would be driven to the county jail. There he was booked and given an inmate number. He was now just part of the institution. He was taken to the classification wing, where the administrator, seeing that he was a criminal defense lawyer, placed him in a segregated tank, all by himself, on the sixth floor of the jail.

Lucas asked to be put into the general population, but the administrator remembered the last time they had put a criminal lawyer in with the regular inmates, all sorts of problems started. The inmates filed numerous writs against the sheriff, complaining about everything from not being allowed to play basketball eight hours a day to being denied kosher food. That wasn't going to happen again.

By eight o'clock, Lucas was now all alone, locked in cell A-14 on the sixth floor of the county jail. He had a narrow bed, a toilet, a sink, a pair of underwear, and a pair of white prison overalls. A trustee later brought him a toothbrush, some Colgate toothpaste, a towel, and a bar of soap.

He just sat on his hard bed until well past midnight. Then he laid on his back and stared at the ceiling. It had been a hard day, and he was exhausted. He was tired of practicing law, tired of fighting the judges, the prosecutors, and the police. He didn't want to do it anymore. He fell fast asleep, dreaming that he was a surfer, fighting one wave after the next, trying not to drown, but they never stopped, never stopped coming, one after the next. Finally, his board just broke, and he fell deep into the sea.

"Wake up! Wake up! It's breakfast time," screamed the trustee, a young white man with a goatee.

He handed Lucas a breakfast tray through the bars. Lucas thanked him and placed the tray on his bed. Moving to the sink he brushed his teeth. He felt a whole lot better. Even in jail he enjoyed brushing his teeth. Sitting on his bed he ate his breakfast of two waffles, a slice of cantaloupe, and a glass of orange juice. Then he lay back down and just stared at the ceiling. He figured that he'd probably get a visit that day from his one friend, John O'Reilly. But most likely it would be after work, sometime after five. The day passed slowly. That evening he awaited John's arrival, but he never showed. Lucas just lay in his cell until well past midnight when he finally fell asleep.

The next night, he was given permission to use the pay phone on the floor. He called the O'Reilly house collect, but

John refused to accept the charges. Lucas was furious. He called Jill and asked her to keep an eye on his townhouse while he was in jail. He told her to use the key that he had given her, and to go inside and take the five-thousand dollars he had hidden under his mattress. "Pay my rent to the landlord for the next five months. There will be some money left over; you can keep it."

He told her that she could use his car until he got out, but warned her not to drive it if she was drunk. She was thrilled because she could now save money from cab fares to and from work each night.

She told him, "Hang in there, baby," which made him feel like she really cared about him.

He didn't have any more communication with Jill—or anyone else, until the mail arrived four weeks later. It was a certified letter from the State Bar of Texas. He thought, *Oh fuck*, and opened it up.

Sure enough, it was a grievance filed by his favorite federal judge. It was accompanied by a letter from the grievance committee telling him that his law license would be suspended for a period of two years unless he wished to contest the charges. He had one week to give notice that he wished to contest the grievance; otherwise, the suspension would take effect.

He sat there and stared alternately at the letter and the ceiling. He had always loved the practice of law, the thrill of fighting the government. Yet, he was ready to give it all up if forced to, by those who control such things. He knew that he'd have no chance at a grievance hearing. The blue-blooded committee members would never understand why he acted the way he did in the Ralph Pond trial. They would scold him for being so bold and wild, then proceed to punish him as severely as their powers would allow. So he crumpled the papers into the palms of his hands and tossed them between the metal bars of his cell into a passing trustee's waste basket. He now realized it was time to move on, wherever, east or west, that the winds might take him. He just couldn't handle his life in evil Texas any longer. Once he was released from jail, he would leave forever.

TEN

Lucas heard the rattling of brass keys, and then the sound of his cell door being unlocked. Propping himself up onto his elbows, he turned his head towards the entryway. A young, redheaded sheriff deputy yelled, "Get up! You're going home today."

Looking surprised, Lucas asked, "Why? I haven't finished my full sentence yet!"

The deputy responded, "It's the day before Christmas. The Sheriff is releasing a lot of you inmates short of completing your sentences. Does it every year. It lets people be with their families over the holidays, and it helps clear out the jail for the start of the new year."

Climbing out of his bed, Lucas asked if it would be okay if he brushed his teeth before leaving his cell.

"Yeah, go right ahead."

As he leaned over the sink, the deputy told him, "Hey, don't cuss out any more judges when you get out of here! This isn't the place for a guy like you."

Spitting the toothpaste into the sink, Lucas responded, "It's not that bad. I'd rather be in here than in front of some of those whore judges we have to deal with!"

The deputy chuckled as he and Lucas left the cell together. Lucas asked, "How long will it take me to get out of this fucking place?"

"An hour or so, before you're actually on the streets."

When they reached the end of the hallway, the deputy pointed to a black metal chair across from a large desk. He told Lucas to sit down, that the processing deputies would take care of him. Shaking Lucas' hand, he told him, "Have a Merry Christmas, Counselor," and then he briskly walked away.

To Lucas Lustick, Christmas meant nothing. Having never celebrated it in his life, it was just another day. He wondered what he would do once he walked out of the jail. He hadn't talked to Jill in months, but he needed to get his car back from her. After that, he wasn't too sure what he was going to do. Maybe, he'd drive to New York, Florida, or Maryland. Possibly go back to California. But, wherever he went, he figured that he would be there for a long time.

The processing deputy interrupted his train of thought, asking, "Do you have any aliases that you go by?"

"No."

She then handed him his wallet, keys, and three-hundred-and-forty dollars in cash which were in his property inventory. She then pointed to a small room which stored the clothing he wore when he was booked in. She told him to go inside and change into his clothes. He did so and then sat back down in the black metal chair. Looking closely at his visitation list, the female deputy commented, "It doesn't look like you've had any visitors during your stay. Is that correct?"

"No ma'am, no visitors, that's correct."

She then told him that he was free to leave and wished him a Merry Christmas. Nodding, he said, "Thank you."

Getting up, he quietly left, knowing that the lady felt sorry for him because nobody visited him while he had been housed in solitary confinement. As he walked outside, he felt the cold morning air up against his face. It was very refreshing. Crossing Franklin Street, he was almost run over by several passing cars. He wondered how he was going to get home. Spotting a phone booth, he decided to call a cab. Once he lifted the receiver, he went through his pockets and realized that he didn't have a quarter. "Fuck," he muttered under his breath. Slamming the receiver back onto the phone, he continued walking up Jefferson Street. A cab was coming in his direction, so he flagged it down. Jumping into the front seat he screamed, "It's freezing out here!"

The cabbie asked, "Where's your fucking coat! What do you think, it's summertime?"

Lucas, staring at him said, "Take me to Richmond and Fountainview."

The cabbie asked in his gruff voice, "Are you a jailbird?" while his cab was still in park.

Looking into his eyes, Lucas asked, "What do you mean by that?"

"Well, are you just getting out of jail? I picked you up wandering in front of the jail. You're dressed like it's fucking summertime! To shoot straight with you, buddy, do you have the cash to pay for your fare, or are you going to stiff me like some other payroled jailbirds I've picked up here before?"

Looking across at the heavyset driver, Lucas calmly answered, "First of all, Einstein, the word is paroled, not payroled; and to answer your question, yes, I've got enough cash in my pocket to pay your fare, and probably enough to buy the fucking trailer you live in!"

The cabbie, glaring at him, angrily replied, "Look, motherfucker, don't fuck with me or I'll knock your fucking head off, throw you in the street, and then run over your fucking ass! I don't have time for your bullshit! You show me a twenty or get out of my fucking cab!"

Opening the door, Lucas stepped out and started to walk off.

The cabbie screamed, "Shut the fucking door, you asshole!"

Lucas just kept walking away without looking back. He heard the driver cussing him and threatening to kill him, but he just kept walking away. Nearly a half block away, he heard the car door loudly slam shut and the last echoes of the driver's obscenity-laced voice. As he continued walking, he realized how much he hated mankind. He had been happier locked up in his little holding tank with dirty walls where he didn't have to mix it up with other members of this so-called civilization. There, he was free from everybody's anger, rudeness, competitiveness, and mean-spirited thoughts and expressions. Free to think by himself, to imagine things with his own creative mind. He had enjoyed the jail time. But now, he was out, and he could do whatever he so desired, everything except practice law in Texas. *Fuck law*, he thought, *I'm done with that business.*

As he continued walking down Jefferson Street, he felt his hands getting very cold. He put them into his trouser pockets, holding his shoulders straight and high as he crossed over to Main Street. As he was walking, he saw another cab. He waved to the driver that he needed a ride. The cab pulled up and he slowly got into the back seat. Pulling out a twenty-dollar bill, he handed it to the driver, and asked, "Is this enough to get me to Richmond and Fountainview?"

The driver answered, "That ought to get you there, buddy," and he then stepped on the gas pedal and drove off. An Italian, New Yorker-type, the driver asked, "Where's your coat? It's cold out there!"

Shrugging his shoulders, Lucas answered, "I'm a convicted, just-paroled inmate fresh out of jail! I don't have a coat."

The cabbie, looking back over his shoulder, asked, "Oh yeah, what were you in for?"

"I killed my wife," Lucas paused. "She drove me crazy. I finally just had to blast her during halftime of a Monday night game!"

Nodding back to him, the cabbie said, "I understand. They can sure be pains in the ass during football season. How much time did you have to do?"

"I did ten flat years, but it was worth every last second of it. Now I'm out, and I'll never have to listen to her again."

"It sure sounds like it was well worth it."

Smiling, Lucas said, "You cabdrivers really understand life. That's what I like about you guys."

The driver pulled off the freeway onto Richmond Avenue where he then headed towards Fountainview. He asked, "What's the exact address?"

"It's 4918 Fountainview; a townhouse, all red brick-like. Turn right there."

Lucas pointed to where he wanted him to go. The driver made the turn and kept going until he saw a group of red brick townhouses. Slamming his brakes, he stopped in front of the one which had the number "4918" painted in black on the curb out front. Lucas asked if he owed any more money for the ride, to which the driver replied, "No sir, the twenty takes care of everything."

He got out, thanked him for the ride, and walked up to the front door of his townhome. He placed his key into the lock, but it wouldn't turn. He fiddled with it, but the door still wouldn't unlock. Looking over his shoulder he saw that the cab driver still hadn't driven off. He yelled to him, "Hold on, don't leave yet! The door isn't opening!"

Again he tried to open it, this time using more force, but still the lock wouldn't give. He started thinking that maybe the landlord changed his lock, possibly even evicted him. Maybe, Jill hadn't told him of his predicament. Now, he was angry, ready to start cussing, ready to kick in the door. But, something inside of him told him to stay calm, be patient. This something told him that he lived in a cruel world, one that cared only about the bottom line, one that had no compassion for those down on their luck.

Standing there, he wasn't sure what to do. The curtain inside the living-room window was slightly open, so he walked over to see if he could peek inside. Standing on some wet mulch between the shrubberies, he leaned forward towards the window and looked inside. There was a large Christmas tree in a corner of the living room, and a piano up against a wall. Also, a couch, a chair—all sorts of furniture filled the room. Pictures were hung on the walls. Lucas remembered that all he had in this room was a television set on top of a milk crate and maybe a few large pillows on the floor. He walked back towards the cab.

The driver asked, "Do you need a lift anywhere else?"

Nodding his head, Lucas got back into the cab and directed the driver to continue down Fountainview. Once reaching Westpark Drive, he told him to turn right. They drove several blocks on Westpark before he asked him to stop at a rundown apartment complex on the left side of the street. Jumping out of the car, Lucas told the driver to stay put while he checked to see if anyone was home in this particular unit facing the street. Walking up to the front door, he knocked three times. The cabbie watched him, wondering what he was up to. Was this a friend's house or what? Lucas knocked again, only this time louder; still nobody answered. Several more seconds passed and then finally the door opened.

There, stood an attractive blonde with a maroon bathrobe wrapped around her. She stared straight at Lucas but said nothing. She was puzzled about who he was, and what he wanted on this cold morning.

He asked, "Is Jill here?"

The girl angrily replied, "No, she doesn't live here anymore!"

Lucas looked down at the heavy wool socks on the girl's feet. Feeling uncomfortable talking with her, he wouldn't look into her eyes. She made him feel like he was wasting her time, sort of ruining her day. She had that nasty look to her which good-looking girls had when they wanted to be left alone. He asked, "Do you know where she is?"

"Who are you? Am I supposed to know who-the-fuck you are?"

Slowly raising his head, Lucas now looked directly at her. He was about to cuss her out, but chose not to do so. As angry as her attitude made him, he decided that it wasn't worth it. It was as if he had lost some of the inner anger and fight from deep within himself. It wasn't worth going toe-to-toe with the idiots of the world. The world sucked, the people of the world sucked; let them all go to hell! Turning around, he slowly walked back to the cab. The driver watched the girl waiting for Lucas to get back to the cab. Then she slammed her door shut.

"What was that all about?"

"Nothing, nothing at all. She's some bitch. Can you please take me to a K-Mart or Woolworths? I need to get a few things. Here's forty more dollars towards my fare."

The cabbie took the money and then drove to a large K-Mart several miles away. Lucas got out and asked him to wait while he went inside. Upon entering the store, he was immediately overwhelmed by the chaos and commotion which surrounded him on this morning, the day before Christmas. People were everywhere, doing their last-minute shopping.

Grabbing a shopping cart, he headed to the men's clothing department, where he found a pair of blue jeans, a black pair of extra-large sweat pants, two packages of underwear, and ten pairs of white gym socks which he tossed into his cart. Walking towards the athletic department, he found a size twelve pair of black, high-top sneakers and two Spalding gym bags, one larger than the other. As he headed to the long checkout lines, he passed the toiletries and picked up what he needed.

Once he reached the lines, he just waited his turn, watching the hundreds of people scattered throughout the store, buying last-minute things for Christmas. There were men, women, and children everywhere, all looking merry on this final day before Christmas. It was extremely noisy because of the combination of Christmas songs piped into the store, everyone talking, children laughing, carts rolling, and registers ringing. He thought to himself, *If only I had a bomb, I'd blow this whole fucking place up. I'd end Christmas for all these loud, happy, obnoxious people. End it quickly!*

He leaned forward on his shopping cart. Gazing down, he shut the whole world out. Slowly, he edged forward as the line shortened. He realized that he had become more antisocial than ever. Jail had only reinforced his strong love of being alone. The many hours of deep meditation only strengthened his hatred of the world around him. He thought of John O'Reilly, and then Jill, and their betrayals of him. He daydreamed of beating the crap out of John. And Jill, the whore, wherever she was, he imagined her violently crashing his car and burning to the bone.

These retaliatory thoughts kept racing through his mind, one after another. He had no control over them, but he wanted none. These thoughts gave him an inner peace and a sense of fulfillment. The feelings were nothing but pure unadulterated anger. Both of his disloyal friends were fair game for his vengeful imagination.

Finally, he reached the cashier, who rang up the merchandise in his cart. She placed everything in one shopping bag, except the two gym bags, which she placed beside the shopping bag inside his cart. He paid her and started rolling the cart out into the parking lot where the cabdriver was still waiting.

Before getting in, he stuffed all the items he had just purchased into the larger gym bag. Then he got into the cab, holding both bags. Handing the driver another forty dollars, he told him, "Take me to Texas United Bank, downtown on Lamar Street."

"No problem, I'll have you there in fifteen minutes."

Getting onto Highway 59, the cabbie headed downtown. As he exited the freeway ramp and was heading towards the bank, he asked, "What are you going to do, rob this place?"

Laughing, Lucas asked, "Do I look like a robber to you?"

"Yeah, you've got a crazy look about you."

"I've heard that before."

When they reached the bank entrance, Lucas told him, "I'll be right back; just stay put."

The driver then buried his head into the sports page as Lucas stepped out from the cab. Holding the empty gym bag, he entered the bank. Immediately, he caught the eye of an off-duty policeman who was working security at the bank as an extra job. The officer approached him as he stood in the front lobby near the elevator, asking, "Sir, what are you doing with that gym bag?"

Lucas, looking at him, thought, *It's none of your fucking business!* But he didn't want to give this cop a chance to throw him in jail, so he answered, "I'm going downstairs to clear out my safe-deposit box."

The officer, satisfied with his explanation, said, "I'm sorry to have bothered you, sir. Have a Merry Christmas."

Lucas then rode the elevator down to the basement where he told a bank clerk sitting behind a desk that he desired access to his safe-deposit box. The clerk checked his identification and then asked for the key to the box, which Lucas handed to him. After getting the bank's key, the clerk asked Lucas to walk with him into the vault where he would then unlock the box. There, he pulled the box out from the wall and handed it to Lucas. It was a rather large box. He asked if he wanted a private room where he could open it.

"Yeah, that would be great."

The two walked out from the vault area and the clerk led Lucas to a tiny room where he went inside and closed the door. Standing in front of a mahogany table, he put down the safe-deposit box, and then placed the gym bag beside it. Opening the box, he reached inside and pulled out handfuls of hundred-dollar bills which he placed into the gym bag. He didn't count the money, but figured it to be close to three-hundred-thousand dollars. Some of it was from drug-dealing clients who paid him in cash, and some of it was from gambling winnings accumulated over the past two or three years. Now was the time to withdraw it since he was leaving town for good. Zipping up the gym bag, he walked out and handed the empty safe-deposit box back to the bank employee.

Then he left the area and walked over to the elevator which he rode back up to the bank lobby.

There, he moved into line, waiting his turn to see a teller. Standing patiently, he was forced to listen to Christmas carols being piped throughout the bank's main lobby. Christmas Eve was fast approaching and everyone seemed to be so jovial. He was thinking to himself, *It sure seems like the newspapers always report a lot of suicides around this time of year. But hell, everybody in the bank sure seems happy.*

When he finally reached the front of the line, he stared at the four tellers who were waiting on customers in front of him. They were quite attractive young ladies. He thought, *Why aren't they all working in a dancing joint or some whorehouse? These girls could be making some real money. Why would they want to work in a bean-counting place like this?* One of the tellers motioned that she was ready to wait on him.

He approached and she said, "Merry Christmas, sir. How can I help you today?"

"I need to close my account. I want a cashier's check for the money in my account."

The young girl asked for his account number. Running it on her screen, she looked up and commented, "Why, sir, you have a lot of money in this account. I need for you to fill out a withdrawal form, and I need to see some identification. Then, I'll show it to my manager and get you a check."

Taking the withdrawal form she handed him, Lucas wrote on it that he wanted to close his account. He wasn't even sure how much money was in it. He handed the form and his driver's license to the young girl, who stepped away momentarily. She soon returned and told him that she would get him a bank check for his balance, and explained that a bank check was very similar to a cashier's check.

"Fine, but please hurry. I've got a cab waiting outside."

She prepared the check and took it back to her manager's office to get the proper signature. Returning, she handed it to Lucas.

He told her, "Thank you," and then rushed out from the bank, relieved to see that his cab was still there. As he was hurrying to get into it, he heard his name echoing somewhere in the distance. Turning around, he didn't see anybody.

"Lucas, Lucas," he heard again; now it sounded clearer to him. Again, he looked around. There, walking towards him from across the street, was Rickie, hand-in-hand with Mikey. Beside the two of them was an attractive young girl, whom Rickie, upon reaching him, introduced as Sarah, their nanny from England.

Lucas extended his hand to Mikey, who did not reciprocate. The boy just stared at him, not knowing who he was. Lucas asked, "Do you know who I am? I'm your Uncle Lucas."

But, Mikey just kept eyeing him, not saying anything. Lucas looked at Rickie and commented, "Well, I guess he doesn't really know me."

Rickie, looking down at Mikey, told him, "Say hi to Uncle Lucas."

But, Mikey still said nothing.

Lucas could see Amy in his face. The same jaw line and mouth; the same dark, beautiful eyes; but where Amy always had a sparkle in her eyes, Mikey had a lifeless look in his. He didn't quite seem to connect to the world. Letting go of Rickie's hand, he started briskly walking by himself towards the bank. Sarah chased after him. Rickie remained and told Lucas that he had brought Mikey and Sarah into town so that Mikey could see Santa Claus, who was supposed to be at the bank. He explained that even though Mikey was Jewish, he believed that it was a good idea to let him see Santa Claus.

Lucas assured him, "Yeah, it's good to expose him to other religions. It'll never hurt him to see how different the religions all are."

Rickie, nodding his head, asked, "So what are you up to? I haven't seen your name in the paper recently."

"Well, check the *Bar Journal* next month. I lost my license."

"Why? What happened?"

"Lets just say I had it out with some lady federal judge. It's fine, I'm done practicing law. I'm leaving Texas. In fact, I'm leaving today."

"Where are you going?"

Shrugging his shoulders he answered, "I don't know. I just know I'm leaving."

"But, Lucas, you're the best criminal lawyer in the city. You need to rethink this."

"Nope. My decision has already been made. Let's talk about Mikey. What's up with him? Is he doing okay?"

Rickie suddenly became very sad, and lowering his voice, answered, "No. He has had a lot of problems since Amy's death. I started him in school, but he couldn't handle it. He stuck out, didn't fit in with his classmates, wouldn't interact, wouldn't do anything with the other children. The kids started making fun of him, teasing him, calling him names. He couldn't take it anymore. He'd cry everyday when Sarah picked him up. Finally, I just took him out. I couldn't put him through the torture. Now he stays home with Sarah. She's great with him, but she's not his mother. He still has these hysterical fits where he cries out for Amy at night. He still misses her so much."

Lucas, shaking his head, said, "Man, that's sad. I could tell at the funeral that it would be hard on him. I'm really sorry. He's like my family. You know, he's Amy's kid; Amy was like my sister. She would die if she saw him like this; well, you know what I mean."

Rickie, looking more dejected now, answered, "I know."

Seeing that Rickie was getting so upset, Lucas told him, "I've gotta go now. My cab is taking me to the airport. I'm splitting Texas. You are the only person who knows that I'm leaving. I doubt anyone cares, but if you see anyone who asks where I am, just tell them you haven't seen me. Please, do that for me. I don't want anyone to know that I left, or anything else about me."

Rickie nodded and assured him, "I'll honor your request."

"And I'll tell you what," continued Lucas, "wherever I end up, I'll send you a letter with a phone number where I can be reached. If I move again, then I'll send you another phone number where I can be reached. You will always be able to find me. But you must keep my number a secret, and you need to promise never to use it unless something bad has happened to Mikey or he needs me for something. Don't just call me to see how I'm doing, or to talk about the Forty Niners being in the Super Bowl some year. I'm cutting all ties to my life down here, except to Mikey if he ever needs me. Is that okay?"

Nodding, Rickie said, "Lucas, you're one of a kind. I hope I never have to talk to you again." The two shook hands and went their separate ways.

Getting into the cab, Lucas told the driver, "Take me to the airport. I need to get out of this fucking town!"

"No problem, but where are you going to fly on Christmas Eve?"

"I don't know. I'll either go to New York, or maybe Maryland, maybe Florida. Whichever place has a flight taking off sooner. I've lived on the West Coast, and here in fucking Texas. It's time I live back East somewhere. Hell, that's where this country got started. That's where I need to go, somewhere back East."

On the way to the airport, he asked the cabbie to pull off the freeway at the Laura Koppe exit, where he then directed him to an old, worn-down building with a sign in the window which read, "Uptown Pharmacy." Lucas told him, "I know the pharmacist here. I need to get some pills from him."

He entered the pharmacy and was back in ten minutes. "No more stops. Just straight to the airport."

ELEVEN

As Lucas strolled through the airport, people from behind were readily passing him. Everyone was in a big hurry to make their flights. Even little kids passed him as they trailed behind their moms and dads. The holiday season brought a certain frenzy among the many last-minute travelers. But Lucas was in no hurry. It was just him alone, lugging two gym bags, not knowing for sure where he was going. He knew that he was going to try to catch a flight somewhere, preferably New York or Baltimore, possibly even Florida. All three places were known for having good horse racing. He figured he'd be spending a lot of his days at the track. Fate would determine exactly where he ended up. New York had Belmont and Aqueduct, Baltimore had Pimlico, and South Florida had a place called Hialeah.

Walking up to the ticket counter, Lucas was greeted by a young, female ticket agent who asked him if he had reservations.

"No, I don't. I need to fly somewhere on the East Coast. I just need one ticket."

"Sir, can you please be a little more specific? Where would you like to fly on the East Coast?"

Shrugging his shoulders, he answered, "New York, Baltimore, maybe Miami."

Punching into her keyboard, she informed him, "New York is sold out, there is a seven-thirty-five flight available to Baltimore, Miami is completely sold out. I have one seat available to Baltimore."

"I'll take it."

"When would you like to return, sir?"

"I'm not returning," he said. "Just one way."

After asking his name, the agent punched out his ticket, and told him the cost was two-hundred-and-fifty dollars. Reaching into his gym bag, Lucas pulled out three hundred-dollar bills which he handed to her. She gave him his ticket and change. Then she informed him, "You'll be departing from gate 9B. Your seat is in row 38, seat A. That's toward the back of the plane, next to a window. I hope you don't mind."

Nodding, Lucas said, "That's fine, thank you." Then he left thinking, *That stupid bitch; window seat in the back, she hopes I don't mind. Hell, that's the best seat on the fucking plane!*

Fifteen minutes later, he boarded the plane and shuffled his way towards the back. Then he placed the larger of his two gym bags into the overhead compartment and the smaller one beneath his assigned seat. Nobody had yet taken the two seats beside him.

Lucas watched the people as they boarded the plane. Staring at each one of them as they walked down the aisle, he wondered what their plights were in life. Why were they on this plane? Some looked happy to be getting on, others sad or scared. Lucas had a hard time distinguishing the sad people from the scared ones. He figured the two mind-sets ran fairly close together. But, those who looked happy were easy to spot. Their smiling faces expressed that they were going home to Baltimore for the holidays to visit family members whom they really wished to see. One middle-aged gentleman was wearing a gray winter jacket and a Baltimore Colts cap. It was obvious that he was returning home.

Identical twin girls boarded, both wearing blue Rice University jackets. Lucas figured they were probably going home to visit their parents for the holidays. Closely watching the girls as they walked down the aisle, he thought, *Fuck, they look exactly alike! How could anyone possibly tell them apart?*

As both girls eased their way to the back of the plane, one of them held up her boarding pass and told the other, "There's row 38."

The two sisters took their seats next to Lucas. Turning his head away from them, he looked out his window. However, for some reason he really wanted to stare. He wanted to make comparisons, see if they were really exactly alike. Instead, he kept staring out the window, waiting for the plane to start moving. Even their chattering voices sounded identical to his ears.

Legal Vengeance

Once the plane was in the sky and the lights were turned off in the cabin, Lucas tried to catch a glimpse of the sisters. But it was too dark at first to see them. After several seconds his eyes adjusted to the darkness and he found himself staring at them. Never before had he given much thought to identical twins. Now, he wondered how God could have created two exactly alike people. Amy had studied genetics; she must have done some work on identical twins. The subject seemed fascinating to him, much more so than he had ever realized.

He started thinking about Amy and how good she'd always been to him. He thought of Mikey and the empty look in his eyes outside of the bank. The attractive nanny would hopefully be good to him. Poor Mikey was going to have a rough trip through life. Lucas, knowing how tough the world could be, worried whether Mikey would be able to cope with its viciousness.

Closing his eyes, he started daydreaming of what it would be like to have the two twins in bed with him at the same time. He could conduct an experiment to see if they were alike. Did they enjoy the same things? Did they mirror each other? *Hell, I could benefit science! I'd be, "Lucas Lustick, the research scientist." Wow, what a thought! But, I'm sure that some other lucky guy has done that experiment before.* He guessed that there were probably scores of gents who had hacked on identical twins before, plenty who could write volumes on the subject. Anyway, it was sure nice to think about, dream about. Then he fell into a deep sleep.

Before he knew it, he was awakened, and the plane was descending into Baltimore. Looking out the window he could see ice and snow everywhere. The skies were dark, but the ground was white. Placing his hand up against the window, he could feel the frigid air of the East Coast. Then he leaned his forehead up against it. "It must be zero degrees in this fucking town!" he said aloud.

The twin sitting next to him looked at him and said, "Excuse me?"

Looking back at her, Lucas repeated, "I said it must be zero degrees in this fucking town."

The young girl appearing shocked by his language, asked, "Sir, would you please watch your mouth? I don't appreciate it!"

Lucas angrily answered, "Don't tell me what I can and can't say, you pompous, little Rice bitch!"

An older flight attendant suddenly appeared, telling Lucas, "Sir, control your language or we will have you arrested when you step off this airplane!"

Lucas clenched his fists to control his anger as he looked up at her; otherwise, he would have lashed into her, too. Looking back at the girl sitting next to him, he heard her sister whispering to her, "Leave him alone, he's not right. He's crazy; let him be."

Slowly, he unclenched his fists, trying to slow down his breathing. He didn't want to spend anymore long days locked up in the slammer. Staring out his window, he could see that the plane was close to landing on the runway. He thought that he had better learn to control his anger and bad language around people. There was so much hatred built-up inside. He never wanted to be told what to do; never wanted to be crossed by anybody.

But, he realized that he didn't need to always get back at everyone. Looking up to the dark sky, he promised himself that for the rest of his life he would learn to control his anger. Even when he was done wrong by others, he would control himself and show no emotion. Sometimes, he would just try to forget the wrong done to him. Other times, when it was necessary, he would get even. But getting even would always need to be done in a quiet way. Cussing folks out would never get him anywhere.

After the plane landed, Lucas nudged the twin sitting next to him, telling her that he was sorry for what had happened earlier. "I'm under a lot of stress and just lost it."

The girl looked away, refusing to accept his apology. Lucas then tried to apologize to her sister, and she, too, just looked away. So, he looked back out his window, mumbling to himself, "Those fucking whores."

Catching himself, he didn't say another word. After the plane landed, the cabin emptied row by row, but he sat patiently in his seat. There was no hurry, for he had nowhere to go. After the last person exited the plane, he finally stood up and pulled down his gym bag from the overhead compartment. Picking up the other one from under his seat, he started walking up the aisle. He feared the police might be waiting for him when he stepped off the plane, but that was not the case. Briskly he walked to the terminal.

Once inside, he kept walking alongside the crowd towards the baggage pickup area. It was there he figured he'd be able to hail a taxicab. Once at the pickup area, he exited the terminal into the cold night air. A bearded taxi driver pulled up, and he quickly hopped in. Shivering from head to toe, he told the driver, "It's freezing here! This is fucking unbelievable!"

The cabbie asked, "Where are you from?"

"Texas. Houston, Texas."

"It doesn't get this cold down there, does it?"

Lucas now taking his hands out from his pockets, answered, "Fuck no!"

"Where to?" asked the driver as he chomped on his cigar and rolled down his window to let some of the smoke escape.

"I need a place to stay for a couple of days. Any decent hotel, but somewhere near Pimlico Racetrack."

Looking over at him, the driver asked, "Why near Pimlico?"

"Because I want to go there tomorrow for the races."

The driver guffawed, "What, are you crazy? First of all, Pimlico isn't racing this time of year. It don't open 'til March or April. Bowie is running now, but it's closed tomorrow for Christmas."

Lucas was disappointed and didn't hide it. "What do you mean there's no fucking racing tomorrow? That's when they ought to be open! People aren't working and can go out there."

"That ain't the way it is. The folks who work there, you know, the horsemen, the ticket sellers, the touts; they all want off to celebrate with their families. Hell, I don't blame 'em!"

Lucas asked, "Where's Bowie? Is it near Pimlico?"

"No way, not even close. It's on the other side of town. Thirty miles from downtown, towards D.C."

Lucas, visibly upset, told him, "Just take me to a hotel somewhere downtown. I may as well settle in."

The cabbie began driving. "What brings you to Baltimore?" he asked.

Lucas thought a second and answered, "Well, I just got out of jail. I'm trying to start a new life for myself. I heard good things about Baltimore."

"What have you heard good about this town, other than we've got the Colts and The Block?"

Lucas appearing puzzled, asked, "What's The Block?"

"Baltimore is famous for The Block! You really don't know what The Block is? You're pulling my leg, aren't you?"

"No, I'm not."

The driver, now very excited, told him, "It's a city-long street consisting of nothing but whorehouses. One next to another, a whole city-block long. Good women in all of them. You just go into anyone of them, you can't go wrong!"

"Hell, it sounds like my kind of place!"

"Do you want me to take you there now?"

Lucas hesitating, answered, "Nah, not tonight."

He really wanted to go, but knew it wouldn't be wise to take his cash-filled gym bag into some whorehouse on this place called The Block. He'd been rolled in those types of places before. No, before he started catting around town, he was going to see to it that his money was safely stashed into some bank. He told the driver, "Just take me to some half-ass decent hotel, somewhere near downtown."

The cabbie dropped him off a block from the old Hilton on Charles Street, and he got out and paid his fare. The driver told him, "I can't get any closer because of this construction. Enjoy Baltimore!"

Lucas thanked him. It was freezing cold outside. His feet were suddenly soaking wet as he trudged through the slush on the sidewalk in front of the hotel. His toes were quickly becoming as stiff as piano keys. When he finally entered through the front door, he went straight to the fireplace in the front lobby. Standing in front of the burning firewood, he held out his arms, slowly inching closer so that his feet could warm up. After ten minutes of enjoying the fire's warmth, he walked to the front desk and asked the clerk for a room for the night. He told her that he might need the room for several days, but wasn't sure. She had numerous vacancies and asked him which floor he'd prefer—the first, second, or third.

"The third."

The lady then did the necessary paperwork and Lucas tendered the cash. With a key now in hand, he headed towards the elevator. He pushed the Up button and waited for the elevator door to open. Looking around to see if anyone was watching, he indulged a strong compulsion to keep pushing the button. He didn't know what had come over him.

The elevator finally arrived and he stepped into it. Anxiously, he pushed the button with the number 3 on it. The light lit up and the elevator moved upwards. As it did so, he kept pushing the 3 button over and over. The elevator stopped on the second floor and two men got on. He now refrained from pushing the button, but felt tremendous pressure building inside his head to keep pushing it on the ride to the third floor. The pressure didn't stop until he got off the elevator.

As he walked down the hallway, he stopped in front of his room and unlocked and opened the door. Walking inside, he flipped on the light and then reached into one of his gym bags to get out his toothbrush and toothpaste. Walking into the bathroom, he turned the water on and started brushing away. *Why did I have that bizarre urge to push the elevator button over and over again?* He assumed it must have been stress. After brushing his teeth, he got undressed and took a hot shower. The water pressure was strong, which he liked. He held his head under the showerhead just to feel the hot water crashing upon his scalp. Finally he got out, dried off, shut off the lights, and climbed under the covers. Now he felt calm, relaxed, and ready to fall into a deep sleep. Instead, he tossed and turned all night, back and forth, back and forth.

Finally, he sat up in the bed. It was still dark inside his room. The alarm clock showed seven o'clock, straight up. The curtains in the room were drawn shut, but a glimmer of light made its way inside. Getting out of bed, he went into the bathroom, turned on the light, and stared at himself in the mirror. He looked over to the light switch and hastily pushed it down, cutting off the lights. Then he proceeded to switch the light on and off ten times in rapid succession.

Finally, he left it on and started brushing his teeth, wondering why he felt this need to keep switching the light on and off, on and off. Then, all of a sudden, he had an urge to press his elbow up against the bathroom mirror in front of him. *What the hell was that?* It was a powerful urge, one beyond his control. After he finished with his teeth, he leaned over the sink, placed his right elbow up against the mirror, then tapped it against the mirror ten times before stopping. It allowed a release of the terrible pressure which had built up inside his head. *Why am I having these weird urges?* He felt compelled to carry them out; otherwise he felt like his head would explode. Never before had he experienced these types of obsessions. They confused him—they scared him! Not knowing what brought them on, he wondered, *Am I going crazy?*

Walking to the large window, he pulled the maroon curtains apart so that he could see outside to the streets of Baltimore. Touching the glass with the palm of his right hand, he could feel how cold it was outside. The large snowflakes were generously falling from the sky. They hit the wet pavement below, immediately dissipating upon contact. The streets were wet and deserted. Just looking outside made him shiver. Pulling the drapes back together, he sat down on his bed.

Several minutes later he turned on the large television set. All three channels were saturated with coverage of Christmas Day parades, so he turned it off and got back into bed. Within minutes, he felt that same awful sensation of pressure building up inside his head. He felt this uncontrollable need to get back up from the bed and switch the television on and off, on and off. He had to succumb to it. Getting up, he switched the television set on and off fifteen times, thus releasing the pressure. Then, he hopped back into bed, pulled the covers over himself, and started thinking about all the things he needed to do. He had to find a bank to stash his money. He needed to find a place to permanently live. He had to buy a car. Most importantly, he needed a warm coat to wear. *Getting a coat is first on my list. I'm gonna freeze to death otherwise. But, it being fucking Christmas Day, everyplace is closed. Fuck Christmas!*

He felt very depressed being cooped up in this hotel on this cold day. Even if he owned a coat and decided to walk the streets, he'd have to leave all his cash in his room. Then he would worry that somebody might come in and steal it. The racetrack, the banks, the stores, the restaurants, the bars; hell, everything was closed. Any possible enjoyment from television was out of the question, because each channel had nothing but Christmas parades.

And these compulsive feelings which forced him to keep switching the television and lights on and off, to keep tapping his elbow on the mirror; these scared him. He feared that his mind was being overtaken by some outside forces. He hated his life and his present situation. Standing up, he reached into the larger of the two gym bags, pulled out a small pill bottle and opened it. Pouring out five or six small, white pills into the palm of his hand, he then walked to the bathroom sink and looked at himself in the mirror. Mumbling, "Lustick, you fucking loser," he placed all the pills upon the back of his tongue. Cupping his hands together under the running faucet, he filled them with cold water which he then forcefully chugged into his mouth. The pills were effortlessly washed down his throat, all at once, where they would soon take effect in putting him to sleep.

Looking at himself in the mirror, he smiled. These pills would end his miserable life for good, or at the very least, they would close down the workings of his system until this horrible Christmas holiday had passed.

TWELVE

The loud knock at the door accompanied by a deep male voice screaming, "Open up the door! Open up the door!" was enough to awaken Lucas from his deep sleep. It was dark in the room. He had no idea what day or time it was. Naked, he got up and walked gingerly towards the door.

"Who's there?" he asked.

"It's the hotel manager. Are you all right?"

"Yeah. What day is it?"

"It's Monday, the twenty-eighth of December." He went on, "You owe three days rent for your room!"

"Let me shower, and I'll be downstairs in a few minutes. Then I'll pay your fucking ass."

"Don't try to leave without paying or we'll call the police!"

Lucas felt like he had been sleeping for months. He felt groggy and tired as he limped into the bathroom to brush his teeth and take a hot shower. As he was brushing, suddenly he had that strange urge to again press his elbow up against the mirror. It consumed him. Finally, he gave in and proceeded to tap his right elbow against the mirror exactly ten times.

Once he completed the tapping, there was a great release of pressure from within his head.

After showering, he dried himself off and put on a pair of jeans and a white T-shirt. He knew that he would need to buy some warm clothes if he was going to stay in this godforsaken ice town. Finding a warm coat was still the number one item on his agenda. He decided that he'd look for one, and then find a bank where he could deposit his money. Then, he would hail a cab to take him to the racetrack to see what Maryland horse racing was all about. He still felt slightly disoriented due to the carryover effect of the pills. Nevertheless, he felt a renewed energy burning within to take on the day.

He walked out of his room, leaving everything behind except the cash-filled gym bag which he held in his left hand. As he rode the elevator down to the first floor, he was constantly pushing the buttons in front of him. He walked to the checkout desk and told the clerk that he needed to stay a few more days. The clerk informed him that he needed to pay his bill for the nights he had already stayed. Reaching into his gym bag, he pulled out five one-hundred-dollar bills which he placed on the counter. The clerk gave him his change and a receipt, which he stuck in his pocket.

Walking towards the entryway of the hotel, he stepped outside. To his right was a red-faced bellhop, dressed in a black, full-length winter coat, covering all of him except from his calves down. Lucas called to the young man, "Hey, kid, come on over here."

The boy obediently complied, "What can I do for you, sir?"

"What did you pay for that coat you're wearing?"

"Nothing, my mother bought it for me."

"I'll give you two-hundred bucks for it."

Smiling, the boy said, "But sir, this coat isn't worth anywhere near two-hundred bucks!"

Lucas then pulled a couple hundred-dollar bills from his gym bag and handed them to him. "Here, take these," he said. "Just give me the fucking coat! To me it's worth the money."

The boy slowly took off the coat and handed it over to Lucas, who immediately put it on. As he wrapped it tightly around himself, he felt its warmth trickle through his body. He thought, *What a steal for only two-hundred bucks!* He looked at the young bellhop who was now two-hundred dollars richer, but visibly trembling from the below-freezing temperatures. He told him, "Boy, if you are ever in a desert and are lucky enough to have a gallon jug of water, don't sell it for even a million dollars."

The boy responded, "No sir, I wouldn't. But sir, if you are ever in the desert and have a million dollars, and you see a boy with a gallon jug of water, and if there is a store that sells water within walking distance and the store sells the water for ten dollars a jug, you might just walk to the store and buy the water."

Lucas snapped, "Get me a cab, wise guy, and I hope you freeze your fucking ass off!"

The boy answered, "Sorry, sir, I'm freezing," as he tiptoed back inside the hotel.

Lucas was now left by himself standing on the curb in search of a ride. Five minutes passed, then ten, and still there wasn't any sign of a cab. The two-hundred-dollar coat didn't seem to be doing so great a job of keeping him warm. It seemed as if the winter air was now overpowering the coat's thermal capabilities. He was shivering beyond control. Finally, he spotted a cab and waved to it. The driver saw him and pulled up. Lucas opened the front door and got in. "Nearest bank, please. I need to get to the nearest fucking bank."

The driver responded, "No problem, buddy, calm down. You don't need to call it a fucking bank. Bank without the adjective will get you there just as quickly."

The driver, now feeling that he had properly corrected Lucas, turned the cab onto Calvert Street and headed towards a Bank of Maryland branch several blocks away. Stopping in front of the bank, he told Lucas, "Your fare is two-ninety, sir."

Handing him three dollar bills, Lucas told him, "Keep the fucking change," as he stepped from the cab.

Slamming the door shut, he walked into the main lobby of the bank. Once inside, he stopped and looked around. It was an elaborately decorated bank with deep, plush, gray carpet throughout the huge lobby. The ceiling seemed to reach the sky, adorned with hundreds of beautiful, yellow-brass chandeliers reflecting light around the room. The walls were of a dark, cherry wood, adding to the upscale decorum. *This bank looks a lot different from the fucking banks in Texas.*

The Texas banks were also big, but they had a western gaudiness to them. He remembered the signs in those banks reminding everyone how proud they were to be Texans. Signs which read, "Proud Texans Invest at Bank of Texas," or "True Texans Get Their Home Loans Here." Nowhere at this Bank of Maryland did he see such signs. There were no signs period, let alone ones which read, "Proud People of Maryland Bank Here," or "True People of Maryland Buy CDs Here." Lucas liked this bank's classy style.

Walking to the customer-service lines, he stood behind two other customers and waited his turn. He looked down to the gym bag he was holding. He wasn't sure what to say to anyone about opening an account since he hadn't thought it out.

The teller asked, "Can I help you, sir?"

Lucas nodded, "Yeah, I need to open an account. I need a safe-deposit box, too."

"Sir, to open a new account you need to go across the lobby to one of the two men sitting over there. They will be more than happy to help you."

Lucas nodded, and then started walking across the lobby where he made eye contact with one of the bank officers sitting behind a large desk.

"May I help you, sir?"

"Yeah, I need to open a checking account, and I need a safe-deposit box."

"Have a seat, sir. I will be most happy to help you. My name is David Lewing. I'm an officer in charge of new accounts. What's your name, sir?"

"Lustick, Lucas Lustick."

"Where are you from, sir?"

"Texas."

"Mr. Lustick, how do you like our weather?"

"Mr. Lewing, I'm not here to talk about the weather. Would you just give me the necessary paperwork to open a checking account, and a key to a safe-deposit box?"

David Lewing was taken aback by Lucas' abrasiveness; however, he remained very professional. He gave him the necessary paperwork which Lucas quickly filled out.

"Where's a deposit form for my first deposit?"

Mr. Lewing immediately handed him one.

Lucas pulled out his bank check written by his Texas bank and endorsed it. Next, he took ten-thousand dollars in cash from his gym bag and handed the deposit slip, the bank check, and the cash to Mr. Lewing, who stood up and walked to the main teller's windows where he would open the new account.

Lucas looked around the huge room, and believing that nobody was watching him, started tapping Mr. Lewing's desk with his right elbow. He did this twenty times and then changed to his left elbow which he tapped on the desk twenty more times. Then his eyes circled around the bank lobby, hoping that nobody had seen him. It didn't appear that anyone had watched him. He felt that he had released the pressure from within his head without anyone knowing.

Several minutes later Mr. Lewing returned and handed him a check register and some temporary checks. He explained that the bank couldn't mail him regular checks or a statement because he didn't list an address on his application other than, "Maryland." He told him that he needed to be more specific about his address.

Lucas assured him that once he had a place to live, he'd come back to the bank and give them the information. Mr. Lewing then handed him a key with the number "1402" engraved on it and informed him that the safe-deposit boxes were in the basement of the bank. Lucas followed him to a large marble stairwell located towards the front of the bank lobby. There, they walked downstairs to an area where an armed guard was sitting outside the safe-deposit room.

Mr. Lewing greeted the guard, and then proceeded to open the door to the room with a key from his pocket. He assured the guard that Lucas was with him as the two entered into the dimly lit room. Mr. Lewing pointed to box "1402" and asked, "Sir, is this big enough for you?"

Lucas nodded and Mr. Lewing then turned one of the locks with his key, and instructed Lucas to place his key in the adjacent lock and turn it. He did so and the safety-deposit box opened. At that point, for privacy concerns, Mr. Lewing politely stepped outside of the room. Lucas scooped nearly ten-thousand dollars in cash from the gym bag and stashed it inside his coat pocket. The rest of the money he carefully placed inside the box, which he then closed and locked. Next, he walked out from the room carrying his gym bag, and headed to the stairwell that led to the bank lobby. He passed Mr. Lewing and the guard without even acknowledging them. Once he got to the top of the stairs, he briskly exited the bank.

After hailing a cab, he asked the driver to take him to a Ford dealership. The cabbie took him to the Brooks Robinson dealership near the harbor. There, he purchased a used black Mustang with thirty-thousand miles on it. After paying cash for it, he looked as happy as a pig in mud as he drove off the lot. Now he had a coat, a car, a bank, and he finally was ready to go to the racetrack!

Pulling out from the car dealership, he drove down a side street. He saw a cab at a stoplight and beeped his horn to get the driver's attention. Jumping out from his car, Lucas approached him, asking, "Hey man, how do I get to the horse track?"

The gruff cabbie responded, "What do I look like, a fucking tour guide? The track's nowhere near here!"

Lucas pulled out two twenty-dollar bills and said, "Take this and just lead me to the track. I'll follow you."

The cabdriver took the money and said, "It's a twenty-minute ride."

Lucas followed him out of downtown and for several miles on some freeway. He had no idea where he was going, but followed the cab as it exited the freeway onto a feeder street.

There, the cabbie turned right onto a two-way street which he traveled upon for three miles before pulling over onto the side of the road. Lucas stopped his car right behind him.

The cabbie exited his vehicle and walked back to Lucas, telling him, "Stay on this road for about three miles and then you'll see the signs to the track. It's Bowie Racetrack; you'll see the signs."

Lucas nodded, "I appreciate your taking me out here."

"No problem."

Lucas drove until he saw the Bowie signs which led him to the grounds of the racetrack. He felt excited when he initially saw the track. Adrenaline was rushing through his body as he pulled into a parking space. Exiting his car, he walked towards the track's entrance. It was freezing and he took in a large breath of the cold air. *Wow!* he thought. *How do these fucking horses run in this weather?*

After paying his admission, he walked into the grandstand. It was an old track which looked like it was built in the early 1900s. He watched the folks who clamored inside the grandstand in-between races to avoid the subfreezing temperatures. They were all bundled up with coats, scarves, knit hats, gloves, whatever it took to help stay warm when they went outside to stand at the finish line and watch their horses run. Even covered in heavy winter garb, there could be no mistaking these people for what they really were—degenerates to the core. These were gamblers who frequented the track on weekdays, a far cry from the types who came on weekends.

The weekend players at least had jobs during the week. Ninety-nine percent of the weekday players didn't hold real jobs; most lived off government assistance or income derived from part-time labor. The racetrack was their whole life. It was a place to spend the days. Besides the dream of hitting a big race someday and winning a lot of money, the track gave these folks a society all their own. Some were loners who kept to themselves, while others were very social, constantly chattering about which horse should win the next race. They were well aware of each other since they were all at the track every day. They shared a certain camaraderie that only downtrodden, veteran horse players would understand. Their families had abandoned them, all because of their addiction to the track. They were losers, but they always kept trying, always thinking they had a chance.

Lucas knew there was no difference between the weekday horse players here and those he used to see in California. He liked being around these types of people. He was comfortable within this element and knew that most of these folks were basically decent. Because of the way he was, he knew that he would never actually be friendly with any of them. But, he knew that he could coexist with them everyday in this type of environment. They'd bet their horses and he'd bet his. They'd all stand at the finish line together, crunching their tickets as race after race of horses stampeded down the stretch. He would stand side-by-side with these total strangers. Never again would he stand in a courtroom where he could be abused by mean women judges. He'd be right here, forever, watching horses run.

THIRTEEN

Lucas never moved out from the hotel. He stayed for years, paying his bill every two weeks. It provided him with what he needed: a bed, television, forceful shower, toilet, and a sink. Maids cleaned his room each and every day. What else could he want? He didn't need a kitchen since he never cooked anything. There were soft drink machines in the lobby if he got thirsty. There were plenty of Chinese restaurants and delis within walking distance when he was hungry. He became very familiar with The Block, where he could walk in less than five minutes from his hotel lobby. No doubt, he was living in a prime spot of Baltimore.

Over the years, he decorated his walls with posters of powerful racehorses and graceful ballerinas. Living only two blocks from the Baltimore Ballet Company, he'd often walk to watch the performers practice. It gave him great pleasure. He had always loved watching ballerinas. When he had lived in Berkeley, he and Amy often crossed the bridge into San Francisco to watch the San Francisco Ballet Company perform. He never thought much of the male dancers; to him, they were just props for the sleek, ultra-feminine ballerinas.

He saw a great resemblance between the ballerinas and the four-legged creatures with numbers pasted to their saddles at the tracks. Both ballerinas and racehorses were strong, powerful, and graceful, and both held their heads high when performing. Both had long slender legs which though appearing very fragile, were yet very strong. Both wore tiny shoes to protect their feet. Both showed tremendous heart in doing what they did best.

Basically, Lucas was very content during his years in Baltimore. On a typical day he'd wake up in the morning, go eat breakfast at a deli, and arrive at the track by one o'clock, in time to bet the daily double. He'd stay through the eighth race and then be back at his hotel by five.

Some evenings he would go watch the ballerinas practice; others, he would go to The Block looking for girls. He usually ate dinner around nine o'clock at one of the many downtown restaurants. As he ate, he'd always study the next day's *Racing Form*.

He had other interests besides sex, horses, and food. When the Colts or Orioles were in town, he'd often go to Memorial Stadium to watch them play. Sometimes he'd bet the games with a bookie named Fly, whom he had met on The Block. Fly also ran a whorehouse on The Block called "Boots." Lucas respected the way Fly was entangled in two vices.

On some evenings, Lucas would visit the Johns Hopkins undergraduate or Medical School libraries to read about various subjects he found interesting. He'd read about anything which he wanted to learn about. Having an insatiable appetite for knowledge, he'd often sit in the libraries for hours, reading whatever he came across. Students would at times try to engage him in conversation, however, he'd never say anything back to them. He'd just sit at one of the pinewood desks, burying his head into whatever book or journal he was reading.

People often wondered who he was. He appeared too old to be a student, but he looked scummy and degenerate enough to be a professor or a career academic of some sort. Most any subject interested him, and he absorbed the most complex and difficult disciplines with the greatest of ease. He read everything he could about chemistry, biology, philosophy, and physics. He became fascinated with the study of human genetics, often indulging in scientific books which differentiated the chemicals which carried various genetic codes within cells.

Lucas was quite aware that he had been born with a great intellect, but he was also aware that all was not well inside his head. His compulsive behaviors, which began with the excessive pushing of elevator buttons and tapping of the bathroom mirror with his elbow, had become much worse over the years. These were no longer just occasional occurrences here and there. They became constant and controlling afflictions which worsened over time until they totally controlled his day-to-day activities.

When he walked, he would need to bang his knees together with each step. If he failed to do so, he'd feel that same terrible pressure inside of his head. Wherever he walked, whether it be on the streets, at the racetrack, The Block, or even inside his hotel room, he always walked with the inside portions of his knees touching each other with each step. He walked slowly, and that made it less noticeable to those who watched him. But, you couldn't miss seeing him shrugging his shoulders.

Whether he was walking or simply sitting, he would constantly shrug his shoulders in a twitching manner. He'd do this approximately every two-to-three seconds. He did this whether in public or alone; it was beyond his control. It got worse over time, to the point that he seldom left his hotel. If he didn't twitch, he'd feel that awful pressure ready to burst inside of his head. So he would twitch, twitch, and twitch again, all day long, all night long, just to keep the pressure away.

He'd walk to The Block, but instead of visiting whorehouses, he'd visit liquor stores, bringing half-gallon jugs of Jack Daniel's back to his place. He would often drink himself to sleep, awakening only to the miserable compulsions which were within his head. Wherever he went, people would watch him and wonder what was wrong with him. Some people taunted and laughed at him. Rowdy teenagers would call him "Twitchy" or "Jack in the Box." He would look back at them but never respond. Nobody realized how brilliant a man this was who clumsily walked and shrugged his way through the streets of Baltimore. His appearance was that of a mentally disturbed, disheveled streetwalker with a severe neurological disorder of some type. Nobody realized the inner turmoil that possessed him.

Only one who studied the mentally ill would have ever dared to approach him. And on a cold Sunday afternoon in December, that's just what happened. It was at a Colts game at Memorial Stadium. Lucas sat by himself in the lower box seats near the fifty-yard line. He had bought the ticket from a scalper standing outside the stadium for triple the face value. It was a great seat. Sitting next to him, to his right, was a bald-headed, elderly gentleman bundled up in a full-length gray coat, his neck and chin wrapped in a black scarf. He had dark-gray eyes, and the skin under his cheekbones appeared to be aged and deeply pitted. He and Lucas made eye contact with each other when the game started.

For the next three hours or so, the two would sit next to each other and watch the football game. The man couldn't help but notice Lucas' constant twitching movements. As the game went on, he was twitching beyond control. During the fourth quarter, the man switched seats with a younger woman who had been sitting on the other side of him. She was a tiny woman, at the most, five-feet tall, maybe ninety-five pounds. She was covered up, wearing a tan leather coat and a knit hat which entirely covered her hair except for some loose strands which fell onto her oily forehead. She appeared to be in her early, maybe mid-thirties. Lucas noticed her and wondered why she switched seats with the old man.

He noticed that she had permanent acne scars similar to the deep pits he'd seen in the old man's face. He assumed that this woman was the old man's daughter. He thought, *What a waste of a good ticket bringing a woman to the game! But on the other hand, it was nice of the old man to bring his homely daughter out somewhere.* Lucas kept amusing himself with his terribly mean thoughts about the way the woman looked. He'd watch the game, then turn and look at her, laughing inside as he thought awful things about her looks. Then he'd turn and watch the game again, all the while, still uncontrollably twitching away.

The woman noticed that as Lucas was twitching, he'd occasionally start laughing when he looked at her. Then he'd turn his attention back to the football game. She continued to observe his behavior until the game ended. At that point, she stood up and said to him, "My name is Sarah Lombardi. I'm a psychiatrist here in town and I can't help but notice that you seem to have a type of nervous disorder which I've done a great bit of research on."

Lucas didn't say anything, but he let her continue. "I'd love to help you if you can visit my office sometime during the week. I won't charge you a cent. I just want to help you."

Mumbling, Lucas asked, "Where's your office?"

"It's in the medical center, downtown. Here, let me give you a card with my phone number on it." Pulling out a card from her purse, she handed it to him. "Just call tomorrow and talk with my nurse; she'll give you an appointment. I'm very much looking forward to helping you."

Quietly he said, "Thank you, ma'am," and with that he turned to his left and walked down the row until he reached the aisle. Now, he was so ashamed of himself for having laughed at this woman during the game. People had made fun of him his entire life, and here he was doing the same cruel thing to someone else. He feared he was becoming wicked like most of the other people on Earth.

Walking up the stairs he focused his attention on how much he hated the fact that he was always twitching. He never thought that there was anything he could do about it; it had just become part of him. But, now he saw an opportunity from this kind, homely woman, to end the internal torture that he'd been going through for years. She seemed confident; she didn't even hesitate. She seemed to know that she could help him. It was worth a shot. Anything to make his miserable life better. He would call her office the next morning at nine o'clock sharp and hopefully get an appointment.

FOURTEEN

Lucas sat on the black leather couch across from Dr. Lombardi. Not dressed like a doctor, Sarah wore simple black shoes, a long green skirt, and a green and black sweater. Her greasy hair was pulled behind her head where it was confined by a sturdy rubber band. Her skin was pale; she didn't wear any makeup. There was no effort to cover up the acne scars which road-mapped her face. Lucas noticed that she had the same dark-gray eyes as the old man who was sitting next to her at the football game. He still wondered if the old man was her father. Sitting with her legs crossed in an unpainted wooden chair five feet away from him, she asked, "How are you doing?"

"Okay," Lucas answered, "except that these bastardly afflictions are totally making my life unbearable."

As he talked, he continuously twitched. He explained to her about the strong pressures he repeatedly felt inside of his head, and told her what he felt compelled to do to rid himself of them. The tapping of his elbows on mirrors, turning the light switches on and off, and continuously banging his knees together as he walked; he described all these strange behaviors which he engaged in at different times to alleviate the awful pressure within his head.

She asked him if he had felt this pressure his entire life and he told her, "No, it all started not that long ago, but it has gotten progressively worse."

She inquired about what type of work he did. He told her, "I don't have a job."

"Have you ever worked?"

"I used to be a criminal lawyer down in Texas."

"Why aren't you doing that anymore?"

"I got sick of it and just quit."

Dr. Lombardi asked him where he lived, and he told her about the hotel. She inquired about his family, and he told her he really didn't have one.

At this point, she left to go into another room to get a notepad so that she could start taking notes. Normally, she didn't take detailed notes when she met with patients, but instead just jotted things down in her files after interviews. But here, she felt that in doing his history, things were going to get slightly more complex than usual. She would need to take contemporaneous notes as he spoke. When she returned, she settled into her chair with a yellow legal-size notepad.

He told her that the notepad was fine with him, that it wouldn't at all interfere with his telling her about his background. She explained that she needed to know his entire past if she was going to try to rid him of this serious nervous disorder which was so disrupting his everyday life. He needed to be totally candid. Holding a blue ink pen, she told him, "Let's start from the beginning."

He just sat there for several moments, and then began shrugging and twitching uncontrollably. He told her that he was sorry but that he couldn't stop himself. She assured him that it didn't bother her and to just start talking.

He began, "I'm not sure if I was born in California or Nevada. It was either in Oakland or someplace near Reno, Nevada. My mother, she was a beautiful woman. Before I was born, she lived in Haight-Ashbury with two of her girlfriends. Both of them were very pretty, too. They had all grown up in the Bay Area, but none of them finished high school.

"My mother and her two girlfriends, when they were about eighteen, worked at a place called the Graduate Club, which, to my understanding, was some sort of a hangout located on Haight Street. It was a place where so-called intellectual, older men would gather at night to discuss the problems of the world, drink whiskey, do drugs, and hustle young girls if they so desired. My mother worked there as a hostess. She told me that some of the finest minds from the various academic institutions of Northern California would gather there.

Many of the men were professors from Berkeley, Stanford, and other area institutions, and she would often sit around and listen to them talk about various things that she never really understood. Most of these men were scientists. She told me that she basically served them drinks and made them sandwiches when they were hungry. There were other girls who worked there who were prostitutes. But, of course, she may have been lying to me; she may have just as well been one herself, for all that I know.

"My father was one of the men who frequented the club. He was a physics professor at Berkeley, and not just a regular physics professor. She told me that he was a candidate for the Nobel Prize back when she first met him. She claims that she fell in love with him, and they started seeing each other when he would come over to the club every week. According to her, he was a brilliant man, and he was very kind to her.

"She said that he wasn't a handsome man by any means; in fact, he was rather ugly. However, there was something about his intelligence which attracted her to him. But, he had a family. His wife, too, was a professor at Berkeley. They had three children and my mom said she knew he was never going to leave her. But he had an eye for youthful beauty, and his wife, though supposedly attractive when she was young, had lost her girlish looks as she grew older. Anyhow, he and my mom had an affair, and she became pregnant with me.

"When she told him that she was carrying his baby, he gave her money and told her to go get an abortion. But my mom refused. The same thing happened to one of her roommates with another Berkeley professor. She, too, decided she didn't want to have an abortion.

"My mother never really told me all the details about what happened next, but somehow, she and this roommate of hers ended up moving in with some group of people who lived across the bay in Oakland. They were some sort of a cult. There were two men who were the leaders. They knew my mom's and her friend's situation. They were aware that both of them were pregnant, and that the biological fathers were both college professors. My mom and her friend, they were pretty girls, but I don't believe these men took them in for any sexual pleasures. They gave them shelter, food, money, and a feeling that they were part of a family. They basically took care of them. I don't know what else happened in Oakland. I don't know if I was born in Oakland. I may have been. But, I may have been born in Nevada."

At this point Lucas paused for several minutes and Dr. Lombardi asked, "Are you okay, Lucas? Are you okay talking about this?"

Looking up at her, he said, "I've never really told anybody this whole story. I'm sorry if it's not totally clear, I'm doing the best I can. My mom told me all of this later in life, so I'm going on what she told me she remembered."

"Lucas, can I get you something to drink?"

He nodded, "Yes, can you get me a glass of water."

As she stood up, he was twitching uncontrollably. She left the room and returned, handing him a glass filled with ice water. Sitting back down, she asked, "Are you ready to go on?"

He continued, "Well, somehow my mother and this cult she joined, and by the way her best friend that I told you about earlier, her name was Betty; they all settled somewhere outside of Reno, Nevada.

"I can remember a little bit about my childhood. I recall me and Amy were always together. Amy was Betty's little girl. She was born near the same time as I was. She and I always shared a room, along with a boy named Agnew. I told you how Amy and I got there, but I don't know how Agnew did. The three of us were always in this same little room together. It was like a fort. We had mattresses on the ground, and there were blankets and clothes in this room. The only time we were allowed to leave the room was when one of the men in charge came and got us. My mom and Amy's mom, and I guess Agnew's mom, all slept in another, like, fort. And the men in the cult, they had three or four forts. Their forts were about an eighth mile from ours. There were seven or eight men in the cult.

"We didn't go to school, but the men would quite often take us to one of their forts and teach us things. I remember this one man, Rudolf, he taught us how to read and to do arithmetic. He taught us things almost every day. When he taught us, if we didn't know the answers to his questions, he would hit us with a cane. I always knew all the answers and Amy did also. I guess that was because our fathers were so smart. But Agnew, he had learning problems of some sort and he used to get hit with the cane all the time. Rudolf would hit him hard on his back, and his butt, and his legs, and Agnew would scream in pain. There was nothing Amy or I could do to stop Rudolf. Agnew was beaten all the time."

"Did your mother ever help at all in your education?"

"No, the women never helped us with our learning."

"What else do you remember about your childhood, Lucas?"

"Well, Rudolf and some of the other men cult members would take us out into the woods where, I guess, I can remember back to when I was about five years old. They would bring us little animals, sometimes rabbits, sometimes kittens or puppies, and we would be forced to stand around a big wooden chopping block. They would put one of the little animals on the chopping block, and for example, would tell me and Amy to hold the animal down, and then they would give a butcher knife to Agnew and tell him to cut the animal's head off while we held it down.

"Sometimes, Agnew and Amy would hold the animal on the chopping block and I'd have to decapitate it. Amy, when it was her turn to do it, she would cry, and I remember she would never do it until one of the men would hit her with a stick on the back of her neck. Then she would do it. We killed lots of little animals. I don't know why they wanted us to do this so much. It was like they didn't want us to have any feelings. It always bothered Amy to slaughter these animals and it bothered me sometimes, but Agnew for some reason seemed to enjoy it. I remember there would be times we'd go out to the woods to play, even when the men weren't around.

If Agnew would see a little bird, he'd grab it, and then snap its neck back. I don't know why he would do this; he just did."

Shaking her head sideways, Dr. Lombardi said, "It's close to five o'clock now, Lucas. You told me a lot today. Let's knock it off and meet back tomorrow around the same time."

Standing up, he asked her, "How much do I owe you?"

"Nothing. I told you when I saw you at the stadium that I was going to help you. You don't owe me anything."

"Thank you," he mumbled as he headed out the door.

He felt very tired and drained as he walked outside. Walking very slowly, with his knees banging against each other, he headed towards Baltimore Street. Not hungry for dinner, he turned into Boots, sat at the counter, and ordered a Jack on the rocks. There was a beautiful girl dancing in front of him, but he never even looked at her. He just sat with his head down, sipping his drink. He couldn't stop twitching. After ordering a second, third, and fourth drink, he finally left. Stumbling back to his hotel, he went straight to his room. There, he got out a bottle of Jack and started chugging from it until he finally passed out.

He didn't wake up until two o'clock in the afternoon the following day. Heading straight to the bathroom, he started to violently brush his teeth, brushing with more force than he had ever used before. He started to feel that terrible pressure from within his head, so he began tapping his right elbow on the bathroom mirror. It made the awful feeling go away. Then he took a shower, got dressed, and headed out for the day.

He started the long journey to Dr. Lombardi's office, stopping at a diner where he ordered a sandwich and a drink. When he arrived at her office, the receptionist told him to follow her back to the same room he had been in the day before and to have a seat on the same couch. There, he patiently waited for Dr. Lombardi.

Several minutes later she came in and sat in the same chair she had the day before. She smiled at him. He had never seen her smile; it appeared she was happy to see him. She seemed like she really wanted to hear the rest of his story. She asked how he was doing, and he told her,

"Not so well, but I'm ready to go on."

"Okay, go ahead."

"I think I left off yesterday telling you what they made us do to the little animals. Last night, I tried real hard to think back. There were some things that I didn't tell you. These men in the cult, they were some sort of Germans. They had all grown up in Germany. They all had accents. I remember they had distinctive German accents, and even to this day, some people ask me if I'm from Germany because I learned how to talk around these men. I still have some hint of a German accent even though I've tried to get rid of it over the years.

"Rudolf, I told you he taught us reading and math. He also taught us German history. He displayed great joy in teaching us that subject. He taught us more of that than American history. I remember the leaders in the cult were always telling Amy and me that we were far superior to other people.

They told us that we were smarter and, because of that, we were superior. They told us that intelligence meant everything.

"I also remember at nighttime that we would hardly ever leave our fort. It was me, Amy, and Agnew in our fort every night. I remember we weren't allowed out unless one of the men came to get us and took us out. We would usually just sit in our room and look out the window at the stars. Sometimes we would talk about the lessons we were taught. We had lots of books to read before it turned dark outside. Amy and I read all the time. But, once it was dark we couldn't read anymore. We didn't have electricity in our fort, or running water.

"I never once brushed my teeth my entire childhood. Now I do it every chance I get. I'm addicted to it." He paused. "Anyhow, getting back to what we were talking about."

Hesitating, he looked down at the floor as he continued, "Sometimes we would talk about our mothers. We didn't see them often. We would see them occasionally, but they were gone most of the time. We never knew where they were. I would sometimes ask my mom where she would go all the time, and she would just tell me that she went to work. I'd ask her what she would do at work and she would just say that she cleaned people's houses. Amy's mother told her the same thing, but they were gone all the time at nighttime, and we wondered whose houses they were cleaning so late at night.

"When I got older, my mom told me the truth. It wasn't until I was in college that she told me that these men had forced her and Betty to work in a bordello not that far from where we lived. She told me that they would work as prostitutes and were brainwashed to give all their money to the men of the cult. They worked for years as prostitutes, and Amy and I never knew. I told you my mom was beautiful when she was young, and so was Amy's."

Dr. Lombardi was shaking her head back and forth as Lucas was telling her this. She said, "Your poor mother!"

Lucas looking at her, nodded, but didn't say anything. He paused for several minutes, then went on. "Another thing which I think is important to tell you is that at night, Rudolf and Leon, he was another one of the cult men, would sometimes come to our fort and take either Amy or Agnew off with them. I remember that usually they would just take one of them, but occasionally they would take both of them. They never made me go with them.

"I remember Amy coming back many times, and she would be crying. And I remember her being scared some nights, and she would be bleeding from her private parts. I remember sometimes giving her a towel to stop the bleeding. We didn't have a bathroom or sink in our fort, but there was a running stream of fresh water behind our fort, and I remember going with her to get some water to put onto the towel on some nights. I would ask her what happened to her and she wouldn't ever tell me. I knew what they were doing to her, and I knew that they scared her. They told her that if she told anybody, they would kill her. I remember Agnew many times being taken away, and when he came back, he, too, would be crying. He told me that his butt hurt and there would be blood coming from it. Sometimes Amy and I would walk with him to the stream where we would put some water on a towel so that he could clean up the blood from his butt."

Dr. Lombardi asked, "How old were Amy and Agnew when this started happening?"

Lucas paused, "We were all about the same age. We were eight or nine, the best that I can remember, when Rudolf and Leon started this. It went on for a few years. It didn't happen every night, but it happened like once a month or so. They seemed to have enough time for their bodies to heal in-between the times when they were taken away at night."

"But they never took you away at night, Lucas?"

"No, I was basically ugly, like I still am today. I was fat, flabby, whatever. Amy, she was a pretty little girl, and Agnew was a handsome child, very lean, well-built. The men desired them, not me."

Dr. Lombardi asked, "Did you or Amy ever tell your mothers what was happening?"

"No, we were too scared. But, when we were all around twelve years old is when we got our revenge; that's when it happened. We knew that Leon and Rudolf lived in the same fort; it was the closest one to ours. We heard them one night carrying on. They were drinking heavily. We could hear them outside of their fort. They were very, very drunk; I mean, they were wasted. I remember some man in another fort screaming at them to be quiet and to go to sleep. They both went inside, but we could still hear them. Then it became silent. We waited an hour or so and then quietly got up from our mattresses.

"Me, Amy, and Agnew. Agnew and I each had butcher knives. Amy was scared. Agnew and I were, too, but not as much. We knew what we had to do. We had it all planned. We quietly crawled to their fort. Amy then slid open their door and looked back to us and nodded. That told us that both Rudolf and Leon were fast asleep. If they had been awake, she would have gone in and started crying to them about something, and we would have retreated back to our fort.

"Anyhow, Amy backed away from the door, then Agnew and I crawled in. I got behind the pillow where Leon was sleeping and Agnew stood behind Rudolf. Both of them were asleep on their backs. We looked at each other, and at the same time lifted our butcher knives with both hands two feet above our heads, and then simultaneously, with as much force as our bodies could muster, plunged those knives into the windpipes of both of those Nazis! I distinctly remember the feeling of my knife cutting straight through Leon's neck. I remember pulling it towards myself as I cut through the bone and tissues of his neck.

"Then I looked over at Rudolf. Agnew had totally severed his head from his body. I looked up at Agnew; he had this big grin on his face. We had just murdered these two mean motherfuckers. Excuse me, I mean these two Germans. It was a cold-blooded killing, but these two guys needed to die for what they did to Agnew and Amy. Plus, the way we did it, there was no sound, no screaming, nothing. It was fast and quick, just like they taught us how to do those little animals I told you about.

"We quickly got out of their place, and Amy was standing there. I remember she was crying. She didn't see what had happened to Rudolf or Leon, but she knew what we had done. I remember she was wearing a blue dress. Her knees were shaking. Her long, blonde hair was dangling to her waist. She looked frightened to death.

"We didn't know what to do, so we just ran. We ran away into the darkness of the night. We ran and we ran and we ran. It seemed like I had extra energy because I never got tired. I must have been pumped up with adrenaline or something. It seemed like we ran all night long, and I remember Amy, she stayed up with us. And I remember the look on her face; she looked so tired and afraid. We were all so afraid.

"We knew that if we got caught by the other men from the cult, they would kill us. And we were afraid, of course, of anyone else finding out we had just committed these two murders. But we had no idea where we were running to."

Lucas paused for several moments and then continued, "I remember that we came across some railroad tracks. We saw about a mile away from us, a long row of railroad cars. These cars weren't moving, they were just still. We ran all the way 'til we reached them. We had never seen a train; we had read about them in our books, but we never knew that they'd be so big.

"This wasn't a passenger train; it was a freight train. Some of the boxcars, I remember, carried large amounts of steel in them. These cars were open on the top. But one of the boxcars was closed on top. We slid open a door on the side of it. There were lots of car and truck batteries in this car; it was half-full of these batteries. We climbed inside, all three of us, and we just slid the door shut. We left it open an inch or so to be able to get air. It was dark in there, but we felt safe. We were thirsty; we hadn't had anything to drink all night. I'll never forget how thirsty I was sitting in that boxcar. We whispered to each other, wondering where this train was going. It didn't move for at least thirty or forty minutes, but then it started to lurch forward. I remember holding Amy's hand as it started to shove off."

Dr. Lombardi then interrupted him, "Lucas, let's stop here for a second. I want to go back and ask you some questions."

She hesitated and then asked, "Do you know exactly how old you were when this incident happened?"

"I remember I was around twelve, maybe almost thirteen."

"Do you remember when you were growing up in that cult, if you had much interaction with your mother?"

"No, I hardly ever saw her. She was one of the women at the complex, just like Amy's mom, but she seldom did things with me. She never made dinner. Well, sometimes she would help the men in preparing dinner. On occasion, we would all eat together, but we hardly ever did so. Usually one of the men would just bring food to our fort and leave it for us to eat. We ate lots of fish and vegetables, and tons of rice."

"Do you recall if your mom ever hugged or kissed you?"

"No, never. My mother never kissed me, she never hugged me. Leon and Rudolf taught us that any showing of affection was a sign of weakness. I never even wanted to hug or kiss my mom. The only affection I ever felt was for Amy because she looked so scared all the time."

"Did Amy's mom ever show her any affection?"

"No, never."

"During this time, did you children ever go anywhere, for instance, shopping, or go out to any restaurants?"

Shaking his head, he answered, "No, we didn't even know what a restaurant or store was when we were growing up. I remember there was nothing near where we lived except mountains, trees, animals, and streams. We would wander off and hike in the mountains. I remember when it used to snow; it snowed a lot in the winter. It would get ice cold. We had some heavy jackets to sleep in, and we would also wear these same jackets when we went out in the snow. I remember when I was nine, I got a new one. It was so warm, I wore it all the time. I loved that jacket. One of the men had given it to me. Amy, Agnew, and I would all play together in the snow. We would have snowball fights, and we would bury each other in it. So when thinking back, hiking and playing in the snow are my best memories of that time."

"Did you feel bad after you killed Leon?"

"No, I didn't feel anything except scared that we might get caught. It wasn't any different than the times I had to kill the little animals. It was the same type of feeling. I didn't feel too guilty at all. Those men were cruel to Amy and to Agnew, and they needed to be killed.

"Looking back now, I think both of them would have been proud of us for the lack of feeling we had when we executed them."

"Do you feel any guilt today for what you did to them?"

Staring straight into her eyes, he answered, "No."

She then looked away, and asked, "What happened with the cult members when they found out that Rudolf and Leon had been murdered?"

"Well," he continued, "I found out many years later that the other men just took them and buried them. You see, this cult was an anti-government group, and they weren't going to bring in the government or police to try to solve their problems. They knew that we had killed them, but they knew that we were gone. They also knew that we could survive on our own, all three of us. They knew how mentally tough we all were. They didn't want to find us and bring us back to the cult. We had shown them that we didn't agree with the type of existence they were living."

She asked, "Where did the train finally take you?"

"The train ride was long and noisy, and it was very tough for us. We were in that damn boxcar for probably four hours.

Then the train just stopped! I remember we edged open the door to look outside and we saw all these hills, and we saw buildings, and we saw smoke in the sky. We didn't know where we were, but it turns out we were in South San Francisco. It's an industrial town, south of San Francisco. We all got out of the boxcar and started walking.

"We saw roads. I remember even seeing a freeway with lots of cars driving on it. I had never seen real cars. I had read about them when we lived at the cult. Like I told you, I read a lot. There were all these books there, and I don't know where they came from, but I had read a lot of them. Rudolf had taught me to read well. I'll say that much about him. Anyhow, we walked up to the freeway and started walking along it.

"I remember, we were looking for a stream, hoping to get some water. I was exhausted, as we all were. We didn't see a stream anywhere.

"Then, I remember, a car, a big black car, pulled off to the side of the road and there was a pretty lady in it. She asked us where we were going. And we told her we were just walking, and that we were looking for a stream so we could get some water. She could tell that we were totally worn out. She told us to get in her car and she would drive us somewhere to get some water. She took us to a small store.

"At the time, we had never seen a store, or been in one, but I had read about them in books. She took us inside this store and bought each of us a can of Coke. At the time we didn't know what Coke was. I thought it was water, and I remember the lady opened the can for me, and I took a big gulp. I immediately spit it out; it was disgusting! I remember getting angry and telling the woman that I wanted water. I asked her what that crap was that she had just given to me. Amy and Agnew, they never tried their drink.

"The lady working at the store then took us into the back of the store and turned on something which I now know was a faucet. But then, I had never seen running water coming out of a wall, and I remember, she gave us each a paper cup. We filled these cups with this water coming out of the wall, and I remember how good it tasted. We drank a lot of it. She let us have all we wanted.

"The lady who picked us up in the car asked us where we lived. I remember, Amy told her that we didn't live anywhere. We had made a pact in the railroad car that we wouldn't tell anybody anything about us, except our names. We only had first names. I was Lucas, Amy was Amy, and Agnew was Agnew. We wouldn't tell anybody where we lived, what had happened where we lived, nothing. We had agreed that if anyone asked us any questions, we would say that we were just "here." We were afraid that if we told people anything about where we came from, they would find out somehow about the murders, and then we'd all be in big trouble.

"So we told this lady that we didn't live anywhere, and she told us that we must have parents somewhere, that we should tell her the truth, and she would help us find them. We told her that we had no parents, that we were just "here."

She kept questioning us, asking us where we lived. We told her we lived "here." We told her we just lived outside; we didn't live with anybody. So she said okay, and she drove off, leaving us outside of the store. Then fifteen minutes later, a police car drives up.

"We, back then, didn't know anything about the police, except what we had read in books. I remember these two police officers asked us the same questions that the lady had asked us. We gave them the same answers. They didn't believe us; they wanted to know where we lived. We told them we just lived outside by ourselves.

"Of course, the next thing we knew, they took us downtown in their patrol car to some juvenile detention center in San Francisco. They put us in some room, and a lot of people came in and started talking to us. They asked us questions about who we were, where we lived, who our parents were. Basically, they thought we were runaways, and they thought that they could get us to talk. But they didn't know how we were. They didn't know about the pact we had made on the train. I remember they separated us later that evening. A lot of people came to talk to me, just by myself, trying to find out who I was and where I came from.

"They brought in women to talk to me, religious people, even some other kids my age, but I wouldn't tell anyone anything. Eventually, they put all three of us back together, and I talked to Amy and Agnew, and they told me that they had been pretty much put through the same routine. They left us together in this little room all night, and in the morning they brought us water and food. These people were very nice to us. I remember the police coming in and taking lots of pictures of us. I remember them taking our fingerprints with lots of ink. I remember them making us open our mouths and taking pictures of our teeth.

"Then we were brought into some room and there was some man wearing a black dress, and there were lots of people around him. He was sitting high up in the air. He was an old man.

"That's what we were thinking at the time. Of course, now, I know that he was a judge, and the people around him were court personnel, and we went in front of him. At first, he was very nice. He asked us lots of questions, but he wasn't happy with the answers we were giving him as to who we were, and where we came from.

"He then picked up this wooden hammer and hit it on top of the wooden table he was sitting at. I remember, he raised his voice and tried to scare us into answering his questions. Amy, Agnew, and I all looked at each other and we knew that we weren't scared of him, and we knew we weren't going to give him any information. We were used to people trying to scare us.

"We refused to talk to him. He angrily ordered the policemen in the court to remove us, which they did. They took us to some holding tank in the building and had us sit there.

That afternoon these policemen walked us to another building.

"When we got there, they separated Amy from Agnew and me. We didn't see her for the next couple of days. They put Agnew and me in the same room. We each had a bed and we stayed in this room for a few days. A lot of people visited us. Some were police, some were social workers, some were doctors; I imagine that they were psychiatrists. These people asked us a lot of questions as to who we were, and where we were from, but we never told them anything. Finally, they brought us back to that judge.

"He was angry at us and I remember him ordering us to be taken to some orphanage until they figured out who we were and where we came from."

Dr. Lombardi commented, "You were some strong-minded children!"

Lucas nodded, "Yeah, they had no chance of ever breaking any of us down."

Dr. Lombardi, looking at the clock on the wall, saw it was five o'clock. "I'd like to keep going if you can, rather than break it off now. This was an unbelievable childhood you had. It's amazing what you went through."

Then Lucas told her, "I'd like to finish the background stuff tonight so that maybe you can start my treatment." Dr. Lombardi asked him to continue.

"The next thing I knew, we were all at some orphanage in San Francisco. We were there with about thirty other kids.

At first it was strange, but it was very nice compared to what we were used to. We had three meals a day: breakfast, lunch, and dinner, and the food was great. We had never had such good food. There was a room which had a television set. None of us knew what a television was until then. I watched movies and cartoons and game shows. I remember when I started watching sports on it, like football and basketball. At first, I didn't know what those games were. I liked the bright colors of the different uniforms worn by the players.

"The orphanage sent us to a public school. That's when they gave me the last name of Lustick. I had always been just, Lucas. The people at the orphanage said that I needed a last name since I was going to school. I don't know where they got Lustick from, but I've always used it for my last name. I remember that the kids all treated me badly because I was from the orphanage. I didn't have any friends in junior high. I went to classes where the teachers gave me books to read, and then they gave me tests. I remember I got perfect scores on all the tests they ever gave me. I don't think I ever missed a problem on any test they ever gave me. School was very easy for me.

"I basically hated all the other kids at this school. The girls, they were mean to me all the time. A lot of them were pretty, but all they cared about were their looks, and I was basically fat and ugly, so they didn't want to have anything to do with me. I also disliked all the boys at the school. I was alone all the time. But Amy, she did just great in this school.

She also made friends. Agnew, he didn't like it. He fought a lot of people. He badly beat up some kids."

"Did you have any social life whatsoever?"

Lucas shook his head. "None, and it never changed all through high school. I never had any girlfriends, not even in high school. On weekends I would just stay at the orphanage and watch television. I'd watch every football, baseball, or basketball game that was ever on. I was fascinated with these sports. I had never played them, but all I wanted to do was watch other people play them. I became obsessed with watching sports.

"I knew that I was too uncoordinated to play; I had tried in gym classes in school. So I became an expert in watching. I thought of becoming a football coach. I totally understand football better than anyone, just by watching it and reading coaching books that I've checked out from libraries. I should have become a football coach. I'd probably be coaching in the NFL now if I'd of gone that route.

"Anyhow, all three of us stayed at the orphanage until we finished high school. The high school was about two blocks away from the orphanage. I remember I had perfect grades and graduated early. I took the SAT test and got close to a perfect score on it.

"I didn't have any money to go to college, but a lot of schools were offering me full scholarships. I remember my high school counselor telling me that I could go to any college in the country on a scholarship. The same for Amy.

She was a straight-A student and she and I decided we'd go to the same college. We decided to stay in the Bay Area and attend Berkeley. It was a State school and the State would pay for everything. So when we were seventeen, we both left the orphanage and moved into dorms at Berkeley for our freshman year.

"Agnew left the orphanage, too, but he never went to college. He got a job somewhere in San Francisco. During my years in college I saw Amy quite often. Agnew, I'd see him occasionally, either at Golden Gate Fields or Bay Meadows, which were two horse tracks in the area. Golden Gate Fields was right in Berkeley, cushioned up against the Bay.

"I spent many afternoons at the track. I love horse racing. To this day it's my favorite pastime. I love the way it's each man for himself at the track. Each man can bet on whatever he feels like betting on. I remember Agnew, for whatever reason, used to love betting 2-8 as an exacta in almost every race. He would always bet 2-8, no matter who the horses were.

"Those have always been his numbers. I remember I started calling him, "2-8." I thought it was so funny that he always bet the number 2 horse to win and the number 8 horse to run second. But that was his right, the freedom of the racetrack, to do whatever the hell he wanted.

"Anyway, back to my days at Berkeley. I liked my classes. I majored in history. Read hundreds of books, maybe even more on history. I loved it. I graduated with a 4.0 and got a full scholarship to law school at Boalt Hall; that's the Berkeley Law School. Amy stayed at Berkeley also and worked towards her Ph.D. in molecular biology. She, too, got a full scholarship. I had no social life throughout college or law school. Never had a girlfriend. But I saw lots of hookers. I always thought that was the perfect trade-off, sex for money. It's been going on ever since the days of cavemen. I never wanted a full-time girlfriend. I don't know why I was like that; I still am.

"I remember the summer before starting law school, I hitchhiked to Nevada. I was looking to see if I could find the area where I had been raised. I remembered the forts we had lived in, and I knew they had been somewhere near Reno. I recall that I walked for two-to-three days all around these areas outside of Reno, but couldn't see any spots which I remembered from when I was a kid.

"I hitchhiked on some back roads and some trucker picked me up and told me that he was going to some whorehouse in the area. He said it was a legalized one. I told him I'd go with him. I had some money in my pocket. He drove up to this building which had a bunch of signs posted outside. They said something like, Bunny Ranch, so we got out of the truck, and the guy rang the doorbell, and then we walked into this building. A lady came out to greet us, and she looked to be close to fortyish. She was wearing a long black dress, and she told us that the girls would be out shortly, and to have a seat. I looked at this woman, and she looked right back into my eyes, and I knew just who she was. She was my mother.

And she knew who I was. I said to her, 'You're my mom.' And she said, 'Lucas!' It was so unbelievable!

"Then, all these girls came out wearing negligees and bathing suits. I remember the guy who gave me the ride, he pointed to one of the girls and said that he wanted her. I looked at the girls, but didn't desire any of them. I just wanted to talk with my mother. So, I told her that I didn't want to be with any of the girls. I just wanted to wait for the man to finish his business because he had given me a ride. I remember my mother dismissing all the other girls, and the guy who had given me the lift had already gone into the back with the girl he had chosen."

Pausing several moments, he continued, "It was just me and my mom in this big waiting room. She asked me what I was doing in Reno, and I told her that I had just come back to visit. I filled her in on everything I had been doing since I left the cult when I was little. She told me all about her life since then, and what she had been doing. We got along really well. We were both happy to see each other. It was like we were very close to one another. She was excited for me that I was in law school. She filled me in on what happened with the cult. She told me she knew that we had killed Rudolf and Leon, but she understood why.

"She told me all about my dad, all about who he was. This was when I learned that he was a physicist at Berkeley. This was when she told me about when she had met him at the Graduate Club. She explained to me about how she joined the cult with Amy's mom, all the things I told you yesterday, she filled me in on them. She told me how the cult men had forced her into prostitution at this brothel, and how she worked as one of the girls for many years. When the cult broke up, she stayed, and as she got older, the owner made her the madam.

"She took me back into some security room, and she was laughing about how much fun it was being a madam. She showed me that there was a hidden camera in the front room of the brothel which filmed any customer who came in through the front door. She told me that the patrons never knew that they were being filmed, and that she had thousands of pictures of men who had visited. She showed me pictures of some famous people whom I recognized. I saw the governor of California. I saw the NFL commissioner, and lots of famous actors and professional athletes. She thought it was cute that these men didn't know that she had pictures of them. I personally thought that it was bullshit that a man couldn't go there without having his picture taken by some hidden camera. I asked her if she took my picture when I walked in. She said, 'Yeah,' and showed it to me. There I was, standing in the front room at my mother's whorehouse!

"Anyway, about an hour or so later, the man who had given me the ride finished up with his girl and was back in the waiting room. I told my mom I was going to get a lift back to the freeway from him and would then hitch a ride back to California. She told me not to, and called me a cab. I told her,

'No, I'll hitch a ride,' but she said, 'No way,' that she would get me a cab and that she would pay for it. Anyhow, some cab driver showed up, and she gave him four-hundred dollars to take me back to San Francisco. I remember, she wanted my telephone number. I gave it to her and she gave me hers, and I left.

"When I was in law school, I visited her twice. Even to this day, she's still the madam at the same place. I visit her every two-to-three years. I never 'do' any of the girls there. I just visit her and we talk. We're good friends."

Dr. Lombardi then asked, "Lucas, what about your father? Did you ever meet with him?"

"No. I knew who he was. I never took any physics classes when I was in school so I never really had any reasons to go into his building."

"You were right there at Berkeley and never once wanted to meet your dad?"

"No. I'm not mad at him at all. In fact, I understand that he just accidentally got my mother pregnant. I knew that he had his own family, and I never wanted to make him feel uncomfortable knowing that I was a student at the university where he taught. I never had any bad feelings towards him.

"Law school was a breeze. I seldom went to lectures, but I graduated at the top of my class. I spent most of my time at the racetracks and gambling on football and basketball. I figured out a way to make money betting on these sports but don't want to go into it now. When I graduated, all the big law firms in California wanted me to work for them, but I just wanted to work for myself. Amy got her Ph.D. in three years and took a job down in Houston, Texas.

"Her fiancé at the time, Rickie, couldn't leave the Bay Area for another three weeks. She had no way to get to Houston, but I had a car by this time, so I drove her there. When we got down there, I decided that since she was going to be there, I'd stay also. So I studied for the Texas bar exam, passed it, and started practicing law as a criminal defense lawyer in Houston."

Lucas explained to her about his years in Houston and why he eventually left. She saw the anger in him when he talked about leaving Texas and giving up the practice of law. He told her about his years in Baltimore up to the point where he had met her. He looked at her and said, "That's it."

He was exhausted, and was twitching incessantly as he sat there.

Dr. Lombardi, looking at him, said, "You're a disturbed man, but at least we know why. As I am sure you know, you're suffering from what we call an obsessive-compulsive disorder. You twitch constantly, and you keep banging your knees together. In an attempt to avoid the pressure or tension within your head, what you're doing is yielding to these compulsions. You're giving in to such a degree that these compulsions have interfered with your being able to enjoy anything in your life. There is a medication which I want you to start taking which is made by Eli Lilly & Company. It is called Prozac."

She wrote out a prescription and handed it to him. "Take one twenty-milligram capsule every day. Hopefully, it will be disruptive to these compulsions of yours. It may take two-or-three weeks to start having an effect, but be patient. This drug has been very successful treating your type of disorder. I want to see you in four weeks to see if it's working."

She warned him of possible side effects and told him to contact her if he experienced any of them. Lucas slowly got up and thanked her for all of her help. He shook her hand and she gave him a warm smile as she walked him to the doorway. After leaving, he headed to the nearest pharmacy he could find. He had a good feeling about taking this medication, totally optimistic that it would work.

He started taking the Prozac that same day, and after two weeks noticed a significant decrease in his compulsive behaviors. He didn't twitch nearly as much, he stopped banging his knees together, and he no longer felt an urge to tap his elbow on the bathroom mirror. This medication had helped out more than he could ever have imagined. He was almost normal again.

On his follow-up visit, Lucas told Sarah that he wanted to pay her for her services, but she refused any payment. She was absolutely thrilled with his progress. Although he still twitched some, it was nothing like it had been a month earlier. She wrote him a prescription for another three months of the medication.

After leaving her office late that afternoon, he walked into a Chinese restaurant halfway between her office and his hotel.

After finishing dinner, he stopped at a bar on Baltimore Street where he enjoyed a beer. Then he walked back to his hotel, feeling great. He wasn't banging his knees together. Absent was that terrible pressure from inside his head.

When he got to the hotel, he waved to the desk clerk on his way to the elevator. The clerk yelled to him before he reached the elevator down the hallway, "Mr. Lustick! You had a telephone call."

Lucas was startled. Nobody had ever called him, he had no friends. He assumed that the clerk must have been mistaken. He walked back to the front desk, and the clerk repeated, "You had a phone call. I took down the person's name and number. Here it is."

He handed the piece of paper to Lucas. Pulling it up close to his eyes, he could see the call was from Rickie. There was a Houston phone number scribbled on the paper. He remembered having sent the hotel's phone number to Rickie when he had first arrived in Baltimore. *Why would Rickie be calling?*

In his hotel room he placed the call immediately.

"Hello," Rickie answered on the other end.

"Rickie, it's Lucas. What's up?"

"Mikey, he's in big trouble! He's seventeen now. He's a special education student in high school. Several months ago, he got caught delivering some cocaine for some boys he knew. He did it because he wanted to fit in. He's set for sentencing this

Friday, and John O'Reilly is his judge. I hired him a good lawyer, but I remember that you and O'Reilly used to be real close."

Lucas stopped him, "That's enough. I'm coming down in the morning. I'll take the first American Airlines flight out of Baltimore. Pick me up at the airport, downstairs at the baggage claim area. Okay?"

"Okay," Rickie answered. "I'll see you there."

After hanging up the phone, Lucas just stood there. He thought about how Dr. Lombardi had helped him when he was in need. Now, he could help someone in return—not a stranger, but instead, Amy's boy!

FIFTEEN

After riding an escalator down to the pick-up area, Lucas scanned the entire floor looking for Rickie. Finally, he saw him, and the two approached one another and shook hands. Rickie had aged considerably. Lucas could tell that life hadn't been easy.

The first thing Rickie said was, "I can't tell you how much I appreciate that you've come down here."

Lucas didn't respond. The two started walking towards the parking garage. Rickie then asked what he had been doing all these years.

"I've been taking it easy. Been living in Baltimore, Maryland, ever since I left. I go to the horse track every day. Live by myself. Basically, I'm just letting the years pass until I die."

"Are you practicing law in Maryland?"

"No, I've stayed away from the law. Gave it up way back when I left Texas."

Rickie then inquired, "Are you married?"

"No, of course not. What about you. Did you ever get remarried?"

"No. Ever since Amy died, I've done very little dating. I've had no interest in falling in love again."

Lucas nodded and then asked, "What about Mikey? What happened?"

By now the two had reached Rickie's BMW. Rickie opened the trunk and Lucas placed his suitcase inside. As they drove out of the garage, Rickie quietly said, "Mikey is in trouble. He's in some serious trouble." He then was silent.

Lucas said, "Go on. I need details."

"Well, you remember Mikey when he was little? Remember something wasn't right with him?"

"Yeah, I remember."

"As he grew up, he had severe learning disabilities. Never understood things in school no matter how hard he tried. I've hired some of the best tutors that I could find, but something in his mind just doesn't click. No matter how hard he tries, he has very limited abilities. He's been in special-education classes ever since elementary school, but he's not retarded; he just has learning problems. Besides that, he's had a series of other problems growing up. He's afraid of the dark, and he's afraid of heights. He has a severe fear of being in closed-in places."

Lucas remembered back to the day of Amy's funeral when Mikey was trying to open the casket after it had been placed in the ground. He wondered if that, maybe, had something to do with his being claustrophobic.

Rickie went on, "Mikey has never had any real friends. He's always wanted to have some. He would do anything to fit in. Anything, if he thought it might help him make some friends. That's been a big problem, especially since he became a teenager. That's how he got into this trouble."

As the two were driving down Highway 45 towards downtown Houston, Lucas interrupted him and asked, "Will you drop me off at a hotel?"

"You don't have to stay at a hotel," Rickie replied. "You're more than welcome to stay at my place. I've got a big house with plenty of room."

"Thanks, but I'd rather stay in a hotel. I'd be more comfortable there."

"Okay, I'll drop you off at one of the nicer ones near the Galleria."

Lucas then asked him to continue about Mikey.

"Some boys who were athletes, you know what I mean, jocks, at his school, arranged to sell some cocaine to some other boys who they thought went to another school across town. The boys had made arrangements to sell their cocaine for two-thousand dollars to these other kids. It was to be a simple transaction whereby the buyers would come to the school parking lot, and the deal would be done there. The jocks got Mikey to carry the cocaine to the parking lot, and he was supposed to give it to these boys who would, in return, give him the two-thousand dollars. He would then bring the money back inside the school and give it to the jocks.

"Mikey wasn't going to get anything out of it; he was just doing these other boys a favor so that they would like him. That's how he is. Like I said, he would do anything to have friends. He didn't realize these jocks were just using him. Anyhow, it turned out the boys who were supposedly from the other school were actually undercover narcotics agents from the DEA. They arrested Mikey in the parking lot at his school."

"Oh shit," Lucas mumbled.

"Lucas, it's the worst thing that's ever happened to me. It's as bad as when Amy died. I didn't know what to do, so I hired a lawyer name Russell Smith. He's supposedly the best criminal lawyer in Houston. He was an assistant DA for ten years before going into private practice. He's been working on the case for the last three-to-four months."

"I remember him from when I was down here," said Lucas. "He was a prosecutor then. He was alright. What I recall of him, he was a 'Texas boy' all the way. Went to UT for college and law school. He knew what he was doing when he was a prosecutor. What's he doing for Mikey in his case?"

"He told me that the case was a slam dunk for the prosecution. Said there was no chance that we could win if we went to trial. So last month, he had Mikey enter a plea of guilty before the judge, who, like I told you over the phone the other night, is John O'Reilly. I understand that he's a real tough judge, especially on drug cases."

"That fucking O'Reilly finally made it to judge?"

"Yeah," answered Rickie. "Anyhow, Mikey is going to be sentenced by him this Friday. It's a first-degree felony that he is charged with. O'Reilly can give him anything from probation up to life in prison. We're hoping that he gives him probation because of the circumstances."

"Where's Mikey now?" asked Lucas.

"He's in school. He's terrified about going to court. He's a very timid boy; you'll see when you meet him. He's five-eight and only weighs a hundred-and-twenty-five pounds. Has no self-confidence. He's just plain scared to death about going to court this Friday. That's why I called you, Lucas. I don't know what you can do to help, but I know that you and O'Reilly used to be real close. If there's any way you can talk to him, I would deeply appreciate it."

At this point, Rickie pulled into the parking lot in front of the hotel, and the two just sat in the car.

Lucas told him, "Just leave me here and go pick up Mikey from school, then bring him back here to visit this evening. I'll talk to him and then I'll go visit O'Reilly in the morning. Sentencing is not until Friday, is that correct?"

"Yes."

"Today's Tuesday, right? Rickie nodded, "We've got time." The two shook hands and Lucas strolled into the hotel.

He walked up to the front desk and asked the clerk for a room.

She inquired, "How many nights do you need?"

"I'll be leaving Saturday morning."

"Do you have a credit card, sir?"

"No, I don't."

"How are you going to pay for your room?"

"How much will a room cost through Friday night?"

"Five-hundred-and-twenty-four dollars."

Lucas reached into his pocket and pulled out the exact amount in cash, which he handed over to her. She handed him his room key along with a receipt.

After entering his room, he walked over to a large window and looked outside. It was beyond all belief that he was back in Houston, Texas. He remembered the terrible times he had experienced years back. His old pal, John O'Reilly. He thought back to when they used to hang out together during their law school days and as young lawyers. He recalled when they bet horses together, and when they were involved in fixing football and basketball games, and even when they did prostitutes together.

What would John be like now? After all, he was now The Honorable John O'Reilly. Did he still bet on football games? Did he still do whores? Was he as pompous as he was when he was an assistant district attorney? Lucas figured that he probably stopped participating in all of his vices once he became judge. John had always wanted to be a judge, and certainly would know that the only way to actually lose his bench would be if he were caught in some sort of illegal gambling or prostitution situation.

Lucas wasn't surprised to hear that John had a reputation for being a very harsh judge on drug cases. He remembered that John was that way back when he was a prosecutor. However, it didn't overly concern him. He knew that John would pretty much do as he asked in Mikey's case. Lucas Lustick was not one to ask people for favors. But here, he was going to ask John to sentence Mikey to probation. It would be the only time in his life that he ever asked John to do something for him.

Walking over to the television set, he turned it on. There was a mid-afternoon news flash, live from the Houston Astrodome, about the rodeo. On the screen was a bull rider being thrown off a bull. Lucas thought, *Fuck this cowboy shit*, as he turned off the television. Next, he walked into the bathroom and turned on the shower, staying in it for nearly an hour.

After getting dressed, he sat in a chair and just stared out the window for another hour or so. It felt strange being back in Houston. Deep down to his core, he still hated Texas. He wasn't in town to enjoy anything. He had come only because he wanted to help Mikey.

Amy crept into his mind. His chin dropped to his chest when he thought about her. He had visions of her as a little girl, when they were like brother and sister. He wondered if she had lived longer, whether she would have made great discoveries as a scientist. He thought of taking a cab over to the graveyard where she was buried, but decided not to.

As the evening approached, he phoned downstairs to the front desk, informing the clerk, "I'm expecting guests this evening. When they arrive, just tell them which room I'm in and send them upstairs."

About an hour later, there was a knock at his door. Jumping up, he opened it, and standing there were Rickie and Mikey. The first thing he noticed when he looked at Mikey were the sad, brown eyes. Staring closely, he saw how much he still resembled his mother. He told both Rickie and Mikey to come inside and be seated on his bed. Turning his chair towards the bed, he sat down and asked Mikey, "Do you remember who I am?"

Mikey shook his head, "No."

Lucas told him, "I knew your mother very well. I grew up with her. She was like my sister. I've known your mom and dad from way before you were born."

As he was talking, Lucas was thinking how frail Mikey appeared. His hair was cut even with his ears. It was soft and wispy-looking, falling onto his forehead. The bone structure of his face was feminine for a boy. His body-build didn't appear to be that of a seventeen-year-old, but rather what you would expect in an eleven-year-old. Lucas knew that there would be no way this young boy would ever survive in a Texas prison; he would be eaten alive.

He then asked Mikey to tell him exactly what happened when he got into trouble. Mikey started shaking. He was terrified even before saying a word. Lucas told him, "You're safe here. Just be calm and tell me what happened."

Mikey started crying. He held his hands out, gasping for air; tears were freely falling from his eyes. Rickie wasn't sure what to do, so he put his arm around him and tried to comfort him.

Mikey then screamed, "I'm sorry, Daddy! I'm sorry, Daddy!" He cried for several moments before finally calming down. He was simply worn out.

Rickie told him to just lie on the bed. Sweating profusely, he curled his knees up to his chest and put his head on a pillow. Rickie kissed him and said, "Just rest."

He then asked Lucas to step out into the hallway. There, he told him, "Mikey can't talk about the case; it's too upsetting to him. You can see how immature he is. He's afraid that he may have to go to jail. He's never been away from me in his life except when he's with Sarah, our nanny. I've worked very hard to protect him. He's my whole life! I've been his whole life! If we were separated, there's no way he could make it."

Lucas nodding, told him, "There's no way he could survive in prison."

Rickie asked him, "Is there anything you can do to make sure he gets probation?"

"I'll go talk to O'Reilly tomorrow. I feel there's a ninety-nine percent chance he'll get probation. John surely won't send him to prison."

Legal Vengeance

Rickie then asked, "Before you meet with him, do you think you ought to talk to Russell Smith?"

"No, I don't need to talk to him. I am sure he's doing everything he can to represent Mikey. What I'll be doing is something he can't do. I'll be talking to O'Reilly, not as a lawyer, but as an old friend. I totally believe that John will do what's right in this case. Mikey is obviously in no condition to go to prison. He doesn't have the use of all of his mental faculties. Trust me, I'll see to it that John does the right thing on Friday. Don't even tell Russell Smith what I'm doing. He doesn't need to know about it."

Rickie then extended his hand, telling Lucas how grateful he was that he had made the trip to Texas to help out. The two reentered the room, and Mikey was still lying on the bed. Rickie grabbed his hand and helped him get up. Lucas took his other hand and held it with both of his. Mikey looked right into his eyes, as Lucas assured him that everything would be fine on Friday. Mikey asked, "Do you promise?" It was the type of question that Lucas would expect from an eight-year-old, not a seventeen-year-old.

Nodding, he told him, "Yes, I promise." Mikey seemed to force a smile. Lucas again thought to himself how much he looked like Amy when she was a child.

Lucas told Rickie, "If there are any problems tomorrow, I'll call you. Otherwise, I'll see you in court on Friday."

Rickie and Mikey left the room and walked towards the elevator. Lucas shut the door behind them, opened his suitcase, and pulled out a bottle of bourbon which he finished off. Finally, he turned in for the night, knowing that he had an interesting day ahead.

SIXTEEN

Lucas stepped out of the cab on the corner of San Jacinto and Preston and just stood there. An awkward-looking figure, he was dressed in a pair of black slacks and a wrinkled, white button-down shirt. Totally unshaven, he wore neither a tie nor belt. His black penny loafers were in need of a good shining. He appeared to be some common criminal who had been dropped off in front of the courthouse to attend his court hearing.

Standing on the corner, he watched the front entrance to the courthouse. It was eight-fifty in the morning and lots of people were rushing to get inside the building. Everybody needed to make it to their courts by nine o'clock. Lucas focused on the ones carrying leather briefcases who looked comfortable wearing their suits. He figured that these would be the lawyers and wanted to see if he recognized any of them from when he practiced law. There were men and women, some old, some young, but not one person looked familiar to him.

He remembered the days when he, too, rushed to get into this building. It seemed like it was so long ago. But now he just stood still and watched. There were clerks, bailiffs, judges, prosecutors, defense lawyers, and probation officers who worked here everyday. There were citizens charged with committing the same types of crimes with the same motives as when Lucas had practiced law. There were killers, sex offenders, druggies, thieves, and drunken drivers. Nothing had changed since he left, except for the faces. If nature allowed it, he could come back in two-hundred years and things would still be the same.

He thought back to how fine a lawyer he had been as a young man. He remembered fighting for the rights of his clients. But all that meant nothing now. Today, Lucas Lustick was just some beaten-down old man standing in front of 301 San Jacinto. He realized that he meant nothing to anybody, well, except to Mikey. No doubt, Mikey was counting on him. He'd help him, and then head back to Baltimore.

Finally, he decided to enter the courthouse. It was past nine and the traffic into the building had slowed considerably. Once inside, he walked through the lobby and stepped into one of the four elevators. He asked the elevator operator which floor Judge O'Reilly's court was on. She told him, "The sixth," and then she pushed the button and they headed upwards to the sixth floor. As he stepped off, he saw four huge walnut doors, each one leading into a separate courtroom.

He opened the one which had a sign above it, reading, "Judge John O'Reilly, 189th District Court."

The spectator part of the large courtroom was filled with people sitting in wooden rows of seats, separated by a railing from that part of the courtroom where defense lawyers and prosecutors gathered to discuss cases. Lucas looked around the large room and then focused upon the judicial bench where John was sitting, wearing a black robe. At first sight, John looked practically the same as he had years earlier except that his hair was now gray.

Lucas didn't stare at him and wasn't sure if John even recognized who he was. Walking to his right, he sat in the last row of seats in the courtroom. There, he watched the lawyers and prosecutors in front of him carrying on their everyday business. Occasionally, two of them would approach the bench and engage John in conversation about some case. Lucas couldn't hear what anybody was saying.

After nearly twenty minutes, he noticed that John was staring at him. Maybe he had finally recognized who he was. Lucas looked back at him. He could tell that John was trying to be sure it was him. Lucas figured that he was probably ninety-percent sure who he was, but not one-hundred-percent. If he were absolutely sure, then he would have definitely waved to him to approach the bench. But he would feel stupid if he called him up and then realized that he had called up a stranger.

That's the way John had always been; afraid of making mistakes, fearful of looking stupid. So he kept glancing to the back. Lucas thought to himself, *Maybe John's hoping it isn't me. After all, he's wearing the black robe he always dreamed of wearing. I've got lots of dirt on him from our younger days. He's probably wondering where I disappeared to, and why I'm suddenly back in town.*

Lucas finally just waved at him. John now knew who he was and motioned for him to come up to the bench. Lucas stood up and started walking forward. As he passed by the lawyers, they all stared at him, wondering who the hell he was. Nobody from the audience would ever dare approach this judge unless accompanied by an attorney. John O'Reilly ran the most formal courtroom in the county.

The three young prosecutors assigned to the court all stopped what they were doing and crept towards the bench so that they could hear the conversation between Judge O'Reilly and this awkward-looking man. They watched John stand up and lean forward, extending his right hand to Lucas. With a big smile on his face, he greeted him, "Lucas, after all these years, it is so fine to see you."

Lucas, shaking his hand, told him, "It sure has been a long time."

In a strange way Lucas was happy to see that John had succeeded in life. Years earlier he had been angry with him for not visiting him while he was incarcerated. But time had a way of healing old wounds and that seemed to be the case. He no longer felt much anger towards him.

"Where have you been, Lucas?"

"I've been living in Baltimore, Maryland, for a long time, ever since I left Texas. I haven't been doing much, just getting by. What about you? It looks like you've done good for yourself."

John shrugged, "Life has treated me pretty well over the years. I really can't complain." He continued, "Lucas, come by my chambers, in the back, around noon. We break around then. That will give us time to catch up."

Lucas answered, "I sure will." Then he turned and slowly walked out of the courtroom.

The three prosecutors, bursting with curiosity, all immediately approached John. "Judge, who was that guy?" one of them asked. Each of them was grinning. They had never seen their judge act as he just had. They had never seen him smile. He was never so informal in the courtroom. Everyone knew him as a tough, prick-of-a-judge, who was never friendly to anyone. He had always been unapproachable to them and to everyone else. But now, having seen him act so differently in greeting this old, degenerate-looking man, they seized the opportunity to attempt being personable with him. But the Honorable Judge O'Reilly would have nothing of it. He didn't like them gathering in front of him asking questions. Though he knew he didn't owe them any answers, he gave them one anyway.

"His name is Lucas Lustick. Practiced law way back when I did. Back when y'all were at home cuddling with your mothers, he was down here trying lawsuits. Lustick was a real trial lawyer, an old-school lawyer, by far the best I've ever seen. He'd kick every one of your asses in trial if he was still in the business. Absolutely hated prosecutors! He'd chew you up and spit you out before you ever knew what was happening! And there wouldn't be a damn thing any of you could do about it."

All three prosecutors now had a look on their faces as if they were sorry they had asked who the stranger was. Walking away from the bench, they started working out their cases with the defense lawyers.

When the noon hour hit, Lucas walked through a door which led him into the back hallway behind the courtroom. He walked slowly until he came upon a closed door with a sign on it which read, "Judge John O'Reilly's Chambers." He knocked on the door and heard John yell out, "Come in." Entering the room, he saw John sitting behind a huge desk, still wearing his black robe. Lucas sat down on a couch directly across from him. He told him, "O'Reilly, why don't you take off your robe? It looks ridiculous on you."

John didn't immediately answer him, appearing surprised by the comment. Biting down on a toothpick, he said, "I prefer to wear it even when in chambers, out of respect for the office."

Lucas just looked at him, nodding his head. It seemed to him that John was acting quite arrogant. Evidently he was dead serious about wearing his robe. No doubt, John O'Reilly was still the same prick he had always been. Lucas told him, "I'll just get down to business with you. There's only one reason I'm back in Texas."

John interrupted him, "I know why you're here." He paused and then went on, "You're here for the sentencing of Amy's boy, that little retard, 'Mikey something.' I've got to sentence him this Friday. You're here to help him, aren't you?"

"Yeah, that's exactly why I'm here. I'm here to ask you to give him probation on the case. I met with the boy last night. It's apparent to me that he wouldn't make it long if you sent him to prison. He'd be killed; he's not tough enough. He was Amy's only child, and I don't know how he got himself into this mess, but I'm asking you to place him on probation instead of sentencing him to prison. That's all I'm asking."

John stood up and slowly walked towards a large Texas flag which was hanging in the corner of his office. He said, "The people of this county elected me to fairly administer sentences in criminal cases arising within this jurisdiction. I will sentence the boy to what I think his proper sentence ought to be. As you know, Lucas, it's improper for you to be back here talking to me about any case. I feel very uncomfortable with you coming back here trying to sway my judgment on a case currently pending on my court docket."

Lucas looking him square in the eyes responded, "I'm sorry, John, that you feel this way. I don't mean to make you feel uncomfortable, but you and I did a lot of illegal shit together when we were young. Don't be getting so ethical all the sudden. I'm just asking you to grant me this one favor. I haven't practiced law since I left Texas. It's real important to me that the boy receives some sort of probation in his case."

Getting up, Lucas walked over to where John was standing near the Texas flag. Neither man was in any mood for small talk. Lucas simply shook his hand, thanked him for his time, and then turned around and walked out. After leaving the courthouse, he grabbed a taxi ride to his hotel. John's demeanor didn't totally surprise him. He was as arrogant as Lucas had feared he might be. However, he felt pretty sure that he would give Mikey probation in his case. He felt that his message had gotten through.

He got back to his hotel and called Rickie to let him know about his meeting with John. He told him that everything went relatively well and that he was sure that Mikey would be given probation at his sentencing that Friday.

Rickie seemed very pleased and told him that he didn't know how he could ever repay him.

"You owe me nothing. Just take care of Mikey when he starts his probation."

Rickie asked if he needed a ride to the airport.

"No. I'm going to stay in Houston and attend the sentencing on Friday. It would be better if I'm in court."

Deep down, Lucas had some bad vibes from his meeting with John. He didn't feel one-hundred-percent positive that John would actually give Mikey probation. He felt ninety-nine-percent sure, but there was a slight chance of John double-crossing him. He figured that by appearing at the sentencing, John would be pressured into giving probation. His showing up would make it one-hundred-percent certain.

Rickie said "Lucas, let's go to dinner tonight."

"No thanks, I'm just staying here at the hotel. I'll see you and Mikey in court on Friday. Tell Mikey that Uncle Lucas will be sitting in the back of the courtroom."

Rickie again told him how grateful he was for all his help and hung up the phone.

Lucas then dialed downstairs for a bellhop. One arrived at his room several minutes later and Lucas gave him forty dollars and told him to go buy a fifth of Jack Daniel's. The young man left and returned thirty minutes later with the Jack and a large cup of ice.

Staring out his window he realized how much he still hated Texas. Pouring some Jack Daniel's into his cup, he held it up to his nose. It had a beautiful smell to it. He finished off the whole bottle and by midnight had passed out.

He didn't wake up until one-thirty, Friday morning. He was still wearing the same clothing he wore when he had met with John. Everything was wrinkled. Walking into the bathroom, he looked at himself in the mirror. His eyes were bloodshot, his skin pale. Reaching for his toothbrush, he squirted toothpaste onto it, and started brushing his teeth. Taking off his clothes, he tossed them on the floor as he stepped into the shower, ducking under the spraying water.

He loved the feeling of the hot water pounding onto his head; it helped soothe his bad headache. After nearly fifteen minutes in the shower, he dried himself off and got back into bed. It was still dark outside. Unable to sleep, he just layed there and waited for the sun to rise.

Shortly after seven, light oozed through the drapes. Getting up, he put on the clothes which he had earlier thrown onto the floor. He went back into the bathroom and started brushing his teeth again, spitting the toothpaste back into the sink with such force that it splattered all over the mirror. He felt extremely tense for whatever reason, and his head started twitching even though he was taking his medication. Something about being back in Houston really upset him. At eight-thirty, he went downstairs and hailed a taxicab.

The cabbie dropped him off in front of the courthouse. He knew he looked very untidy; however, he had no other dress clothes to wear. Besides, he was just going to sit in the back of the courtroom. After entering the building, he rode the elevator up to the sixth floor. Quietly entering the courtroom, he grabbed a seat in the back row. He saw Mikey and Rickie sitting in the first row with an attractive dark-haired woman whom he assumed was the nanny. The same three prosecutors who had been in the courtroom earlier in the week were all standing in the attorney's area, holding files and speaking with defense lawyers. John had not yet come into the courtroom.

Lucas watched all the chaos which was going on, thankful that he was no longer a lawyer. He kept looking towards Mikey and Rickie to see if they noticed he was there. Rickie turned around and spotted him. He winked at Lucas and nudged Mikey on his arm as he whispered something in his ear. Mikey then turned around and saw him, too. He couldn't hide his excitement as he waved to Lucas with a big grin on his face. Uncle Lucas would see to it that he wouldn't go to prison. Lucas smiled back at him. Mikey then turned around and sat quietly with his father.

It was well past nine-thirty when the bailiff announced John's entry into the courtroom. Everyone else stood up, but Lucas just sat there. He wasn't going to rise for John O'Reilly's entry into the courtroom. One of the bailiffs noticed that he had not risen. The bailiff walked over to him and told him that he was supposed to stand up when the judge entered the courtroom. Lucas just stared at him. The bailiff then asked, "Did you hear me?"

Lucas still didn't respond.

The bailiff said, "I guess you're just a deaf-mute," as he walked away from Lucas.

John called his prosecutors to the bench and asked whether any of them had any jury trials which they were prepared to start that afternoon. One of them told him that he wanted "to go" on a theft case. John asked whether or not the defense lawyer associated with the case would be available. The prosecutor told him that the lawyer had announced "ready" prior to his taking the bench. John told one of his bailiffs to be sure that a jury panel would be available after lunch.

He then asked his prosecutors if they were ready to proceed on any other matters scheduled for that morning. The chief prosecutor, Scott Heck, told him that there was a case set for sentencing that morning. He told him that it was a drug case and that the lawyer representing the defendant was present in the courtroom. John told him to ask the lawyer to approach the bench. Scott walked over to Russell Smith, who was sitting in the corner of the courtroom, and asked him to approach the bench with him. The two did so, and John greeted Russell. He asked if he was ready to proceed on his client's sentencing. Russell told him that he was.

In a loud voice, John announced, "I now call the case of *The State of Texas versus Michael Kassell* to come before this court for sentencing. Will the parties now approach the bench?"

Lucas was watching all of this from the back of the courtroom. He saw Russell Smith get Mikey and Rickie to have them approach the bench. A bailiff stopped Rickie and told him, "Go sit down! Only the defendants are allowed to appear before the judge for sentencing."

Mikey looked visibly upset that his father couldn't come with him. Lucas could see the tears rolling down his cheeks.

He had expected that his father would be with him when he had to go before the judge. He didn't want to do it alone and appeared frightened.

Lucas angrily approached the bailiff who was now standing next to the railing that separated the attorney section from the spectator section of the courtroom. He told him, "Let that boy's father stand next to him. The boy's got some mental problems."

The bailiff angrily replied, "Sit down, or your ass is going to jail! Don't tell me how to run this fucking courtroom!"

Lucas had thoughts of decking him but decided against it. Instead he just sat down. For some reason he felt very agitated in this courtroom. He felt a certain anger when he saw the flag of the State of Texas hanging from one of the walls in the courtroom. Coming to Texas basically brought out the worst in him. He wanted John to just hurry up and sentence Mikey to probation. Then he'd be able to leave this godforbidden place and go back to Baltimore.

From where he was sitting he could see Mikey standing directly in front of the judge. On one side of him stood Scott Heck, on the other side, Russell Smith. Lucas thought that Scott Heck appeared to be pretty laid-back. He didn't look like an overly aggressive prosecutor. Lucas watched Russell Smith, who in his late forties seemed very polished. He looked more like a civil lawyer rather than a criminal one. It was obvious to Lucas that Russell wasn't a street-fighting lawyer, but rather a well-connected mouthpiece who was capable of getting good deals from judges and prosecutors when his clients pled guilty.

John asked, "Are both sides ready to proceed in this sentencing hearing?"

The prosecutor and Russell Smith simultaneously answered, "Yes sir."

"Very well, we will proceed at this time." Peering down from the bench, John focused in on Mikey, who stood directly in front of him. He paused for several seconds before beginning the hearing. Lucas watched him from the back of the courtroom. He knew that John was thinking to himself that standing before him was Amy's boy. It wasn't just another person who had committed a crime; it was Amy's boy. Lucas knew that John wouldn't do anything to harm him.

John then looked at both attorneys and asked if everything he had reviewed in the pre-sentence report was correct.

Russell Smith nodded his head and told John that the report was accurate. Scott Heck then told him that he had no objection to the report.

John then asked, "Does either side have any argument at this time?"

Russell Smith spoke up, "Yes sir, Judge. I am asking this honorable court to place my client on probation. He is young, and as you are well aware from the pre-sentence report, he has had a lifelong history of psychiatric problems. He has been a special-education student his entire life. He has grown up without the benefit of having a mother. His father, Rickie

Kassell, is a prominent civil lawyer here in Houston and is more than willing to assist him in taking upon the challenge of probation.

"I know that the court has reviewed the psychiatric records, which are attached to the pre-sentence report. I'd like to highlight to the court a section in the records, which pertain to my client having been diagnosed with, and to be currently suffering from, an acute case of claustrophobia. To lock him up in prison would be a torturous hell to him.

"My client has shown great remorse for having been involved in the commission of the offense to which he has pleaded guilty. He realizes that what he did was wrong, and I can assure this court that he will never again get into any trouble. I am asking that you find that it's in the best interest of society and of this defendant, that he be placed on some sort of probation. I have nothing further to say, and I thank you for your consideration in this matter."

John then looked at Scott Heck and asked him if he had anything to say.

He looked back, and shrugging his shoulders said, "Judge, I've reviewed the pre-sentence report and have no objection to this young man receiving probation. I believe that he is a good candidate for it."

Lucas was surprised that Heck didn't even ask for penitentiary time. This being a drug case, a lot of prosecutors would have. He thought that Scott was totally cool in telling

John that probation was fine by him. This meant that there was no pressure put on John to send Mikey to prison.

After Heck spoke, John paused for several seconds. He looked down at Mikey and asked him, "Young man, are you ready to be sentenced?"

Mikey nervously answered, "Yes sir."

John then stated, "This court has heard all the evidence and has reviewed the pre-sentence report before it. I have a very difficult decision to make. I view the crime you have committed as being very serious in nature. I find trafficking in narcotics to always be very serious. Your fine lawyer has presented mitigating circumstances as to why I ought to grant you probation. Many people have come forth on your behalf. This case is very difficult for me as a judge. I am elected by the people of this county to make decisions on cases like this one." He then paused. He remained silent for the next thirty seconds. Finally he spoke, "I hereby sentence you to fifteen years in the State Penitentiary in Huntsville, Texas. Do you have any reasons why this sentence should not be carried forth?"

Mikey started screaming, "No! No! No!" He kept screaming as he fell to his knees. He was trembling before the bench.

John yelled to the bailiffs, "Lock him up!"

Two bailiffs came up from behind and grabbed Mikey under his shoulders and started carrying him to the holding cell behind the court. He was screaming as they were doing so.

Rickie ran up to him but one of the bailiffs stopped him, angrily telling him, "Get away from here or you're going to jail, too!"

Rickie turned around and walked back to the spectator section of the courtroom where he made eye contact with a stunned Lucas, sitting in the back row. Walking back to him he desperately asked, "What do we do now?"

Rickie was sweating profusely and seemed to be in shock. Lucas didn't answer him; he just looked down at the ground. A million things were going through his mind; he had never been so angry. Lucas finally told him that there was nothing which could be done right then, and for him to talk to Russell Smith about appealing the court's sentence.

At that point, Rickie turned and walked up to Russell, who also appeared bewildered. Lucas watched Rickie and Russell Smith whispering to one another.

Lucas finally stood up and walked out of the courtroom into the hallway where he stood for several minutes pondering what he was going to do next. He was beside himself with anger. He wanted at that moment to kill John O'Reilly. Walking into the men's restroom, he looked at himself in the mirror. After hitting the mirror with the palm of his hand, he spit into it. Pacing around the bathroom, he was talking to himself, calling John a "motherfucker," and saying, "The bastard needs to be killed."

Pushing open the door to the bathroom, Lucas walked back into the hallway, his anger escalating with each passing moment.

He kicked his foot into the floor and clenched his fists. Never had he been so angry.

He walked through the door which led into the back hallway behind the courtroom. Heading straight to John's chambers, he saw John still wearing his black robe. Rushing in, he stood a few feet away from him and yelled, "You're a motherfucker!"

Then he pulled his arm back and punched John squarely in the nose. John had not anticipated the punch. His knees buckled from beneath him and he hit the ground hard. He came to, dazed, holding his face as blood gushed down onto his hands. He screamed, "Help! Help!"

Lucas then kicked him as hard as he could. Two bailiffs rushed into the chambers. They grabbed Lucas from behind and slammed him into the wall. One of them grabbed his ears with both hands and kept banging his head into the wall. His forehead was cut open and blood poured down his face. Other bailiffs came to assist, but they were not needed; Lucas had surrendered. He knew he was going to jail. He had momentarily lost control of himself, but now he had settled down. The deputies holding him sensed that he was no longer combative. They removed him from the judge's chambers.

The prosecutors from the courtroom were now standing outside John's chambers. They were curious to see what had happened. Scott Heck walked in and asked if he could be of any help. John told him, "I think he broke my nose, but I'll be alright. Just make sure that the crazy bastard gets charged, and see to it that his bond is so high that he can't get out."

Scott asked, "Judge, why did he do this to you?"

"I guess he was pissed that I didn't give that 'little shit' probation in his case. Fuck him. I don't need any kid like that on probation in my court."

The deputies took Lucas to process him into the county jail where he was charged with assaulting a public servant. Bond was set at one-million dollars. He was booked in just like any other inmate. He would be housed on the sixth floor in the regular population. He asked to be taken to the medical floor to obtain treatment for the lacerations to his forehead, but his request was denied. He was placed in a tank with sixteen other inmates. There were only twelve beds there, which were already taken. He was given a blanket and a pillow, which he placed on the floor in between two of the beds. This would be his quarters for as long as he was in this county jail.

Most of the inmates in the tank were younger. He didn't actually fit in; nobody talked to him. He made eye contact with a few of the prisoners, but he went no further than that. He just stayed in his spot on the floor and stared up at the ceiling. He couldn't believe that he had sucker-punched Judge John O'Reilly, but he was glad that he had even though he was now going to have to do some time. The last time he was incarcerated, he was housed in solitary. This time he was in the general population. The men in his tank seemed to be a fairly quiet bunch; they weren't too rowdy. Most of them just sat there reading books or watching a black-and-white television set which was set up in the tank.

At six o'clock the local news came on, and there he was, bigger than Dallas, smack right across the television screen. The feature story was on how he punched out Judge John O'Reilly. There was no mention that he was a disbarred lawyer or that he had known the judge from the past. The news portrayed him as a disgruntled family member of a criminal who had thought that the judge was too harsh on sentencing. It told how he slipped undetected into the judge's chambers and attacked the judge.

Once the story finished, Lucas was accepting congratulations from the other criminals in his tank. He suddenly was a very popular inmate. Nobody there liked Judge O'Reilly. He was known as, "Maximum John." One of the inmates told Lucas that he wasn't sure, but he'd heard that O'Reilly had even sent his own grandmother to prison. Lucas told everyone, "O'Reilly has been a prick his whole life and that's why I leveled him."

Everyone roared with approval. He'd leveled Maximum John with a solid right to his face. One inmate asked, "How did it feel?"

Lucas smiled at him, "It felt great!"

That evening, around eight o'clock, a guard came and told Lucas that he had a visitor. Opening the door to the tank, he told him to step out. Once he did so, the guard told him to turn around so that he could handcuff him. Lucas complied and the guard escorted him to the part of the floor that was set up for visitation; then, into a small room where he removed the handcuffs. Closing the door, he locked Lucas in.

Lucas sat on a metal chair inside of the room. It was very uncomfortable, but at least there was something to sit on. In the tiny room there was a window with three metal bars across it. On the other side of the metal bars were some old plastic chairs which were there for visitors. Lucas sat for nearly ten minutes just staring out from inside the tiny room.

Then Rickie appeared, dressed in a suit. He was being escorted by a guard who showed him where to sit. The guard advised him, "You cannot pass anything back and forth with the inmate. If you do so, you will be banned from any visitation in the future."

The guard then left, and Rickie stuck his hand in between the bars to shake hands with Lucas. He told him, "I'm surprised that there isn't glass between us and that we don't have to talk on some telephone."

Lucas told him, "That's how it normally is at visitation. But since you're a lawyer, they brought you to this room where lawyers get to meet their clients. Even though you're not my lawyer, I guess they're extending you the courtesy of meeting me in this booth, which is pretty decent on their part." Lucas paused, then asked, "How's Mikey?"

"I don't know. I came up here to visit him. He's staying on the third floor. They told me I couldn't see him right now; they said that he was being checked out and I should go back to his floor in about an hour. So I figured I'd come visit you."

"Thank you. I appreciate it."

"Lucas, what happened between you and O'Reilly?"

"That motherfucker pissed me off so much I just laid into him. I'd of killed him if I'd had a gun. He's a double-crossing motherfucker!"

"Lucas, you were doing me a big favor coming down here. I feel bad that you got yourself into this situation. I'm going to hire a lawyer to represent you."

"No, no, no. You're not hiring me a lawyer. Under no circumstances are you going to hire me a lawyer. I'm just going to take a court-appointed one. That's all I want, some court-appointed motherfucker. Don't send me some lawyer; I won't use him."

"Why not? Don't you want to get out of here?"

"Yeah, I want to get out, but I can sit for awhile. I'm going to do some time; I know that. Let me deal with this by myself. Is that clear?"

"Okay, Lucas, I'll adhere to your wishes. But, if at anytime you change your mind and you want a hired lawyer, you let me know and I'll get you a good one."

Lucas looked down to the ground and then back up at Rickie. He asked, "Can you do me a big favor? Please call this number I'm going to give you."

Rickie pulled out a pen and scratched the number on a piece of paper he pulled from his pocket.

"Joseph ought to answer the phone. He works the desk where I live up in Baltimore. Tell him that I got into some trouble down here in Texas and that I won't be back for awhile. Tell him to go into my room and throw everything away that I have, just toss everything out.

"Tell him to rent out my room, and convince him I'll settle up with him for what I still owe for this month as soon as I can. I would really appreciate it if you could do that for me."

"It will be done in the morning." Rickie just sat there for several moments. He then asked whether he thought Mikey had a chance in appealing the sentence.

Lucas paused, and then answered, "I haven't practiced law down here in a long time, but my gut reaction is that there's nothing you can appeal. That motherfucker O'Reilly, he just simply fucked us. But talk with Russell Smith; if there's anything that can be done, he can try to do it."

At that point two men walked up behind Rickie. Lucas looked up. One was a deputy, the other one was dressed in a black suit. He looked like he might be a jail Chaplain; there was a peaceful look to him. He didn't appear to be in law enforcement.

The deputy asked, "Are you Rickie Kassell?"

Getting up from his chair and turning to face them, he answered, "Yes, I am."

The deputy then asked if he would please come with them. Rickie quickly turned back to Lucas and said, "Remember what I told you about a lawyer. I'll call that number in Baltimore you gave me. If you need anything else, here's my card, call my office collect. If I'm not there, just tell my secretary what you need." He then shook Lucas' hand, turned around, and walked off with the two men.

Lucas just sat there in the small holding cell. Several minutes later he heard screaming which sounded like it was coming from somewhere on the floor. It was a loud scream of, "No! No! No!" As loud as the screaming was, it was muffled to some extent. But, then again he heard the same, "No! No! No!" cried out from somewhere. He wasn't certain where it was coming from. It could have been an inmate who was in a fight. Maybe it was somebody receiving some sort of medical treatment. But he feared that it could also be Rickie after hearing some bad news from the two men who had come up to talk with him. He just sat still, but he heard nothing further.

Finally, thirty minutes later, a deputy came and opened the door to the visiting room. He told Lucas to put his hands behind his back and to turn around so that he could be cuffed. He did so, and while the officer was cuffing him, asked, "What was all that screaming about a few minutes ago?"

"That's none of your business. Come with me. You're going back to your tank."

The deputy then escorted him back to his tank where he unlocked the door and pushed him inside. He locked the door from behind and then stuck his hands through the bars and removed the handcuffs.

Lucas asked the other inmates if they had heard screaming on the floor. They all responded that they had not. He then sat down on his blanket and didn't talk to anybody. A million thoughts were going through his mind. *What was all that screaming about?* He tried convincing himself that it was just some inmate. But, he was worried that it had been Rickie. He just sat there until the news came on at ten o'clock.

First there was the lead-off story, then another story, and another. Lucas felt relieved that there weren't any reports about anything bad happening at the jail. But, then after the first commercial, there stood a newswoman, appearing live, in front of the Sheriff's department. She reported that earlier that evening, a young inmate had hanged himself in his cell. Next, a booking photograph of Mikey appeared on the screen. Then, the station went on to another story.

Lucas just sat, staring down at his blanket. He grabbed it with both of his hands and with all his strength, tried ripping it apart. But any strength he had possessed was now somehow zapped from his body. He sat there in total confusion. It was unbelievable; Mikey was dead. Other inmates tried talking to him, but he was in a catatonic state, oblivious to those around him.

SEVENTEEN

Lucas lay on his blanket all night, never closing his eyes. At five o'clock in the morning, two deputies screamed, "Everybody up!" Several jail trustees brought breakfast plates for the inmates. Everybody stood up to get one, except Lucas, who never moved. After the inmates finished eating breakfast, they started taking turns using the two toilets and two sinks which were located in the back of the tank.

Even then, Lucas never got up to brush his teeth. He looked over at the sinks and thought about it. There were new toothbrushes still in their boxes lying near the sink, and there were tubes of toothpaste. But he didn't get up. He just couldn't.

He was thinking of Mikey. *Being locked up in this jailhouse must have terrified him. The fear which he experienced prior to killing himself must have been awful.* Lucas wiped away the tears descending from his eyes. He knew that Mikey would be buried this day because Jews bury their dead right away. Thinking of Amy, he saw her in his mind. Surely, Mikey would be buried right next to her. However, he wouldn't be able to attend the funeral since he was here in jail.

He wondered how concerned John O'Reilly was about Mikey having killed himself. Having once been close to Lucas, John would know his feelings about retaliation. He would know that this wasn't the end of the story. Mikey's death at some time, in some fashion, would be dealt with one way or another. Lucas was thinking of simply having John killed. He thought of the different ways it could be done.

His thoughts again focused on Mikey. He envisioned his casket being placed above the earth right next to where Amy was buried, and a rabbi chanting prayers about his death. He envisioned Rickie and the other mourners shoveling dirt on top of the coffin, and poor Mikey flat on his back in the ground, knowing that he had escaped serving fifteen horrible years locked up in the state penitentiary.

After a while, a deputy came into the tank and yelled out his name to go to court. Lucas got up from the floor and walked over to him. The deputy handcuffed him and led him out of the tank. They both walked down a long corridor and got into an elevator, which they rode down to another floor where the deputy then led him to another hallway. Once at the end of this hallway, he was cuffed to a large group of inmates. The group was then escorted by several deputies across the street from the jail to the courthouse. There, they all entered into an elevator which took them up to the eighth floor, where they were taken behind the 140th courtroom. There, the deputies unlocked everybody's handcuffs and locked everyone into a holding tank.

There were at least thirty inmates in this small holding cell. There wasn't enough room for anyone to sit or lie down; everyone had to stand straight up. Lucas was squashed between four other inmates. There was a lot of chatter, which was very irritating to Lucas. Finally, a deputy came back and shouted into the tank, "Court is starting! Everyone in here needs to shut the fuck up!"

The noise subsided temporarily, but before long it got loud again. Occasionally, a deputy would come and take one of the inmates into the courtroom to appear before the judge. Lucas was waiting his turn. Eventually, an overweight gentleman wearing a blue sports coat came back to the holding tank and called out, "Lucas Lustick!"

Lucas looked at him and held his hand up. Lucas then shouldered himself through several inmates so that he could stand in front of the iron bars, where he could talk to the man.

He told Lucas, "My name is Jimmy Pitts. I'm your court-appointed lawyer. Do you know what you've been charged with?"

"I think assaulting a public servant or something of that nature."

"That's close enough. Basically you're charged with decking Judge John O'Reilly. It carries two-to-ten years in prison. The prosecutor thinks that O'Reilly is a prick, so he's willing to reduce your case to a misdemeanor assault if you're willing to do one year in the county jail." He looked at Lucas and continued, "That's a great deal. You need to take it."

"Do you want to know why I hit him?"

"I don't really care why you hit him. I've got a lot of cases to handle today. Do you want to take this deal for a year in the county jail or do you want me to reset your case? And I'm warning you that if we reset your case and go to trial, you'll get the maximum, ten years in prison. You can't just whack a judge and not expect to get the max if you go to trial. You better take the year on a misdemeanor."

Lucas hesitated, not saying anything for several moments.

Finally, Pitts told him, "You've got thirty seconds to take this deal or I'm just going to reset your case. You could come back in a month or so and get ten years in prison. I don't give a fuck what you do! It's your decision."

Lucas quietly told him, "Bring me the plea papers."

Pitts disappeared back into the courtroom. About fifteen minutes later, he reappeared holding several sheets of paper which were stapled together. Holding them up in front of Lucas, he told him, "These are your plea papers. Sign on the line on the last page."

He then handed Lucas the papers and a pen. Lucas started reading them, but Jimmy Pitts stopped him. "I don't have fucking time to stay here while you read every word on all of these pages. I'm your lawyer. By signing these papers, you're admitting that you're guilty of assault. You're getting a plea bargain, and a damn-fucking-good one at that. You only have to do one year in the county jail. You're not even convicted of a felony. You're only getting a misdemeanor, and you ought to be damn grateful to me for that!"

Grabbing the papers from Lucas, he flipped to the last page and told him, "Just sign right here!"

Lucas knew that he was getting a pretty good deal, so he signed where Jimmy Pitts told him. Pitts then grabbed the papers and the pen from his hands and left to go back into the courtroom.

Within minutes a deputy came and got Lucas from the holding cell. He led him into the courtroom where he stood in front of a judge by the name of Doyle Halpert. On one side of Lucas stood Jimmy Pitts, and on the other side stood the prosecutor, a middle-aged, gray-haired man.

The prosecutor looked at him and whispered, "I just want to let you know that for whatever reason you punched out O'Reilly, it made my day."

Judge Halpert looking down at Lucas asked, "Mr. Lustick, how do you plead to the charges brought against you of assault?"

"Guilty."

"I hereby sentence you according to the plea agreement to one year in the county jail." Lucas was then taken by a deputy and placed back into the holding tank. He stayed there until noon when he and the other inmates were brought back to their tanks in the county jail.

There he sat down on his blanket, his mind buried in deep thought. He thought about his court-appointed lawyer, Jimmy Pitts. He didn't even care why he had punched out O'Reilly. But the deal for one year in jail was pretty good. It kept him from being convicted of a felony, and it kept him from going to the state penitentiary. He knew that he could handle the county jail—it was like a camp.

The state penitentiary, on the other hand, would have been a totally different story. There, he knew he would've been housed with hard-core criminals, guys who were serving life terms for offenses such as murder, rape, and robbery. Everyday there, he would have to fend for his life. Here in the county jail, he would be doing time with petty criminals, guys who were in for drunken driving, stealing, assault, things of that nature. Here, he knew that he could apply for a job, maybe as a kitchen worker, a maintenance man, or even as a barber. Before he knew it, his time would be up.

That evening, a jail supervisor, Gina Gilbert, asked Lucas if it was true that he was at one time a criminal defense lawyer.

"It is," he answered.

She then told him that the law library, which was down on the third floor of the jail, needed a librarian to work there. "It's a seven-day-a-week job, and the hours are nine to nine."

Nodding his head, Lucas let her know that he was listening.

Gina continued, "We have one of the best law libraries of any jail in the state. Inmates are allowed two hours a week in the library if they so desire. I'd say about twenty-five percent of the population here takes advantage of this privilege.

"If you accept this job, when these guys find out that you used to be a lawyer, they're going to be asking you to help them in their various legal dilemmas. Some of them are really smart on the law, and some don't know their asses from a hole in the wall. It will also be your responsibility to keep all the books and journals updated. It's a tough job being the law librarian, but it can be very rewarding."

Lucas liked the idea. Slowly nodding his head, he told her, "I'll take the job. When do I start?" She told him that someone would be by his tank in the morning, right before nine o'clock, to bring him down to the third floor. He could start working right away.

The following morning, at five minutes before nine, a deputy got him and brought him to the law library. There, the deputy unlocked the door, and Lucas entered. The library was in a small room without any windows. There were two wooden tables, each surrounded by four wooden chairs. On these tables were legal pads, pens, and pencils. The only lights were those which hung from the ceiling above the two tables. There was a set of *Southwestern Reports* which cited every case ever published in Texas. Other law books and journals were available to assist inmates pursuing various aspects of their appeals.

During the next twelve months, Lucas became very involved in helping inmates perfect their appeals. He researched law which helped in the appellate courts of the State of Texas and in the federal courts. When he had practiced law, he had been a trial lawyer, mainly fighting cases in the courtroom. He was never interested in the appellate process, always believing that appeals were handled by bookworm-type lawyers.

Now, he was fascinated with appellate law. He loved assisting inmates in appealing their cases. He read every book in the library which had anything to do with appeals. He could always be found in the law library. He ate his lunch and dinner there and often counseled inmates as he was eating. He became totally obsessed with appellate law, putting all his heart and time into learning it.

His only visitor during the year was Rickie, who first visited him several days after Mikey's funeral. The first thing he told him was that Mikey was laid to rest right next to Amy. Rickie was as depressed a man as Lucas had ever seen. The dark circles under his eyes indicated that he hadn't been sleeping. Lucas feared that he might take his own life, but Rickie was tougher than that. Over the months, he totally dedicated his life to working long hours at his law firm. He visited Lucas every few weeks, trying to give him moral support. He also saw to it that he was taken to the psychiatric section of the jail each month so that he could be administered the Prozac which he so desperately needed. Lucas enjoyed Rickie's visits even though the two men had such different lifestyles. They had suffered together over the years.

The one-year jail sentence went rather quickly. Before he knew it, Lucas was putting on the same clothes he wore the day he had punched out Judge John O'Reilly. A female deputy walked him to a metal door and pulled it open. She told him, "Good luck out there!"

Lucas stepped outside the jail; it was morning, the air was crisp. He looked around for a cab but didn't see one. Not sure which way to start walking, he headed down Franklin Street. There was a dark-blue Cadillac coming towards him on the opposite side of the street. The car pulled up on the curb right next to him. The driver stopped and got out. It was Rickie, who had a big smile on his face as he walked up to Lucas.

Lucas asked, "What the hell are you doing here?"

"I knew you were getting out this morning, so I came to pick you up. This is your car. I bought it for you."

Lucas looked shocked. Nobody had ever bought him anything before.

"You didn't have to do this."

"I know I didn't have to, but I wanted to. Just get inside and drive me home."

Lucas jumped in and closed the door; Rickie got in on the passenger side. They drove off. "Do you remember where I live?"

"I remember your part of town, but when I get into your neighborhood you're going to need to give me directions."

"Lucas, look in the back seat." There sat the same suitcase which he had traveled to Texas with a year earlier.

"How did you get my fucking suitcase from the hotel?"

"When you went to jail, I went to the hotel and they gave me your stuff."

"They just gave you my things?"

"Well, I presented them with a Power of Attorney where I signed your name giving me permission to take possession of all your property at the hotel."

Lucas just laughed, thinking it was hilarious that Rickie, as straight as he was, would forge his name to a Power of Attorney. But he sure appreciated it. This way, at least, he had some clothing to wear.

Rickie asked him what his plans were now that he was out of jail. He was surprised when Lucas told him that he planned on getting his law license back and staying in Texas.

"I really enjoyed doing appellate work while I was the jail librarian. I'm going to specialize in appellate cases only. I'm not going to do any trial work; I'm too fucking old. But my mind is still sharp. I'll beat those bastards in the appellate courts."

"Can you make any money appealing cases for criminals?"

"I don't know," he answered, "but I've got plenty of money in my bank up in Maryland. I don't need the money; I just want to help guys who were fucked over by the government. Did you know that there are over five-hundred men on death row in this redneck state? I bet at least fifty of them aren't even guilty. They're stuck with court-appointed appellate lawyers who don't give a damn about them. They're just waiting to be executed by this backwards, fucked-up State of Texas. It just pisses me off. I'll represent them all for free."

"I think it's very noble on your part to work for free, but isn't it a waste of your time? It's my understanding that death penalty cases aren't ever reversed by the higher courts."

Lucas didn't answer him.

Rickie then told him, "I know that if any lawyer can get one reversed, it's you, Lucas."

As they were entering into his neighborhood, Rickie gave him directions on how to get to his house, and then said, "You can stay with me as long as you need to."

"Thank you. I'd like to stay with you for a few days before I return to Baltimore to close my account and take care of a couple of things. Do you know a lawyer who can help me get my law license back?"

"There's one I know of. His name is Victor Adams. I'll call him and make an appointment. The word is that he's got connections with the State Bar folks and supposedly can get anything done."

In the house, Rickie opened the refrigerator and asked Lucas if he wanted some grapefruit juice.

"No thanks, but I'll take one of those bottles of Budweiser I see in there."

"It's kind of early for drinking beer, don't you think?"

"I've been locked up for a year in that hellhole. It's not too early to have one."

"I guess you're right. Here you go."

Lucas opened up the bottle and sitting at the kitchen table, started pouring it down. Rickie sat next to him, drinking a glass of orange juice. Then Lucas called Victor Adams' office and made an appointment for three o'clock that afternoon.

Lucas got up from the table and walked into the den. There, he saw pictures of Amy and Mikey. He remembered some of them from the last time he had visited. That was back when Amy was still alive. Now there were a lot more pictures of Mikey on the walls. It was apparent how important Mikey was to Rickie. There were pictures of them in various places all around the world. There was one in Disney World; one in New York City; one in front of the Palace in London; one next to the Eiffel Tower in Paris; there was one of them white-water rafting somewhere in Colorado.

There was a picture of Mikey running in the Special Olympics. Another was of him competing in the long jump. Next to these pictures were two silver medals. Rickie, who had come into the den, pointed to the medals and told Lucas how proud Mikey was after he had won them. Lucas could see the pain in his eyes when he talked about Mikey. The fact that Mikey had mental disabilities had made his and Rickie's relationship that much closer.

Rickie started talking about the funeral. "It was the saddest day of my life; sadder than when I buried Amy. It was much worse when it was Mikey's turn. I can't describe to you the pain that comes with burying your only child. I was so numb that I didn't even notice who was there and who wasn't.

There were a lot of people there, but I couldn't talk to any of them. I just remember the rabbi saying the prayers, and then we shoveled dirt onto his casket. He was put to rest right next to Amy. I buried him holding a picture of her in his hands."

Lucas could tell that it was time to stop talking about Mikey because Rickie couldn't handle it, so he changed the subject. "Whatever happened to that nanny who worked for you?"

"Oh, Sarah ... the poor girl took it really hard when Mikey died. She went into shock—she collapsed right here on this floor. It was terrible."

Lucas just shook his head.

"When she came to, she was still totally out of it. She had become very close to Mikey; she went insane after it happened. She just locked herself up in her room for the next few months. Seldom came out except to eat. She'd stay in there all day and all night. When I'd see her, she'd always be wearing black clothing. It was like she was in mourning. You couldn't talk to her, she wouldn't say anything back. She had this glassy look in her eyes which she never had before. She seemed to stay in this state of shock, so I had a psychiatrist come to the house to check on her. He said she was in bad shape, so we civilly committed her to the State Hospital."

Lucas told him, "Damn, that's unbelievable!"

"After she left for the hospital, I went into her room where I found some strange things. There were ten or so books on witchcraft. Also there was this doll; it was like a stuffed animal, except it was a 'man.' Across this doll's chest, in black ink, it read, 'Judge O'Reilly.' There were at least twenty needles stuck into it. Anyhow, it seems as if she was into voodoo."

Lucas asked, "When is she getting out of the asylum?"

"She's been there for nearly nine months. The doctors say she may be released soon. I visit her every few weeks. I told her she can stay here forever. She's like family to me. I just pray she's okay."

"Do you see all the collateral damage that fucking O'Reilly caused?" Lucas asked.

Rickie nodded.

Lucas asked which room he should use. Rickie led him upstairs to one across from Mikey's room. He placed his suitcase on the bed, opened it, and pulled out his toothbrush and toothpaste. He walked down the hallway into the bathroom, where he turned on the faucet and started brushing his teeth. Afterwards, he walked back to his room and moved his suitcase from the bed onto the dresser. Then he lay down and just looked at the ceiling, wondering why the door to Mikey's room was closed. The house was very quiet. Several minutes later, Rickie walked in and handed him a key. He told him that he was free to come and go from the house as he so pleased. Lucas stood and thanked him. They shook hands and then hugged each other. Rickie told him that he was leaving to go to his law office.

Once he left, Lucas lay back down on the bed. He kept staring at the ceiling and thinking about Mikey. *Maybe I'll go into his room. I wonder why the door is shut?* He had this eerie feeling about going into Mikey's room. He wanted to open the door but for some reason was afraid to do so.

At two-thirty he left the house, heading to Victor Adams' office. He pulled up to a tall building located on Main Street. Parking on the street, he walked inside and rode the elevator to the twenty-fourth floor, where he located Victor Adams' suite. The reception area was quite elegant; the furniture was top-of-the-line. The carpet was plush; even the lamps looked like they cost thousands of dollars. It was quite apparent that Victor Adams was going to be an expensive attorney.

Lucas walked up to an open window where he saw a receptionist sitting on the other side. She was an attractive young girl who asked, "May I help you?"

Staring at her, he replied, "I'm Lucas Lustick. I have an appointment with Mr. Adams."

"Have a seat, sir, and I'll be with you shortly."

Lucas sat on a couch, and several minutes later the receptionist came into the waiting room and asked him to follow her. She was wearing a very short skirt. Walking behind her, Lucas checked out her long legs. She made him think of racehorses. He envisioned her with the number "8" pasted to her skirt.

His daydreaming subsided as she led him into Victor Adams' office. Victor was sitting behind a desk. Standing up, he extended his hand for Lucas to shake. As Lucas did so, he

Legal Vengeance

looked down at Victor Adams, a very tiny man, barely five-feet tall. Victor asked him to have a seat. Lucas couldn't get over how small he was. He thought that if he wasn't a midget, then he was the next closest thing.

Victor politely asked, "So, what brings you here today?"

He seemed friendly, with a genuine way about him. Lucas told him about how his law license had been suspended following the trial in Federal Court before Judge Ann Hudson. He told him that it was suspended for two years, but that he had never attempted to get it reinstated when the two years were up. He continued, "It's been a long time since I was suspended. I don't want to have to retake the bar exam. I just want my license reinstated so that I can practice law again."

Victor then asked him to explain in detail everything he had been doing during the years since his license had been suspended. Lucas did so. Victor then asked him if he had been in any trouble with the law since the time of his suspension. Lucas told him, "Yes, I have." He described to him about when he had leveled John O'Reilly. "I know that's going to be a problem in getting my license back."

"Normally that would be the case if you hired any lawyer except me. I am confident that I can get you past that hurdle, but my fees are very high. You either can afford me or you can't. I'll charge you twenty thousand, and you'll have your law license back within sixty days."

"Are you sure? I don't want to blow twenty grand if you can't get the job done."

"Hey, big guy, look at me. See how small I am? Do you think I'd make you a promise, take your money, and not come through?"

"You're hired. I'm driving to Baltimore in the morning. I'll send you a cashier's check within a week. Then you can start working on my case." Both men stood up and shook hands. Lucas then left his office.

He drove back to Rickie's house and sat down at the kitchen table. He decided that it was time to go to Maryland; there were things he needed to do. There was no reason to stay in Texas at this time. Picking up a pad of paper, he wrote Rickie a note, thanking him for picking him up at the jail and for buying him the new car. He indicated that he would be gone for two-to-three months.

He went upstairs and got his belongings. Walking out of the guest room, he stood outside of Mikey's door, pondering whether to open it. Finally he did so, and gingerly he walked inside. It was dark, but he could see because of the light which eased in from the hallway. The blanket was pulled back from the bed. There was clothing on the floor. An opened soft-drink can was on the desk. Obviously, Rickie hadn't changed anything since the day Mikey killed himself. He tiptoed over to the desk. There was a note which was written on jail notepaper. It read, *"Dear Daddy, I am sorry. You are my best friend that I ever had. I can't stay in here -- too scared. I can't be here for fifteen years. I will go and be with Mommy. I love you."*

Mikey had signed the note. It was obviously the note he had left in his jail cell the night he killed himself. Lucas wiped tears from his eyes as he put the note down where he had found it. He pulled the door behind him, walked down the stairs, and left the house. Tossing his suitcase into the backseat of his car, he slowly backed out the driveway. He felt a strange mixture of sadness and anger as he drove away.

Lucas wasn't sure of the fastest route to Maryland. He started driving on Interstate 10 East and by sundown had reached New Orleans, a city he had never visited before. Driving downtown, he came upon Bourbon Street where he parked in a tiny parking lot. He started walking around. People were everywhere. Some were young, some old, most everyone carried drinks in their hands. After stepping into one of the bars, he ordered a bourbon on the rocks. Sitting at a table by himself, he watched a jazz band perform. He stayed put for several hours, and before he knew it, ten o'clock was approaching.

Deciding he wanted a woman, he left the bar and walked up and down Bourbon Street. But the women he saw weren't what he was looking for; they all seemed to be party girls. What he wanted was a good, old-fashioned, Southern street whore. But he didn't know where to find one, so he looked for a taxicab. He knew that a cabbie could tell him where he needed to go. But for some reason he started thinking about Mikey's note to Rickie. It so depressed him that he no longer had the desire for a girl. As he thought about John O'Reilly, he felt his whole body tensing up. He wandered up and down Bourbon Street, looking for his car. When he finally found it, he got back on Interstate 10 and headed east.

He drove all night, through Mississippi and Alabama, and by morning reached Jacksonville, Florida. There he drove to the beach area where he could look out and see the Atlantic Ocean. It was simply beautiful. He went into a small store where he selected two beach towels and a bathing suit. After paying for them, he asked the store owner if there was a room where he could change into the bathing suit. She pointed towards the bathroom, and he walked into it, undressed, and put on his new bathing suit. Carrying his shoes, socks, and pants with him, he left the store and tossed everything into his trunk. Removing his shirt, he threw it in also. Then he walked barefoot out to the beach, finding a good spot in the sand to place his towels. He looked around; the beach wasn't too crowded.

Slowly, he hobbled towards the seawater. He felt broken down, not just mentally, but physically. His knees hurt, his shoulders were weak, his skin was pale. Finally he reached the water, creeping into it until it came up to his chest. Jumping into the air, he allowed himself to fall freely into the ocean. There he remained submerged for several moments before coming up for air—it was so soothing to him. Pushing his hair back from his forehead, he could feel the salt penetrating into his skin. It had a cleansing feeling to it. He strayed further out into the ocean, and the water was now up to his neck. He stood there for nearly ten minutes.

He was still extremely sad, but he felt less tense. His muscles and bones still ached, but now they felt slightly rejuvenated. After looking up at the sun, he looked down at his arms. He knew that if he stayed out much longer, he'd end up sunburned. The ocean, just like everything in life, had the bad with the good. It was time to go.

He cruised through Florida on Interstate 95; by nighttime, he was well into Georgia. He kept driving straight through the Carolinas without stopping for anything except gasoline. When he finally took a break, it was near Richmond, Virginia. There he went into a restaurant to eat. He wasn't all that far from Baltimore. After he finished eating, he continued on his trip.

As he was driving he thought about the order in which he was going to do the things which needed to be done. He knew that he had to visit the bank so that he could take care of paying Victor Adams. He needed to visit Dr. Lombardi to tell her where he had been the past year. He had to go hang out at Pimlico; it was why he had come to Baltimore in the first place. He really missed watching the horses run. Of course, he was going to watch the ballerinas practice. Also, he would eat at his favorite restaurants and, most certainly, visit The Block.

As he approached downtown Baltimore, he got off the freeway and headed to his old hotel on Charles Street where he parked out front. He went inside and there was Joe, sitting behind the desk. He walked up to him and asked, "Hey, Joe, remember me, Lucas Lustick?"

Joe never stood up or showed any emotion. "Yeah, I remember you; of course, I remember you. What do you need, a room?"

Lucas was disappointed by his attitude. He figured that Joe could have been a little nicer to him after all the years he had roomed there. But no, Joe wasn't even the least excited about him being back. He had always thought Lucas to be a bastard. He asked, "How long do you plan on staying this time?"

"Two weeks."

"That will be nine hundred up front, plus you owe me five hundred from last year when you skipped out."

Lucas angrily responded, "Fuck you, man! I didn't skip out! I got thrown in fucking jail down in Texas."

"Well, whatever, you owe me fourteen hundred."

Lucas was confused. *I thought Rickie took care of this ...* then he remembered, *He found out about Mikey right after leaving me ... he forgot ... Mikey's death drove it out of his mind.*

"I'm sorry, here's everything I owe, plus a bit more for the trouble I caused."

His room looked exactly like the room he had lived in before. Exhausted, he flopped onto the bed and immediately fell asleep.

The next morning he walked to one of his favorite diners. After breakfast he went back to his hotel room and just sat on the bed. Then he decided to call Sarah. Hopefully, she'd be in her office and could make time to see him. Her receptionist answered, and he asked if Dr. Lombardi had any appointments available that afternoon. She told him that two o'clock was available. He said he would be there.

Driving to a downtown department store, he bought various items of clothing which he needed. Then he was off to the bank, where he opened his safe-deposit box and took out sixty-thousand dollars. Next, he went to one of the teller's windows and placed down twenty grand. He told the young lady that he needed four cashier checks, each in the amount of five-thousand dollars, made out to Victor Adams. She informed him that before doing this, he would need to fill out several federal forms since he was doing a transaction involving over ten-thousand dollars in cash.

Angrily he answered, "Just forget it. I don't need to fill out any government forms. Them bastards don't need to know any of my fuckin' business!"

Picking up his money, he left. His front and back pockets were stuffed with the cash. Next, he walked to a Federal Express office across the street from the bank. There he got two envelopes and stuffed ten-thousand dollars into each one of them. Closing them, he addressed them to Victor Adams in Houston, Texas. After paying Federal Express fifty dollars to send the two envelopes, he walked back out into the street.

He felt comfortable in downtown Baltimore. It was his home. He looked up at the Bank of Maryland, telling himself,

Yep, this will still be my bank. Maybe he was going to be living in Texas, but he would never be a Texan. Never would he use their banks, never would he drink their beer, never would he wear Texas-style clothing. He'd visit Baltimore every few months; it would always be his home. He walked the downtown streets for the next few hours, feeling a certain excitement about his appointment with Sarah. He knew that she'd be surprised to see him.

At two o'clock he walked into her office. The receptionist led him back into a room where he sat on a couch. There he looked around at the various diplomas which were hanging on the walls. After about ten minutes, there was a knock on the door. Sarah walked in, and he stood up to greet her. She looked very happy to see him. The two hugged each other; there was a certain odd chemistry between them. They were both so barren and homely in the physical sense, yet both so brilliant mentally.

She asked where he had been, and he told her the entire story about his trip to Texas. He explained to her what had happened to Mikey, and about the hatred he was still feeling towards John O'Reilly. He told her about the year he spent in jail, and all about his job in the law library working on appeals. Sarah liked his enthusiasm about getting his law license reinstated and then practicing appellate law.

"I'm sure that you can be as excellent an appellate lawyer as you were a trial lawyer," she assured him.

She asked him how his compulsions had been in the past year. He said that he was doing fine and had received his medication while in jail. She told him that she would write him a prescription for his Prozac for the next six months, but then he had to see her again. He promised her that anytime he was in Baltimore he would visit her. He told her that he now wanted to start paying for his visits, especially since he was going back to work. Shaking her head, she told him that she would never take his money; it wasn't good in her office.

"You were the first real patient I ever had. I remember when I met you at the Colts game with my father. He saw that you were sick, and he wanted me to help you. He had put me through college and medical school so that I might be able to contribute to society. After I treated you, I told him how I helped you. He was so proud of me for making a difference in somebody's life. He felt that I had really done something special with my medical degree. He knew that I could help lots of people throughout my life."

She then paused as tears rolled down her face. "Daddy died three months ago; I was at his bedside. He had a certain comfort as he was going, that I, his only child, was going to be fine, that I'd be a good doctor. He was always worried about me." She paused, "I held his hand when he left, and I could feel that he was so at peace."

Staring into her eyes, Lucas could see the pain she was feeling. He told her how sorry he was for her. She then quickly changed the subject and told him, "I'm very concerned about the anger you harbor towards that Judge O'Reilly, and I want you to control it. Whatever hatred you feel towards him, keep it under wraps. It will do you absolutely no good to go through your life hating him."

"But I hate him, and I want him dead. He double-crossed me!"

"Even though you can't stand him, hurting him will never bring Mikey back; we both know that."

Lucas just stared at her, not saying anything. He knew that she didn't understand his concept of revenge. Changing the subject, he asked, "How is your practice doing?"

She happily answered, "It is starting to grow."

There were patients waiting to see her right then in the reception area. Also, she was teaching part-time at Johns Hopkins, which was very rewarding to her. Lucas stood up and thanked her for meeting with him and told her that he'd set up an appointment the next time he was in town. Then he hugged her and left.

It was two-fifty, and he decided to stroll over to the Maryland Ballet to watch the ballerinas practice. When he reached the studio, he walked inside and grabbed a seat. The girls were hard at work dancing. It had been over a year since he had last visited. Some of the girls he remembered, but a lot of them were new. Their gracefulness still had the same calming effect on him as it had in the past. He still loved watching them do their routines. He thought, *Tonight I'll watch the ballerinas; tomorrow I'll watch the horses.*

Eventually he left and went to his favorite Chinese restaurant on Baltimore Street. Before going inside, he purchased the next day's *Racing Form*, which he studied while he ate. Afterwards, he went back to the hotel, got drunk off a bottle of Jack Daniel's, and passed out.

When he woke up the next day, he picked up the telephone and called Victor Adams in Texas. The receptionist answered and put him through. Lucas asked if he had received the two Federal Express packages. Victor told him that he had, and that he appreciated him sending cash. "Call me back in thirty days for an update."

"Will it be thirty or sixty days before I get my license back? You told me before that you thought it would be sixty."

"It may take up to sixty days, but I'm going to try to get it for you in thirty. That's why I'm saying to call back in thirty days."

"Thank you. I'll get back with you."

That afternoon Lucas drove to Pimlico where he saw the same guys who had always hung out there. Nobody asked him where he'd been for the past year; nobody cared. Everybody was just studying the *Racing Form*, deciding which horses to bet in the next race. The whole afternoon he never talked to anyone. That's what he loved so much about the track. The true degenerates who frequented the grandstand only cared about one thing in life—which horse to bet in the next race. The peacefulness he felt at the horse track could never be equaled anywhere else on the face of the earth.

* * * * *

Lucas spent the next two weeks indulging himself in the things he liked most. He ate in his favorite restaurants, bet fortunes at Pimlico, spent late afternoons watching the ballerinas, and at night poured down whiskey and patronized the finest whorehouses on The Block. He knew that he so desperately needed to drown out the combination of anger and sorrow he had acquired while in Texas. After these two weeks of full-time decadence, things were going to change. No matter how much he loved his life in Baltimore, it didn't matter. He had to leave. There were things that needed to be taken care of elsewhere.

EIGHTEEN

It was just past midnight when Lucas walked out of the Hilton Hotel. Carrying a suitcase in one hand and a gym bag in the other, he walked past Joe without so much as a goodbye. Once outside, he got into his car and slowly drove off. Things in his life were going to change. It would be a long, lonely trip to Las Vegas, Nevada. It would be a straight drive without any stops except when he needed to refill his tank or grab a bite to eat.

By sunrise he was already in Ohio, and by nighttime he was passing through Illinois and heading towards Kansas City. It was in Kansas City where he finally decided to stop. After finishing a late dinner, he took back to the road and continued driving through Kansas, Colorado, and into Utah. He ate lunch the next day at a restaurant off the highway, not too far from the National Forest. He knew that Nevada wasn't far away. After lunch, he continued his journey southward on Highway 15 into Las Vegas. He had been on the road for nearly forty hours and had traveled almost twenty-five-hundred miles. Finally, sitting in front of him was the city of Las Vegas.

It was late in the afternoon, and there was no question in his mind as to where he was going to stay that night. He drove straight downtown and parked outside of Binion's. Then he strolled inside its downtrodden hotel lobby, approached the desk clerk, and told her that he needed a room for the next three nights. Once he paid, she gave him a rusty room key.

A musty smell greeted him as he entered his room on the sixth floor. *This will take a while to get used to.* The furniture was rundown much like the gaming tables downstairs in the casino. Exhausted, he lifted the thin blanket from the bed and climbed onto the sheets. He then pulled the blanket back over him, placed his head on the pillow, and before he knew it, was fast asleep.

It was well past midnight before he finally awakened. His eyes were barely open as he crept out of bed. Opening his suitcase, he removed the things which he needed. He showered, brushed his teeth, and put on a pair of jeans and a T-shirt. Placing his wallet into his back pocket, he walked out of the room, took the elevator down to the lobby, and headed to the casino area.

He went directly to the dice tables looking for Agnew, but didn't see him anywhere. Ordering a Jack Daniel's on the rocks, he sat at a bar not too far from the dice pits. It was now one-thirty or so in the morning. There he watched for Agnew for the next few hours, but never saw him.

The next two days were basically the same. He would sleep in his room all day and then hang out near the dice pits at night, pouring down Jack Daniel's and waiting for Agnew. Occasionally, he'd walk over to one of the tables and play for a short while, but he bet very lightly. This was not a trip in which he was going to do battle with the casino. He was focused on finding Agnew. He pondered going to other casinos looking for him, but knew it would be a waste of time. If Agnew was anywhere in Vegas, he'd be at Binion's.

After three days, he extended his stay another three. He followed the same routine, but there was still no sign of Agnew. He tried to guess where else he might be. Maybe he'd be at one of the horse tracks in southern California. Possibly, he'd be in Reno; with its overabundance of rundown casinos and whorehouses, it would be an attractive city to him. Was he possibly just wandering around the country? Maybe he had even been killed somewhere.

With still no sighting of Agnew, Lucas extended his stay another two days. He continued watching the dice tables hoping that Agnew would somehow suddenly appear, but he never did. Finally, he checked out of his room and left town, heading north. He drove almost eight hours before reaching Reno. Upon entering the city, he started to have flashbacks of his childhood. This happened whenever he came to Reno. But this time, as he was driving towards the downtown area, he repressed them and focused on the mission ahead of him, finding Agnew. He decided that he would first check into a hotel, take a short nap, and then hit the streets that evening looking for him.

Parking on the 300 block of North Virginia Street, he walked into the old El Dorado Hotel, approached the front desk clerk, and paid for two nights. Taking the elevator to the fifth floor, he got out and briskly walked to his room. The furniture was rundown, but elegant in its own sort of way. Getting into bed, he immediately fell asleep.

When he awakened, it was dark outside. Having no idea what time it was, he picked up the phone and called down to the front desk. The clerk told him that it was almost midnight. Getting up, he slowly walked towards the bathroom where he took a hot shower and brushed his teeth. Then he put on some blue jeans, a fresh white T-shirt, and his black high-top sneakers. Now he was ready to go.

Leaving the hotel, he started walking down North Virginia Street. There were eight other casinos located between First and Sixth Street. He went into each one of them looking for Agnew, but there was no sign of him. It occurred to him that he had forgotten to go into the casino at the El Dorado, so he went back and checked there, but there was no Agnew. He continued walking the streets of Reno until nearly three a.m.

At three, he went over to Harold's Club where he ordered a Jack on the rocks and then plummeted into a chair near the bar. Though totally exhausted, he watched the crap games. After finishing off three more drinks, he got up and left. Feeling defeated, he walked down Virginia Street wondering if he would ever find Agnew.

Then he had a sudden idea. Walking to his car, he started it up and drove off, looking for a taxicab. Finding one, he got out of his car and walked over to the cab driver. He told him that he was looking for a whorehouse which was located somewhere outside of Reno, but not too far. Having not been there in years, he knew that he wouldn't be able to find it by himself at night, especially since he had been drinking. He described to the cabbie the place he was looking for, but told him that he didn't remember its name. He did say that it was known as the best whorehouse in the area.

The driver told him, "I know just what you're looking for."

Lucas handed him sixty dollars and told him, "Just let me follow you there."

The two cars pulled off from Virginia Street. Fifteen minutes later the cab stopped in front of a house surrounded by a metal gate. Lucas immediately recognized it as the right place. Waving to the cabbie, he yelled, "Thank you!"

Getting out of his car, he walked to the metal gate. A buzzer sounded and he pulled back the gate and walked to the front door of the house. It slowly opened, and there stood his mother.

She appeared surprised to see him this late at night, but he could tell by the look on her face that she was happy he had come. After giving him a big bear hug, she invited him inside.

"What on God's earth brings you here at this time of night?" She asked, laughing as she led him to a couch.

He told her that he was in town looking for Agnew. He asked, "Do you remember him from when I was little? Remember? It was me, Amy, and Agnew."

She nodded her head. "Of course, I remember Agnew, the skinny little boy with the long fingers. Whatever happened to him?"

Lucas answered, "He's living somewhere in this part of the country. I really need to find him. Have you seen him come in here?"

She hesitated, "Lucas, I wouldn't recognize him if he did. I knew what he looked like when he was a little boy, but I don't have any idea what he looks like now that he's grown. As you know, we have a hidden camera which takes a picture of every man who comes through the front door. I've got boxes and boxes of photos. You are more than welcome to go through them and see if you can find him amongst them. Each picture is dated. You will definitely know if and when he came through here."

Lucas looked at her and nodded his head. He asked her where the pictures were.

She then led him into a room where there were hundreds of boxes of pictures. Telling him to sit at a table, she then brought him two boxes which she said contained photos of men who had patronized the house during the past sixty days. Then she left him alone so he could glance through them.

As he was doing so, one of them caught his attention. Calling his mother into the room, he showed her the photograph, asking if she knew who the man was.

"Sure, I know who he is. He's been a regular here for the last three years. We call him Lefty. He always asks for the same girl, Rebecca. Always wants her, nobody else."

Lucas asked, "Why do you call him Lefty?"

"Because his right arm is crippled. It just hangs there, he can't move it."

Lucas then asked, "Do you know where he's from or what he does for a living?"

"I don't know where he's from. I know he lives here now. I don't have a clue what he does for a living, but I can introduce you to Rebecca. I'm sure she can tell you whatever you need to know about him."

She paused, and then said, "I don't think Rebecca really likes the guy. She told me once that he says cruel things to her, that he has a mean streak in him or something. I don't remember exactly why she doesn't like him."

Lucas asked if he could meet Rebecca right away.

"No, she's with a customer."

The doorbell rang and Lucas' mother left the room while Lucas continued browsing through the photographs in search of Agnew. But he was unable to find a picture of him. Finally, he got up and walked back to where his mother was. She poured him a drink as they conversed about what each had been doing for the past several years. As they were talking, a blonde girl appeared in the front room with a customer whom she was escorting from the house. The girl kissed the man as he left. At that point, Lucas' mother said to the girl, "Rebecca, I'd like you to meet my son Lucas. He's visiting from the East Coast."

Lucas stood up to greet the young girl. Though her complexion was rather pale, she was attractive, with sparkling blue eyes and full lips. She wasn't statuesque, but she had curves in the right places. Lucas thought that she would be great to fool around with, but knew it wasn't going to happen. But she might be able to answer some of his questions about Lefty. He asked her if they could go somewhere private. She led him back into her room where they talked for nearly thirty minutes. Then he handed her three-thousand dollars for her help.

Once back at the El Dorado, he was too wired to fall asleep; he kept thinking about Rebecca and how feminine she was. He went into the dining area of the hotel where he ordered breakfast. Picking up a newspaper, he pulled out the sports section and started flipping through it. There was an article about a horse race at Santa Anita Racetrack near Los Angeles. Thoughts crossed his mind about driving there; however, this wasn't the right time. He needed to stay in Reno, since he had to meet with Rebecca again. Santa Anita would have to wait.

For the next two weeks, he stayed at the El Dorado, sleeping during the days and carousing at night. Always in search of Agnew, he was never able to find him. One night he drove from Reno to Carson City, where he checked out the small casinos. There was an odd-looking character at the Nugget Casino on North Stewart Street wearing a black baseball cap.

From a distance, he thought it might be Agnew. But once he got closer, he saw it was not. He thought about driving to Lake Tahoe, but knew that it would be a waste of his time. Tahoe wasn't Agnew's type of town.

He found himself very worried about Agnew, really wanting to find him. He thought back to his childhood. *It was always Amy, Agnew, and me. Amy is gone. Maybe something has happened to Agnew, too. Where is he? He's not in Vegas, Reno, or Carson City. The only other place where he might be is California. Finding him in California will be no easy task. He might be in San Francisco, Oakland, Los Angeles, maybe even Berkeley. But I'm not giving up. Whatever it takes, I'm going to find him.*

Even though he hadn't found Agnew yet, his trip to northern Nevada hadn't been a total waste. Rebecca had given him some extremely interesting information about Lefty. Tantalizing thoughts now crossed his mind. But first, he needed to visit Laredo, a town on the Texas/Mexico border. Lucas had never been there before, but had some idea about where it was. He wasn't sure of the quickest way to get there, but he just started driving east on Interstate 80 through Nevada.

Eventually, he found himself in Salt Lake City, Utah. After checking into a hotel, he walked the downtown streets, feeling totally out of place in the Mormon capital of the world. He had heard about Mormons, but hadn't ever met one. He knew that some of the men had lots of wives. He'd heard that Mormons weren't supposed to drink whiskey, and that their women, though good-looking, weren't into prostitution. Salt Lake City wasn't his type of town. He found a restaurant where he ate dinner. Afterwards, he hurried back to his hotel room and went to sleep.

The following morning, he was on the road by six o'clock, heading east on Interstate 80 until he reached Cheyenne, Wyoming. There, he caught Highway 25, which he took south. Speeding through Colorado and New Mexico, he finally decided to take a break in Albuquerque. There, he rented a motel room off the side of the highway—two hours for twenty dollars.

After a short nap and a shower, he was on the road again, continuing on Highway 25 until reaching El Paso, Texas. Once there, he caught Interstate 10, traveling east until reaching San Antonio. He felt himself wearing down. The long drive was now taking its toll on his body. Totally exhausted, he still had nearly two hours of driving before reaching Laredo. He drank a cup of coffee at an Exxon station, hoping the caffeine would help keep him awake. He headed south on Highway 35. Once he made it to Laredo, he pulled into a Holiday Inn three miles from the Mexican border.

After checking into a room, he fell fast asleep and slept for a long time. When he finally awakened, he brushed his teeth and quickly showered. Glaring at himself in the mirror, he saw that his hair had grown very long; he hadn't shaved in months. *I look like some sort of wild man—beyond degenerate, downright scary.* Finally, he dressed and went down to the front lobby. He asked the desk clerk if she knew where the Department of Vital Statistics was located.

She told him that she had no idea, so he stepped outside to see if there were any cabs around. A cabbie would be able to tell him where he needed to go. Unfortunately, there were none. Walking back into the hotel lobby, he called directory assistance on a pay phone to get the phone number for the Department of Vital Statistics. One call and he had the address.

Leaving the hotel, he drove to the 2600 block of Cedar. There sat the City of Laredo Health Department. Walking inside, he went straight to the area where the Department of Vital Statistics was located, approached the front desk, and asked for assistance. A Mexican woman who spoke very little English greeted him. It surprised him that the city would even hire somebody who couldn't speak English fluently. The woman simply led him into a dingy back room with thousands of files and left him there. He wasn't even sure what he was looking for. Eventually, he figured things out. After two hours in the room, he walked back out to the waiting area holding two sheets of paper.

The Mexican lady asked him if he needed copies.

"Yes. Can you please make me a copy of each of these two documents?"

Copies in hand, he then drove back to his hotel room. There was a certain degree of exhilaration racing through him which was both physical and mental at the same time. He had never experienced this sensation before. It lasted ten or so minutes before going away.

That evening he decided that he would cross the border into Mexico. After getting dressed, he went down to the lobby of the hotel and went outside looking for a taxicab. To his surprise there was one there. He told the driver that he wanted to go to a liquor store, and then he wanted to visit Mexico.

"No problem, sir. Mexico it is."

The driver would take him into Nuevo Laredo, to wherever he wanted to go, and then return him back to the hotel. He informed him that the fare for the evening would be a hundred dollars an hour, and that he needed to pay at least two hundred down. Lucas pulled out four one-hundred-dollar bills, handed them to him, and asked, "Will this get me started?"

"Yes sir! Where would you like to go?"

"First, take me to a liquor store."

"I'll take you to one on the other side of the bridge. Booze is cheaper down there."

"Fuck that!" Lucas roared. "Take me to the closest liquor store. I don't give a fuck what it costs!"

The cabbie then drove to a rundown store two blocks from the hotel and Lucas jumped out and went inside. He came out carrying a fifth of Gentleman's Jack bourbon. By the time he got into the cab, he had already opened the bottle and was taking a swig from it. Handing the bottle to the driver, he asked him, "Hey, you want some?"

The driver happily answered, "Sure," and took a hit. He said, "This tastes like fucking Jack Daniel's."

Lucas laughed, "Yeah, except it's smoother."

By now they were on the International Bridge heading into Nuevo Laredo.

The driver asked, "So let me guess what you want to do here in Mexico."

"Go ahead."

"You want to go to Boystown and get laid."

Lucas took another swig from the bottle and asked, "What's Boystown?"

The cabbie explained, "It's an area of the city where all the whores work. There are hundreds of them, pretty Mexican girls. That's where you go to get some."

Lucas nodded, "Yeah, that's where I want to go! Take me to that place!"

It was a ten-minute drive from the bridge. Once there, the cabbie pulled inside a gate. "This is it," he said.

Inside these gates were numerous bars, all of which appeared to be seedy from the outside. The driver pulled in front of one of them and told him, "This place has the best-looking girls. You go in there, you pick out the one you like. You buy her a beer and give her some money. Then she'll take you into one of the rooms behind the bar. In the meantime, I'll just wait out here."

Lucas got out of the car, walked inside, and sat at a small table. There were twenty or so young girls, all wearing dresses, scattered throughout the smoke-filled room. A waitress came up to him, so he ordered a beer. Glancing around the room, he saw a girl whom he found to be the most attractive and motioned for her to come over to his table. She did so, sitting down in a chair next to him. He told her to order a drink, which she did. He then told her, "You're the prettiest girl in here."

Shaking her head, she said, "No English."

Lucas pulled out a one-hundred-dollar bill and put it into her hand. That, she understood.

Standing up, she led him into the back of the club where there were tiny rooms with beds in them. She took him into one of them, shut the door, took her clothes off, and then helped him take off his. They got into bed, Lucas lay on his back, and the girl climbed on top of him.

Goddamn ... she is good! And so fucking pretty.

Upon finishing, she got dressed and he handed her another hundred-dollar bill. She then walked him back into the bar where he sat down and ordered another beer. After finishing it, he got up and went back out to the cab, telling the driver, "I had a beautiful girl. She was great! Thanks for bringing me here."

"Well, what do you want to do next?"

"Just take me back to my hotel."

Lucas drank the whole way back. When he got out of the cab he was totally smashed.

The next morning, he woke up and checked out. After going to a diner for breakfast, he then headed back onto Interstate 35 North towards San Antonio. Once there, he drove west on I-10, which would take him all the way to Los Angeles. It would be a long drive through Texas, New Mexico, and Arizona. But he was mentally fit for the trip. Things were turning around in his life, he was feeling young again. He was happy with life; he wasn't shaking or twitching, and he was once again enjoying getting drunk. And soon, he would be practicing law again in Houston. He relished the thought of doing appeals for people who had been convicted of wrongdoings by the entity he referred to as the "Fucked-up State of Texas."

As he drove, certain things crossed his mind, such as where he should live when he made it back to Houston. For sure, he was going to rent an apartment, but he wasn't sure in which part of town. He thought about where he might open his new office. Maybe, he'd simply practice law out of his apartment. He'd hire a girl as a secretary and let her work in his dining room. There was no plan whatsoever to represent people who were accused of committing crimes. He only figured on doing people's appeals after they had already been convicted. Most of his clients would be in prison.

There wouldn't be a need for an office for clients to visit. If he wanted to visit somebody, he'd just go to the prison.

He knew that he would spend a lot of his time at the county law library. There, he would have access to any books which he might need to prepare his appeals. He could do his research and writing there, and then bring it back to his secretary so that she could type it.

He started thinking about John O'Reilly. How was his marriage with Tammy? What had his little girl Megan grown up to be? He assumed that Megan was probably out of college by now. She probably had attended SMU, Vanderbilt, or some similar school which catered to the southern elite. He hoped that she hadn't grown up to be anything like her father. He envisioned John walking into a room and seeing Megan hanging from the ceiling by a belt. It would be the truest form of revenge for what he had done to Rickie and Mikey, the Biblical "eye for an eye." He thought of the pain John would feel in seeing his only child hanging from a ceiling, cold and dead.

He then stopped his idle daydreaming and started thinking about his mother. She had lived a pretty rough life, the way she was treated by the Germans, being forced to work as a prostitute. Now she was still in the same business. She seemed happy, content with what she was doing. *I wonder if she loves me. What does she really think of me? She is such a beautiful woman. Why didn't I inherit any of her good looks?* He wondered whether his life would have been different if he had taken after her in looks. Maybe he would have had girlfriends when growing up. Just maybe, he wouldn't harbor the same hateful thoughts towards women if he had been born beautiful.

His thoughts then wandered to Dr. Lombardi. Sarah Lombardi, what a truly good woman she was. How she had helped him straighten out his life. She was a beautiful woman inside; she had helped him and never wanted anything in return. But on the outside, she was so unattractive. *That's why she was at the football game with her father and not with a boyfriend.* He thought how unfair life was, the premium placed on looks. *If Dr. Lombardi had been born beautiful, would she still have grown up to be a doctor? Or would she have been a housewife, a model, or even a hooker instead? Who knows.* The way things balanced out in life was intriguing to him.

Lucas never stopped, except for coffee and gasoline, on his trip to Los Angeles. When he finally reached LA, he checked into a cheap motel about twenty minutes from Santa Anita Racetrack. It had just turned dark and he immediately fell into a deep sleep. Around ten-thirty the next morning, dressed in blue jeans and a red tank top, he found a cozy diner across the street. Grabbing a copy of the *LA Times*, he pulled out the sports section and handed the rest to the hostess.

After ordering four fried eggs and a double order of bacon, he started flipping through the newspaper and saw that the first post at Santa Anita was at one o'clock. Adrenaline was rushing through his body. Soon he would be at Santa

Anita, also known as the "The Oaks," one of the most famous and prestigious tracks in the world.

After breakfast, he headed northeast towards Arcadia, the actual city where Santa Anita rests. Its beauty, as viewed from the parking lot, awed him. Sitting behind the track were the beautiful San Gabriel Mountains. Being a weekday, the parking lot was still relatively empty. It was early, an hour or so before the first post.

Several other low-life types were also paying their admissions at the grandstand entrance. He strolled through the grandstand until reaching the outside pavement near the finish line of the racetrack. There he sat down and stretched out. He felt the sun glaring through the smog. Deciding that he wanted to get a cap, he walked back into the grandstand. At a souvenir shop he bought a gray cap which said "Santa Anita" on it. Putting it on, he walked back to the grandstand area, bought a copy of the *Racing Form*, and sat down at a table. There he started to handicap the various races that were going to be run that afternoon.

As one o'clock approached, the track was getting more populated. People were starting to walk through the aisles into the grandstand area. Lucas was watching, hoping that he might spot Agnew. Most of the people entering looked like weekday horse players. There were lots of them, and by the time the first race started, the grandstand area was crowded.

Lucas bet the first race, but his horse finished out of the money. In between the first and second race, he walked everywhere, trying to find Agnew. As usual, no luck.

He bet the second race and, once again, his horse finished out of the money. In the third race, he bet a horse named "John U. to Berry." He figured that the horse was named after the famous Baltimore Colt pass-catch combination of Johnny Unitas and Raymond Berry. The horse won the race and Lucas collected nine hundred for the hundred he bet on the horse. He bet the fourth and fifth races, but lost both.

After the fifth race, he noticed guys who appeared to be regulars hanging around the grandstand area. Walking up to them, he asked if anyone knew a guy who frequented the track by the name of Agnew. He talked to twenty-or-so men who were in the area. Lucas hadn't seen Agnew for a while, but he still tried to describe what he looked like. He knew that most track regulars didn't know each other's names, that they recognized one another only because they saw each other so often. He described Agnew as being skinny and as having very long fingers. He emphasized how important it was that he locate him.

Some of the men acted like they sincerely wanted to help, but they didn't know to whom he was referring. Finally, Lucas told them that the guy liked betting the "2-8" exacta in any race where he could.

At that point, two black guys started laughing. One of them said, "We know just who that motherfucker is! That motherfucker is here a lot. We call him ET because of his long, motherfucking fingers!"

The other one said, "Yeah, he bets 2-8 every race, no matter what! He hit a big exacta here two weeks ago and I haven't seen him since. It was 2-8, he bet it in the eighth race, the feature race on a Saturday. It paid over six-hundred dollars on a two-dollar ticket. He had twenty dollars on it. I remember telling him that he was one lucky motherfucker. He'll be back, I don't know when. It may be weeks, a month, but he'll be back. That motherfucker has been coming out here for years."

Lucas then asked the two men to walk with him out to the front area of the track so that he could talk more privately with them. Once there, he told them that he would give them each two-hundred dollars right then.

"All you have to do is, when you next see ET, have him contact me in Houston, Texas. I don't have a number there, yet, but I will within a week." He got two sheets of paper and a pencil from the admission-gate lady and wrote on each sheet of paper, "Lucas Lustick, Houston, Texas."

He handed them each a sheet of paper along with two-hundred dollars. Both were extremely thrilled with this easy opportunity of making two-hundred bucks. They probably would have helped for nothing. Lucas knew that, but figured the money would make them much more conscientious about getting the information to Agnew. He explained that he was a lawyer and that it was urgent that he heard from the ET fellow.

Both men shook his hand and told him that he could rest assured that as soon as ET came back to the track, they would give him the information and tell him to call.

Then all three of them walked back into the grandstand area and went their separate ways. Lucas now believed that he would be hearing from Agnew in the near future. He spent the rest of the afternoon placing bets, but didn't hit any more winners.

After the last race he went back to his motel. He wasn't sure whether to spend the night. He could catch a Dodger game but decided not to. Instead, he was going to start driving to Houston. He felt that he had at least accomplished something on this trip; Agnew would be calling.

Leaving the motel, he drove east on Interstate 10 through California, towards Arizona. Looking at his speedometer he saw that he was only going fifty miles an hour. Usually, he drove eighty, but for some reason he was now driving slowly. He was heading back to Houston, Texas; he couldn't believe it, but he was, with lots on his mind.

The possibility of "turning the tables" on John had put him in a state of turmoil. He thought how much he had changed over the years since moving to Baltimore. Before then he had been young, brash, and hateful towards the world around him. It was as if his conscience had never fully developed as it should have. Maybe it was because of his childhood, maybe not. But for whatever reason, as he aged in Baltimore, he somehow developed a new sense of morality within his value system. He had more of an awareness of pain as others felt it. He thought back to when he was growing up. He had flashbacks of slashing the throats of little kittens. But he now felt that he could never do such a thing again. Now he could empathize with the kittens.

He wasn't sure that it was a good thing that he had changed. Maybe he was just losing his toughness. He knew that he wanted to get even with John O'Reilly for what he had done to Mikey. But if he did so, it would be in conflict with his new set of morals. He had a good idea about how to even the score, but wasn't sure if he should really carry it out. He continued driving slowly as he crossed into Arizona. For him, time was standing still; there was no hurry at all.

Early the next day, as he was passing through New Mexico, he pulled up to a roadside restaurant off the freeway. It was blistering hot outside. He went inside and ordered lunch. After finishing, he got back onto the freeway, but was only going forty-five miles an hour towards Texas. Cars were passing him at high speeds; some honked at him trying to get him to speed up, but he didn't care. He was in his own world.

He started thinking about John. *How easy it would be to just put a bullet in his head. One shot, that's all it would take to end his life. But what good would it really do? He wouldn't feel any pain.*

As he continued his eastbound trip, he found himself pulling off the freeway from time to time, just to observe nature. Several times he pulled into small towns and just drove around, seeing life in its simplest forms. That evening he crossed from New Mexico into Texas. He thought about getting a motel in El Paso but decided against it. He continued his slow journey towards Houston, driving all through the night. He realized that he was very confused about what would be right and what would be wrong in dealing with John.

At sunrise, he was about a hundred-and-fifty miles west of San Antonio. There, he pulled off the main highway and onto some dirt road. He saw a tall, crusty-looking farmer holding a rifle, standing in a field. He wore overalls and a white T-shirt. The butt of his rifle was on the ground and the barrel was pointing up towards the sky. He waved to Lucas, who stopped his car and slowly got out.

The man yelled over to him, "Good morning, pardner."

Lucas yelled back, "How's it going?" As he stretched his muscles, he saw two lambs lying dead on the ground. Both had fresh blood all over them. Their attacker, a large black wolf, lay nearby. Lucas asked the farmer, "What happened here?"

"A lot of my sheep have been getting eaten alive at night over there." He pointed across the field to a large white farmhouse.

Lucas could see flocks of sheep grazing in the grass next to the farmhouse. He then asked, "How did these two little ones end up way over here?"

"Well, I put them out here as bait to draw this damn wolf." He pointed his rifle at the dead wolf. "I hated to give them up, but I had to. I've been hiding over here since five this morning, for him to show up. He came all right—I ran out and blasted him."

Lucas told him, "That's great, but I sure feel sorry for these little lambs."

"I feel sorry for them, too, but sometimes you just have to do what you have to do. Now this wolf won't hurt anymore of my sheep."

Lucas nodded his head. *Just like I need to do what I need to do.*

The farmer then asked him where he was headed.

"Houston."

The farmer asked, "What's wrong with the Astros this year? They're just awful, especially their pitching!"

Lucas told him, "I don't know what their problem is. I haven't been following them."

Then he said that he needed to get back on the road. They shook hands, then he took the country road back to Interstate 10.

As he headed towards San Antonio, he thought about the old farmer. He had spent only a few minutes with him, but they were very moving. The short time seemed to settle some conflicts within his mind. Looking down at his speedometer, he saw that he was now going over seventy. By the time he passed San Antonio and was heading towards Houston, it read ninety!

NINETEEN

It was nearly one o'clock in the afternoon when Lucas reached the city limits of Houston. He went straight downtown and parked his car on Main Street. He walked into Victor Adams' building, rode the elevator to the twenty-fourth floor, and then walked down the hallway to his office. He asked the receptionist if he could see Mr. Adams.

"Do you have an appointment?"

"No, I don't."

She then explained, "Mr. Adams doesn't see people unless they have an appointment."

"I need to see Mr. Adams. I don't need an appointment. I just arrived in town, and I'm sure he will see me. Tell him it's Lucas Lustick."

Lucas remained very calm as he spoke with her. This was the new Lucas Lustick, calm and collected. No longer would he cuss people who angered him.

The receptionist curtly told him, "Hold on," as she stood up and walked into another room behind the reception area. Two minutes later she returned and informed Lucas that

Mr. Adams would be happy to see him. She then led him into the back. Victor Adams greeted him and asked him to have a seat. Smiling, Victor said, "Everything went great with the State Bar."

Reaching underneath his desk, he picked up a legal file. He opened it and pulled out a gold card which read, *State Bar of Texas* across the top of it and *Lucas Lustick* across the bottom. Handing the card to Lucas, he said, "Congratulations!"

"Does this mean I'm a lawyer again?"

Nodding, Victor answered, "It sure does."

"Were there any problems in getting me reinstated?"

"Yes, Judge O'Reilly tried to hurt you. He objected to your being reinstated. Told the Board in a letter that you were of unsuitable character to practice law."

Lucas just sat there. Then he mumbled, "That motherfucker, I'm not surprised. But how were you able to get me reinstated with him trying to fuck me?"

Victor looked up at him and answered, "That's why you paid me twenty-thousand bucks. I told you that I could get the job done."

Lucas looked at him and smiled as he nodded his head. He knew that Rickie had referred him to Victor for a reason. He stood up, thanked him, and then left the office. Driving away from downtown, he headed south on Highway 59 past Kirby Drive. He needed to find a place to stay.

Pulling off the freeway onto Hillcroft Avenue, he drove several miles looking for an apartment complex. He came across a large one on the corner of Hillcroft and Bissonett Boulevard. The whole place looked to be the size of several football fields. After pulling into the parking lot, he drove around and finally found the leasing office.

Inside a young woman greeted him. He told her, "I need to rent an apartment."

She told him to come sit in her office, that she was the leasing agent. She then handed him an application which he filled out.

Reading it, she asked, "So, you're looking for a one-bedroom unit, is that correct?"

He simply nodded his head.

"Where did you used to live, sir? You have no references listed here."

"The last fifteen years or so I've lived in a hotel. I lived in Baltimore, Maryland for a long time. That's my only reference, the hotel."

"Where do you work?"

"I'm a lawyer, but I'm just starting up my practice. I don't have any clients yet."

"I'm very sorry, but we can't rent to you."

"Why not?"

"Because you don't have steady employment."

"But, lady, I can pay half a year's rent, up-front, right now!"

"Well ... I'm sure we can do something."

"Just tell me how much I need to give you."

The lady picked up a pen and started scribbling some numbers on a notepad. She then told him that the total cost for six months would be forty-two-hundred dollars, which would include his electricity. Lucas reached into his pocket and pulled out a wad of bills. Counting them, he then handed her the full amount. She pulled a leasing contract from a drawer, filled in some blanks on it, and wrote at the bottom that Mr. Lustick had paid six months rent in advance. Lucas signed the leasing contract, and she then gave him a key and told him where his unit was located.

After thanking her for her help, he walked out to his car and drove to the unit. It was a two-story building, but his apartment was on the ground floor. Walking up to it, he opened the door. Inside, it was very hot and humid. There was a kitchen, a living room, and a bedroom. The carpet was dark gray, and it was brand new.

Lucas turned on the air conditioning and then walked back out to his car to get his suitcase. Tossing it on the floor in the bedroom, he then walked into the bathroom, turning on the shower to make sure it worked well. The water rushed out of the showerhead with great force. He shut it off, thrilled that it suited his needs. The apartment was starting to cool off.

He lay down on the floor for several moments, but then got back up. Walking outside, he got into his car, drove back onto Highway 59, and headed towards downtown. He felt like he needed a drink, but knew that he first had to take care of several things. Pulling up to a large department store, he went inside. There, he purchased a king-sized bed, a small table with chairs, and a wooden desk. In all, it cost him nearly fifteen-hundred dollars. The salesman assured him that they would deliver the furniture to his apartment the following morning.

Next, he walked throughout the store with a shopping cart, picking up certain things which he needed: some bed sheets, pillows, a blanket, a set of dishes, silverware, and some plastic cups. After paying for these items, he exited the store and placed them into the trunk of his car. He started speeding back towards his apartment complex. On the way, he visited a liquor store where he bought three large bottles of Jack Daniel's. Then he stopped at a convenience store and purchased a dozen-or-so candy bars, several bags of potato chips, and a six-pack of Coke.

Back at his apartment he was delighted to find ice in his freezer. He put some in a plastic cup, poured it full with bourbon, and before long he was passed out on the floor.

When he came around, it was dark outside. He had no idea what time it was. No clocks. No television. He had forgotten to buy them. Walking into the bathroom, he brushed his teeth and took a hot shower. Then he put on a pair of gym shorts and walked out the front door of his unit. There wasn't anybody else walking around. Crickets were chirping.

He went back inside and stretched out on the floor until sunlight finally appeared.

He knew that sometime near eleven o'clock that morning the department store would be delivering the furniture. In the meantime, he got up and went shopping for a television set and a clock radio.

He was back home by the time the deliverymen from the store arrived. After they left, he flopped onto his new bed to see how much bounce it had. Then he pulled out the sheets, blanket, and pillowcases and made the bed. Walking out to the living room area, he looked at his new wooden desk. It needed a chair. Walking over to the kitchen table, he took one of its four chairs and carried it over to the desk. Sitting in it, he leaned his elbows upon the desk; it was just what he needed.

Across the room was the television set which he had bought that morning. He had removed it from the large cardboard box, turned the box upside down, and then placed the television on top. It amazed him how sturdy the box was, easily supporting the seventeen-inch set. Getting up from the chair, he walked into the kitchen and grabbed a Milky Way bar from the freezer and a Coke from the refrigerator. Then he sat down at his new kitchen table and enjoyed the candy bar and the drink.

This place was just right for Lucas; he was now settled in. The number-one thing he needed next was new clothes, especially suits. Also, he needed pads of paper and pens. He walked into his bedroom to see what time it was. His clock radio was on the carpet, plugged into the socket near the window. It was twelve o'clock.

He decided to drive downtown and check out the Harris County Law Library. He would be spending a lot of time there. Maybe he'd even set up his law office there. He'd find a table in some obscure part of the library and just start keeping his things there. He'd keep his books, legal pads, pens, and pencils at this table. The librarians would eventually know who he was, and he figured that nobody would mess with his things. There would be several chairs at his table, and if he ever had to meet with a client's family, they could come and sit around his table while discussing the case.

Downtown, he parked near the library, which was located in the County Administration building. He then walked into the building and rode the elevator to the eighth floor. Down the hallway was a door which led into the law library. Pulling it open, he walked inside and looked around. To his left was a lady sitting behind a large computer, wearing a white tag which read: "Law Librarian." He looked directly at her, but she never looked up. She appeared to be in her fifties; her hair was graying and she was wearing a grayish smock dress. Lucas kept staring at her, but she still never looked up at him. Thinking to himself, *What a bitch*, he walked further into the library.

Exploring the entire floor, he was quite impressed with the quality and quantity of research sources which were readily available. This was one of the finest law libraries he had ever seen. There were tables everywhere; several were away from the main portion of the library. He thought that maybe he would camp out at one of these tables, make it his law office. Sitting in one of the chairs, he looked up at a sign which was pasted on the wall. It read, "All Tables Must Be Cleared Off by Closing Time. The Library Is Not Responsible for Anything Left on the Tables." *Not a good idea to set up my office here. .... Don't want my work thrown out every night.* He now knew that he'd have to look for an office somewhere else in the city.

Outside, he walked towards Main Street, in the general direction of the county courthouse. Two blocks away from the courthouse, he saw a yellow sign in one of the windows of an old brick building located at 412 Main, which read, "Office for Rent." He decided to check it out. Inside he saw a door with a sign which read, "Law Office of Joe Jackson." He walked into the reception area. It was a small room consisting of two rundown chairs and a leather sofa. The carpet was totally worn through to the hardwood floor. The walls looked like they hadn't been painted in forty years. A musty smell permeated the place.

A young girl asked if she could help him. She was thin and had bleached-blonde hair. Lucas thought that she had a white-trash look to her.

"My name is Lucas Lustick. I'm looking for an office to rent."

"Are you a lawyer?" she asked, thinking, from his appearance that he was probably a bum walking in from the street.

Nodding, he answered, "Yeah, I'm a lawyer."

"I'll get Mr. Jackson."

Leaving the reception area, she walked into the back and told Joe Jackson, "There is a man named Lucas Lustick in the waiting room looking to rent the extra office."

Joe Jackson looked surprised, "That's a name from the past! If it's the same guy I'm thinking of, he was a great trial lawyer here some ten or fifteen years ago, one of the best this city's ever seen. Then he just fucking disappeared. Nobody knew where the hell he went. Let me see if it's the same guy."

Standing up, Joe walked from his office into the reception area and looked straight at Lucas. Recognizing one another from years earlier, the two of them shook hands. Lucas knew just who Joe Jackson was. He was a three-hundred-pound cop-out lawyer who never wanted to go to trial. He was an old-timer back when Lucas first started practicing law. Lucas asked him if he had an office available to rent.

"Sure, come with me."

Leading him into an empty room behind the reception area, he said, "This is it. I'm renting it for eight hundred a month, which includes Heather answering the phones and doing general secretarial work. She types sixty words a minute."

"When can I move in?"

"You can move in whenever you want. I've got an extra desk if you need it, and some wooden chairs you can use for your clients."

"Okay, I'll take it." He pulled eight-hundred dollars out of his pocket and handed it to Joe Jackson.

Joe then asked him to come have a seat in his office, where he lit up a cigar. Looking at Lucas he said, "I remember you from way back. You were one of the best young lawyers around. You used to win all your cases, fucking kicked ass around here. What ever happened to you? You just plain disappeared."

Lucas paused; he wasn't sure he wanted to tell Joe Jackson his life story. He told him, "I quit practicing law because I simply got tired of dealing with the system. I moved up North, now I'm back. I'm going to try again, but I'm not doing trial work—just appeals, nothing else."

Joe looked at him and asked, "Where do you think you're going to get business? Business is tight around here, especially on appeals. If you don't do DWIs and misdemeanor assault cases, you won't be able to survive. That's still the bread and butter of this business. I'm telling you the truth; you won't be able to survive just doing appeals."

"Well, if I don't survive, then I just don't. I'll head back up North and you'll be looking for a new tenant."

Joe then told him, "I'm pulling for you and sure hope you can make it doing solely appeals."

Lucas stood up and asked, "Where are the desk and chairs?"

Joe called Heather into his office and told her, "Show Lucas the storage room."

Heather helped move the wooden desk and two chairs into his office. She then brought in a telephone, put it on the desk, and wired it back to her desk where she connected it to Joe's phone system. She asked, "How do you want your phone answered?"

"Law Office of Lucas Lustick, Appellate Lawyer."

Lucas then sat by himself in his new office. He had a desk and a wooden chair to sit in. Across from his desk was the other wooden chair. He thought that he should look for one more wooden chair, but that would be for another day. Today he was happy to have found an office. It wasn't fancy, but it would do.

Finally he got up to leave. On his way out, he stopped and asked Heather if she would call the phone company and set up his line under his name. He needed to be listed in the phone book as an attorney so that his clients and, of course, Agnew would be able to find him. She assured him that she would take care of it in the morning.

During the next several weeks, Lucas' workdays were rather routine. He'd spend several hours each day in the law library, then he would go to his office and just sit behind his desk. He didn't have any cases to work on.

The fact he was back in town was circulating amongst the legal community. The old-time judges and lawyers all remembered him. Everyone was wondering why he was back. Lawyers ran into him at the law library and on the street. They asked him the same questions, "Where have you been, and why are you back all of a sudden?" But, nobody referred any cases to him. Lucas was remembered as a great trial lawyer; nobody knew him as an appellate lawyer. There were other well-known appellate lawyers in Houston.

Finally, he had an idea on how to drum up some business. He sent a letter to the *Death Row* newspaper in Huntsville, Texas, which they printed in one of their editions. The newspaper is circulated among the inmates on death row. The letter asked if there were any innocent inmates who had been falsely convicted. It informed such inmates that there was an attorney in Houston that might be willing to work on their case, free of charge. It instructed them to explain their situation in great detail and to send their correspondence to: Lucas Lustick, 412 Main Street, Houston, Texas.

Within a week, Lucas received over forty responses. He read each one of them. One in particular appeared to have some merit. It was from a man by the name of Robert Jack who had been sentenced to death two years earlier by a Jackson County jury of twelve for the shooting death of a local schoolteacher.

Legal Vengeance

In his letter, Mr. Jack claimed that he had been incarcerated in Ann Arbor, Michigan, at the time of the killing in Jackson County. He wrote, "It is a case of mistaken identification, and the lawyer who represented me in trial and on appeal never checked into my alibi." Mr. Jack swore that if anybody ever looked into it, he'd be cleared of the murder.

Lucas remembered all about Jackson County from the days when he had practiced law. It was a redneck county nearly ninety miles south of Houston. The county seat was Edna. Lucas remembered that a lot of Klansmen lived there. He also recalled that there were only three lawyers practicing criminal law in that county, and that they all were Klan members. He wondered if Robert Jack was black. Lucas decided to call the warden on death row to arrange a visit.

Several days later he drove to Huntsville and was allowed to meet with Mr. Jack. Two prison guards stood ten yards from him and Robert Jack. They weren't there to listen to what Robert told Lucas; in fact, they didn't care in the least. They were there for two purposes: first to see to it that Lucas didn't hand Robert anything, and second, to provide protection to Lucas if Robert tried to hurt him. The guards were well aware that death-row inmates had little to lose; they were just waiting to be executed.

Robert Jack was thrilled to meet Lucas. It was like a dream come true.

Astutely, Lucas looked him up and down. Robert Jack was a thin man. He stood close to five-feet, ten inches and was as black as coal, as dark a man as Lucas had ever laid eyes upon. There was nothing soft about the way Robert Jack looked. He had the look in his eyes of a man who could kill in cold blood. Lucas could see that based on his looks alone, this man never had a chance in Jackson County. Even if he was as innocent as the day was long, he never had a shot in that redneck town. He asked Robert about his trial in Jackson County.

Robert told him that he had been given a court-appointed lawyer named Billy Joe Smith. He told Lucas that he had informed Mr. Smith that at the time the teacher was murdered, he had been in jail up in Michigan. Robert said that Mr. Smith never even looked into it, "Never did nothin', nothin' at all for me! Even on appeal, again I told him to check out my story about Ann Arbor, but he never did. Man, I don't know nothin' at all about that white-lady teacher bein' killed in that town!"

Lucas sat and listened. He couldn't believe that Billy Joe Smith never checked into the alibi. He figured he must have looked into it and wasn't sure whether to believe Robert Jack or not. He told him that he was going to call Mr. Smith and see if it was true that he never checked into the alibi. If not, he himself would check into whether Robert was incarcerated in Michigan at the time the schoolteacher was murdered in Jackson County.

When he got up to leave, Robert shook his hand and told him, "Mr. Lustick, sir, I wouldn't waste your time looking into this if it wasn't true. I want to thank you for helping me. I feel like I owe you something."

Lucas replied, "Robert, if it's true you were in jail in fucking Michigan when that lady was killed, you don't owe me anything."

Back at his office in Houston, he tried to call Billy Joe Smith, but he wasn't in his office that afternoon. "Call back tomorrow," his receptionist said.

"It's very important I speak with him immediately."

"Well, that ain't gonna happen, cause he's at a cattle auction in Cuero."

"I'll call back in the morning."

Finally he had a client. He wondered if Robert Jack's story would pan out. As he was sitting at his desk, he heard loud curse words coming from Joe Jackson's office. It sounded like Joe's voice, so he got up to check on him. Joe was in a manic rage, slamming his fist on his desk and yelling, "I'll kill that little motherfucker! Fuck his ass, that whore-motherfucker!"

Lucas asked, "What's wrong?"

Trembling, Joe blurted out, "Just give me a minute to settle down. Right now I want to kill the motherfucker! Just hold on."

Lucas told him, "Just take your time."

Finally, after a few moments, Joe sat down behind his desk. Still raving mad, he said, "This morning I had a case in John 'Cocksucker' O'Reilly's court. I was representing this poor black kid from the fifth ward; the boy isn't but eighteen years old. He was charged with aggravated assault on a police officer. I pled him last month to a PSI which was set for sentencing today."

Lucas interrupted and said, "You never should have done a presentence investigation to that motherfucker."

"I know that now! I thought for sure that he'd give this kid probation in this case. The cop beat up on the kid and then filed an aggravated assault charge against him. It was total bullshit! I should have tried the fucking case to a jury."

Lucas asked him why he didn't.

"I guess because the kid only paid me two-hundred bucks to represent him. I couldn't try a case for two-hundred fucking dollars. I just figured that O'Reilly would give him probation. But the motherfucker gave him six years in the joint. The kid's mother was screaming in the courtroom. O'Reilly had the bailiff arrest her for disorderly conduct. I was so pissed off I had to walk out of the courtroom; otherwise, I would've cussed out the motherfucker."

Lucas just sat there a while, but didn't say anything. Then he shook his head, got up, and walked out of the office. He knew exactly what Joe was feeling. Going back into his office, he sat behind his desk and stared at the wall until Heather walked in and told him that she was leaving for the day. He gave her a blank stare. After she left, he continued to stare at the wall for well over an hour. Finally he got up and left for the day.

The next day he was back in his office by ten o'clock in the morning. He called Billy Joe Smith's office and the receptionist put him through.

"Billy Joe Smith, can I help you?"

"Yes sir, my name is Lucas Lustick. I'm a lawyer up in Houston, and I'm calling about one of your clients by the name of Robert Jack."

In a deep southern drawl, Billy Joe said, "Robert Jack, yes sir, Robert Jack. I represented him on a capital murder he committed here in Jackson County. The jury gave him death. Now I'm working on his appeal."

"Yeah, that's him. The reason I'm calling is that he wrote me from prison and told me that he had been in Ann Arbor, Michigan, at the time the murder in Jackson County occurred for which he was convicted. He claims that he was locked up in Ann Arbor and that you've never actually looked into it. Is there ..."

Billy Joe interrupted him, "First of all, I don't know you, and I don't know why you are intermeddling in my case." His voice grew angrier as he continued, "That boy wasn't in Michigan when Mrs. Coleman was murdered. That's a fucking lie! He was right here, raping and killing one of our white schoolteachers. He told me about Michigan, but I knew he was lying. Two eyewitnesses from here positively identified his black ass. They were both one-hundred percent sure he was the killer!"

Lucas then asked him whether he had investigated the Michigan alibi.

"I didn't need to. I knew that he was lying! Stay away from my fucking case!"

Lucas just hung up the phone. He now knew that Billy Joe Smith had never even looked into the Ann Arbor alibi. He thought about driving to Michigan where he could go directly to the Sheriff's Department to see if there was any truth to Robert Jack's story, but instead decided he would hire a private investigator who worked in Ann Arbor.

He got on the phone and called directory assistance for the city of Detroit. He asked the operator for the phone number of the Detroit Police Department, Homicide Division. He called and spoke to the receptionist, telling her that he needed to talk with a detective. She put him on hold for several minutes. Finally, he heard, "Detective Ricks, can I help you?"

"Detective, my name's Lucas Lustick, I'm a lawyer down here in Houston, Texas. I need to hire an investigator who can help me on something in Ann Arbor. I'm not exactly sure where Ann Arbor is, but I believe it's somewhere near Detroit. I'm wondering if you know of any ex-cops who are private investigators."

The detective told him that Ann Arbor was actually southwest of Detroit and not too far. He continued, "I know a damn good investigator named Sebesta—Danny Sebesta. He used to work here in homicide. Now he's private. You're not going to find anyone better than him."

He gave Sebesta's number to Lucas, who thanked him for his help. Lucas then dialed the phone number and a man answered, "Danny Sebesta."

"Hello Danny, I'm Lucas Lustick ..." and he explained the entire situation to him.

Sebesta told him that he could easily verify if Robert Jack's story was true or not. He told Lucas that he would need to wire him a five-hundred-dollar retainer through Western Union, and he would then start working on the case. Lucas assured him that the money would be there within the hour. He then gave Sebesta all the identifying information which he needed on Robert Jack.

Across the street was a store which had a Western Union sign out front. There, he wired the money, copied the control number, and went back to his office to call Danny. Danny made a note of the control number, thanked Lucas, and told him that he would call as soon as he had the information from Ann Arbor.

The very next day, Lucas received a call from Danny Sebesta. Sure enough, Robert Jack had been in jail on the day the capital murder of Mrs. Coleman occurred in Jackson County. Sebesta said that he was ninety-nine percent sure of it. He told

Lucas that to be totally positive, he would need a copy of Robert Jack's fingerprints.

Lucas told him that he didn't have them but he would try to get them. He thanked him for the good information and told him that he would get back with him in the next few days. It was about one o'clock in the afternoon. Lucas left his office and jumped into his car. It was time to take action. He got on Highway 59 South and headed towards Edna, Texas. It took him a little more than an hour before he reached the Jackson County line. Once there, he drove another fifteen miles, where he pulled off at the Edna exit. He pulled into a small convenience store where he got directions to the Jackson County District Attorney's office. It was only two miles from where he was. He drove down Main Street until he saw the county courthouse. The District Attorney's office was located on the second floor.

As he walked into the office of the Jackson County District Attorney, he saw a beautiful, dark-haired girl behind a desk. He asked her who the District Attorney was, and she told him it was Joe Bob Nixon.

Lucas asked, "Is he working today?"

"Yes, I'll go get him."

As she stood up, Lucas thought, *Damn! This DA sure knows how to pick a beautiful secretary!*

Several moments later, the young lady returned with a rather youthful-looking gentleman who introduced himself simply as Joe Bob.

Dressed just like Lucas, he was wearing blue jeans and a white button-down shirt. He had short, dark hair and was athletic looking. Lucas shook his hand and asked for several minutes of his time.

Joe Bob Nixon smiled and said, "Come on," as he led Lucas back to his office.

Lucas sat in a chair across from Mr. Nixon. He looked at the diplomas on the wall. Joe Bob Nixon had graduated from Texas A & M University and Baylor University Law School.

Joe Bob asked, "What do you need to visit about?"

"It's my understanding that a while back you prosecuted a man named Robert Jack for the capital murder of a schoolteacher."

Joe Bob nodded his head. Lucas then went on and explained why he thought Robert Jack was innocent of committing the offense. He told about his visit with Robert Jack and of his subsequent hiring of Danny Sebesta. He told him that it appeared that Robert Jack had been in jail up in Michigan when the murder in Jackson County occurred. He asked Joe Bob if he would be willing to look into the matter for himself.

Joe Bob Nixon stood up and looked Lucas in the eyes. He said, "The last thing I want to do is send a man to his death for something he didn't do! That's not why we've got that poison needle up in Huntsville. I'm going to send my Texas Ranger up to Michigan with a set of Robert Jack's fingerprints. If it turns out that he was locked up when this horrible crime happened down here, then I'll surely cooperate with you one-hundred percent in getting Robert Jack off death row."

Joe Bob asked Lucas if he had conveyed this information to Billy Joe Smith. Lucas told him of his telephone conversation with Billy Joe.

Laughing, Joe Bob said, "That sounds like Billy Joe."

Lucas then gave Joe Bob his phone number in Houston, and Joe Bob assured him that he would contact him as soon as he received any information from his Texas Ranger.

It took only two days before Lucas heard back from Joe Bob Nixon. He told him that Robert Jack's alibi did check out; that the Texas Ranger carried a copy of Robert Jack's fingerprints to Ann Arbor, and sure enough, he had been in jail up there on the date in which the murder had occurred in Jackson County.

"I feel terrible about having convicted an innocent man. I'll see if I can bench warrant Mr. Jack back from death row to court here next Monday."

Lucas told him, "That sounds great to me. I can come down and substitute in as his lawyer for that sorry-ass, court-appointed lawyer whom y'all gave to him."

Joe Bob then suggested, "Why don't you just prepare an out-of-time Motion for New Trial? The judge will grant it, and then I'll just dismiss the case."

Lucas asked, "What if your judge down there refuses to grant the Motion?"

"Don't worry about that. The judge here, Judge Gilbert, will do whatever I tell him. Down here the DA runs the court, not the judge."

"I'm sorry; I forgot how you small towns are."

Joe Bob told Lucas, "Hold on for a second."

Several moments later he got back on the phone and told Lucas, "My secretary says everything is set for Monday. We'll bring Robert Jack back to court. It will be at nine o'clock. Is that all right with you?"

"I'll be there." He paused and then asked, "Can you please call the court-appointed lawyer down there, Billy Joe Smith, or whatever his name is, and let him know that I'm substituting in on Monday?"

Joe Bob assured him that he would, and Lucas thanked him and hung up the phone.

He just sat at his desk. He was back, batting a thousand. His only client, Robert Jack, was getting off death row. It wasn't miracle-working on his part; he had simply done his job.

The following Monday he drove to the Jackson County Courthouse and arrived shortly before nine. He walked into the building and went straight to the courtroom on the second floor. There wasn't a judge sitting on the bench. He saw Joe Bob Nixon talking with several newspapermen who were writing down what he was telling them. Lucas handed him a copy of the Motion for New Trial and then gave the original to the clerk of the court who was seated next to the judge's bench.

One of the newspapermen approached Lucas and told him that he was a reporter from one of the Houston newspapers. He asked whether he had an extra copy of the Motion he had just filed. Lucas told him that he did not. The reporter then asked him how he got involved in this particular case in Jackson County. He asked him to explain how it was that he had met Robert Jack. Lucas didn't answer him.

Joe Bob Nixon then approached Lucas and asked if he would like to talk to Robert Jack, who was in a holding tank behind the courtroom. He then led Lucas there. A sheriff's deputy unlocked the door and told Lucas to go inside. Robert Jack was just sitting there, his left hand cuffed to the bench. He could tell by the look on Lucas' face as he walked in that he had good news. Lucas shook his hand but didn't say anything at first. The two men looked at each other, eye-to-eye. Lucas then told him, "You're going to be home tonight! Everything you told me checked out!" Then he handed him a paper to sign, enabling Lucas to replace Billy Joe Smith as counsel of record.

Robert Jack then asked, "Is that pitiful motherfucker going to show up this morning?"

Lucas, shaking his head sideways, answered, "I doubt it."

As they were sitting there talking, a bailiff came and told Lucas that it was time to go before the judge. He uncuffed Robert Jack from the bench and led him into the courtroom.

Lucas closely followed. The two went and stood at the counsel table. Judge Gilbert asked Lucas and Joe Bob Nixon to step closer to the bench. He told Lucas that he knew what the Motion for New Trial was all about; Nixon had filled him in on the whole situation the night before.

Judge Gilbert told Lucas, "I don't want to make a big production out of what's happening here. The locals don't need to know all the details. We don't need Billy Joe Smith being embarrassed by this whole situation. You just stand there with your client and ask me to grant you a new trial. I will do so, and then the District Attorney will dismiss the charges against Mr. Jack. I am gagging you and the District Attorney from discussing anything about this case with the media. All they will know is that the District Attorney's office dismissed this case against the defendant because the District Attorney believes Mr. Jack to be innocent."

He then looked at Lucas and Joe Bob Nixon and asked, "Gentlemen, do you both understand?"

Both Lucas and Joe Bob Nixon nodded. The judge then said, "Well, then, let's go!"

Lucas stepped back and stood next to his client. The judge then proceeded, "I now call the case of 'The State of Texas versus Robert Jack.' I have before me a Motion for New Trial which has been filed in this court. I have reviewed it and at this time will grant such Motion. I order that the Motion so filed in this court be sealed and kept within the records of this court. It is so ordered that nobody can unseal this Motion without the permission of this court."

Joe Bob Nixon then told the judge, "At this time, Your Honor, I'm dropping any charges in this case against Robert Jack."

He then handed the clerk a written Motion to Dismiss, which the judge signed.

The judge then looked out into the courtroom and announced, "At this time, I am placing a gag order on anybody associated with this case; they are not to discuss anything related to this case with the media."

Judge Gilbert then got up and left the courtroom. Lucas turned and looked into the spectator section of the courtroom where there were a dozen or so people standing. He didn't recognize any of them. Several of them had notepads. Everyone was confused as to why Robert Jack's case had been dismissed. Lucas then looked at Robert and asked, "Do you need a ride anywhere?"

Robert just laughed. He said that he had a brother who lived in Houston. Lucas told him that he would drive him to his brother's house. As Lucas and Robert were walking out from the courtroom, Joe Bob Nixon walked directly up to Robert, extending his hand.

He told him, "From the bottom of my heart, I'm sorry about what happened here." Robert shook Joe Bob's hand and forced a small smile. Lucas shook Joe Bob's hand, too, and thanked him for his help in resolving the case. Lucas and Robert Jack then walked down the stairs and left the courthouse.

The newspaper reporters followed them outside, asking numerous questions, but Lucas and Robert ignored them. The reporters were totally confused as to why Robert Jack had been set free. There were two cameramen who were snapping pictures of them as they walked. Once they reached the car, they both got in, and Lucas slowly drove away from the Jackson County Courthouse.

TWENTY

Tammy yelled, "John, honey, hurry up and come on downstairs! There's something you have to see in this morning's paper!"

John didn't answer her; he seldom paid much attention to anything she said. He continued shaving and then put on a white button-down shirt. Stepping into his closet, he picked out a red-and-black-striped tie to wear. Tammy hollered again for him to come downstairs. He still didn't answer her. He finished putting on his tie, making sure that it fit perfectly on his shirt. Then, he flicked off the lights and walked out to the stairwell. Nonchalantly, he walked down the steep flight of stairs and strolled into the kitchen. Tammy was sitting at the kitchen table by herself.

"John, come on over here and—look!"

He started walking towards her. She said, "There's your dear friend, Lucas Lustick!" Pointing to the picture on the front page of the newspaper, she said, "Why does he have that god-awful-looking beard?"

John picked up the paper and stared at the picture. "That son-of-a-bitch! I can't believe he's practicing law again. I knew he tried getting his license back, but I objected like hell to the State Bar. I can't believe they gave it back to him!"

John angrily left the kitchen and walked into the living room holding the newspaper. There, he sat down on a black leather couch. Again he looked at the picture of Lucas and the man standing next to him wearing jail clothes. He screamed to Tammy in the kitchen, "What's this sleazebag doing with this nigger inmate on the front page of our paper?"

Tammy didn't say anything. She had already read the whole story. It made Lucas look like a hero for freeing a poor, innocent man from death row. The article was vague as to how Lucas did it; however, it made it appear that he had pulled off some sort of legal magic.

The newspaper also went into some background information about Lucas. It stated that according to colleagues, when Mr. Lustick was young he was a warrior-type defense lawyer, one of the best ever in Texas; but for some unknown reason in the prime of his career, he quit his practice and just disappeared.

The article then quoted an Assistant District Attorney who wished to remain anonymous, saying, "Mr. Lustick appeared in the Harris County Courthouse for an unknown reason approximately eighteen months ago. There, he and Judge John O'Reilly engaged in mutual combat resulting in Mr. Lustick leveling the judge with one blow. He was prosecuted and sentenced to do one year in the county jail."

The article went on to say that while in jail, according to sheriff's deputies who were interviewed, Lucas Lustick served as the law librarian where he helped other inmates work on their appeals. Once he was released from jail, the State Bar reinstated his license on the basis that he had been rehabilitated; and he once again started practicing law, specializing in appellate matters. There was a quote in the article from Robert Jack saying, "This man saved my life!"

As John was reading the article, Tammy was afraid to leave the kitchen. She just stayed put, knowing not to go near him right then. She listened for him, but didn't hear anything. She knew that he already had enough time to finish reading the article, but for some reason he wasn't saying anything.

Finally, John walked back into the kitchen holding the paper in his left hand. He was so angry that he was shaking. Looking straight at Tammy, he pointed with his right index finger at the picture of Lucas. He screamed to her, "That motherfucker sucker-punched me! There was no mutual combat! If there had been, I would have kicked his fucking ass! I want to find out which prosecutor lied about there being mutual combat between us!"

Tammy got up and walked towards him. She tried to hug him, but he just pulled away. She said, "Honey, nobody cares who won the fight between you and him. He ended up going to jail over it."

"Well, it matters to me! This article makes me look like a pussy! It makes him look like some tough guy, even calls him a warrior. Everyone who reads this will think that I got my ass kicked by this dirty-looking motherfucker."

"John, settle down, honey. You're the judge. You're an elected official in this county. Everyone who reads this will know that he's just a terrible human being—he represents criminals for a living. Just look at that picture of him. He's disgusting!"

John, slamming the newspaper down on the ground, went back into the kitchen and picked up the telephone. He called directory assistance and asked for the number of the State Bar of Texas Disciplinary Committee. After dialing the number, he told the receptionist, "This is Judge O'Reilly of Harris County. I'd like to speak to the individual who is head of the attorney-disciplinary committee. I want to find out how a particular lawyer was ever reinstated by the Bar to practice law."

The receptionist put him through to the head of the committee, Mr. Mike Olsen. John asked about Lucas being reinstated to practice law. Mr. Olsen explained that the committee had voted and that their decision was final. He said, "Anything discussed at committee meetings is confidential and is not open to review by members of the public."

John screamed, "I'm a judge! I have the right to know what went on at the hearing!"

Mr. Olsen responded, "The fact that you're a judge means absolutely nothing. You aren't entitled to know anything that went on at any hearing."

Tammy was watching John as he spoke into the phone. His face was red, his arm was trembling as he slammed the receiver down. Standing up, he punched the refrigerator as hard as he could, yelling, "I'm a fucking judge! I get sucker-punched by some dead-beat ex-lawyer. He gets his fucking license back, nobody tells me about it, and I don't have the right to fucking know anything about why he got it back!"

Storming out of the house, he went into his garage. Tammy watched as he backed out in his black pickup truck. She had seen him angry many times, but never anything like this. Ever since his parents were killed five years earlier in an horrific car crash, he hadn't been the same.

He had inherited all their money and built her this beautiful house, but he seemed to be really lonely and very distant. She remembered how he used to spend weekends talking with Otis for endless hours about the problems of the world. Back then, he was usually in a pretty decent mood; but ever since the accident, it seemed like he was always angry.

He never really confided in her as he had with his father. She was always there for him, but he never had much to say to her. At nights, he would often eat dinner and then just plain disappear. She never knew exactly where he went and never asked. She knew that if he wanted to search out the dark side of life, Houston with its multitude of exotic clubs and single girls had plenty to offer. She figured that if he was up to anything, she didn't want to know anyway.

At the Lustick Law Office, the phone steadily rang. The article in the morning paper sprung an interest from other news media. One call after the next, everybody wanted information as to why Robert Jack was released from death row. Heather fielded all the calls, some from television stations, others from newspapers around the state.

Everybody wanted to talk with Lucas, but he refused to talk to any of the callers. He had Heather tell each of them that he was unavailable. The one call he took was from Rickie, who congratulated him for getting his license back and for his success in the Robert Jack case. Rickie asked him where he was living and about his new law office. Lucas told him to drop by the office someday.

That evening, the Robert Jack case was the headline news story on all three Houston networks. Just like the newspaper article that morning, the televised reports gave Lucas full credit for Robert Jack's release. Though Lucas was asked, he refused to be interviewed by any of the networks. All three stations showed a picture of him standing with Robert Jack outside the Jackson County Courthouse. Lucas was watching one of the broadcasts and thought that with his unkempt beard and long hair, he looked mighty grubby. But, on the other hand, he thought he looked quite professor-like.

For a moment, he thought about his father in Berkeley; he hadn't thought about him in a long time. There weren't any hard feelings against him at all; he just wished that he hadn't inherited his looks. *What would my life have been like if I was good looking like my mother?* As he continued thinking about his dad, he poured himself a glass of McAfee's bourbon whiskey. Sitting in his apartment, he just stared at the walls. Before he knew it, it was well past midnight and he was wondering where he was going to get his next case.

The following morning he went to his office where Heather told him that he had several phone calls from prospective clients. Laughing, she said, "Now that you're famous, everybody wants to hire you."

Lucas returned the calls. One man wanted him to represent him on a cocaine delivery charge; two more calls were for DWIs. Lucas told all three callers that he wasn't doing courtroom work, only appeals. Throughout the rest of the week he had over twenty phone calls from people who wanted him to represent them in court. However, he turned them all down because they didn't involve appeals.

He was receiving lots of letters from inmates on death row. It seemed like everybody there wanted him to work on their case. He was a big celebrity in Huntsville, for he had represented Robert Jack for free, and now Mr. Jack was back on the street.

Death row in Huntsville, Texas, was a horrible place to be. Inmates were locked down in small cells for at least twenty-three hours a day. Some were allowed out for recreation an hour each day, but that was left up to the warden. Many of the condemned were never freed from their small cages. They just stayed put, awaiting the day for the State to execute them. All they grasped onto was hope that somehow their case might be reversed on appeal.

Lucas reviewed each request for his help. Two cases stood out as ones in which he wanted to get involved. He also took his first private appeal, that of an elderly woman convicted in Harris County for possession of cocaine. In that case, the police burst into the old lady's house with a search warrant. She was fast asleep in her bedroom. The lawmen found twenty-four kilos of cocaine in her garage. She was charged, convicted, and sentenced to life in prison. Lucas was hired by her son-in-law, who paid him fifty-thousand dollars up front. He visited the old lady in prison.

She told him that it wasn't her cocaine; it had been placed in her garage by her son-in-law. Furthermore, she didn't want to get her son-in-law in trouble; she'd rather do the time in prison since he and her daughter had four young children at home. She wanted to appeal her case only if she was assured that her son-in-law wouldn't get into any trouble.

In her appeal, Lucas would simply argue that there wasn't an affirmative link between her and the cocaine found in the garage. There would be no mention as to whom the cocaine might belong.

Over the next three-to-four months, Lucas worked on his three new cases. He visited death row several times to meet with his two clients and spent numerous hours in the Harris County Law Library researching the law for his cases. He had no social life; he had no friends. He visited a female psychiatrist at Baylor to follow up the treatment started by Dr. Lombardi.

She tried to talk to him about what was going on in his life, but he was uncooperative with her. He didn't want to share the things he had shared with Sarah. He told her to call Sarah if it made her feel more comfortable in prescribing Prozac for him. As time passed, he was becoming more introverted and antisocial. His days were all work; at night he drank heavily. Occasionally, he would go to a topless club where he would drink and watch the women dance.

One evening he met Rickie for dinner at a local steakhouse. Rickie was dressed in a suit, but Lucas just wore jeans and a T-shirt. As the two ate, Rickie watched Lucas carefully, worried about him because he was so unkempt looking. He tried to make conversation with him, but Lucas wasn't saying much; he seldom even looked up from his plate. Rickie had always known him to be a bit strange, but now he seemed to be even worse. When the two finished eating, Rickie paid the bill. They left the restaurant and walked out to their cars.

Rickie told him that it was nice seeing him. Lucas forced himself to smile. Rickie noticed that Lucas' two front teeth looked like they were rotting away. He asked, "When was the last time you saw a dentist?"

"Oh, it's been about fifteen years."

Rickie asked if his teeth were causing him any pain.

Lucas nodded his head.

Rickie warned him, "You need to take care of those two front ones or you're going to lose them."

"Yeah, you're right."

It was another three months before Lucas visited a dentist. The dentist had to pull out both of his front teeth. He then told Lucas that he needed to get dentures. Lucas refused to even talk about it. When he showed up at his law office the next day, Heather asked, "What happened to your front teeth?"

He told her, "Mind your own business," as he went back into his office and shut the door.

It was quiet and he was able to work on his cases. Eventually, over several weeks, he finished writing briefs on all three of his pending cases. He knew that it would take months, possibly years before receiving answers on them from the appellate courts. He felt that he had chances to win all three cases. It was just a matter of waiting for the rulings to be published.

One late afternoon, he was sitting in his office staring at the walls. He received a phone call from Rickie who told him that one of their law firm's wealthiest clients had been arrested and charged in three aggravated rapes. The man, currently sitting in the county jail without any bond, had called Rickie and asked him to refer him to the best criminal-defense lawyer in the state.

"Lucas, I told him it was you. The guy's a multimillionaire." Rickie paused, "I know that you said you're not doing courtroom work, but this is going to be a high-profile case. What do you think?"

Lucas hesitated, and then said, "I appreciate your thinking about me, but I'm not really interested."

"Oh, I forgot to tell you. The case is in John O'Reilly's court."

"It's in that motherfucker's court? In that case, I may take it. What's the guy's name?"

"John Sears."

Lucas then told Rickie that he would visit Mr. Sears at the county jail. He thanked him for the referral.

That evening Lucas visited John Sears in the county jail. Sears was a dapper-looking man, even in his orange jail-suit. He was around five-feet, nine-inches tall, approximately one-hundred-and-sixty pounds. He had blondish hair and a neatly trimmed mustache. He told Lucas that he had been to court that morning and had told Judge O'Reilly that he needed to hire a lawyer.

"I've been told you're the best. Money is not an issue. I'll pay you whatever you need to properly represent me."

Lucas asked him what the case was about.

"I'm a suspect in the rapes of three different girls at the University of Houston. The girls were all attacked on different nights. I was stopped one evening by some campus police who said that I fit the physical description of the rapist."

He paused, "They were suspicious as to why I was on their campus at nighttime, so they took me into custody. Took some of my blood and put me in a lineup. None of the bitches could identify me."

He paused again, waiting for Lucas to say something, but he remained silent. "The blood they took, they did some sort of DNA testing with it. Supposedly, they found semen in all three of the girls who were raped. The testing they did came back that I was the one who raped each of them. They say that the odds are four-billion-to-one that I'm the guy."

Lucas told him, "You know that if that DNA process is done right, it's one-hundred-percent foolproof. It's unbeatable."

John Sears nodded, "I understand that. That's why I need a good lawyer!"

He was waiting to see if Lucas would ask him if he was guilty, but he never did. John Sears told him, "Just let me know how much it's going to cost and I'll have my brother drop a check by your office in the morning."

"I'm charging you two-million dollars."

John, appearing surprised, told him, "That's a lot of money!"

"You're in a lot of trouble. I'll do whatever I can to get you off."

"Can you beat this?"

Lucas assured him, "I can."

The two shook hands and Lucas left.

He went right home and started drinking from a bottle of bourbon. He was excited, not because of the money, but because he was going to go to trial in John O'Reilly's courtroom. Looking at himself in the bathroom mirror, he started cussing out John right there, "You dirty motherfucking asshole. You fuck with me in this trial, motherfucker, and I'll lay your motherfucking ass out again."

He had his fist up as he watched himself in the mirror throwing punches. He was feeling the effects of the alcohol. He thought about going to a topless bar, but was too drunk to even find his keys. Finally, he just passed out on the floor in his living room.

The next morning he went to the office. Heather told him that someone had dropped off a check, which she handed to him. She acted like she didn't know it was written for two-million dollars. He just took it and walked into his office.

He and Heather didn't have a very good working relationship. He knew she thought he was rude and condescending. Since he had been officing there, he realized that she had on numerous occasions tried talking with him, but he would very seldom engage in conversation with her. He treated her like she was merely someone who answered his phone.

He was aware that he was a bastard to her, but that was just the way it was. He also had a strained relationship with Joe Jackson; he seldom talked to him except when paying the rent each month. There would be times when Joe would go into Lucas' office, sit down, and try to talk with him about things. But Lucas would just look away from him, rarely saying anything back. Joe would finally feel uncomfortable and leave. Lucas knew that Joe thought he was an anti-social prick, but again, he just didn't care.

That afternoon, Lucas called John O'Reilly's court and spoke with Bessie, the court coordinator. He asked her when the next court date was for John Sears. She told him that Mr. Sears was on Friday's docket. She never asked him who he was; she just rudely hung up the phone after giving him the information requested.

Looking out the window of his office, he had a giant grin on his face. He couldn't wait to see John's reaction when he showed up in court to represent John Sears. He would be pissed, seeing Lucas in there on such a high-profile case. It would upset him enough just seeing him. It would be a thousand times worse seeing him on this particular case. First of all, John would know that there would be no deal-making; the case would involve a jury trial. He also would know that Lucas, as was his style, would irritate him throughout the whole trial. He would object to everything the prosecutors did; he would object to everything John did. Basically, John would know that a trial with him would be a living hell!

When Friday came, Lucas appeared in court wearing a black suit, white shirt, and a black tie. His hair was long, and he still hadn't shaved. When he first walked into the courtroom, he walked past the spectator section and into the attorney section which was located in front of John's bench. There, he stopped and just looked around. John was sitting behind his bench looking down at him. He wondered what the hell Lucas was doing in his courtroom. He called Bessie over and asked her if she knew why Lucas Lustick was there. She told him that she didn't know. She walked over to Lucas and asked, "Sir, which case are you here on?"

"I'm here to represent Mr. Sears. Tell the judge I've been paid two-million dollars."

She then walked back to John and gave him the news. He didn't show any expression, but inside he was furious. He looked up at the ceiling as if asking God what he had done to deserve this. This was an interesting case; why couldn't he enjoy it? It was now quickly turning into a nightmare. As Lucas stood there, Tom Jones, the newly assigned head prosecutor in the court, walked up to him and asked him which case he was there for.

"I'm here for the John Sears case."

"So you're representing that rascal. He's one sick puppy!"

Lucas asked, "When do you plan on taking him to trial?"

Tom answered, "I want to try him as soon as you and I are both ready. Let's approach the bench and ask the judge."

Lucas, nodding, answered, "Okay."

Tom had no idea who Lucas was. He was wondering how such a low-life lawyer got hired on this type of case. He and Lucas walked up to the bench. Tom told the judge, "This lawyer here is representing Mr. John Sears, and we were wondering when you wanted to set the case for trial?"

John, at first, didn't answer. He looked at Lucas, still in disbelief that he had the gall to appear in his courtroom. John knew that there wasn't a thing he could do about it. He was thinking that there must be some way in which he could screw Lucas over. Looking at Tom, he asked, "How complex a case is this?"

"It's very complex, Your Honor; it involves DNA testing. There's going to be an expert witness explaining the theory of DNA to the jury. As you well know, we have training sessions at the District Attorney's Office where we've been taught all about DNA, so I personally am very familiar with using this type of evidence. I'm sure that the defense is going to need plenty of time to become familiar with it, so I have no objection in giving counsel as much time as he needs to learn about DNA evidence."

John O'Reilly had never presided over a trial involving DNA evidence. But, he assumed that any defense lawyer would need time to prepare for a case involving it. He figured that Lucas would want three-to-four months to prepare for trial. He would need to learn the scientific theory behind DNA identification; then he would need to hire an expert to help him attack the prosecution's evidence.

John, looking down at Tom, told him that the case was going to trial the upcoming Monday. John looked over at Lucas, who stared back at him with a blank expression. Lucas then angrily turned around and walked out from the courtroom.

Tom stayed in front of the bench and asked, "Your Honor, you've got to be kidding. I don't have any witnesses subpoenaed yet. How can you expect me to be ready by Monday?"

John, standing up, whispered, "Follow me into my chambers."

The two left the courtroom through a side door. Once they were in chambers, John shut the door. He said, "We're going to pick a jury on Monday. Have your witnesses ready to testify Tuesday or Wednesday. It's just the three girls, a couple cops, and the forensic expert from the police laboratory. You'll have no problem getting everyone down here." He paused briefly, then continued. "That lawyer who's out there, Lucas Lustick, you didn't see him on television and in the newspapers a while back?"

"No," Tom answered. "I never read the newspapers, and I seldom watch television."

John informed him, "The guy disappeared from the courthouse scene for a long time. But when he was young, back when I was a prosecutor, he was the best trial lawyer in town. He looks like a scumbag, but don't let that fool you. He has tremendous talent in the courtroom. You haven't seen anyone like him, believe me. I tried a murder case against him when I was young and he kicked my ass in trial. I personally hate the motherfucker, but I have to admit he's a great lawyer. Trying this case on Monday gives you a huge advantage. Lustick is big in preparation, and this way, he doesn't have any time to get ready for this DNA shit. You don't want him to learn about it. Just be ready to go on Monday!"

"Well, thanks for the warning. I'll do whatever I can to be ready." Tom then left the judge's chambers.

While John was meeting with Tom, Lucas had walked back to the holding tank to talk with John Sears, who did not want to go to trial on the following Monday. He couldn't believe that the judge was pushing the case so fast.

Lucas told him, "No doubt, he's just an asshole, but fuck him. I'll be ready by Monday. What that motherfucker doesn't know is that I know all about DNA identification. I used to study up on it when I lived in Baltimore. I used to read books that scientists read about DNA. These books weren't even written for fucking lawyers. Most lawyers wouldn't ever understand the shit I used to read on DNA." John just nodded. Lucas went on, "You paid a lot of money for me to represent you. I told you I'd get you out of this, and I'm going to stick to my word; you wait and see." He then shook his hand and told him that he would see him in court on Monday.

John then asked, "Are you going to visit me this weekend so we can put together my alibi?"

"No, I'm not. You don't need a fucking alibi."

John suddenly appeared very angry. "I paid you two-million dollars to represent me and you're not even going to visit me in jail to help me with an alibi! What the hell did I pay you for?"

Lucas told him, "Calm down."

But John was now even angrier. He said, "What the fuck do you mean, 'calm down'? My whole life is at stake and you're not even gonna help me with my alibi? I'm thinking of firing your ass!"

Lucas, looking directly into his eyes, quietly said, "Look, you hired me to be your lawyer because you know that I'm the best. You just do the raping and let me do the lawyering!"

John was now furious, but he knew that Lucas was right, he was guiltier than sin. His only hope was that Lucas could somehow out-lawyer the prosecutor. That's why he hired him; he was supposedly the best there was. He needed to let Lucas take total control of the case.

He said, "Hey, I'm sorry I lost it. Just please try to get me out of this."

Lucas told him, "I have a lot of work to do before Monday. Let me get out of here. Don't worry; everything is going to be fine."

O'Reilly had fucked him by setting the case for trial that Monday. Lucas knew that he could have asked for a continuance. All he had to do was put it on the record that he wasn't prepared for trial because of the complexity of the case; then John wouldn't have had any choice but to grant it. John was playing a dirty trick on him, but he wasn't going to allow it to interfere with his representation of John Sears. He would work all weekend, and then be ready for trial on Monday.

Lucas walked to his car and then drove to the medical center. There, he looked for the University of Texas Medical School bookstore. Hustling inside, he purchased several books which had information about the forensic use of DNA. He left and drove back to his law office. At three o'clock that afternoon he received a phone call from Tom Jones, who told him that he was shocked that the judge had set the case for trial so quickly.

Lucas told him, "That's because he's a fucking prick! You ought to know that; you're in there everyday!"

Tom replied, "I want you to know that my file is open, and you're welcome today or even tomorrow to come over here and read it. I think it's unfair what the judge did to you today, and I want to be as fair to you as I can."

Lucas wondered about this. *Why would Tom try to help me prepare my defense by letting me read the State's file?*

Lucas told him, "I appreciate it, but that's okay. I'll just wait to hear the evidence in court on Monday." He thanked him for calling and then hung up the phone.

Tom was shocked that Lucas didn't take him up on his offer. He had never known of a case in which a lawyer went to trial without having read the State's file. This file, in particular, had scientific reports and charts in it that were essential to understanding the case.

Lucas stayed in his office all night gathering information from the books which he had purchased. At two a.m. he drove home. In his mind, he was ready to start trial. He knew he had a total understanding of DNA fingerprinting from a scientific standpoint. He would be able to cross-examine the prosecution's expert and show the jury that DNA evidence was not as foolproof as the expert would try to make it out to be.

He knew that once he was in the courtroom, his superior legal skills would outmatch those of the prosecutor. He would convince the jury that there were flaws in the State's case which constituted a reasonable doubt. That's all he needed to do to win the case for John Sears. He spent the rest of the weekend sleeping and getting drunk. He only left his apartment once, when he had to go to a nearby liquor store to buy some more bourbon.

On Monday, Lucas showed up in court at nine o'clock. The judge had John Sears brought out from the holding cell. He was wearing a dark-blue Brooks Brothers suit with a white shirt and red tie. He hardly looked like a man capable of raping anybody. Lucas sat next to him at the counsel table, wearing a pair of blue slacks and a black corduroy jacket.

At nine-fifteen, the jury panel started assembling in the courtroom. The jurors' eyes were focused on the table where Lucas and John Sears were sitting. Across from them sat Tom Jones, who was scribbling things onto a legal pad. As the jurors were still filing in, Tom looked over at Lucas, who didn't have any notepads in front of him, didn't even have a pen. He was amazed that Lucas had nothing to aid him. He had never heard of a lawyer going to trial without as much as a legal pad and a pen. It seemed kind of freaky to him.

John O'Reilly called for Lucas and Tom to approach the bench. He asked if both sides were ready for trial. Tom announced, "The State of Texas is ready."

John now looked down at Lucas, waiting for a response; however, he still didn't say anything.

John asked him, "Mr. Lustick, are you ready for trial?"

Lucas whispered back to him, "You bet your fucking ass I am."

Tom looked at him incredulously. He couldn't believe what he had just heard Lucas say to the judge.

John then angrily warned Lucas, "If you get out of order during this trial, I will hold you in contempt of court and put your sorry ass in jail!"

Lucas just looked at him, but didn't say anything.

John told both lawyers to go back to their counsel tables. He then introduced himself to the jury pool and thanked them for appearing. Next, he asked Lucas and Tom to once again approach the bench. He whispered to them, "Before I go on, I need to know whether you are trying just one of the cases, or all three of them at the same time?"

Tom answered, "By golly Judge, I'm not sure. Mr. Lustick and myself never discussed it."

Tom looked at Lucas who was just rubbing his beard.

After several moments, Lucas looked back at him and said, "Let's try all three cases together."

Tom responded, "That's fine with me."

Lucas felt he had just obtained a tremendous strategic advantage for his client. Though the jurors would hear about all three rapes, if he were able to win three acquittals, then the prosecution would be forbidden to try John Sears again.

If the State proceeded on just one case and Lucas beat it, then they could try John Sears two more times. The prosecution basically would have three shots to obtain a conviction. Doing them all at once would give them only one bite at the apple. True, the jury would hear from all three victims in one trial, but Lucas knew that if he could convince the jurors that DNA evidence was not reliable, then John Sears would be set free. Lucas knew how reliable DNA evidence actually was, and he assumed that it would be nearly impossible to convince three separate juries of its unreliability. With one jury he figured he had a chance. The judge ordered Lucas and Tom back to their counsel tables.

John then *voir dired* the panel on various aspects of the law which they would need to understand if chosen to be one of the twelve jurors. He talked about the burden of proof being upon the State of Texas. He defined reasonable doubt the best he could. He explained that in a criminal case, the defendant had the right to remain silent and not testify in court, and that the jurors could not hold that against him. Once he finished explaining these and several other basic legal principles, he then allowed Tom Jones and Lucas time to talk to the jury.

Tom talked with the jurors first. He asked them as a group whether they would be able to convict John Sears if he brought them enough evidence to prove that he was guilty as charged in all three cases. The jurors all nodded that they could if they believed there was sufficient evidence. He then explained that in certain cases there might not be eyewitness identification, and that the State might rest its laurels solely on scientific evidence. He asked the panel members whether they would be able to convict if they were convinced beyond a reasonable doubt of a defendant's guilt based on evidence derived solely from scientific findings. The jurors each acknowledged that they would be able to do so. Tom talked with the panel for about thirty minutes and then sat down.

Lucas then stood up and slowly shuffled to the podium where he introduced himself to the jurors. Pointing to John Sears, he told everyone that Mr. Sears was innocent of committing the three rapes for which he was charged. He then pointed over to Tom Jones who was sitting at the counsel table, and told the jurors that Mr. Jones was trying to get a life sentence against an innocent man. This totally teed-off Tom, who stood up and angrily objected to Lucas telling the jurors that John Sears was innocent.

The judge sustained the objection and told Lucas to continue.

"That prosecutor is going to want you jurors to convict my client based solely on some flimsy, hocus-pocus type of evidence."

Again, Tom stood and loudly objected. He was furious at Lucas.

Lucas knew that he was getting under Tom's skin. The judge instructed him not to give his personal opinion as to the reliability of any evidence which the State intended to rely upon in the trial. Lucas then talked to each juror individually about some of their life experiences. He wanted to know where each person came from. What was their background? Were they conservative or liberal-minded people?

He wanted jurors who were less likely to be impressed by complicated scientific evidence. In his mind, he preferred people with the least amount of education. He wanted folks who had never even heard of DNA evidence; they would be less likely to convict based upon it. He knew that well-read jurors would most likely be acquainted with DNA and would know that the scientific community felt it to be infallible. Once he finished talking to the jurors, he made his strikes and then handed his list to the court's clerk.

Tom Jones then turned in his strike list.

John waited for the clerk to hand him the names of the twelve jurors who remained after both sides struck ten jurors whom they found unsuitable. He then called out the names of the dozen folks who were going to serve in this particular case. All twelve of them walked forward and took a seat in the jury box. John made them swear to give a true verdict based solely upon the evidence. The rest of the panel was then excused.

John then asked Tom Jones if he had an opening statement. He stood up and answered in front of the jury, "No, Your Honor, my case is so strong I don't need one."

Lucas, jumping out of his chair, screamed, "Screw him, Judge! I object to him saying that!"

He was seething mad. He started toward Tom Jones, looking as if he was ready to slug him. John then yelled to his bailiff to clear the jury out of the courtroom. After the jurors left he angrily looked at Lucas, telling him, "If I see another outburst from you like what I just saw, I will hold you in contempt of this court and place you in the county jail for a hundred-and-eighty days! Am I clear, Mr. Lustick?"

Lucas didn't answer him.

"Mr. Lustick, if you're not going to answer me, that's fine. I'm giving you notice that the next time you get out of line, that's it. This trial will be over. I'll declare a mistrial, and you'll go to jail for one-hundred-and-eighty days."

He then told the bailiff to bring the jurors back into the courtroom. After they took their seats, he told Tom Jones to begin presenting his case. The first three witnesses were attractive, young college coeds who all told basically the same story. Each one had been on the University of Houston campus late some night, when grabbed by a masked man holding a knife who dragged her to an isolated area behind the campus football stadium. There, each girl was forced to perform oral sex and was then violently raped. Each was threatened that if she went to the police, he would come back and kill her.

Nevertheless, each girl testified that she immediately contacted the campus police. In all three cases, the girls were taken to Ben Taub Hospital in the Houston Medical Center, where they were examined by physicians. All three testified how their lives had been affected since the incidents.

Throughout the girls' testimony, Lucas just watched them. They were all the preppy types he didn't like back when he was in school. He had no compassion for any of them. He didn't care that they were raped, but he knew that the jurors didn't share the same feelings. He could sense that they, as a group, had tremendous sympathy for the girls. He wanted to cross-examine them just because he could, but he knew it wouldn't be wise so he didn't ask them any questions.

Following the girls' testimony, the next witnesses were the three women doctors who were each on call at the Ben Taub Emergency Room on one of the nights when a girl was brought in. They each testified about the physical exam they performed by using cotton swabs, hoping to find any seminal fluid left by the attacker.

When Tom Jones passed each doctor for questioning, Lucas stood up and said, "I have no questions."

Following their testimony, the next witness was the same University of Houston police officer who accompanied each girl to the hospital. In all three cases, this officer transported the envelopes containing the cotton swabs taken by the doctors to the City of Houston Crime Lab, where he placed them in a lockbox. Following his testimony for the prosecution, Lucas told the court, "I have no further questions of this witness."

The arresting officer took the witness stand and told the jurors about the night he detained John Sears for lurking on the campus, "I was suspicious of him. I asked him if he would consent to giving a sample of his blood, and to my surprise, he consented. A nurse took a vial of his blood which I drove directly to the city crime lab where I dropped it off."

Lucas refrained from asking this officer any questions.

It was nearly five o'clock in the afternoon when John recessed the trial until the following day. He told the jurors to return by nine o'clock in the morning to continue hearing testimony. Standing up, he walked off the bench.

That evening, during dinner, Tammy asked John how his day in court went. She knew that there were apt to be some problems between him and Lucas.

He told her, "Things went pretty well; Lustick got out of line early this morning, but I set his ass straight. I told him I wasn't going to take any of his bullshit and that I'd throw him in jail if he carried on. He seemed to get the message. He didn't say much the rest of the day."

He paused, "All three of the victims testified, and Lucas didn't ask a single question of any of them, which surprised me. The girls were all sweet, pretty college girls, the type he used to hate when we were in law school in California. I thought he would fuck with them on cross-examination just for kicks, but he didn't.

"The three doctors from Ben Taub who examined the girls, and the police officer involved in the cases, he didn't ask any of them a single question. He could've fucked with them on chain of custody regarding the physical evidence, but he didn't."

Tammy then said, "Maybe he's just changed as a lawyer. He's gotten a lot older. Maybe he's lost the attitude he had when he was younger."

John looking at her, said, "No, I don't think so; he's up to something. I don't know what it is ... but it's something.

He reads jurors like a hawk. There was a reason why he didn't ask any questions today."

The following morning, the jury was in the box at nine o'clock sharp ready to listen to testimony. Everyone was anxious to begin, except Lucas, who hadn't shown up yet.

He arrived at nine-fifteen and sat down at the counsel table next to John Sears. He was wearing the same clothes he had worn the day before. The jurors were all watching him, wondering where he had been all night. Tom Jones looked at John who was sitting at his bench. Tom knew that Judge O'Reilly was a stickler for lawyers being in court on time. He expected him to lash out at Lucas for being late, but John knew that's exactly what Lucas wanted him to do. That way, he might get some sympathy from the jurors. John looked down at Tom and told him, "Call your next witness."

He called Shannon Simpson to the stand. Shannon ran the Houston Police Department's Forensic Laboratory. He was the expert on running the tests which compared DNA evidence recovered at crime scenes to that of possible suspects.

He told the jurors about his background in forensic science, giving them a detailed accounting of the many courses he had taken which prepared him to do DNA laboratory testing and comparisons. He told the jurors that he had conducted DNA comparisons in over two-hundred cases.

Tom Jones asked him to explain DNA fingerprinting to the jury. Tom told him that he could use the chalkboard in the courtroom to help explain it. Shannon then stood up and walked over to the chalkboard. He picked up a piece of chalk and looked over at the jurors, ready to educate them on the subject of DNA. He told them that every cell contains DNA, and that DNA is a chemical that carries a genetic code. He told them that cells had chains of DNA molecules which had millions of "bases" which were listed as either A, T, C, or G. He explained that these bases were different in their sequences for everyone on the planet, except for identical twins.

Lucas then objected to the witness "testifying in the narrative." He asked John to order the prosecutor to proceed in question-and-answer form. John overruled his objection.

Tom then asked Shannon, "Will you explain to this jury what type of test you run to see if a suspect's DNA matches that found at the crime scene? Try to be specific to the facts in our cases."

Shannon told the jurors that in these particular cases, DNA was extracted from the semen recovered from the three swabs which were turned over to the crime lab. He said that the defendant in this case, John Sears, following his detention by campus police, gave a sample of his blood to the laboratory from which his DNA was extracted. Once he had the three swabs which contained the "unknown DNA," he needed to see if any of them matched the "known DNA," that being John Sears' DNA.

He told the jurors that he used restriction enzymes, which were chemicals which cut the DNA to find the sequence of the

A, T, C, and G bases. He explained that the sequence might be C, C, G, A, T, T in a particular DNA strand, or that it might be another sequence in another strand.

He said that once he had a sample of the DNA, he would put some of it onto a gel base and use electric force to move the DNA fragments to different parts of the gel. The specific patterns on the gel would then be placed on a nylon membrane which he would treat with radioactive chemicals.

Lucas looked over to the jury panel. He was pleased to see that they were totally confused. They were trying to understand what Shannon Simpson was explaining to them, but were finding it very difficult. *What's he thinking ... that these jurors are fucking molecular biologists?*

Shannon continued with his testimony, explaining that the nylon membrane was held against x-ray film for three days, and this recorded the radioactivity involved. Finally, he testified that he could compare the "unknown DNA" from the crime scene to that of the "known DNA" taken from the suspect, John Sears, and could determine whether there was a "match." He explained what a match was between two DNA samples. He said that in this particular case, there was a positive match of John Sears' DNA to that of all three samples of DNA recovered from the swabs taken from the three crime victims.

He then gave a statistical analysis as to what he thought was the probability that John Sears committed the three rapes at the University of Houston. He told the jurors that the chances of John Sears being the culprit were four billion-to-one. Tom Jones then asked him to be seated back on the witness stand. Next he told the court, "I'll pass the witness."

Lucas began his questioning by tearing into Shannon Simpson with an exhaustive cross-examination like Shannon had never before experienced. In past trials testifying about DNA, the defense lawyers rarely asked him any questions. That was not the case here. Lucas, holding up his medical books, approached Shannon and attacked all the procedures which were used by the crime lab.

He pointed out to the jurors that Shannon's work-product fell far short from what it should have been. He shoved the books in Shannon's face, asking him to explain why he didn't follow the same procedures which were used by forensic scientists at Harvard and Johns Hopkins. He asked to see all of Shannon's notes, and then spent two hours displaying them to the jury so that everyone could see how sloppy his work was.

Finally, he attacked Shannon's conclusion that statistically there was a four-billion-to-one probability that John Sears was guilty. Lucas was an expert on statistical analysis. Approaching the chalkboard, he asked Shannon if he would join him there. He then asked him to write on the board the statistical equations which he used in reaching his conclusions.

Shannon knew that he wasn't all that great at statistics. He could tell how sharp Lucas was on everything. He wanted to quietly leave the courtroom and go home, but he knew that he couldn't. There he stood, next to the chalkboard, only feet away from the jury. Next to him was a crazy-looking lawyer who was getting ready to rip into him. And that's just what Lucas did. In one of the most blistering cross-examinations ever seen in a Texas courtroom, Lucas reduced Shannon to tears. He readily admitted that his statistical analysis was way off. He admitted that the probability of John Sears having committed the three rapes at the University of Houston was actually only thirty-to-one.

When Lucas finished his questioning, he walked back to the counsel table and sat down. He was sweating profusely, his perspiration dripping from his face onto the counsel table. John Sears looked over at him and knew that he had gotten what he had paid for. Lucas Lustick had raised a reasonable doubt.

It was four o'clock in the afternoon and the judge asked Tom if he had any more witnesses to testify.

"No sir, the State rests its case."

John then looked at Lucas and asked, "What says the defense?"

Standing up, Lucas said, "The defense rests."

John then gave the jurors a ten-minute recess, informing them that when they returned he would read them the jury-charge, and then each lawyer would make a final argument. During this recess, he and Tom retreated into chambers where he gave Tom some ideas for final argument. Tom wrote them down on a pad so that he would remember what to argue before the jury. John assured him that he would still gain convictions based on the evidence presented.

During the recess, Lucas walked out to his car. Finding a bottle of Jack Daniel's in his trunk, he started drinking from it. He knew he'd already won the case; he could see it in the jurors' eyes. There was no need to even make a final argument. There was no way that this jury was going to convict John Sears. He took a couple more hits from the bottle and then walked back into the courthouse. After riding the elevator, he slowly walked inside the courtroom and sat down at the counsel table. Judge O'Reilly and Tom Jones were still in the judge's chambers working on the prosecution's final argument.

It was nearly thirty more minutes before they appeared in the courtroom. Lucas had fallen asleep in his chair while he was waiting on them. John Sears had to kick him to awaken him.

Judge O'Reilly read the jury charge to the jurors. Lucas had the chance to argue first. He stood up and fell backwards; the alcohol combined with the hard day's work had taken its toll on him. Regaining his balance, he walked in front of the jury. Looking at them, he didn't say anything. He stood there for a long time; everybody was waiting for him to speak.

Peering into the eyes of several of the men jurors, he could tell that they were on his side. The women jurors, on the other hand, he wasn't so sure about since he wouldn't look them in the eyes. His instincts told him that he shouldn't say much. These jurors knew what was up; they saw him rip apart the State's case. Finally, he asked them, "Will you please find my client not guilty?"

He then nodded to the jurors and sat back down at the counsel table.

Tom Jones was next. His final argument lasted over forty-five minutes. He went into great detail on how John Sears had ruined the lives of the three coeds. He told them that the poor girls would never again feel safe alone. He talked about the nightmares each would have to live with. He mentioned the fine work done by the police and doctors involved in the cases. He added, "As for Shannon Simpson's testimony, the defense lawyer's personal attack upon him was unnecessary and proved nothing. It was simply showboating by Mr. Lustick in an attempt to confuse you."

Tom emphasized how reliable DNA evidence was, and argued that in all three cases there was a positive match with DNA extracted from John Sears' blood and the DNA extracted from the semen found inside the victims' bodies. He then pointed at John Sears and screamed, "You are a serial rapist!"

Lucas shot out of his chair, "I object, Judge, to his calling my client that. To hell with him!"

John immediately picked up his hammer and started banging it on the bench. He yelled at Lucas, "Sit down, Counsel!"

Lucas looked at him and their eyes met. He didn't want to fight with John, for he was too exhausted and was feeling the effect of the Jack Daniel's. Today was not the day to do battle with John O'Reilly. He quietly sat back down.

Tom finished up his argument by asking the jurors to find John Sears guilty in all three cases.

Judge O'Reilly then told the jurors that they should go back into the jury room, elect a foreman, and begin deliberations. At that point, the twelve jurors looked at one another and started nodding their heads. An overweight man in his fifties rose up from his chair. He told John that the jurors didn't need to leave the jury box to deliberate. "Your Honor, we already have a verdict in this case."

John looked at the jurors; each of them nodded to him. He was very surprised for he had never seen this happen before, a jury deliberating right in the jury box.

He then asked the juror, "What is the verdict in each case?"

"Not guilty in each case, Your Honor!"

Tom dropped his head down on the counsel table in total disbelief. He had just completed what he thought was his best final argument ever. John Sears had a giant grin on his face. Standing up, he thanked the jurors while they were still in the box. John O'Reilly got off the bench and left the courtroom.

Lucas shook hands with John Sears and left the courtroom ahead of the jurors. He went out to his car and grabbed his bottle of Jack Daniel's, took a drink from it, and then drove off. He got onto the freeway and started driving home. Unfortunately, he got stuck in rush-hour traffic. While he was sitting in his car, he started having a craving for a white-trash, blonde-headed woman. Immediately he pulled off the freeway onto Richmond Avenue and went into Tiffany's, a well-known topless club. There, he ordered a drink and looked around the club at the various dancers. A young blonde in a black miniskirt caught his attention. Calling her over, he asked her to give him several lap dances. He really liked the way she looked and the way she moved. He asked her how much money she expected to make that evening.

"Five-hundred dollars."

He then offered her two-thousand in cash to come spend the night with him. She agreed, and the two of them left the club together. Driving her own car, she followed him to his place. Once they arrived at the barren apartment, he showered while she sat down at the kitchen table and drank a beer from the refrigerator.

He came out wearing only a pair of boxer shorts. He lit up a cigarette, poured himself a drink, and sat down at the table with her. She asked him what he did for a living. He said he was a banker. He really didn't desire to have any conversation with her. He got up, went to his bedroom, and then came back and handed her two-thousand dollars in one-hundred-dollar bills. He then led her into the bedroom, shut the door, and had his way with her. When he was finished, he passed out asleep on his bed. The young girl got up and quietly left his apartment to go back to work at the club.

Across town, John O'Reilly was at home pouring down shots of Johnnie Walker Black.

He, too, was exhausted from the two long days in court. He sat across from Tammy who was nibbling away at the lasagna she had made for dinner. John kept pouring down drink after drink without saying anything to her.

It was obvious that Lucas had won the case in court that day. Tammy knew how much it upset her husband. Finally, he said something to her; the liquor had taken him off his guard. "Tammy, I've never seen anything like it. As much as I can't stand Lucas, he's by far the finest lawyer I've ever seen in court. Today, his client was guilty as sin. Guilty of violently raping three college girls, and that fucking Lucas convinced that jury to cut him loose."

Pouring himself another drink, he continued, "What he did to this expert witness was unbelievable. He's just so fucking talented. He did everything off the cuff. Never even took a note throughout the whole fucking trial! I've never seen anything like it. When it was all over, the jury never even wanted to go into the jury room. They voted right in the fucking jury box!"

Tammy then told him, "There's nothing, honey, that you could have done about it. You've always known how fine a lawyer Lucas is."

John didn't say anything else. He just sat at the table staring at the bottle of Johnnie Walker.

TWENTY-ONE

It was two days before Lucas regained consciousness. The trial, in combination with the bourbon and blonde-headed girl, totally zapped him of energy. Stumbling out of bed, he showered, got dressed, and opened the door to his apartment. It was light outside. He thought it was Wednesday morning. Getting into his car, he drove to a nearby diner. Before going inside, he put some change into a newspaper dispenser and pulled out the morning's paper. Only then did he realize that he had slept through Wednesday, and it was now Thursday. Walking inside the diner, he grabbed a seat and ordered breakfast.

After eating, he drove downtown to his law office. There he walked in and was greeted by Heather, "Well, here comes the celebrity! Your phone was ringing off the hook yesterday. Everybody wants to talk to you."

"What are you talking about?" Lucas wasn't in any mood to be called a celebrity. He thought she was poking fun at him.

"Did you see yourself in the newspaper and on television yesterday? That case with John Sears was splattered all over the news! Everyone's been calling here, wanting to talk to you."

"What did you tell them?"

"I told them that you weren't here, that I didn't know where you were."

"Well, keep telling that to anybody who calls. I don't want to talk to anybody about anything."

Regardless, over the next hour, he had numerous phone calls from people who wanted to hire him as their lawyer. One was from a local baseball star for the Astros who was charged with assault. Lucas refused to talk to anyone, instructing Heather to simply tell folks that he wasn't taking any new cases. The John Sears trial had worn him out, and now he wasn't sure what to do with his life. He promised himself that he would never again step into a courtroom to do a trial. Having deposited his fee from the Sears case into an account at Wells Fargo Bank, he was basically set financially. There was also plenty of money in his bank in Baltimore.

On Friday morning, instead of going to his office, Lucas headed to Lyons Avenue, a rough part of town just north of downtown Houston. The area was frequented by drug dealers and prostitutes. Lucas knew that on Lyons Avenue he could pick up a street hustler for a fifty-dollar bill. That's what he was in the mood for that morning, just quick sex from a street girl.

Spotting an attractive black woman standing on the side of the street, he took her to a motel room which he rented for twenty dollars. When he finished with her, he dropped her back off where he had found her.

Then he cruised down several blocks and came upon an industrial part of town which he had never paid attention to. There were wrecker yards and scrap-metal yards on both sides of the roadway. He pulled into one of the scrap-metal yards just out of curiosity. There was a large sign which read in bold letters, "SHAPIRO SCRAP YARD," raised above the entryway. Pulling inside the gate, he parked his car.

Sitting there, he watched the men who were working. They each wore blue shirts which said "Shapiro Metals" on them. The workers were all extremely filthy, their hands and arms covered with dirt. Several of them were pulling heavy metal drums, one was operating a crane, others were loading a truck.

The only job Lucas had ever known was that of being a hired mouthpiece for people who were in trouble. Having never had any other job, he wondered what it would be like to work for Shapiro Metals. Sitting in his car, he kept watching the workers and thinking. *Now these are real men who work hard for a living. At the end of the day they wash off the dirt and sweat from themselves and go home to wherever they came from.*

Finally, he got out and walked to the main office. Opening the door, he walked inside. Behind the counter was a man wearing a white shirt and a pair of work pants. He asked Lucas, "What can I do for you?"

"I was looking for a job."

"Have you ever worked for a scrap-metal yard before?"

"No."

"Well, what kind of work have you done in the past?"

"I'm a lawyer, but I don't want to be one anymore. I want an honest job."

The man, thinking Lucas had quite a sense of humor, said, "You're telling me that you're a lawyer, but you want to work in this rat hole?"

Lucas nodding his head, answered, "I need the work."

The man assumed Lucas was simply an old bum lying about being a lawyer. Basically, he was amused by him. He told him, "I can put you to work in the metal house; we need another man back there. You need to show up here tomorrow morning at eight. I'll pay you fifty bucks at the end of each work day."

Lucas told him that he'd be back in the morning, and the man handed him one of the blue shirts just like he'd seen the other guys wearing. Lucas took it and left the office. He walked out to his car and backed out from the dusty yard. He was so excited about starting his job the next day that he drove to a local department store to buy some work clothes. There, he purchased three pairs of beige work pants, a pair of steel-toed boots, and a yellow cap which had the word

"CATERPILLAR" across it. He was as wired as he had been in a long time and couldn't wait for the morning to arrive.

After returning home, he watched television until nine o'clock. Then, he set his alarm clock to go off early in the morning. At nine-fifteen he lay down in his bed, wanting to make sure that he had a good night's rest before starting his new job. He had a hard time falling asleep, but eventually did so.

When he got up in the morning, he put on his work clothes. Particularly, he liked the Shapiro Metals shirt; he kept admiring himself in the mirror. This job would be a whole lot different than going to the courthouse. Leaving his apartment, he drove to Lyons Avenue where he parked his car inside the gates of Shapiro Metals. Walking into the front office, he found the man who had given him the job the day before. The foreman didn't say much to him other than, "Come with me."

He led Lucas through a dusty yard behind the front office and into a wooden building where he introduced him to a middle-aged black man named "Punch." He informed Punch that Lucas would be his new assistant in the metal house.

Punch was angry that the foreman had hired a white man to work with him. Punch had worked for Shapiro Metals twenty years and had always had black men working with him in the metal house. As the foreman started walking back to the office, Punch followed after him, asking, "Why are you giving me this fat, weak-looking, white motherfucker to work with me back here? This motherfucker won't be able to help me at all!"

The foreman told him, "Just see how it works out. If he's lazy, we'll get rid of his ass."

Punch hurried back into the metal house where he immediately started bossing Lucas around. He ordered him to empty out a large metal drum which contained copper tubing attached to yellow brass fittings. He told him to cut the copper from the brass and to separate them into two separate drums. Lucas used a large cutting shear to help do this. It was almost noon when he finished the job. Punch then told him that he was leaving for lunch and that he wanted him to separate all the yellow brass from the red brass in two large drums. Lucas turned the drums over, and by the time Punch returned from lunch, he had separated all the yellow brass from the red.

Punch was impressed by the work of his new assistant. Looking at Lucas' filthy hands, he tossed him a pair of gloves and said, "Wear these when you work; they'll help keep your hands from getting cut."

Lucas took the gloves and put them on. Punch then led him out behind the metal house where there were old car batteries stacked on top of one another. The stacks reached over eight-feet high. There must have been a thousand batteries piled up; they were all different colors. They were nasty-looking, some with acid spilling down the sides. A large truck was backed up to the stacks. Punch told Lucas that his next job was to load all the batteries onto the truck.

Lucas asked, "What are you guys doing with all these batteries?"

"People bring their dead car batteries here, and we buy them because they've got lead in them. Also, gas stations bring them here. Once we get enough of them, we load up this truck and ship them to Dallas, where a bigger yard buys them from us. We make good fucking money out of these batteries. The lead has good value to it."

Lucas then started picking up the batteries one at a time and loading them onto the truck. Some of them were soaked in acid and when he picked them up, the acid would slip underneath his gloves and burn his hands. But he continued doing his job, loading the batteries onto the truck one at a time. Each battery he would carry from the pile to the truck. Then he would have to climb onto the truck so that he could neatly stack the batteries in rows on top of one another.

It was hard labor. He had never worked like this before and was exhausted. But he kept going, even surprising himself with his perseverance. Sweat was dripping from him—he felt like a real working man. Two young black men wearing Shapiro Metals shirts came over and started helping him load the batteries onto the truck. He welcomed the help since he was close to passing out. The heat was getting to him. He asked if there was anyplace he could get a cup of water.

One of the men led him to a shack way in the back of the scrap yard. He told Lucas to go inside, that there was a toilet and also a water cooler. Lucas walked in and got a paper cup which he filled with cold water and then quickly gulped down. There was a mirror on the wall in the shack which he looked into. He was absolutely filthy; his face and beard were soaked in sweat mixed with dirt. His shirt and pants were drenched in sweat and acid. He loved the way he looked. Heading back out to the battery pile, he continued loading batteries onto the truck.

One of his co-workers asked, "What's an old motherfucker like you doing working out here with us niggers?"

"I just needed a job."

After the truck was fully loaded, Lucas walked back into the metal house and informed Punch that they had finished loading the truck. Punch then screamed out into the yard to the two workers who had helped load the truck to come back into the metal house.

Once they did so, Punch closed the door, and then pulled out a large, flat sheet of aluminum. He placed it on top of a large drum and pulled out a pair of red dice. The two workers had big smiles on their faces as they stood across from Punch. They each pulled out dollar bills from their pants' pockets.

Punch told Lucas, "At the end of the fucking day we always shoot craps back here. The boss man up front, he don't know; that's why we shut the door, so he can't see back here."

Lucas watched as Punch and the two other workers started the game. Then he asked if he could join in. Punch responded, "Sure, just pull out your money!"

Lucas pulled out twenty dollars and joined the game. Punch was shooting the dice and needed to roll a ten. Holding the dice between his two hands and talking to them, he shouted, "Baby needs a new pair of shoes."

He then rolled the dice on the aluminum sheet where one of them came up six and the other came up four. He grabbed money out of everybody's hands. When the game was over, Lucas had lost his twenty dollars, but had the time of his life doing so. After work that day, he went with Punch to a bar across the street from Shapiro's. There, he drank bourbon and shot pool until sundown. Then, he and Punch went their separate ways.

Lucas drove down Lyons Avenue heading out to the freeway. He must have passed by fifteen or twenty street walkers, but he felt he was too dirty to pick up any of them. He went home, took a shower, and lay down. He was totally exhausted. It was the hardest day of work he had ever had. Being a blue-collar worker seemed to suit him well. Placing his head on his pillow, he fell fast asleep.

The next day he was back at work. The foreman had Punch and him take the truckload of batteries to Dallas where they would drop them off at another scrap-metal yard. Punch did the driving and Lucas sat in the passenger seat. Once they reached the yard, Lucas assisted several young men from there in unloading the batteries from the truck. Punch occasionally came back and helped, but mostly he just chatted with the foreman of the Dallas yard while the truck was being unloaded. Once the job was finished, they headed back to Houston. Along the way, Punch asked, "Can you drive this truck?"

"Yep."

Punch pulled off on the side of the road. The two changed positions and Lucas was now behind the wheel. He sped off, reaching speeds of nearly seventy miles an hour on Interstate 45. Both windows were rolled down on the cab; he could feel the force of the air hitting his face. This was as much fun as he had ever had. Once he got back to Houston, he pulled the truck into the yard at Shapiro's. Punch then told him to go back into the metal house and sweep up the floor; then he could leave for the day.

For the next year, Lucas worked at the yard. It was a job he fell in love with. He still had a law office, but seldom went there. He worked on several appeals during the evening hours. He no longer considered himself to be a lawyer. In his mind, he was a junkyard man, a blue-collar worker. He showed up at work each morning, put in his eight hours, and then went home. He had moved from his apartment in the southwest part of town, to a ghetto apartment not too far from work.

He and Punch became close friends during this year. They worked together during the days and often went out together at night to neighborhood bars where they would shoot pool and get drunk. Sometimes, they would pick up street walkers and bring them back to his apartment where they would stay up all night.

During the time Lucas worked at Shapiro's, he won two of the appeals which he had filed. One was for the old lady who had been convicted in the cocaine case. She was set free because the court held that there wasn't an affirmative link between her and the cocaine found in her garage.

The other case involved one of the men on death row who was awarded a new trial due to technical mistakes made by the judge in his trial. The Appellate Court applauded Lucas for uncovering these errors. He had now won two appeals for death-row inmates. No inmate had ever been released from death row, except the two men whom Lucas had represented. It was now well accepted amongst the legal community that he was the top appellate lawyer in the state, if not the entire nation.

As great a lawyer as he was, he no longer had any interest in practicing law. He much preferred his blue-collar job and had no intentions of going back to handling courtroom cases. But, he would keep an open mind and possibly take some appeals if they interested him. He still maintained his law office and called Heather every two weeks or so to get his messages.

There were always lots of calls from people who wanted to hire him to represent them in court, for Houston was a hotbed for criminal activity. Hundreds of people were being arrested each day, and many of them had plenty of money to hire top-notch defense lawyers. Lucas Lustick was thought to be the best money could buy. However, he simply wasn't taking on any new cases.

TWENTY-TWO

It was the hottest summer that Houstonians had ever experienced. There was a sweltering heat, the type that drove everybody inside. But even then, air conditioners had little success in keeping people cool because the humidity was just plain uncontrollable. Hundreds of people were dying from heat stroke, many more had to be hospitalized. The rising temperature was paralleled by a rising homicide rate. By mid-August there had already been over fifty killings committed in Houston during that month alone. Homicide detectives worked overtime trying to solve the cases.

But there was one particular killing which had investigators both angered and baffled. It involved an eight-year-old girl who had been abducted from a neighborhood swim-team meet. The child's body was recovered near an area bayou. She had been sexually mutilated by a soft-drink bottle which was found near her body. Her throat had been cut, and semen was found splattered on her face. Houstonians were outraged by this brutal killing and put tremendous pressure upon the police department to catch the perpetrator of this horrible crime. The top-two detectives within the homicide division put their heads together and were trying to solve it, but so far had been unsuccessful. They lacked even a clue as to who had committed this heinous crime.

"We've got to catch the sick bastard who killed this little girl! This case really bothers me," said Detective Jack Dean with a sigh as he got up from his desk and walked towards Mike Sandell.

Stepping in front of Mike's desk, he continued, "In our twenty years in this division, this is the sickest case I've ever seen. It's not just some ghetto or wetback killing. It's not some guy killing his wife for whatever reason. It's totally sick!"

Leaning forward, he rested his hands on Mike's desk and continued, "I keep seeing her in my mind when we found her lying near that bayou. She looked so young, so innocent."

Mike knew just what Jack was talking about. He had been with him when the girl's body was recovered. "We'll catch the sick bastard," he assured him.

Jack, shaking his head, said, "I don't care what the Chief tells us about following the rules. I'll do whatever I need to do to catch this perverted motherfucker!"

He looked down to where Mike was sitting. He knew that Mike realized that this case was by far the most serious of the unsolved murders pending in Houston. They both were committed to solving it as soon as possible. They had been receiving tips from various sources ever since the killing; unfortunately, all of them so far had led to dead ends.

On this particular night it was very quiet in the homicide division. The phones weren't ringing, nobody visited. It was just Jack and Mike doing paperwork. The other detectives were off for the evening or working the streets. The only other person with them at the department that evening was Diana, a secretary whose desk was down the hallway. Their shift lasted until six a.m.

At two a.m. Diana knocked on their door. Mike said, "Come in."

Opening the door, Diana announced, "There's a woman out here who wants to talk to a detective. She doesn't want to give her name, but says that she has reliable information about some murder case."

Jack told her to bring the woman down to their office so that they could interview her. Diana, returning with her, said, "Both of these men are homicide detectives. They can help you."

Both Jack and Mike exchanged greetings with the woman as Diana quietly shut the door and walked back to her desk.

Dressed in all black, the woman was wearing a skirt just above her knees and a sleeveless blouse which was tucked in. Her shoes were simple black flip-flops, the type which one might wear to a pool party. Her dark hair was pulled back into a ponytail. She wore around her neck a thin, black, silk-rope necklace held together by a simple clasp. She had huge, circular, dark eyes, and a very thin, pale, fragile-looking face. She wore no makeup, except a touch of red lipstick which emphasized her lips. She appeared to be in her late twenties.

Jack told her to have a seat across from him. She sat gracefully and crossed her legs. He asked her what her name was.

"I don't want to tell you my name."

Jack looked into her eyes and then down at the floor for several seconds. Finally, he looked back up at her and asked, "Why don't you want to give us your name?"

"I have information as to who killed the little swim-team girl. But I will only give it to you on the condition that I remain anonymous. I want to give you my information only if I'm assured that I will never again be contacted." She paused, and then continued, "Unless you make me that promise, I'll leave right now."

Jack looked over at Mike who was slowly nodding his head. Jack then told the woman, "We'll honor your wishes. Give us whatever information you have. You can then leave and we'll never call you back. I'm giving you my word."

The mysterious woman looked back at him, not saying anything. Jack thought that she was beautiful in a gypsy sort of way. He was intrigued by her looks and also eager to hear whatever information she might share with them.

She asked, "How can I believe you detectives when you tell me that I'll never be called back after tonight?"

"I can't make you believe me," answered Jack. "All I can do is give you my word that I will never make you come back."

"I will trust that you and your partner will do just as you both promise me."

"Thank you." Jack paused, and then asked, "Will you please tell us what you know?"

She began, "I'm a call girl to very wealthy gentlemen. Most of my clients live either in Dallas or Houston. They pay a lot for sessions with me. They're all very different in what their needs and desires are. I do whatever they ask of me as long as it's not dangerous."

She then paused for a moment before continuing, "I've got one particular client here in Houston who recently did some very strange things to me. I saw him just prior to when that little girl was kidnapped from her swim-team meet. He came over to my condominium for his regular session. In prior meetings with him, he always wanted me to wear lingerie. But on this particular night he wanted me to wear a one-piece bathing suit. I know this man pretty well; I've been seeing him for almost three years. On this night, he tied my wrists together with some rope, which was normal for him. A lot of my clients are into this."

She paused and stared into Jack's eyes. Then she looked away from him, down at the carpet, and continued, "He then pulled my arms behind my head, and he started kissing me on top of my bathing suit where my breasts and stomach are. Then he reached into this gym bag which was beside the bed and pulled out something. It was so dark in the room, I didn't know what it was. He pulled my bathing suit aside, and then he put something inside of me which felt very strange, like hard and cold.

"I asked him, 'What are you putting inside me?' He told me that it was a Pepsi bottle. I've been with a lot of strange men before, so I knew not to act surprised. I knew he would never hurt me, for he was just playing out a fantasy. He moved the bottle around, inside of me, but after a while he started doing it harder. It was hurting, so I screamed at him to stop, which he did. I asked him what he was doing. He told me, 'Just be quiet.' So I just lay there, and I saw him doing himself." She paused and continued, "He was as excited as I'd ever seen him. After several minutes of this, he came all over my face."

Jack told her, "He sounds like one sick bastard!"

She continued, "I asked him afterwards what had gotten into him. He's always been honest with me, figuring that whatever he tells me is in confidence. He told me that he had a strange desire to abduct a little girl from a swim team; it was something he felt he needed to do, something he felt like he had no control over. That's why he play-acted it out with me. He figured that it would keep him from actually doing it. But, it was only a week later when I heard that little girl was kidnapped and killed. I'm not sure if he's the guy, but I just felt that I had to come down here and tell somebody about the experience I had with this man. He could be the guy. I really don't know."

Jack assured her, "You're doing the right thing by coming down here. He sure might be the guy! It's our job to look into all that."

Mike asked, "Who is this man?"

She didn't look over to him. She looked at Jack and told him, "His name is John O'Reilly. He's a judge here in town."

Mike snapped, "What? You've got to be kidding me!" He seemed as if he didn't believe her. He stood up and started approaching her. She looked scared.

Jack scolded him, "Mike, sit down and relax! Just sit down!"

The woman then asked if it was okay for her to leave because she had nothing else to say. She appeared to be frightened by Mike. Jack told her she could go, and she opened the door to the office and walked out.

Mike looked at Jack and asked, "You don't believe a word that whore says, do you?"

"No, but we need to look into each and every lead we get."

Mike cried out, "Come on, he's a fucking District Court Judge. He's the best one we've got. He doesn't hang out with women like that—he's a married man!"

Jack told him, "I know and I agree with you. But, let's do one thing. Let me call George Rao over in Vice. He works late and he knows every fucking whore in the city. Let's just run it by him and see if he has any information on O'Reilly."

Shaking his head, Mike told him, "I'm not for it. I think it's all bullshit! But you do what you think you need to do."

Jack picked up the phone and dialed. A woman answered, "Captain Rao's office." Jack asked to speak with George Rao.

"George Rao. Can I help you?"

"This is Jack Dean in Homicide."

"Hey, Jack, it's been a long time. How are things over there?"

"Things are busy. I need some help. But what we talk about has to remain confidential. Is that clear?"

"Yeah, no problem."

"Do you have any information about our District Judge, John O'Reilly, patronizing prostitutes? Anything at all?"

"Shit, yes. I've got a whole file on O'Reilly. He's been doing hookers since he's been on the bench. All types: white, black, Asian, Mexican. They all have one thing in common: they're all high-class types. The judge don't fuck around with street-walking girls!"

Jack then said, "I'll be goddamned. So, O'Reilly has been fucking high-class whores ever since he's been on the bench." He looked over at Mike, whose facial expression was still one of disbelief. He then asked George, "Do you know anything about a dark-haired girl about thirty, thin, looks kind of like a gypsy? Has great legs and a great ass? Do you know any hooker who fits that description?"

George just laughed. "We've got lots of girls in this town who fit that description. You need to be more specific."

Jack told him that he couldn't be and thanked him for the information. Glancing over at Mike, he could see that he was still unconvinced.

Jack told him, "Partner, you might not like it, but the Honorable John O'Reilly is now a suspect in our investigation."

Mike just sat there, saying, "Bullshit. Just because some whore comes in here and tells us about a fantasy session she had with Judge O'Reilly, don't make him a suspect for murdering a child!"

Jack responded, "I disagree. So far we've gotten nowhere in this investigation. We can't rule out any possibility. We can check this out real easily. All we need to do is get some blood from O'Reilly and run a DNA comparison with the semen that was found on the girl's face. If it matches, he's the guy. If it doesn't, then what the whore told us is just another bad lead."

"How the hell are you going to get a search warrant ordering O'Reilly to give us a blood sample? There's no probable cause here!"

"We don't need a warrant. We just need to figure out a way to get some blood from him without him knowing that we got it. Then, we'll run it over to the lab and let them do the testing on it. We just need to think of a plan to get some of his blood."

"Don't you think we need to talk to the Chief before we get into this sneaky shit?"

"No, we can't tell the fucking Chief what we're doing. He won't let us do it. We just need to do it on our own."

After pausing, Jack said, "I've got an idea. I'll call Ned Clausen over at the Health Department; he loves setting up blood drives. I'll get him to send a memo to each judge in the courthouse, asking that he and his staff each donate blood. Hopefully, O'Reilly will agree to participate, and then I'll figure out a way to get a few droplets of his blood and take them to the forensic lab for the DNA testing."

"How are you going to get Ned Clausen to go along with this? He may be suspicious as to what you're up to."

"Don't worry. He and I grew up together. He'll do it if I ask him to. Hell, Ned will be happy about getting all this extra blood for the Health Department. He won't even ask me why I want some of O'Reilly's!"

Mike, totally appalled, said, "You work on your little project, and in the meantime I'll work on some of our other cases!"

Undaunted, Jack told him, "That's fine with me. I'll handle the blood-drive plan on my own."

Two weeks later, the Health Department's blood drive was underway in the basement of the courthouse. Two Filipino nurses were drawing blood from county employees who had agreed to donate. They had set up two stations. Each one had a bed where the donors would lay down to allow the nurses to draw their blood. The beds were surrounded by cloth curtains which gave everyone some degree of privacy as their blood was being taken. These makeshift curtains were nearly five-feet high.

Jack Dean was in the basement at the time the operation started. He found a comfortable couch not too far from where the nurses had set up the stations. Sitting there, he read a newspaper and sipped on a cup of coffee. He was waiting to see if John O'Reilly would eventually appear.

Finally, at eleven o'clock, John O'Reilly got off an elevator and walked towards the nursing stations. Jack acted as if he was still reading his newspaper, but he was keeping an eye on John. He watched him fill out some paperwork and then saw him go into one of the enclosed areas. Once he lay down on the bed, Jack lost sight of him.

Quickly, he got up and walked over to the station where John was lying. Peeking over the cloth curtain, he could see the nurse withdrawing his blood. Neither the nurse nor John noticed him.

When he finished giving his blood, John left and rode the elevator back upstairs. Jack never took his eyes off the blood bag which contained O'Reilly's blood. He actually went up to the nurse who had drawn it and identified himself as a police officer. He told her that he needed to mark something on John's particular blood bag. She told him that it was okay, and she then went to meet the next donor.

At that point, Jack grabbed the blood bag and walked off. He rode the elevator up to the first floor, carrying John O'Reilly's blood with him. Quickly leaving the courthouse, he got into his car and drove away. He couldn't believe how perfectly his plan had worked.

At the forensic laboratory he met with Shannon Simpson, telling him, "I have some blood from a suspect in the Claudia Belfour killing! I need you to do a DNA comparison of the blood in this blood bag with the semen which was recovered in that case. See if it's a match or not!"

Shannon got a lab syringe which he used to remove some blood from the bag. He then squirted it into a test tube which he and Jack both initialed. This was done to preserve the chain of custody of the blood. Shannon then told Jack that he would start the testing that evening and would hopefully have the final results in two weeks. Jack thanked him and returned to his office.

There he found Mike sitting at his desk working on another case. Jack placed the blood bag right in front of him.

Looking up, Mike asked, "What the hell is that?"

Jack laughing, answered, "The Honorable John O'Reilly's blood! It went like clockwork. It was the finest detective work I've ever done. I watched with my own eyes as the judge came to my blood drive and gave his blood! And here it is!"

Mike asked, "Well, what are you going to do with it now?"

"I just brought it over to the lab. Shannon took a syringe-full from it, which he needs to do his testing. Says he'll have the results in two weeks."

"But what are you going to do with this?" Mike pointed at the blood bag.

Jack answered, "We need to save it for the chain of custody if the DNA turns out to match. I didn't want to leave it at the lab because O'Reilly's name is written on the bottom of the bag.

"I didn't want Shannon to see that this is O'Reilly's blood he's testing. He doesn't know whose blood it is. But, I don't know what to do with the blood now."

Mike told him, "This was your idea. You figure out where the hell you're going to put it!"

Standing up, Jack said, "Hold on."

He picked up the blood bag and left the room, returning five minutes later, empty-handed.

Mike asked him where it was. Jack told him, "I went downstairs to the kitchen and I put it into a brown-paper grocery bag and stapled it across the top. I wrote on the grocery bag with a magic marker, 'MIKE SANDELL'S CHINESE FOOD. DON'T FUCK WITH THIS,' and I pushed the bag towards the back of the refrigerator. Nobody will touch it."

Mike shouted, "You're out of control! You've lost your mind!"

* * * * *

The hot summer took its toll on Lucas both mentally and physically. Having lost lots of weight, he was only able to work the morning shift at Shapiro's. He cut off his hair, shaved his beard, and had a picture of a naked woman tattooed onto his right bicep. A black bandana was always wrapped around his head.

He purchased a used pool table from a local bar which he put into the living room at his apartment. There, he spent countless hours practicing each and every imaginable pool shot. He became proficient and eventually started taking his game to the ghetto bars where he could do some gambling. There, he'd play anyone for as much money as they wished to play for. Sometimes he would win, but more often than not he'd get beaten by sharks who had been playing the game their whole lives.

He didn't take the losses too hard, since he realized that he was still basically a novice. The money he lost meant nothing to him; he just liked having some sort of competition back in his life. And, of course, he enjoyed being in the bars at night. He was usually the only white person around, which he didn't mind. He was used to being an outcast. Often, he'd leave the bars with hookers whom he would take back to his apartment.

He enjoyed his life as a junkyard man. Though he disliked the extreme heat of summer, he knew that September was fast approaching, and with it would be cooler temperatures. Then, he'd grow back his hair and beard and gain back the weight he had lost during the dreadfully hot summer.

TWENTY-THREE

The phone rang at Jack Dean's desk; it was Shannon Simpson. "The blood which you dropped off here two weeks ago … I extracted DNA from it and compared it with the DNA we recovered in the little girl's case. It was a match!" Shannon screamed, "Eight billion-to-one, it's the guy!"

Jack Dean couldn't believe what he had just heard. Standing up at his desk, he asked, "Shannon, are you fucking sure? That blood which I brought to you has the same DNA as the semen which we recovered from Claudia Belfour?"

"Yes sir, without a doubt!"

"Wow!" Jack exclaimed, "This is going to be a giant case. Be sure that you keep all the evidence under lock and key at the lab. Please don't lose anything! Make sure everything is kept in order!"

Shannon assured him that he had nothing to worry about. All the evidence was secured.

Jack then told him that he needed to bring to the lab the blood bag which the blood droplets were drawn from so that it could be properly preserved as evidence. "What time will you be leaving work tonight?" Jack inquired.

Shannon told him he would wait there until he dropped off the blood bag.

"I'll be there in fifteen minutes," Jack assured him.

Hanging up the phone, he walked down the stairs to the refrigerator, pulled open the door, and removed the brown-paper bag containing the blood. Briskly, he walked down the hallway and left the building. Jumping into his unmarked car, he headed towards the crime lab.

His heart was pounding. He had caught the swim-team girl's rapist by an ingenious method of obtaining John O'Reilly's blood. He could barely contain his excitement. He couldn't wait to tell his partner Mike. He was on a family vacation in South Padre Island, but was expected to return to work later that evening. Jack figured that, at the moment, Mike was in his car with his wife and screaming children, driving back from their vacation. *Boy, will he be surprised when he finds out that Judge John O'Reilly is their guy!*

Shannon greeted Jack at the door of the lab and led him inside. The lights were dimmed. They were the only two people there. They sat down on a couch, and Jack placed the grocery bag with O'Reilly's blood between the two of them. He said, "I'm going to tell you something which is top secret. You must promise not to tell anybody what I'm going to tell you."

"You got my word."

Jack then opened the paper bag and pulled out the blood bag, handing it to Shannon. He pointed to the name which was written on the bottom of the blood bag.

Reading out loud, Shannon gulped, "JOHN O'REILLY!" Looking right at Jack, he asked, "Is that Judge John O'Reilly?"

Jack nodded that it was.

Shannon screamed, "Fucking unbelievable! Judge O'Reilly is the swim-team girl rapist!"

Jack was still nodding his head. He told Shannon, "I'm going to initial this bag and date it today. Now you initial it, and then put it in your lockbox with all the other evidence you've gathered in this case. Just be careful and keep everything under lock and key."

Standing up, Jack walked towards the door. Shannon placed the blood bag on a desk. The two shook hands, then Jack thanked him for staying late and left. He got into his car and started driving back to the police station. It would be several hours before Mike came to work. Hopefully, he would help draft the arrest warrant for John O'Reilly.

Back at his office, he sat and waited for Mike to show up. It was slightly past ten o'clock when he finally arrived. Slumping in his desk chair, Mike said, "It's sure nice to be back at work. Vacations wear me out. I'm sick and tired of hearing my wife screaming at the kids. I can handle it for a day or two, but after that, it just drives me crazy!"

Jack didn't tell him the news right away. He asked, "Did you get some fishing in?"

"Yeah, I did, but Julie came along. It's no fun fishing with your wife. The fish won't bite."

"I understand. That's why I'm no longer married! But, at least you got to spend time with your boys."

Nodding, Mike said, "I guess you're right."

He then asked, "Anything interesting going on here since I left?"

"No, nothing. Things have been real slow. A couple of bar shootings and some Filipino guy killed his mistress for talking too much. Other than that, nothing has really happened. I put the Filipino file on your desk so you could work on it. I'll handle the bar cases."

Standing up, Jack walked over to the window in their office. He looked outside and then turned and stared down at Mike; he figured it was time to tell him. "By the way, remember that blood I got from O'Reilly?"

Mike nodded, "Yeah, you put it in the supermarket bag and put it in the refrigerator downstairs."

Jack went on, "Remember, I had Shannon Simpson check it out to compare it? To compare it with the DNA taken from the semen which you scraped from the little girl's face?"

"Yeah, what happened on that?"

Jack then raised his voice, "Well, it was a positive match! O'Reilly did it! Our fucking Judge John O'Reilly is the guy who kidnapped and raped Claudia Belfour!"

Jack was now shaking. Mike just sat there stunned. Finally he asked, "Are you sure?"

Jack told him, "Yes, I visited with Shannon at the lab this evening. He says that it's Judge John O'Reilly, without a doubt. We need to draw up a warrant and get that perverted motherfucker in jail right away. We'll arrest his ass in the morning when he shows up for court. We need to act quickly and get this warrant done tonight so that we can keep him from doing anything to another little girl. You're better at drafting warrants than I am. That's why I've waited for you to come in tonight."

Mike just looked at him without saying anything. Jack was wondering why he wasn't more excited about the case being solved. Finally, Mike asked, "Have you ever heard of the fourth amendment to the United States Constitution?"

Jack responded, "Fuck the fourth amendment! I didn't do nothing wrong in this case. I'm trying to get a sick bastard off the streets!"

Mike, shaking his head in disagreement, said, "The way you got O'Reilly's blood was totally illegal, you know it. You illegally had his blood taken under the pretense that he was donating it to a blood drive; when, in fact, you were taking it so that you could run a DNA analysis on it. That's trickery and it will never stand up in court. A first-year law student could get this evidence suppressed. O'Reilly will hire some lawyer who will not only get the DNA evidence thrown out, but who will also sue your ass and the whole goddamned Police Department on account of your outrageous behavior!"

Mike held his lips tightly together in anger.

"Now settle down," Jack told him. "Once we get O'Reilly in custody and off the streets, and we show beyond all reasonable doubt that he's guilty because of the DNA evidence, there isn't a fucking judge in this county who has the balls to throw this case out of court on a technicality, and allow this sick, perverted child-killer back out on the streets!"

He paused and then went on, "It'll be political suicide for any judge to allow him back out on the streets because of some technicality. You talk about us being sued. Fuck, some killer-rapist is going to sue me and our whole department for the illegal way I caught his ass? A jury wouldn't give him one fucking dollar because I conducted an illegal seizure of his blood!"

"Well, if that's the way you feel about it, draft your warrant, try to get it signed, and go arrest him!"

Jack slowly walked over to Mike's desk and stood before him, saying, "You and I have been partners for a long time. I love you, Man. We've worked on some of the worst cases in this city's history. I don't want to do anything that upsets you, but look at it this way. I didn't necessarily violate O'Reilly's rights in the way I went about getting his blood. Yeah, I tricked him, but some courts may look at it as good police-work on my part. Sometimes, we need to use trickery to catch murderers. The courts, and I'm not just talking about the courts in Houston, but the appellate courts in Austin, and even the United States Supreme Court in Washington may be understanding as to why I did what I did.

"Hell, look at it this way! What if after the blood drive, we had decided to take a sample of everyone's blood who had donated, then extracted DNA from each sample and did a comparison with the DNA found in our case. Let's say that we got a positive match with one of our donor's blood. What would we do? We'd have him arrested!

"There is a legal argument that each and every person who gave their blood, had in effect, abandoned it, and once it was abandoned, we had the right to take it and have it tested. O'Reilly abandoned his blood to the City of Houston to do whatever the City wanted to do with it. We could have given it to a patient at a hospital or, as we did in this case, we could have had it tested."

Mike hesitated several seconds and said, "Your abandonment argument is weak and you know it. You do what you want, but just keep me out of it!"

Jack told him, "As a cop, I have a moral duty to get O'Reilly off the streets. If some judge wants to release him on a technicality, then that's beyond my control!"

Sitting back down at his desk, Jack started drafting an arrest warrant and affidavit which showed that there was probable cause that John O'Reilly was, in fact, the killer of Claudia Belfour. He needed to detail in the affidavit why there was reason to arrest John. He included the information he received from the call girl who had refused to give her name. He wrote about contacting George Rao, who bolstered her story by assuring that John did, in fact, patronize high-class call girls.

He wrote about setting up the blood drive and explained how he walked off with the blood bag and took it to the police laboratory, where Shannon Simpson extracted DNA from it and found that it matched the DNA extracted from the semen found on Claudia Belfour's body. He then signed the affidavit and had it notarized.

There was one last thing he needed to do—get the warrant signed by a Magistrate in the county. He didn't really want one who would carefully read the entire affidavit because deep down he feared that a magistrate wouldn't sign the warrant if he thought there was a fourth-amendment violation. That would kill the entire investigation. He needed a Magistrate who would simply sign the arrest warrant without carefully reading the affidavit. Then, he could have John O'Reilly arrested and put into jail.

The media would go crazy about the case. News of a judge being a kidnapper, rapist, and killer would be sensational! Once the public felt that John O'Reilly was guilty, it would be unlikely for any judge to throw the case out of court because of a fourth-amendment violation.

Jack knew just who he wanted to get to sign the arrest warrant. It was Judge Robert Merchant, a Justice of the Peace in South Houston. Judge Merchant was a drunkard who would sign any warrant without ever reading the attached affidavit. Jack drove out to Judge Merchant's house by himself and knocked on his door. It was nearly one-thirty in the morning.

The judge opened the door and in a slurred voice asked, "What do you want so late at night?"

"I've got an arrest warrant that I need to get signed."

"You got something I can write with?"

Jack handed him a blue ball-point pen along with the arrest warrant. He pointed to the line where he wanted him to sign. The judge complied.

"Thanks. Sorry I had to come by so late."

"Don't worry about it ... I was up drinking anyhow."

Jack left and drove back downtown where he called the Patrol Division and spoke with the Sergeant on duty. He told him that he needed four uniformed patrol officers to meet him in the lobby of the county courthouse at ten o'clock in the morning. He then called George Hightower, the elected District Attorney for Harris County, to tell him what was going on. He explained the whole situation to George and asked if he had any concerns about the way in which he went about obtaining the blood. Hightower told him, "I think it was great detective work on your part."

But Hightower was shocked to hear the child's killer was John O'Reilly. He thought John was a prick, but never dreamed he was a rapist and killer. He told Jack that he personally was going to prosecute the case instead of passing it down to one of his assistants. He asked him to meet with him at the DA's office in the morning so that he could proceed to file capital murder charges.

Jack then got out his telephone directory and looked up the home phone number for Gina Patterson, a news reporter for Channel 11. She picked up the phone after the second ring, sounding like she had been in a deep sleep. Jack had known her for years. He told her that she needed to be at the courthouse with her crew in the morning. She asked him why, but he wouldn't tell her anything except that there was going to be a big news story. She begged him to tell her but all he would say was, "Just be there in the morning at ten o'clock. It's going to be a giant story!"

TWENTY-FOUR

It was ten o'clock when John O'Reilly entered his courtroom. Wearing his black robe, he stood behind his bench and announced that he was going to call the court's docket for the day. The spectator section of the courtroom was packed with defendants out on bond and other interested parties. The attorney section was filled with prosecutors and defense attorneys discussing cases. As John was reading off the names on the docket, he looked up and observed several newscasters sitting in the back two rows of his courtroom. Outside the doorway, he saw several cameramen jockeying for position to get a better look inside. He wondered why so much media was present in his courtroom this morning. He wasn't aware of any high-profile cases being heard that day.

Ten minutes after taking his bench, four uniformed Houston police officers walked into the courtroom. They were accompanied by Detective Jack Dean and District Attorney George Hightower. The six men calmly walked through the spectator section of the courtroom and then into the attorney section, where they rushed straight to John. Two officers stepped behind him and the other two went to his sides. Having no idea what was going on, Judge John O'Reilly looked dazed. Standing up, he looked down at Jack Dean and George Hightower, who were standing directly in front of him. Jack yelled, "We have a warrant for your arrest!"

John angrily responded, "I don't know why you're here, but you better get your fucking asses out of my courtroom!"

Anger and confusion were seething on his face; his whole body tensed up.

Jack then ordered the uniformed officers, "Arrest him!"

All four officers converged on John to handcuff him. He went berserk. He punched one of the officers in the face and was wildly swinging at and kicking the others. It took all four officers to finally subdue him. He was handcuffed behind his back and his feet were roped together.

At that point, Jack read him his rights as he was lying on the floor behind his bench. "You are charged with capital murder. You have the right to remain silent."

John glared at him and yelled, "Fuck you, motherfucker!"

"Anything you say can and will be used against you in a court of law."

John spit at Jack and screamed, "Fuck you!"

"You have the right to hire a lawyer. If you can't afford one, one will be appointed." Jack looked at him, waiting for him to say something, but John just stared at him.

"Any interview you give can be terminated at anytime you wish. Is there anything you would like to say, Mr. O'Reilly?"

John was sweating profusely. He told Jack, "You motherfucker, when I get out of here, I am going to personally kick your fucking ass!"

"Is there anything else you'd like to say?"

"Suck my dick, motherfucker! You're a dead pig when I get out of here!"

At that point, George Hightower instructed the uniformed officers to take John to the third floor of the building where he would appear before Judge Casey Murphy in the 230th District Court of Harris County. George had filed the case earlier that morning and it had been assigned to that court.

The four uniformed officers had to physically lift John off the floor and carry him through his courtroom and into the hallway. There were newscasters and cameramen everywhere. They weren't exactly sure what was happening, but they all knew that some big news was in the making. The officers carried John onto the elevator and rode to the third floor, where he would appear before Judge Murphy.

The news media had taken the stairs to the third floor and had beaten the elevator. They filmed John in his judicial robe, handcuffed and roped, being carried into the courtroom. He was carried before Judge Murphy, who was sitting on his bench. The judge ordered the officers to untie the rope from John's legs so that he could stand. The courtroom was packed with newspeople and courthouse employees, all trying to see what was going on.

Judge Murphy was a lot like John O'Reilly. A law-and-order judge, he was not particularly personable. He had attended law school at the University of Texas, and upon graduation had worked for the United States Attorney's Office for five years. He was then appointed to the 230th by the governor.

As a judge, he seldom had any interaction with John. Their courtrooms were on separate floors in the courthouse. He was fifteen years younger than John, and at the time he was appointed to the bench, John was already the senior judge of Harris County. The two seldom acknowledged each other, even when riding on the same elevator. Casey was now finishing his third year on the bench and was going to need to run for re-election in November. Since he barely knew John, he didn't feel a need to recuse himself from hearing the case.

Judge Murphy asked George Hightower to give him probable cause as to why he should hold John O'Reilly in custody. George gave him the details of the Claudia Belfour case. He said that John O'Reilly became a suspect when a mysterious woman appeared at the homicide division and gave Detective Jack Dean some confidential information, which he investigated and found to be credible.

He explained how Jack Dean then went about obtaining John's blood. He went through the chain of custody of the blood from Jack to Shannon Simpson. He said that Simpson conducted a complex DNA analysis, which proved that the semen which was found on the body of Claudia Belfour was that of John O'Reilly's. He concluded by saying, "There's no doubt in my mind that this man is the one who kidnapped, raped, sexually mutilated, and then killed Claudia Belfour. We ask that no bond be set."

At this point, John was shaking. He was furious.

Judge Murphy told him, "You need to calm down."

John told him "I want to be heard!"

Judge Murphy warned him that anything he might say at this time could be used against him at a future date in this court.

John told him, "I understand that, but I would still like to be heard! First of all, I am asking you to release me from custody because of the illegal manner and means which the despicable Detective Dean used in obtaining a sample of my blood.

"You just heard Mr. Hightower. If Dean had not used trickery and deception, then he would never, ever, have obtained a sample of my blood to have it tested. This is a total violation of my fourth-amendment right to be free from unlawful police search and seizure.

"I am asking you, because of this obvious illegal police conduct, to find that there is no probable cause to detain me at this time."

At this point, George Hightower again addressed the court. "Your Honor, it appears to me that this defendant is attempting to persuade you to release him because of improper police conduct which occurred during the investigation in this case. He's asking you to release him basically on a technicality which has nothing to do with his guilt or innocence in the kidnapping, rape, mutilation, and killing of a young Houston girl. I'd ask the court to defer its ruling at this time on this technicality being presented by this defendant. His lawyer can raise it at the appropriate time for you to rule upon."

John then cut him off, saying, "This is the appropriate time! Dean had no right to trick me into giving up my blood so that he could use it to run a DNA test! As you know, Your Honor, I too, like yourself, am a law-and-order-type judge. But, I also believe in the Constitution of the United States of America. The police conduct in this case is an outrageous violation of the fourth amendment to our great Constitution."

At this point, George looked at John and asked, "Other than this technical defense which you have so eloquently presented to the court, are you guilty or not guilty of killing Claudia Belfour?"

John looked angrily at him for the manner in which he asked the question. Judge Murphy quickly intervened, "We will have none of this type behavior in this courtroom!"

He looked directly at George and told him, "You will never again direct any questions to this defendant without my permission! Is that perfectly clear?"

"Yes sir."

Judge Murphy then stated, "At this time, the court finds that there is probable cause to detain this defendant. Due to this case being a capital murder, where, if convicted, the defendant could be subjected to the death penalty, no bond will be set. My court coordinator will give both sides a date for the next court appearance." Looking down at John, he asked him if he was going to hire a lawyer to represent him.

"Damn right I am. This is the worst injustice I've ever seen!"

"Very well; you will have your day in court to be heard."

The bailiffs took John to a room behind the courtroom. They were accompanied by the four uniformed officers from the Houston Police Department. He was then taken into the hallway, where he and his six escorts entered an elevator. Cameras were flashing in his face; the media was in a frenzy. This was a huge story; a sitting District Court Judge was being held as the prime suspect in the murder of "the swim-team girl"!

At the county jail, classification deputies knew that John O'Reilly couldn't be housed with regular inmates due to his being a District Court Judge. Any inmate whom he had sentenced might retaliate if he were placed into the general population. His reputation as "Maximum John" would haunt him if he were put there; he needed to be housed in solitary confinement. He ended up in a single cell on the eighth floor, where he would never have any contact with other inmates.

* * * * *

That afternoon, the television and radio stations each carried John's case as their top news story. Tammy first heard of his arrest as she was watching the twelve-o'clock news. She couldn't believe her eyes when she saw footage of her husband fighting with police officers right in his own courtroom. Not sure what to do, she decided to just stay home until she heard from John. She figured that he would eventually call, and then she would go visit him.

Getting up from in front of the television, she walked into the kitchen. There, she poured herself a glass of wine. She didn't know what to think. The news made it look like John was totally guilty. She didn't think that he was capable of ever hurting anyone, but she also knew that he was quite often gone at nights. Maybe, there was a dark side to him she didn't know about.

She didn't hear from him all afternoon. The five-o'clock news showed a close-up of him arguing to Judge Murphy that he believed he ought to be released because of the illegal police conduct involved in obtaining his blood. A news reporter stated, "Judge O'Reilly has not once said that he wasn't guilty of committing the offense, but rather is arguing that he ought to be released on a technicality!"

The reporter continued, "The evidence appears to point to the guilt of Judge O'Reilly as charged."

There were also interviews conducted with Claudia Belfour's parents, who, of course, were delighted that their daughter's killer had been caught. Mr. Belfour applauded the

Houston Police Department for the fine work they did in catching this, "... sick, perverted killer." Mr. Belfour was incensed that John was attempting to get off on the basis of a technicality.

Later that evening, John finally called home, telling Tammy, "I need you to come visit me at the jail. I'm on the eighth floor. Come see me as soon as you can!"

"Are you all right?"

"No, please come see me right away!"

"Okay."

She went into her closet to pick out a dress to wear. She thought it odd that he did not say he wasn't guilty. *Why didn't he proclaim his innocence to me? After all, I am his wife.* She felt very sad. She thought that maybe he had done it. The ten-o'clock news came on as she was ready to leave, but she shut off the television and left. She didn't want to hear anyone say how guilty her husband was.

She drove downtown to the jail where she received authorization to visit him. Deputies led her up to the eighth floor and placed her inside the visiting booth. She sat there, waiting for John to be brought out so that she could talk to him. When he finally appeared, she could see him through a glass window. She picked up a telephone to speak with him. He was wearing an orange jumpsuit and looked totally worn out. Lifting his telephone, he spoke into it. "Honey, I want you to know I had nothing to do with this case I'm charged with; I swear to you. Be sure to tell Megan that I'm not guilty. The fucking DA is insane!"

Tammy then told him, "I believe you. You need to know that the television stations have already found you guilty. They're depicting you as a mad-dog rapist. There's no way you're going to be able to get a fair trial in this county."

She had never seen him in this type of situation, and it scared her. She wondered if he would ever be released. She asked, "What are you going to do about a lawyer?"

"Get in touch with Lucas," he said. "Tell him to come down here and visit me. Nobody else, just Lucas; I'm hiring him. Tomorrow, I want you to start selling some of our stocks. Free up at least a million. He's probably going to need that much."

She said, "Okay," then paused, and with tears in her eyes told him, "I love you."

She told him that she had to leave; she couldn't stand seeing him in jail. Placing the phone back on the wall, she walked off.

It took her two days of calling to finally get in touch with Lucas. She told him that John wanted to see him. Lucas told her that he had read about the case in the paper. He gave her his condolences and told her that he would go visit John.

It was another two days before Lucas did so. He sat in the attorney's booth, waiting for John to be brought from his tank.

Finally, John came in and sat down. He was wearing his jail jumpsuit. Lucas was wearing his work clothes.

"Lucas, what the fuck are you doing in that work shirt? Why are your hands so fucking dirty?"

Pointing to the lettering on his shirt, Lucas answered, "I got a job working for Shapiro Metals. I'm a junkyard man now. I do a lot of truck driving also."

John scoffed, "That's nigger work! What the hell are you doing working there?"

"It's a great job; I love it. It's a lot better than practicing law."

Shaking his head in total disbelief John asked, "Have you heard about this fucking case they've put on me? They say I raped and killed some little girl!"

"Yeah, I read about it in the newspaper. I couldn't believe it when I saw it; what's up with it?"

"Lucas, I didn't do it, I swear to God! I didn't have anything to do with it. They're trying to fuck me over!"

Lucas didn't respond. There was total silence between the two men. Finally, John cried out, "The DA is out to fuck me on this! He says he's going for the death penalty! I need to hire you to represent me and get me out of this bullshit. Really, Lucas, I swear to you, I'm totally innocent! Why would I ever rape and kill a little girl? I'm totally innocent!"

Lucas looked at him, still not saying anything. Then, looking down at the floor, he said, "John, I believe you when you tell me you're not guilty. But, you know that as far as I'm concerned, I don't really care if you're guilty or not. It means nothing to me either way. You can tell me if you did it."

"Look at me, Lucas! Look up! I'm telling you that I did not do anything to that little girl. It's driving me crazy being in here! I need your fucking help! I need you to represent me on this case! Will you?"

"John, I'm sorry, but I don't think I can. That last case I tried in your court totally wore me out. It finished me off. I just can't go back into the courtroom. I'm too fucking old."

John then stood up, and staring directly into Lucas' eyes, told him, "This is just like the case you tried in my court. The whole case rests on DNA evidence; that's all they fucking got on me! The guy who did the testing in my case is the same asshole, Shannon Simpson, the same guy you tore apart in that case you tried in my courtroom. You are the only lawyer in this state who can beat a DNA case. You're the best. I'll pay you a million dollars to represent me. I need you to get me out of this mess!"

Lucas just sat there motionless. John could tell that he was in deep thought. Finally, he said, "John, I just can't do it. It will kill me. It's going to be a super-high publicity case. It would wear me down. I just can't take the courtroom pressure anymore. That's why I got this blue-collar job; it's so relaxing to me. I cut up copper tubing in the metal shop, or just haul things back and forth to Dallas in a truck. I can't explain it. You would never understand it, but being a blue-collar worker is just where I am at this point in my life. I'm sorry."

John now had an angry look on his face. He asked, "Are you doing this to get back at me because of what happened to Amy's boy? Tell me if that's it!"

"Of course not. I was mighty angry with you back then, but now I understand that you were just doing your job. You did what you felt needed to be done." He paused and then continued, "By the way, I'm sorry that I punched you that day, but I was so pissed at you at the time, I just lost it."

John assured him, "I've totally forgiven you for what happened then." Hesitating, he said, "I want you to keep thinking about taking my case. I have total confidence in you, Lucas. There's no lawyer that I've seen that's even close to you when it comes down to combat in the courtroom."

Lucas answered, "There are lots of good lawyers who can properly represent you. If you don't want a Houston lawyer, some of the best ones are up in Dallas. Whomever you end up hiring, I want you to know that if he needs any help in beating a DNA case, I'll be happy to consult with him. I won't charge you anything, since you and I go way back. Just tell whomever you end up hiring to call me, and I'll help in any way that I can. But you need to hire a lawyer. I'm not changing my mind about representing you. I just can't go back into the courtroom. I can't do it anymore."

John then seemed to give up on having Lucas as his lawyer. Sitting down, he stared hopelessly at the floor. He thanked him for coming to visit.

Lucas wished him well, got up, and left. As he was driving home, he thought to himself that he had never seen John so down, so totally depressed. O'Reilly was seeing what it was like having his freedom taken away. All these years he had been sentencing people to hard time. Now he was getting a big taste of it. And it would only get worse as time went on; Lucas knew what locking a man up could do to his soul.

The next day John hired a lawyer from Dallas by the name of Nick Harrison. Harrison was the ex-United States Attorney from the Northern District of Texas. He was considered to be one of the top trial lawyers in Texas. He charged John a flat one-million-dollar fee to take his case. John told Harrison about Lucas' offer to help on handling the DNA part of the case; "He tore the shit out of Shannon Simpson's testimony in the case in which I presided over. He made Simpson look like a fucking idiot!"

Harrison assured him that he didn't need any help on the case. "I doubt there's anything Luke Lustick knows about DNA that I don't."

"Well, he's available to help at no cost if you need him. He's an old friend of mine from my law school days."

John appeared in court the following week. There were newsmen and cameras everywhere. George Hightower spoke with Nick Harrison about where they were going to try the case. Harrison wanted a change of venue to another county.

He didn't think he could get a fair trial in Houston because of the bad publicity which had already been generated by the news media. Hightower, of course, thought otherwise. He thought Houston would be the perfect place. The two lawyers approached the bench and spoke with Judge Murphy.

Harrison told him of his desire to have the case moved out of Houston, explaining that he didn't think John could get a fair trial in Harris County. He also said that he wanted to have a suppression hearing because he thought the manner in which the police obtained his client's blood was unconstitutional.

Judge Murphy told him, "In two weeks, we're going to have a hearing on both issues. I'll decide then about the seizure issue and the venue issue." The case was then reset.

Lucas read about the case the following morning in the *Houston Chronicle*. It was the top news story of the day, all across the front page. There was even a picture of John standing next to Nick Harrison. Lucas thought that Harrison was a dapper-looking lawyer. The newspaper article described him as the finest criminal-defense lawyer in the state. That angered Lucas. He knew Harrison, though much more polished than he, wasn't half the lawyer he was. The article portrayed Casey Murphy as being a tough, law-and-order judge. Lucas knew that the fact the case was set for a hearing only two weeks down the road meant that Judge Murphy was in a hurry to get this case tried.

TWENTY-FIVE

Once September finally arrived, the temperature started dropping. Lucas was back to working forty-hour weeks at Shapiro's. He was doing lots of driving, usually hauling large loads of metals from Houston to Dallas. One afternoon, after returning from a trip, the foreman saw an empty bottle of Jack Daniel's in his truck. He asked him whether he had been drinking.

Lucas answered, "No, I don't know where that bottle came from."

The foreman told him, "Nevertheless, I can't have you driving anymore. You just work in the metal shop everyday."

This demoralized Lucas, who walked back to the metal shop with his head bowed, carrying a pair of worker's gloves in his left hand. When he got there, he told the other workers that he had been caught drinking and wasn't going to be allowed to drive anymore. He felt despondent as he had just lost his favorite part of the job. At home that evening he actually broke down crying. He drank bourbon until he passed out on his couch.

* * * * *

The next morning on his way to work he stopped at a diner for breakfast. After picking up a newspaper at the front counter, he grabbed a seat at a booth. The whole top half of the front page was devoted to John O'Reilly's case. Judge Murphy had granted the change of venue and ordered the case transferred to Gillespie County for trial.

Lucas started gagging on the coffee which the waitress had just brought him. He knew just where Gillespie County was. The County seat was Fredericksburg, Texas, a small German town up in the hill country past San Antonio. Lucas had tried a case there earlier in his career. One-hundred percent of the citizens in that county were right-winged, conservative Germans. He figured that Judge Murphy must really want John dead to have moved the case there. Lucas knew that John didn't stand a snowball's chance in hell of avoiding a death sentence in that particular jurisdiction.

The article also reported that much to the dismay of Nick Harrison, Judge Murphy denied the Motion to Suppress, regarding the blood taken from John by the police. The judge ruled that in his opinion, the manner in which Jack Dean sneakily obtained John's blood, without his consent, was not illegal police conduct. In his ruling, he even applauded the method used by Dean as being heroic police work.

Lucas thought the ruling by Judge Murphy was absurd. Nevertheless, it was exactly what he had expected; he knew that Murphy lacked the guts to allow the case to be ruined because of a technicality. As he ate his breakfast, he thought of John. He figured that he must be feeling pretty sick right about now. Not only did his judge lack the guts to throw his case out because of the illegal seizure, but he wanted him to be convicted so badly that he was moving the case to the hideous town of Fredericksburg. John would know he had no chance up there!

The trial was set to begin in early October. It would most likely be finished later that month. Judge Murphy had planned it perfectly; he'd try the case right before election time. He'd get plenty of media exposure as a law-and-order judge, which, of course, would help him get elected in early November. Lucas finished his breakfast and then headed into work.

The days became routine for him at Sharpiro's. Everyday he worked in the metal shop. He'd cut up the copper and the brasses into various grades, then place them into different drums. He used a cutting shear and occasionally a torch to help separate the various configurations of metals which were brought to the yard by plumbers and contractors. He worked hard each day and at night was a frequent visitor at the neighborhood bars. Many folks who knew him wondered how he was able to work eight-hour days since he was always up past two in the morning, usually totally wasted. But somehow he managed.

Lucas followed the news coverage of John's case once the trial convened in Fredericksburg. It was covered in great detail by the television and print media. It appeared that Harrison put on a quality defense in representing John. He brought in DNA experts to critique the work done by Shannon Simpson, but it appeared that Shannon was up to the task this time. He had learned from Lucas to be better prepared in his presentation. He didn't want Harrison to humiliate him as Lucas had.

After two weeks in trial, the prosecution was successful. A Gillespie County jury convicted John of capital murder in the rape, mutilation, and killing of Claudia Belfour. According to the newspaper articles, John went crazy after he was convicted and kicked over the counsel table in the courtroom. It took five deputies to restrain him.

At Harrison's urging, the trial was postponed several days before the jury was brought back to decide whether to sentence John to life in prison or death by lethal injection. When the trial reconvened, it took just two hours of deliberations before the jury assessed the death penalty. Prior to the verdict being read, John was handcuffed and gagged by the bailiffs to avoid another hysterical outbreak on his part.

On the evening in which the death sentence was returned, Lucas watched the late-night news, holding a bottle of Gentlemen's Jack in his right hand. The footage showed John being escorted out of the courtroom following the trial. A news reporter stated, "Judge O'Reilly will be taken directly from Gillespie County to the death-row unit of the Texas Department of Corrections in Huntsville, Texas. There, he will sit on death row with others condemned to die as he waits for his case to be appealed to the Texas Court of Criminal Appeals in Austin."

Lucas shut the television off, happy that John had finally gotten what he truly deserved. He had been so cruel to Mikey. Now things had balanced out. But he didn't feel totally right. His entire body was shaking; something was wrong. He couldn't stop the shaking, he had no control over it. Leaving his apartment, he walked to a nearby bar. There, he drank the night away, not coming home until nearly three a.m. When he got into bed he realized that he had finally stopped shaking. He wondered what had brought it on earlier in the evening, but had no clue. He was just relieved that it had stopped.

Later that week, Lucas was called in from the metal shop to see the foreman of Shapiro's. He was told that his services were no longer needed. He wasn't told why and didn't ask. Receiving his final pay, he slowly placed it into his pocket. Heartbroken, he walked out from the main office and went back into the metal shop to say goodbye to his co-workers. They were all visibly upset that he was being fired. They watched him walk away slowly, get into his car, and drive off.

The following morning he called into his law office. Heather asked him where he had been; she hadn't heard from him in a long time. Not answering her question, he told her, "Tell Joe I'm not paying rent this month. Tell him that I'm closing my office. Also, call the phone company and tell them to cut off my phone."

"What should I do with all your things that are still here in the office?"

"Just throw everything away. I have no use for anything there."

"What should I do if any of your old clients come by looking for you?"

"Anybody who wants to find me, just tell them that I passed away."

Two days later, Lucas packed all of his clothing into the trunk of his car and left Houston, not saying farewell to anybody. He was as dejected as he had ever been because of losing his job at Shapiro's. Getting onto I-10 West, he just started driving. He was going to where he knew he could find peace. It would be Oakland, California, a city where he could go unnoticed attending to his favorite things. There, he could frequent the twenty-four-hour card houses on San Pablo Avenue. He could watch horses run at Golden Gate Fields or Bay Meadows. He could go to San Francisco to watch the finest in ballet. He could watch the A's play baseball, and the Raiders play football. He could drink until his heart was content, and there were loose women everywhere. Oakland was where Lucas Lustick would spend the rest of his life.

Upon reaching Los Angeles, he rented a hotel room so that he could catch up on some sleep.

Once rejuvenated, he continued on through California until finally reaching the Bay Area. He drove through San Francisco, over the Bay Bridge, and into the blue-collar town of Oakland. When he arrived, he checked into a small hotel on San Pablo Avenue. There was a sign across its window which read, "WEEKLY RENTALS $150.00." Checking in, he paid rent for two weeks. His room had a dingy smell to it, but it wasn't too bad. There was a bed, a couch, and a television. He had a strange feeling that this would be his living quarters for a long time. He took a quick shower to make sure that it worked well. If he was going to stay for a while, he would need a good shower. It worked great.

Showered and dressed, he left the hotel and walked about two-hundred yards to a card house called Joe's. There was a sign posted above the entryway which read, "Women Are Allowed, but Are Not Welcome." He walked inside; it was a smoke-filled room. There were fifteen or so card games going on. The games were either five-card-draw-high or five-card-draw-low.

He glanced around the room; the gamblers were a decadent-looking bunch. Half of them were wearing old worn-out Oakland Raider black jerseys. There wasn't a man in there who didn't have hair growing all over his face. There wasn't a woman in the joint other than the two waitresses serving food and drinks.

An elderly employee came up to him and asked, "What do you want to play, high or low?"

"I want to play low." The man then asked him if he wanted to play in a twenty-, forty-, or two-hundred-dollar buy-in game.

"The two-hundred-dollar one."

The man then led him to a table, showing him where to sit. Lucas looked at the six other men who were sitting at the table. They all appeared to be rough, hardcore gamblers. Over the next four hours, he won over fifteen-hundred dollars playing low-ball. But, then he started shaking again; he couldn't stop himself. His head, his hands, every part of him was trembling. He didn't know what had brought it on; as before it was uncontrollable. Leaving Joe's, he went back to his hotel where he went to sleep. When he woke up the next morning, the shaking was gone.

TWENTY-SIX

John was absolutely miserable on death row, where he was housed in solitary confinement for twenty-three hours each day. The one hour he was let out of his cell, he was taken to a secured courtyard behind the main prison building. There, he could breathe fresh air each day. Since he was such a high-profile inmate, no one else was allowed in the courtyard while he was there. The guards fed him three meals a day in his cell.

Extremely depressed, he still had hope that he would beat his case on appeal. He knew that he wasn't given a fair trial. He had written Tammy, telling her to hire Lucas to write his appeal. He knew that Lucas could win it. When she wrote back, telling him that she had gone by Lucas' office only to find out that he had died, it shattered his hopes. It seemed like his whole life was caving in. But, he was still going to fight. Writing to Tammy again, this time he instructed her to hire Lou Dixon, a top-notch appeals lawyer from San Antonio. Lou would fight the State tooth and nail in trying to reverse the conviction. John knew that other than Lucas, Lou was the best money could buy.

Legal Vengeance

For the next five years, Lou attacked every step which the State took in convicting John. He claimed that it was unfair that the case was tried in Fredericksburg. He claimed that illegal police conduct trapped John into submitting blood. He attacked the DNA procedures used by Shannon Simpson. He wrote that there was insufficient evidence presented at trial to convict John. Valiantly he attacked the constitutionality of the Texas death-penalty statute. He argued against the manner in which the death penalty was unfairly administered by the State of Texas.

Unfortunately for John, Lou Dixon lost all of his arguments on all fronts. The Texas Court of Criminal Appeals overruled each and every one of his issues and affirmed the conviction. The Federal Circuit Court in New Orleans did the same. Finally, even the Supreme Court of the United States refused to grant any relief. After the Supreme Court ruling, the trial court set an execution date, one-hundred-and-twenty days away.

Lou Dixon visited John and told him, "I've tried my best, but there is nothing else I can do. I am very sorry."

John finally gave up. He didn't like death row; he was ready to die. Tammy and Megan had stopped visiting him. Because of the DNA evidence, they were convinced that he was guilty. Occasionally, Tammy would send him a letter, but Megan completely discarded him from her life. Despondent, everyday he thought about dying.

One Friday afternoon, a porter dropped a letter into his cell. It was postmarked "Oakland, California." Wondering who it might be from, he tore open the envelope. It was a letter from Lucas. He couldn't believe his eyes. Lucas was alive, not dead like Tammy had told him. In the letter Lucas asked, "How is your appeal going? Write back if I can be of any assistance."

John was ecstatic; standing up, he paced around his cell clenching his fist. Lucas was still alive, and he was now offering to help!

John immediately wrote back, informing Lucas that all of his appeals up to that point had failed. "I'm scheduled to be executed in less than four months."

He informed Lucas that his lawyer was Lou Dixon of San Antonio, and that Lou had all of his files. He said to call Lou and request that he send the files to him in Oakland where he could review them and try to convince the Supreme Court or the Governor's office to issue a halt to his execution. He emphasized in the letter to act quickly, for he had less than four months to live. He thanked him for writing and sent off the letter the next morning. He found it strange that Lucas' address was at a hotel.

When Lucas received John's letter, he immediately called Lou Dixon and asked him to send John's files. Lou told him that he would need to get John's permission before sending them. He assured him that he would immediately write to John and once he gave consent, he would send the files to Lucas in Oakland. Lucas asked him to hurry.

Lucas then wrote a letter to John, telling him that Lou was going to send him the files in Oakland, and that he would work on getting a stay of execution. He also instructed John to list him at the death-row unit as being his attorney of record. That was the only way in which he would be allowed to visit. He said that he wasn't sure when he would visit but promised that he would be there at some point.

John had great confidence in Lucas being able to straighten this whole mess out. He wasn't sure what he would do, but he knew that whatever it was, it would end up exonerating him. Writing Tammy, he told her that Lucas was now his attorney and that eventually he'd be cleared. "With Lucas on my side, there's no doubt the truth will be uncovered!"

As time passed, he never heard anything from Lucas. Six weeks before the execution date, he wrote and asked for an update on what was going on. Lucas never responded. He wrote again three weeks later, but still didn't hear anything back. Frantic, he wondered why Lucas wasn't getting back to him. He prayed for him to visit, but he didn't appear. Even a week before his execution date, he still hadn't seen or heard from him.

Now he was downright scared. He wondered where Lucas could be.

* * * * *

Two days before his execution date, John received a visit from Earl Scruggs, the assistant warden of the prison. Earl told him that on the following day he would be brought to a special building adjacent to the death house which would be where he would sleep on the final night before his execution. Earl asked him what he would like to order for his final meal.

John told him, "I need to talk to my lawyer. His name is Lucas Lustick. He lives in Oakland, California. He's trying to get this whole thing stopped. Can you please try to get in touch with him for me? I'm desperate. Please!"

Earl told him, "If he's working on the case, I'm sure you'll hear from him. It's really not my job to try to find him." He again asked him what he wanted for his last meal.

"I don't want a last meal. Just call my lawyer for me, please!"

Earl told him, "I'm just going to order you a T-bone steak and a baked potato."

As he was walking off, he looked back at John and told him, "You're getting what you deserve for what you did to that little girl!"

John stared back at him, but didn't say anything.

The following day, he was moved into the building which Earl had told him about. In the evening, he was served his final meal which he slowly ate. Afterwards, he totally lost it. Guards heard him incessantly screaming: "Where's my lawyer? Lucas! Lucas! Lucas! Help! Help!"

Three guards went into the room to try to settle him down; however, he wouldn't stop screaming. He fought with them. They had to cuff him around his wrists and his ankles. Even then, he was screaming as he lay on the ground. One of the guards kicked him in the mouth, knocking loose several teeth. He squirmed on the floor until finally his energy gave way. One of the guards put a towel over his mouth to stop the bleeding. He was thoroughly drenched in blood, sweat, and tears.

A nurse was called to check on him. The guards lifted him up and placed him into a chair so she could make sure that he was okay. He just sat there motionless as she examined his mouth. She and the guards then walked out of the room, shutting off the lights behind them.

He was now sitting in this chair, in total darkness, on this, the last night of his life. He thought about his mom and dad; he thought about his wife and daughter. Loudly crying, he couldn't even wipe away the tears because his hands were cuffed together. He stayed awake all night, knowing it was the last night of his life.

At nine in the morning, Earl Scruggs came to visit him. He told him, "Executions here are traditionally held at six o'clock in the evening. But due to the fact that our Warden has a high-school football game he wants to attend in Galveston this evening, yours is set for high noon. I hope that's okay with you."

John just shook his head in disbelief. He asked if he could be uncuffed at least from around his hands.

"No, I'm real sorry, but we're under strict orders to keep you like this until after you've stopped breathing."

John pleaded, "Will you at least please call my lawyer?"

"No, but don't worry, he still has three hours to get here. If he's late, I'll tell him that you were looking for him."

John then muttered, "Fuck yourself!"

Earl called him a "sorry motherfucker," and walked out of the holding area.

The death house was ripe to proceed with the execution at twelve noon. The prison doctor made sure that he had the proper dosages of sodium thiopental, pancuronium bromide, and potassium chloride to inject into John's veins to make sure that he would never awaken. Reporters were starting to arrive outside the death house so that they could cover the execution for the news agencies. Some of them would be allowed inside to actually witness the event.

At eleven o'clock, Claudia Belfour's parents arrived. They were immediately ushered into the death house so that they could personally watch the man convicted of killing their daughter be put to death. Upon entering the building, Mr. Belfour told the reporters that he had waited a long time for this day.

It was eleven-twenty when Lucas Lustick walked through the prison gates and into the Warden's office. He was wearing a baggy, blue suit with a black tie. He probably weighed close to three-hundred pounds. His gray hair was greasy and long, and he looked like he hadn't shaved in weeks. His hands were shaking as he showed the Warden his Texas Bar card and California driver's license. The Warden checked his own records to make sure that he was listed as attorney of record. Once he verified it, he asked Earl Scruggs to check his briefcase for weapons and to then accompany him to visit John O'Reilly. The Warden asked Lucas, "Is everything a go?"

Lucas told him, "I haven't heard anything halting the execution from the Supreme Court."

Then he added, "But we still have over thirty minutes left; anything is possible."

Earl walked with Lucas to the building where John was being held. He explained, "His hands and feet are cuffed because we've had a lot of trouble with him. I'm going to put you in there alone with him to protect y'all's privacy. But, if there's a problem, just scream out, and we'll be in there!"

Lucas told him, "Thanks," and entered the room alone. He was shaking uncontrollably.

John couldn't believe his eyes. He thought he was seeing things. "Lucas, you're finally here. Why are you shaking so much? Are you okay?" He paused a moment and then said, "Fuck, never mind why you're shaking! We're about out of time. Stop these motherfuckers from killing me!"

Lucas quietly mumbled, "John, I'm going to get straight to the point cause we don't have much time. I know you didn't kill that girl. I know you're innocent."

Hesitating for several moments, he then reached into his briefcase with trembling hands and pulled out a folder. He whispered, "Where do you think you were born?"

"Houston ... why?"

Lucas again whispered, "Because you weren't really born in Houston. That's just what your parents told you. You were actually born in Laredo, Texas."

Pulling out a piece of paper from his folder, he showed it to him. It was a copy of a Webb County birth certificate with the name, "John Carney," written across the top of it. It indicated that this infant's place of birth was in Laredo, Texas, on April 24, 1950, and that his parents were a Shirley and David Carney of Midland, Texas. Handwritten on the bottom of the certificate were the following words: "This child was adopted on the day of his birth by Otis and Maggie O'Reilly of Houston, Texas." John, appearing puzzled, asked, "So, where is this going?"

Lucas then showed him another Webb County birth certificate from Laredo with the name "Jim Carney" written across the top of it. The document indicated that the child was also born on April 24, 1950, and that his parents were also Shirley and David Carney of Midland, Texas. Handwriting on this certificate indicated that this infant was adopted at birth by Rita and Kirk Phillips of Carson City, Nevada.

Lucas whispered, "You had an identical twin brother. The two of you were actually the children of David and Shirley Carney. Both of you boys were put up for adoption right after birth in Laredo. Your parents adopted you but never told you so. A Nevada couple adopted your brother; he lives in Reno. Here's his picture."

Lucas showed him the picture which he had come across at his mother's bordello near Reno. John stared at it in disbelief; the man in the photo looked exactly like him. Lucas told him, "When I first saw him, I knew right away he had to be your twin. He was full-time fucking this whore out in Reno, and I paid her to get me information about his past, and to also give me one of his used rubbers after he finished fucking her. I rode to Laredo to verify he was your twin, and sure enough he was!"

John now understood what had happened. He was livid, but let Lucas continue, "By the way, the mystery call girl in your case was the nanny who raised Mikey; you ruined her life, too. Remember Agnew from our days in California? You used to treat him like shit. He always thought you were a prick. Well, Amy was special to him also. Anyhow, he's a cold-blooded killer. He killed the little girl and then emptied out your twin brother's rubber on her. You and your brother have the same DNA; that's why you're here! You deserve all this, and I hope you burn in hell!"

John was now red with anger, screaming at Lucas, "You low-life, murdering motherfucker!"

He tried to move but was totally confined by the metal which restrained him. He screamed, "Help! I need help!"

He was screaming at the top of his lungs, "I'm innocent! I need to talk to someone! Please, I'm innocent! My lawyer set me up! Look in his briefcase!"

Earl Scruggs rushed in with four guards. Lucas told him, "He's losing it since I told him that the Supreme Court wasn't going to stop the execution—he can't handle it!"

Earl yelled to the guards, "Gag him! We can't have him screaming like this when we carry him into the death chamber!"

One of the guards then stuck a white towel into John's mouth, as another one wrapped duct tape around his head and across the towel. It was now five minutes before noon. Earl told the guards, "It's time to carry him into the chamber so that the little girl's family can have their justice!"

Lucas, looking deeply into John's eyes, told him, "It didn't have to be this way," and he walked out of the building.

As he walked off, he heard the heavy footsteps of the guards as they carried John into the death house where he was put onto a gurney and executed.

Lucas left the prison yard and walked to his car. Leaving the prison grounds, he got onto Highway 45 heading south. Shaking uncontrollably, he drove until he reached Interstate 10 and then headed west towards California. As he was driving, he thought about how fine it felt that he had finally gotten his revenge for what John had done to Mikey. *O'Reilly went to his death knowing that he had been set up. What an awful way to die!*

But, Lucas felt terrible sadness and guilt knowing that he had sacrificed Claudia Belfour in order to get this ultimate punishment for John. He remembered the old farmer standing by the two lambs and the wolf. The man told him that sometimes you needed to sacrifice something good to rid the world of something evil. It gave Lucas some solace in what he had done, but not enough. The fact that he had orchestrated Claudia Belfour's killing was something that needed to be dealt with.

When the sun went down, he pulled off the freeway onto a side road. Opening a fifth of Jack Daniel's, he started drinking it. Placing the bottle down on the floorboard of his car, he knew what he needed to do. He grabbed a .38 caliber revolver from under the seat, looked at it carefully, felt the weight of it, the smoothness of the steel. ... then he released the safety. Closing his eyes he thought about Amy and Mikey. *Will I see them again?* he wondered.

www.ingramcontent.com/pod-product-compliance
Lightning Source LLC
LaVergne TN
LVHW040730250326
834688LV00031B/231